Praise for *The Binding Song*

'Brilliant. I had shivers.'
Jenny Blackhurst, author of *Before I Let You In*

'The evocation of place is first class . . . wonderfully
paced, the tension ratchets up to a very satisfying
ending. A thoroughly enjoyable read.'
James Oswald, author of the Inspector McLean series

'Elodie Harper's first novel, set in HMP Halvergate, has
become all the more possible, given what else has been
going on beyond our prison walls. Plotting, pace and
writing render *The Binding Song* a must read.'
Jon Snow

'One of the most chilling, atmospheric debuts I've read.
It was so compelling and creepy my heart beat with fear
at times.'
Claire Douglas, author of *Local Girl Missing*

'Deliciously creepy. *The Binding Song* is a nerve-
jangling treat for fans of Mo Hayder or Stephen King.'
Mark Edwards

'Creepy from the word go, utterly compelling and
hauntingly tragic – but I'll warn you now – you might
have to sleep with the lights on.'
Susi Holliday, author of *The Deaths of December*

ELODIE HARPER

The Binding Song

MULHOLLAND
BOOKS
HODDER

First published in Great Britain in 2017 by Mulholland Books
An imprint of Hodder & Stoughton
An Hachette UK company

This paperback edition published in 2018

1

A CIP catalogue record for this title is available from the British Library

Paperback ISBN 978 1 473 64217 1
eBook ISBN 978 1 473 64216 4

Typeset in Plantin Light by Hewer Text UK Ltd, Edinburgh

Printed and bound in Great Britain by Clays Ltd, St Ives plc

Hodder & Stoughton policy is to use papers that are natural, renewable
and recyclable products and made from wood grown in sustainable
forests. The logging and manufacturing processes are expected to
conform to the environmental regulations of the country of origin.

Hodder & Stoughton Ltd
Carmelite House
50 Victoria Embankment
London EC4Y 0DZ

www.hodder.co.uk

For my mother Suzy Kendall. Big tree, little tree.

Our own wretched state ... is but a wandering about for a while in this prison of the world, till we be brought unto the execution of death

Thomas More
'A Dialogue of Comfort against Tribulation', 1534

Prologue

The break in the trees told him nothing. Ryan had no idea how far he had travelled or in what direction. He longed to sink down into the mud, rest just for a moment, but instead he scuttled across the open patch of long grass, bent double like a crab. He tried not to think about the lorry he'd left behind, the warm seat, the friendly driver. Perhaps if he'd stayed, he could have hitched a lift out of Norfolk. But it had made him nervous when his companion turned up the radio. At every ad break he started to sweat, wondering when his description was going to blare out over the news.

He stumbled as he re-entered the wood. The ugly grey day was getting darker, the trees' outlines bleeding into the dusk, making it hard to see where he was going. He blinked water from his eyes. A fine mist of rain coated his hair and ran like sweat down his face. Every inch of his skin felt damp. Ryan took a few steps deeper into the wood, seeking out a clump of trees that bunched together more closely than the others. Leaning his back against a trunk, he slid down its length, finally coming to rest on the earth. Even if the entire East Anglian Constabulary came crashing through the woods behind him, he couldn't bring himself to walk any further.

With his head against the bark, he listened. Nothing but the wind and the patter of light rain on needles and bracken. Perhaps it was safe to stop for a while. He got out the chocolate bar he had stolen from the trucker, its plastic wrapper rustling as he broke off a piece. Eating some now and saving the rest for tomorrow would give him a little energy, maybe even enough to make his way to the port at Felixstowe.

Focused on the taste, he nearly missed the stooped figure flitting by, some distance away in the wood. It was a woman, small and thin, making no noise as she passed. She seemed to know her way, moving with purpose. Ryan inched himself up on his haunches, trying to make out where she was heading. As soon as he moved, she stopped. He flattened himself against the trunk. The woman turned towards him. She was too far away for him to make out her expression; only the white of her face flashed back through the darkness. For a moment, he thought she had seen him. Then she turned and moved on.

Something about the paleness of her face recalled the dread of Halvergate. Like a flare sent out at sea, it briefly illuminated his thoughts, then sank into the unknown. Inside Ryan had laughed at the other men, but now, alone in the wood, he felt uneasy. He watched the woman continue her journey. A little further and she would be out of sight. Twilight was setting in, so she must know her way. Perhaps she was heading to another road – if so, he could get a sense of his bearings. Deciding to follow her, he scrambled to his feet.

He tracked the woman, treading as quietly as he could. It seemed to him that while she made no noise at all, every twig that snapped under his feet went off like a gunshot. Ryan took out the broken shard of CD from his pocket, sharpened like a knife. He turned it over in his fingers; the keen edge felt reassuring. He didn't plan on hurting her, not unless he had to, but the weapon reminded him that outside Halvergate all things were possible.

Darkness seeped into the wood and it became more difficult to follow his prey. She seemed to be walking faster now, still not making any sound. He struggled to keep up, his only guide the silver bark of the trees, dim in the moonlight. She became nothing more than a shadow at the edge of his vision, a movement that frayed and split in different directions. He stumbled first one way, then the next, before giving up. He stopped. The press of the trees, the silence and the darkness, all stretching out in unknown directions, felt more claustrophobic than prison.

Then he saw it. The woman's pale face. She was watching him through the branches, the white of her skin lit up by the moon. But no light shone in her eyes. Like holes gaping in a mask, her eyes were completely black.

Ryan gasped and stumbled backwards, dropping the broken CD. The image disappeared. Looking back at him was a white strip of bark, two shadowy knots cut like eyes in its peeling skin. You could almost mistake it for a face.

'Stupid bastard!' Ryan spoke the words aloud for comfort, but felt none. The trees closed inwards, silencing him, a hostile force. He had to get out into the open. He squatted down in the mud, feeling for the CD. The pounding of his heart beat loud in his ears and his fingers shook as he scrabbled through leaves and mud. The knife was gone.

Behind him Ryan heard the crack of snapping wood. He swung round. Nothing. He turned back, unsteady on his haunches, and there, crouched in front of him, was the eyeless woman. He saw the white veins standing out in her neck, her face contorted with rage. She screamed.

The sound expanded in Ryan's head, shattering his mind. He tried to stagger upright, but instead he fell, crashing into the mud, the soft side of his neck landing heavily on the upturned spike of his CD. Blood filled his mouth. He tried to pull himself upright, to crawl away, but found himself choking. Above him, the trace mark of branches faded.

Ryan couldn't see the woman, but he sensed her white face, leaning downwards, close to his own. The stranger's dark eyes stared into his, the black spreading outwards as he lost consciousness.

I

There's nothing comfortable about stepping into another person's shoes, particularly when you don't know why they were left empty. Janet slowed her car as she approached the prison's outer gate. A drumbeat of rain played on the roof. She had taken John Helkin's job without asking why he'd left. It seemed too obvious to ask. But now, on her second day at HMP Halvergate, his absence felt like a shadow. The outline of a man with all the rest left blank.

Through the bars of water on her windscreen, the wavering figure of a security guard took shape. She hurried to get her ID card up to the window so he didn't have to wait. 'Dr Janet Palmer,' she said, raising her voice over the rain's heavy tattoo. Water dripped on to her knee as the guard took her temporary pass and peered at it. Underneath his hood, the man's nose was red from the cold, his skin cracked and peeling.

'Just temporary then?' he asked, turning the card over in his wet fingers.

Janet smiled. 'Well, hopefully only the pass, not me.'

The guard said nothing and drew back, his face no longer visible above the line of glass. He handed Janet her ID back through the window, then turned and disappeared into his cubbyhole. Janet stared after him as the barrier rose. He didn't look at her as she passed through.

She drove beyond the disused outbuildings of what had once been RAF Breydon, before turning in to the former airfield. Its wide expanse stretched out in an official no-man's-land, unused by the prison and unleased by the government. Massive grey

4

clouds spread overhead like a blanket hung on a low ceiling. Janet imagined the sky's vastness must once have given a sense of freedom to the airmen who could take to it and escape, but it gave her the opposite feeling. It was oppressive, making her feel exposed, watched from all sides. In the distance, the crumbling control tower brought home the silence.

It had been made clear to her that she was inheriting a department in disarray, but still, she had a feeling HMP Halvergate would plumb new depths of chaos, even for Her Majesty's beleaguered Prison Service. She drew her shoulders back against the seat, gripping the wheel. There was no point worrying now. Being the sole psychologist in charge had been part of the job's attraction, the promotion she had been waiting for.

A row of cars nestled against the outer perimeter fence, sheltering from the rain driving across the barren airfield. Janet parked alongside them and scurried into the cover of the gate lodge, a breeze-block cube with the Queen's insignia above the door. Water pooled beneath her feet on the concrete floor. Behind a wall of glass sat an unfamiliar prison officer. He gestured for her to come over to the desk where he sat, boxed in.

Janet held up her ID. 'It's my second day,' she said, speaking loudly so he could hear. 'I think I'm picking the keys up this morning, if you have them.'

In answer he nodded towards the glass door to his left, which slid open with a thud. Janet headed in, hearing the gate buzz shut behind her. For a moment she stood sealed into the small space, waiting for the next gate to open. She never liked this time in the prison's fish tank, muffled between doors as if passing from one world to the next. She glanced over to the officer and was surprised to see he was watching her through the glass without making a move to let her through. She stared back, her cheeks getting hotter, until he pushed the button and the door in front of her buzzed open.

Feeling irritated, she headed over to the key hatch, pushing her tally, number 268, through the slot. In return the officer slid through a set of three keys. It was her passport to Halvergate. Janet held them so tightly the metal dug into her fingers. The officer, a heavy man in his late forties with a tobacco-stained moustache, leaned forwards against the glass.

'When you get to the VP wing, wait for Terry. He's coming to meet you.'

'Thanks,' said Janet.

She left the lodge and walked across the sterile area, a tarmac square surrounded by high fences and barbed wire, like a giant cattle pen. As she unlocked the gate to the yard, a deafening beeping rang out across the empty space until she closed it again. A large sign by the handle told her, 'Lock it, Prove it!'

Janet faced the jail that overshadowed her. HMP Halvergate was a nondescript 1950s prison, its redbrick dulled by years of battering wind, its small barred windows set like narrowing eyes against the weather. The building looked sullen and unloved. Scaffolding stuck out from one side of it; clearly there was a half-hearted attempt at repair going on. Nobody was working on it this morning, a security lapse she could not imagine occurring at her old workplace, HMP Leyland.

She shook her umbrella slightly, the rain cascading over its edge, and headed for the vulnerable prisoners' wing, D block. At the doorway she looked up at the unwinking eye of the CCTV camera. Another beep, and the heavy metal swung inwards. She hurried in, securing the lock and shutting out the wet.

Stamping her feet on the mat, she put down the umbrella and clipped the keys to the metal chain at her belt. The small entrance hall was empty. No sign of Terry. She waited.

Even standing still, Janet looked restless. All her movements were sharp, like a small bird of prey, alert to every passing shadow. In the rain, her red hair had darkened at the edges, separating into wet tendrils. Dark eyes, fringed by ginger lashes, marked the only colour in her chalk-white face.

Janet became aware of the hum of Halvergate's ventilation system, a deep rumbling that pulsed constantly through the corridors. She looked down at her watch, impatient, when a voice made her turn.

'Dr Palmer?'

Facing her was a lean man with close-cropped curly black hair, greying at the temples. His olive skin had an unhealthy pallor beneath it. Terry Saunders, the specialist officer on D block. She held out her hand. 'Please, it's Janet.' He shook it vigorously, squeezing so hard that the ring on her middle finger dug into her skin. She nearly winced.

'You're starting the assessments today?' He had a strong Norfolk accent and didn't answer her smile with one of his own.

'Yes. I thought we could start with the six men already on the treatment programme, before moving on to the ones you've picked out from the waiting list.'

She found herself talking to the air. Terry had buzzed through to the offices that skirted the housing block and headed down the corridor without waiting for her to finish. She only just caught the barred door before it swung shut between them, scraping her fingers on its edge.

'You know,' she called after his retreating form, 'I'd rather see inmates in my own office.'

'Dr Helkin always liked a more neutral space.'

Janet jogged to catch up. 'If that's how you've set it up for today that's fine, but in future for one-to-one work I'll hold assessments in my office. I find it builds a better rapport.'

Terry stopped, making her jump back to avoid crashing into him. Her eye level only just reached the diamond Prison Officers Association badge on his black tie. She looked up and saw he had freckles spattered across his nose and cheeks, like paint flicked from a brush. They spoke of sunny afternoons and looked out of place on his pinched face.

'Dr Palmer, I know you've done this job before but I know these men. Some of them aren't the sort you want to invite into your private space. You'll have to trust me on this.'

Janet felt tempted to remind the patronising man that she had spent the past four years at a maximum security prison whose infamy left Halvergate in the shade. But there was no point standing on pride, not when Terry held all the answers to her questions.

'Is there anything more I should know about any of the inmates here?' Her dark eyes searched his. 'Dr Helkin's notes have significant gaps. Anything further you can tell me, I'd appreciate it.'

Terry shrugged, then looked away. He talked to the floor. 'I just think you should be careful, is all.'

Janet waited for more, but Terry clearly felt this cryptic remark had ended the conversation. 'Well, in any case,' she said, 'I have to go to my office to pick up my files. I'll need whatever case notes there are to hand.'

'I've already brought them over for you,' said Terry, moving off.

The room set aside for her clinic was not inviting. Icy cold, no carpet, no window; just a couple of ill-matched chairs and a tiny plastic table covered with half-empty folders. Janet tried not to curse Terry as she picked up the first one.

Dr Helkin had left the post due to 'stress', she'd been told, which she took as a euphemism for being given the shove. Her predecessor had left almost no record of his last eight months in the post, which was itself a disciplinary offence. It was all the more perplexing because his first month had been a model of good data keeping. But there was nothing on the spate of suicides in the VP wing at Halvergate, nothing on rapist Ryan Spalding's escape from hospital, and nothing on the latest sex offender treatment programme, which had come to an abrupt end halfway through. When she opened the folders for the five men who had killed themselves – Kyle Reeder, Ahmed Ali, Ryan Spalding, Mark Conybeer and Liam Smith – there were no written observations at all. Instead she found a couple of scrawled notes referencing cases in unnamed volumes. Janet couldn't imagine John Helkin getting a job elsewhere in a hurry.

Collecting information on prisoners was close to an obsession for Janet, and she wasn't used to assessing people with so little guidance. Her old shared office at HMP Leyland came into her mind's eye, its shelves packed with folders, the filing cabinets a hive of meticulously collated data. She redid her ponytail, scraping back the hair until it pulled at her scalp. Opening a new file, she smoothed out the pages.

Janet liked to think of her job as reminiscent of an engineer working in the bomb disposal squad. She approached each inmate as a potentially explosive device whose wiring had to be studied, understood and finally disabled. While her colleagues at Leyland struggled with the emotional pitfalls of working closely with sex offenders, torn between compassion and disgust; Janet knew that her apparent detachment was unusual.

She spent the morning meeting two men who had been on Helkin's treatment programme. The lack of information on either made it a challenge to assess them. But although Majid Ashraf and Duncan Fletcher both complained of the cold in Terry's consultation room, Janet soon lost any sense of it. Concentration took over, and the outside world telescoped inwards to a single point of interest – the character of the man in front of her and the risk he posed.

In the short break before her third inmate she saw with surprise that here, at last, was one man whose notes Dr Helkin had bothered to update, however inadequately. He'd written '*unaffected*' repeatedly for the past three months.

Michael Donovan, a thirty-nine-year-old prisoner, was in for the rape of his partner. The assault had been particularly violent and he'd been up for her attempted murder too, but was subsequently cleared of that. Of course, there was no copy of the judge's comments at sentencing, or anything else that might be useful. Janet wrote a reminder to send off for more details and read on. A university graduate and computer games designer, Michael was three years into an eight-year sentence. He had initially refused to join any rehabilitation courses, but after being transferred to Halvergate ten months ago had agreed to join the sex offender treatment programme. Helkin's notes gave no record of Michael's initial assessment or his progress. On her first day, the deputy governor Richard Smith had broken the news to her that no tapes of the group sessions had been kept.

She drummed her fingers on the table. Her predecessor's eccentric bookkeeping defied belief. And that '*unaffected*' comment was both ominous and unhelpful. Unaffected by what? The rehabilitation programme? Depression? Dr Helkin's own peculiar brand of forensic psychology?

Terry popped his head round the door, holding out a small plastic cup. 'Done a tea run. D'you want one before I bring Michael in?'

She smiled, surprised by the offer. 'Great, thanks.'

Her colleague stepped into the room. 'I'll bring him in then?'

'Whenever you like.'

He hesitated, as if about to say something, then put her tea on the table and left.

'Sod it!' Janet yanked back her hand from the burning cup, spilling tea on her thigh. Terry must have asbestos hands. She bent to brush the drops off her trousers at the same moment that Michael Donovan walked in.

Janet rose to shake his hand, but he stood frozen, staring at her face. He made no move to meet her outstretched arm, leaving it to hang in mid-air. His eyes drifted down from her face to her chest, his gape widening. She glanced down in annoyance, then flushed. Her red enamel cross shone, swinging lightly on its short chain. It must have slipped out from under her jumper when she spilled the tea. Officially, she shouldn't be wearing it. She stuffed it back undercover. She knew what was coming next, the tedious questions about her faith asked either in belligerence or plaintive hope, to which her answer was always the same: 'It's just a necklace, it means nothing.'

But Michael Donovan didn't speak. Instead he continued to stare at the space where the necklace had been, as if it were a charm keeping him rooted to the spot. Janet wondered if the man was well. She gestured across the table. 'Please, take a seat.'

Her voice broke his reverie. 'Not what I was expecting,' he said, looking up and smiling at her. '*Put on the full armour of God, so that you can take your stand against the devil's schemes.*' He laughed at her bemused expression. 'Ephesians, Chapter 6. Forgive me, I'm no Bible basher, but you get time to read all sorts in here, and there's no denying the Good Book's poetry.'

Janet scraped her chair back and sat down. She nodded curtly at him, determined to restore the session to normality. Donovan continued to smile as he folded himself slowly into the seat opposite. Where her previous two inmates had sat upright, look-ing anxious or even aggressive in the uncomfortable chair, Michael Donovan managed to drape himself over it. He was an immensely attractive man, with smile lines around his mouth. The perfect symmetry of his face reminded her of the angels in the Sistine Chapel, and his flesh looked too rosy for the drab light at Halvergate. Janet thought she must seem like a ghost beside him. Whatever had first surprised him about her appear-ance, he now exuded confidence. There was an amused look in his blue eyes, as if he were the one giving the consultation. Perhaps his earlier startled reaction had even been faked, designed to unsettle her. A game player then.

She leaned forwards, her arms resting on the table, watching him. 'My name's Janet Palmer. As you probably know, I've replaced John Helkin as Halvergate's psychologist and I'm here to guide you through the sex offender treatment programme. Any questions about that, or about anything else, we can go over in today's meeting.'

'Janet?' Michael over-enunciated the word, spitting out the consonants. 'What a lovely name.'

'Thank you,' she said, although it hadn't sounded like a compli-ment. She pulled her ponytail tighter. One rust-coloured curl came loose, like a broken spring. 'So, you find reading helpful here?'

He spread his hands in an expansive gesture. 'Of course, I like reading everywhere. But life's other charms are somewhat limited in Halvergate.'

'Are you reading anything interesting at the moment, besides the Bible?' She took up her pen.

There was a beat as he studied her. '*Utopia*, by Thomas More.'

Janet looked up from her notes, surprised. 'Unusual choice,' she said. 'And are you impressed by his ideal society?'

'A little too like Halvergate.' He laughed. 'All those rules. And punishments. So, how about you? Got anything interesting on the go?' He stroked his neck, eyes narrowed.

It was a while since Janet had come across a prisoner who flirted with her so soon, or so obviously. It was never an encouraging sign. 'I'm not much of a reader,' she lied.

'You surprise me.'

'So, you're three years into your sentence for rape, and you've completed the first part of the programme put in place by John Helkin.' She folded her hands. 'How do you feel that went?'

'Presumably you've got his notes.'

'But I'd be interested to hear your perspective.'

Michael sat back even further in his chair. 'Fascinating.'

'Are you able to expand on that?'

'I found it immensely helpful. Especially the role play considering the attack from the victim's point of view.' The corners of his mouth twitched. 'Though of course it made me feel even more guilty.'

The lie seemed less offensive than the lack of effort he put into telling it. For the first time, Janet felt some sympathy for Helkin and his '*unaffected*'. Fine, she thought. Let's see how much Michael felt like smiling at a parole board after failing the treatment.

'It was a violent offence, and one which I understand you denied at the trial. What prompted your change of heart?'

'I've had time to reflect, Dr Palmer. Remorse in my case has been slow, but none the less potent for that.' He stared steadily at her as he spoke. Janet did not believe a word. She made a quick note, *conduct psychopathy checklist*.

'It's encouraging that you're feeling remorse. Of course the flip-side is often depression. Have you been suffering from low moods recently?'

'I'm sure they'll take a turn for the better now you're here.' He tilted backwards, resting his arms behind his head. All he needed to complete the picture of smugness was to prop his feet up on the table.

The sight of him balanced so precariously, with two legs of the chair off the ground, made Janet uneasy. 'Perhaps you could just talk through the offence in your own words.' She tipped her head to one side in a movement that was supposed to be encouraging, but instead was reminiscent of a sparrowhawk.

'Oh, it was terrible,' Michael began. 'I still don't understand why I acted like I did. My girlfriend Karina wanted to try out something kinkier than usual. I tied her up, and then, well.' He shrugged. 'I got carried away.'

Janet knew 'carried away' was a poor description of the violence Michael had inflicted. 'What do you think caused you to hurt her? Were you angry with her for something?'

'No. It just gave me a thrill.'

'What gave you a thrill?'

He stared at her, unblinking, across the small table. 'Seeing the pain in her eyes.'

Without meaning to, Janet put her hand to her jumper, feeling the reassuring shape of the panic alarm hanging round her neck. Michael smiled as if he understood the gesture. 'And what do you think about that pain now,' she asked. 'Does it still excite you?'

'Of course. But I also feel dreadfully guilty about it.' Michael looked down at his hands, running a thumb over fingernails that, Janet thought, looked beautifully manicured for a man restricted to two showers a week. He sighed. 'Poor Karina.'

She had worked with enough rapists to see Michael was still

enjoying a sense of power over his victim, even several years after the event. She paused, writing down his response. 'Was it the first time you had been violent towards a woman, or was it perhaps something you'd wanted to do for a while?'

'It had never occurred to me before, but once you've tried it . . . Well, an experience like that is impossible to forget.' Michael continued to study his fingernails.

'Do you feel that you might want to rape other women, besides Karina?'

'All men want to rape women.' Michael looked up, the words an unpleasant counterpoint to his angelic face. 'If they tell you otherwise, I'm afraid it's just to spare your feelings. The only difference between me and those on the outside is that not all men have the balls to do it.'

Janet felt her own dislike meet his provocation like an electric charge. Instead of holding his gaze she looked down at her papers. 'I've heard that argument in prison many times before, Michael,' she said. 'I'm sure it's a view John Helkin has already challenged, and we'll certainly pick up on it again as a group.' She closed the file in front of her. 'But unless there's anything else you'd like to ask or go over, I think we'll leave it there for today.'

Instead of answering, Michael stood up to leave, towering over her, before she had a chance to rise from her chair. 'Well, it's been a pleasure meeting you, Janey.'

Janet felt a surge of rage, far out of proportion to his rudeness. 'I'm not *Janey*.'

Michael Donovan looked delighted. 'Forgive me. Your first name sounds so harsh. I'm not sure it suits you.'

2

Janet felt tired as she drove out of Halvergate. It wasn't proving to be the best first week ever. The caginess of her colleagues was stifling; some of the inmates had seemed more communicative than her own team. Coming as she did from the close-knit, supportive world of HMP Leyland, the tension of this prison rested like a weight between her shoulder blades. It wasn't a place to be landed with a prisoner like Michael Donovan, alone, without the backup of officers she trusted.

In the winter dark, her road home wound past a thick line of scrubby trees that screened the airfield and prison from view. Janet resisted the urge to put her foot down and speed round the bend. There was no rush to reach her destination. To make the move to Norfolk easy, she had chosen to rent a place ten minutes away in the village of Halverton after the prison's human resources department recommended the landlady. She had barely lived there a week and was already regretting it.

There were no signs of life as she headed down the dismal main street and drew up outside the small modern house. The building lacked any discernible character. It was a clone of any number of 1930s purpose-built pebble-dashed homes, and could have squatted alongside any road in the country.

She trudged up the soggy gravel path, turning her key in the single Yale lock. A faint smell of mould seeped out into the crisp winter air when she opened the door. Janet closed herself into the dank interior, shaking the rain from her coat and hanging it up in the narrow hallway. Kicking off her shoes, she headed into the kitchen and switched on the kettle. She leaned forwards, staring at the grubby lace that framed the window above the sink, the Formica clammy against her palms. Darkness hid the patch of garden outside. Instead her own face looked back at her from the black glass. She drew the curtains, puffs of dust rising when she yanked them across the rail. A bottle of wine clinked at her as she opened the fridge, but she ignored it and reached for the milk.

In the living room, her feet propped on the coffee table, Janet grabbed the remote and switched on the TV for company. It was a huge square box of a telly with a tiny screen, wedged into a purpose-built 1970s cabinet. Next to it, gathering dust, was a white ceramic statue of a human head with the different areas of the brain labelled in black. It was the sort of prop some psychologists went in for but which Janet had never liked. A keepsake from the last tenant.

Janet hoped John Helkin had been given it as an unwanted Christmas present, rather than choosing it for himself. Her land-lady Mrs Slaney had told her that Dr Helkin had left various 'bits and bobs' behind, a fact that hadn't bothered her at first, but which now made her feel pursued by Halvergate into her own home. Not that 14 Cherry Tree Drive felt like home.

Janet set down her tea and reached for the photograph by her feet on the coffee table. Smiling back at her was a much younger version of herself. The photograph had been taken in the hills above Florence, with the cathedral's dome in the distance. The girl in the picture was laughing, her blonde highlights catching the sun, a red cross round her neck. Janet pulled the cross out from under her jumper and put the photograph beside her on the floral sofa.

Loneliness drifted towards her like the incoming tide. In her hand, the screen on her mobile phone was blank. The person she most wanted to talk to, the person she always wanted to talk to, would not answer her calls.

Failing that, there was always Arun. Janet frowned. He'd told her the job would be a terrible mistake, that there must be easier ways of being promoted than moving to the back end of nowhere. He'd told her she'd regret it. Only once had he asked her not to move because he'd miss her. She pressed the keypad and Arun's picture shone back at her, an old blurry one, taken when her phone had fewer pixels and she'd been more certain she loved him.

She thought about the summer they first got together. She thought about Isabel.

They were sitting in their childhood bedroom, Isabel on Janet's bed as usual, rather than her own. The room seemed horribly cramped and childlike after the freedom of university. Janet felt annoyed. Her sister had left up a yellowing poster from an art exhibition they had visited several years ago on a school trip. She didn't like being reminded of the time Izzy was her only friend. And they still had matching pink duvet covers from when they were fourteen or something. That would have to change.

'What's he like then?' Izzy asked, almost bouncing on the bed with curiosity. Janet tossed her dyed blonde hair back, certain her sister could never understand the love she felt for Arun. Isabel who had barely even snogged anyone, who seemed determined to spend her second year at university just like the first, always working in the care home or the hospital, dreaming of being a doctor. 'Oh, you know.' She shrugged.

'I don't know. Tall, clever, funny, good-looking, what?' Izzy's good mood wasn't dented by her sister's rudeness.

'All those things,' Janet said, feeling defensive. Arun wasn't good-looking, not really, but no need to share that detail. She had no intention of introducing them just yet. For once she wanted there to be one person she didn't share with her sister, one part of her life Isabel didn't know everything about. 'We've only just started going out, there's not much to tell.'

'You love him though.'

In spite of herself, Janet felt the urge to smile. 'Maybe.' Even to her own ears her voice sounded like a truculent five-year-old.

'You do, you do!' Izzy laughed, shoving her. 'You've got that grumpy Bagpuss face on, all screwed up and grouchy, but inside you're all smug and smiling.'

'Get off, stupid!'

Izzy hit her over the head with the pillow. 'Smug and smiling! Smug and smiling! Bagpuss face!' As always, her sister's mood was contagious and Janet started to laugh.

'You'll have to get your own boyfriend,' she said, snatching the pillow and thumping Isabel. 'Then you can stop being such a nosy arse about mine.'

An expression she didn't recognise lit up her sister's face. 'Perhaps I already have.'

Janet stood up. There was no point thinking about the past.

She walked across to where the boxes sat stacked in the corner, left exactly where Arun had put them when he helped her unpack. Somewhere inside one of them was the pink duvet she had once wanted to outgrow.

Arun had left them there, refusing to stay the night on principle, instead driving all the way back to London on a Saturday night. 'You'll just have to come home at weekends,' he'd said, shirt sticking to his sweaty chest as he stomped back to the van. She had stood mutely by the door, waiting for him to crack, to turn back and kiss her, as he always did. Only this time he hadn't.

She pressed 'A' and speed-dialled his number. Arun's voicemail promised to get back to her. Janet toyed with the phone. She knew exactly where he was. She hesitated, then called his work number.

'Faraday Lab,' said a high female voice.

'Hi Jean, it's Janet. Is Arun about?'

'Sure.' There was some muttering and scuffling before Arun finally picked up the phone.

'Hi.' His tone didn't invite a chat. She could picture him, glasses wedged on his nose, tapping his foot.

'Hi there,' she said with false cheeriness. 'Just thought I'd say hello, and um, see how you're doing.'

'Yes, OK, fine, thanks.' A pause. 'Look, I'm quite busy, is it important? Or can I call you a bit later?'

'Yes, of course, I mean, no hurry, just calling for a chat, whenever.'

'OK, speak later.' He hung up.

Janet stared at the threadbare orange carpet, a feeling she couldn't name expanding in her chest, chilling her. Few things could have been guaranteed to upset him more than her moving to Britain's most eastern county to pursue a career he had always hated. She wasn't sure their relationship was going to recover from this latest disappointment.

She picked up the TV remote and turned up the sound before wandering into the kitchen. Pouring herself a glass of red, she took last night's couscous and chicken out of the fridge. She couldn't be bothered to heat it up and headed back into the living room to eat it out of the plastic tub.

Thumping down on Mrs Slaney's chintzy sofa, Janet ferreted her laptop out from behind the cushion where she had wedged it the night before. The wine hit the back of her throat, warming her, as she powered it into life. Not for the first time, work would fill the void. With so little information available on the men who had committed suicide, she was going to have to rely on Google. She took a mouthful of food and started with Ryan Spalding's name in the search bar.

A variety of images came up on screen. The most popular showed a bullet-headed man in his late twenties, with blue eyes and a receding chin. He stared at her with the unsmiling, vacant look everyone wears when starring in a police mugshot. In another picture he was walking into Ipswich Crown Court, a coat half covering his head, one eye glaring out from beneath a sleeve, two fingers held up at the photographer. Janet half smiled. Not a man who cared to charm the press.

She clicked through the news reports thrown up by her search, skimming Spalding's crimes. A serial rapist, he had preyed on a number of women in Suffolk, meeting them through a popular internet dating site. *Sex Beast's Death in the Woods,* ran one tabloid headline.

> *Serial sex monster Spalding was found dead in Thetford Forest at 6.30 on Tuesday morning. Local builder Dennis Harman made the grisly discovery. He told our reporter, 'I often take the dog for a walk this way. It was like a scene from* Saw. *Blood everywhere. It looked like the guy had a knife or bit of metal sticking out from the side of his throat . . .*

Janet grimaced and speed-read through the rest of the article. The paper had given Great Yarmouth General Hospital a hard time, questioning why the 'crazed convict' had been able to escape from their care so easily. The fact that Spalding had been referred to the hospital on psychiatric grounds was highlighted with relish but the reporter gave no useful detail. From HMP Halvergate there was 'no comment.'

'No change there, then,' Janet muttered. Making her way through the other articles, she noticed that only the local papers had bothered to follow up with the news that the police were treating Spalding's death as suicide, not murder.

She had just typed Liam Smith's name into the search bar when her mobile rang, jumping about on the sofa, lit up with Arun's picture. Janet gulped down the last forkful of cold couscous.

'Hey there—' she broke off, coughing. Arun didn't rush to fill the pause. 'Sorry, just having dinner.'

'This not a good time?'

'No, it's perfect, you're not interrupting anything. I'm being a tramp as usual and eating out of a tub.'

Arun didn't laugh. He was a fan of sit-down dinners. 'How's the first week going?'

'It's OK, not much going on yet.' Even though it felt impossible to fake huge enthusiasm for Halvergate, she had no intention of complaining and proving him right. 'I miss you,' she added, a fraction too late.

He sighed heavily. 'I miss you too. Look, I'm sorry about being away at the conference this weekend. But I was thinking of coming down the one after that.'

'Really?' Janet was surprised. It was a rare event for Arun to change his mind. 'I thought you said you didn't want to come to Norfolk, that it was up to me to do the travelling.'

'Well, I mean, I won't if it's not convenient. I thought you'd be pleased.'

'No, I am pleased, it's great you're coming.' Eleven years together and they still managed to offend one another. 'We can go out and explore the countryside,' she said, thinking of his love of walking. 'I've not done that yet.'

He didn't pick up on the suggestion. 'Right, yes, maybe. Thing is I'm working next Saturday so I might have to come up and back on the Sunday.'

'Seriously? That's like a six-hour round trip. Why don't you just come up late on Saturday? It's not like you'll be keeping me up.'

'Well, OK. I guess that makes sense.'

Janet said nothing. She began to have an unpleasant feeling about where next weekend might be heading.

'It's nothing awful or anything,' Arun went on, speaking a little too quickly. 'It's just, there's lots of stuff we need to talk about.'

'You can't talk about any of it now?'

'I'd rather not.'

'Well, I'll see you next weekend then.' She waited, but there was no reply. 'Love you,' she said, the words a ritual long worn of meaning.

'Love you too. Take care.'

Janet sat for a moment, staring at the TV screen without taking it in. Instead she pictured the flat she had left behind, the home Arun would be returning to later, filled with memories of their shared life together. The print of Lake Grasmere from their first holiday, the beautiful rug his mum and dad had given them as a moving-in present and, above all, Arun's quiet, studious presence. The smile as he looked up at her from his book. The unspoken comfort of him always being there.

She picked up the remote and turned the television off. She glanced again at the search results on her laptop for Liam Smith, but found she no longer wanted to spend the evening with only the dead for company. She clicked the lid shut, and the heavy dampness of the house surged into the silence.

3

Lee Webster, the governor of HMP Halvergate, leaned back in his chair opposite Janet, clearly in an expansive mood. In his late fifties, he was a stooped grey badger of a man, his stomach hanging over his belt. Small round glasses perched incongruously on the end of his nose, and he peered over them at the world like a miscast Miss Marple.

'We're delighted to have you on board, you know, with all your experience at Leyland. The way you handled that riot. Well, potential riot. Impressive, very impressive. Not like the Strangeways riots though. Now, that was something. I was at Strangeways at the time . . .'

Lee's gaze wandered from his desk as he spoke, drifting past her shoulder. Behind him, a slab of grey sky was visible through the window. Janet wondered why he had chosen to position his desk with the view at his back. She hoped it wasn't so the light got in his visitors' eyes. High up at the front of the prison, the governor's office looked out over the perimeter fence towards the airfield. The control tower stood in the decaying expanse like an aged guard.

He was still speaking, but he seemed to be recounting his anecdote to himself. He rarely looked at her, and when he did his pale fish eyes sometimes fixed on her ear, sometimes her chin, but never on her eyes. It was a disconcerting habit. His voice was so thin and husky she had to lean forward to hear him. Although she was increasingly unsure if it was worth the effort. The man was a dreadful windbag. Why hadn't she noticed that at her job interview? She supposed the Strangeways story had been more interesting the first time round. Then, just as she began to despair, Lee turned abruptly from Strangeways to the present.

'Now, about your notion of restarting the current sex offender treatment programme from scratch.' He wagged a finger at her, like some jovial uncle. 'That's not going to be possible. I'm sure you realise it's one of our key performance targets, getting through two programmes in a year. I've absolutely no doubt you're up to the job of completing the one Helkin started. You shouldn't be worried about that. You'll do fine. Just crack on with it, eh?'

'It's not a question of being up to the job,' Janet said, her sharp eyes fixing on the governor, whose gaze immediately slid away to the side. 'It's about ensuring the treatment's integrity and reducing the men's risk of reoffending. There's clearly been a substantial period of neglect under John Helkin. I don't know if you know just how serious that neglect has been.' Janet could hear her voice rising higher. 'There are no written notes and no video of any of the sessions, and from my initial assessments, I'm certain all six men on the original programme would benefit from restarting it, not to mention the three new ones—'

'But what of the performance target, Dr Palmer?' he interrupted. 'How do you expect me to break that to the rest of the management team? No, first-week nerves are quite understandable, but in this case, misplaced. I have every faith in you, your lack of confidence is entirely, entirely . . .' Lee trailed off, unable to find the word, shuffling the mass of tea-stained papers on his desk. 'And Dr Helkin might have gone off the boil, but he wasn't a bad chap. I imagine he did a reasonable enough job of looking after everyone, even if his notes are, as you insist, a little scanty. Not everyone can be as fulsome as you ladies. He was always a man of few words.'

'Mr Webster, there were five suicides in almost as many months at Halvergate under Dr Helkin's care. Not to mention Ryan Spalding's escape from hospital.'

Lee pushed his glasses up his nose, frowning. 'As I said, Helkin went off the boil. If he never wrote anything down, it would've been impossible to see that coming. And the escape, well, it was from hospital, that's a Department of Health affair, no blame attached to the management here.' He peered at her chin. 'And of course suicides, although regrettable, are not, unlike getting through two treatment programmes a year, part of our performance targets, are they?'

Faced with this appalling logic, Janet found herself unable to reply. Taking her silence for assent, Lee smiled, his eyes twinkling, suddenly the jolly uncle again. 'Look, why don't we strike a compromise? You can restart the programme, but only if you knock out a few sessions. I don't mind which ones, just so long as you make sure we've completed two programmes by the end of the year. Can't say fairer than that, eh?' Lee shambled to the door, flinging out an arm, clearly her cue to leave.

A few seconds later Janet was standing in the corridor outside his office, wondering how the governor had managed to manoeuvre her out of the door so quickly without laying a hand on her.

In her own office, she stood for a moment with her back to the closed door, trying not to think about her old shared room at Leyland, or her colleague Stuart's friendly face, the cup of tea that would have been waiting for her. The massive good-luck card he and the rest of the team had given her sat prominently on the shelves by her desk. It only emphasised the lack of cheer in the empty room.

She flicked on the light. Even though it was morning, the gloomy winter's day barely illuminated the small space. Unlike Lee's office, hers looked over to the side of Halvergate, facing the perimeter fence that flanked the prison. Running along the length of it were some unattractive olive green 1950s prefabs that had once belonged to the RAF. These days they housed the prisoners' workshops, but they looked like glorified Portakabins. She imagined they must be far too stuffy in summer, and freezing in the winter; even the *Daily Express* couldn't complain that the inmates working in them were getting an easy ride.

Janet headed to her desk. It was twenty minutes before she was officially due to start, and a day of thrashing out the group programme with Terry lay ahead. Always an early riser, at Halvergate she'd found herself arriving at work even earlier than usual. This was partly to feel on top of the job, and partly to get out of Cherry Tree Drive. The place depressed her even more than the prison; bad dreams disturbed her sleep, and she kept stumbling across leftovers from John Helkin, which was unnerving. Last night she had investigated the airing cupboard only to find racks of his shirts hanging up, sad and crumpled, swaying slightly from the heat. He must own a lot of shirts to have left so many behind.

She started at a knock on the door. It was Terry.

'Am I disturbing you?' He inched himself over the threshold. 'Saw your car was already here.'

'Not at all. Can I get you a tea or coffee?' Janet headed over to her tiny sink. 'I was just about to make myself one.'

Terry hesitated, staring at the two stripy mugs she was holding out towards him. 'OK, ta. I'll have a tea.'

Janet switched the kettle on and Terry made his way over to join her. The pair of them sat in uncompanionable silence in the two soft chairs by the door, waiting for the water to boil. Despite having turned up uninvited, Terry scarcely looked at her and didn't seem in a hurry to start the conversation.

'What's up then?' Janet asked, as she poured out the hot water. Terry helped himself to four sachets of milk, leaving just two in the bowl.

'It's about the sessions. About who's in the group.' He stared down at his mug, still avoiding her eye. 'It's your call, Dr Palmer, but there's a young man, Ian Fendley, who I think really deserves a chance. I've added him to the list today, hoped you might squeeze him in.'

Janet watched Terry as she sipped her tea. Their group was already full; another new face would be stretching things. Not that anyone in Halvergate's management was going to mind. She thought of her new governor and his key performance targets. Fast-tracking another inmate through the system was bound to win Lee's approval. 'No harm in doing an assessment,' she said. 'As long as you're sure his mental health is robust enough to cope with the programme. Has he been screened by the in-reach team?'

Terry nodded. 'Yes, I got them to have a look at him. Not long after he arrived here.'

'Can I ask why you're so keen we have him in the group? The other three have been on the waiting list, this man's case must be pretty compelling to jump the queue.'

'Ian's just a boy really. Twenty-two-year-old lad, first offence.' Terry raised a hand, as if to ward off any objection. 'I'm not saying that's an excuse, it was a nasty date rape, but I think he's really sorry about it. Not often you can say that.'

'True,' said Janet, thinking of Michael Donovan. 'And there's no other reason I need to know about, you didn't know him on the outside?' She took in the senior officer's shifty expression and felt a stab of misgiving. 'You have to tell me if you know him.'

'I'm not going to lie, he's from my neighbourhood, I've seen him around.' Terry flushed as she continued to stare at him. 'But I never spoke to Ian before he got here, him or his family.'

Janet wasn't entirely sure she believed him, but felt she had pushed the point as far as she could. 'Well, I can't promise, but I'll do the assessment. If you bring over any paperwork about his history, I can see him this morning.'

Terry downed the rest of his milky tea and set the mug down with a clunk. 'I'll go get it now.'

He stood up to leave, but before he reached the door, Stuart's good-luck card caught his eye. He stopped, staring at it. He stayed there so long, she wondered if he was going to pick it up. 'There was something you mentioned the other day. About gaps in Dr Helkin's notes.' Terry had his back to her as he spoke. 'I don't understand it. You see, he was always writing.'

Before she could reply, he left the room.

Janet sat looking at the closed door. Something told her it was the most personal conversation she had yet had with anyone at Halvergate.

When Terry dropped Ian Fendley off at her office, he seemed shy and polite. Floppy-haired, slender and softly spoken, nothing about him would ring obvious alarm bells in a woman's mind if he chatted to her at a bus stop. Of course, it hadn't worked out that way for seventeen-year-old Alyssa Petrovic.

Janet watched him closely, her pen poised, as she asked the familiar question. 'Perhaps you could just talk me through the offence in your own words.'

Ian ran a hand nervously through his sandy hair, a gesture that made him look like the teenager he almost was. 'We'd met a couple of nights before, yeah, when I got her number waiting for the bus home. When I saw her again she looked different, like older, she'd got loads of make-up on, a nice dress and that, and I thought, that's it, I'm in.' He looked embarrassed. 'I know that was stupid now.'

'And then what happened?'

'We got some chips, chatted on the beach, had a bit of a snog. It was late by then, midnight or one maybe.' Ian trailed off, avoiding her eye. 'And that's when it happened.'

'When you assaulted her?'

'Look, I'm not proud of it, am I? I really liked her, I thought she liked me.' His face turned pink. 'I wanted to write, tell her how sorry I was, but she didn't want to hear nothing from me. That's what the lawyer said.'

Janet leaned against the side of the chair, balancing the notepad on her knee. She was careful to keep her expression neutral. 'Can you understand why she didn't want to hear from you?'

'Yeah, I guess I wouldn't have wanted to hear nothing from me neither after that. But I'm sorry, you know?' Ian ran his hands down the sides of his trousers as if to wipe sweat off his palms.

'I only got how wrong it had all gone when she started screaming, and then those kids came running over, and I didn't have a chance to explain.'

Janet nodded. 'So you ran away and left her on the beach?'

Ian slumped down in the chair. 'Yeah, not proud of that either.'

Janet paused to scribble down notes: *reasonable eye contact, apparent sense of shame, some minimising of the offence.* When she looked back at Ian, he was biting his nails, hair half covering his eyes. 'And what are you hoping to get out of the programme?'

'Well, I'm hoping you can help me. You know, help me not do that kind of thing again.' He shook the hair out of his face. 'And like, maybe being on the programme and that, I might be able to get some qualifications or something. Terry said maybe I could do something like that.'

'We can definitely look at that. I'll talk to Terry for you.' Janet put her notebook down. 'You know, the treatment programme is quite intense. We'd have to go over your offence in detail and most of the other men are a lot older, some are repeat offenders. Are you sure you're up for it?'

'Yeah, I'm up for it.' Ian grinned at her, looking more like a schoolboy than a convict. 'And you know, Miss, how much worse can it be? Not like this is Pontins, is it?'

4

Outside her office window, fog had rolled in from the marshes. She could no longer see it in the dark, except where it gathered like a swarm of moths around the lights on the perimeter fence. It was early evening, but felt like midnight. Across the blackness of the airfield, Cherry Tree Drive sat waiting for her. She didn't get up. Instead, for the third time, she scanned down the list of names she and Terry had drawn up for the treatment programme, mentally picturing each man.

They had decided to restart the group sessions with the same six offenders Terry and Helkin had been treating, with Ian Fendley and three other new starters to replace the prisoners who had died or been moved. Terry had lined up a local psychology graduate as the third facilitator, a young woman called Siobhan Trant. Janet was surprised nobody had been available within Halvergate, but Terry only shrugged when she queried him. With Lee's instructions to finish the programme by the end of the year, they would be forced to skip several sessions for the men who had already been through half the programme with Helkin, although they had agreed that one man would be made to restart them all.

Michael Donovan. Seeing his name on the page, Janet again felt the unease that had disturbed her at their first meeting. She closed her eyes, pressing her fingers against the frown lines, where a headache was forming. Not since she had first qualified as a psychology assistant had a prisoner perplexed her so much after just one meeting. It was not, she decided, that she found Michael attractive. This she could accept without guilt and lay to one side.

It was more troubling than attraction. Michael felt familiar to her, as if she might have known him before. She found it impossible to consider him as so many wires and synapses to be re-routed and disarmed. Instead his personality surged through, like an electric current. At Leyland, she would have discussed her reaction with Stuart. Here, there was nobody she knew or trusted enough.

Janet walked to the window. The black glass reflected her pale face back into the room. Her nose felt cold as she pressed it against the pane. She cupped her hands around her eyes to see through. Across the yard, in the middle of the workshops, sat a squat pink building, covered in pebble-dash. It could have been mistaken for another hideous bungalow, but she remembered Terry telling her that it was the RAF chapel. The lights were on, shining through the stained glass. Janet put her hand to her throat, conscious of the cross under her jumper. It had been a while since she'd been in church.

'It's not much further.' Izzy turned round, her face pink and sweaty from the climb. The sun shone bright behind her head, picking up the red in her hair like a halo.

Janet took another swig of tepid water. The walk up from Florence to the hills should have been little more than a gentle stroll, but in the heat it was sweltering. Back in London, she'd had mixed feelings about this holiday, booked before she got together with Arun, but from the moment they arrived she'd found she was enjoying it too much to miss him.

She caught up with Izzy and took her hand. 'Come on slowcoach!' she said, dragging her up the next stone step. Isabel shook her off. 'Ugh, let go, sweaty hand.'

They paused a moment in the doorway, looking back over the city below that shimmered red and blue in the heat. Then Isabel stepped forward into the darkness of San Miniato al Monte, and Janet followed.

She blinked, adjusting to the sudden change in light, the cool air enveloping her like a cloak. Then she stood still, overwhelmed by the beauty and strangeness of the place. The sun breaking through the glass in stripes, the colours of the wooden ceiling dancing in the light, the cold black and white of the marble.

'It's like seeing God,' Izzy said, voicing Janet's thoughts.

Steven Finch, the chaplain of HMP Halvergate, sat at the back of the nave, his head bowed, enjoying the stillness. In his mind, so as not to disturb the silence, he recited the collect for evensong. *Lighten our darkness we beseech thee, Oh Lord; and by thy great mercy defend us from all perils and dangers of this night.*

Steven raised his eyes to the altar, wondering how many times the collect had been said here. Hundreds, maybe thousands of times. Even before he became a Christian, he had always marvelled at the way an empty church never really feels empty. Hope and prayers hang in the air like dust motes, a heavy scent left behind by the congregation, the same way his Auntie Joan would leave a trail of Californian Poppy in every room she passed through. It probably wasn't the thing to compare a cheap Woolies' perfume to the devotions of the faithful, but both, Steven felt, were denser than air.

He was lucky with St Mary's Halvergate. The majority of prison chapels where he'd worked had been depressingly utilitarian, and although this was no Liverpool Cathedral, thanks to the RAF, it still felt like a place of worship rather than a box ticked by the prison service. It wasn't the stained glass, the wooden pews or the altar that Steven felt most grateful for, but the statue. Carved entirely from white stone, her rough surface shining with flecks of silver, Our Lady of Halvergate had stolen his heart. She stood at the front, facing her captive audience during services, but not looking at them; instead, she raised her eyes to heaven. Her features were drawn in the naive style but there was no mistaking the grief in her face. She clasped her hands to her chest, a sword piercing her heart.

The latch clicked behind him. Steven turned. A small, slight woman entered the chapel. The new psychologist, he thought. At first he was so surprised to see her he forgot to say hello, and then something in her expression made him sit back in the shadows. Her hair had separated into wet curls in the rain, surrounding her face like a nest of snakes. She walked swiftly down the aisle and came to a stop in front of the beautiful Maria Dolorosa.

Steven had intended to leave a beat and then say something, but as the woman stood there, unmoving, and time stretched on, he began to feel uncomfortable. This was more than a sightseeing trip. His new colleague appeared to be having a moment, and he was going to look like some sort of stalker when she turned round to leave. He got up noisily.

'Nice, isn't she? Can you believe we've even got some old postcards of her?' His cheery northern voice echoed loudly in the empty space, making the psychologist turn round with a start. Steven strode towards her, pretending not to see the silver lines shining on her face, a mirror of the Madonna's stone tears.

'Sorry if I gave you a fright. Steven Finch. I'm the prison chaplain.' He held out a hand, but for a moment he thought she might not take it. She looked disorientated, like a diver just returned to the water's surface. Then she grasped his hand in hers as if expecting him to pull her up from the deep.

'Janet Palmer, the new psychologist.'

Steven liberated himself from her freezing fingers. 'John Helkin's replacement, then?'

'Did you know him?' Her large dark eyes fixed on him with a stare so intense it felt like an accusation.

'Sorry, before my time. I only got here a month before you.'

'Oh.' She stepped back, her disappointment obvious. For reasons Steven couldn't fathom, this encounter was not going well. He had managed to make absolutely no friends at Halvergate, and as a usually gregarious soul was beginning to fear he had lost his touch. He could not let this potential drinking companion and partner in gossip escape, however peculiar she seemed. He hadn't been this desperate for friends since primary school.

33

'If you like the statue, you might find this interesting.' He beckoned her towards the back of the church.

On the right-hand side of the door, which she'd stalked past as she came in, was the truncated nose of a Second World War aircraft sticking out from the wall. Beside it hung an old propeller shaped and welded into a makeshift cross. Dozens of metal badges engraved with pilots' and engineers' names covered the walls.

'It's the airmen's corner. They left the badges to say thanks for the safe journey home,' said Steven, peering at a few. 'And families left the names of those they lost, to be remembered here.'

There should have been something morbid about the whole shrine, but somehow it had instead a jaunty, laddish air. Janet ran her fingers over the plane's nose, poker-faced. 'It's great.'

'The governor wanted to get rid of it. Security risk or something. The RAF stepped in. Don't think Lee was pleased, he's not been back here since, which is a *shame*, obviously.' Steven cast a sly glance at her, one eyebrow raised in an exaggeratedly camp gesture.

They watched each other for a moment, calculating. Then Janet breathed out a sigh that sent wisps of hair flying from her face. 'It's not just me, then? You weren't riveted by his Strangeways saga either?'

'Nope.' Steven grinned, warmth spreading through his chest like the first sip from a glass of red wine. It was wrong, un-Christian, to bond with somebody over disliking others, and in church too, but he found he didn't care.

Janet smiled back at him, the skin round her eyes crinkling. 'Everyone here just seems so bloody miserable or *weird*.'

'Don't hold back now. Why don't you tell me what you really think?'

'I know, sorry, very unprofessional. It's just this place, it's . . . well.' She shrugged.

'And I bet nobody's suggested anything so civilised as going for a drink?' She shook her head. 'No, thought not. You'll have to come round for dinner on Friday. I live in Norwich, so it nearly qualifies as civilised.' He tilted his head with mock solemnity. 'That's if you're not hanging out with Terry after work, the pair of you making gloomy eyes at each other?'

Janet laughed, and Steven wondered how he could ever have thought her peculiar.

'No, that would be great.'

He scribbled his mobile number and address on an old service sheet. 'Seven thirty do you?'

'You sure it's no trouble?' Janet chewed her lip, a picture of middle-class concern.

'A load of trouble. I've got a crammed social life out here, not sure how I'll cope having dinner with a new colleague.' Steven rolled his eyes. 'Don't be daft.'

She turned to leave. Steven stood in the church doorway, the light behind him. Its glow followed her as she walked along the path that led back to Halvergate.

'Our Lady of Sorrows,' he said to himself, watching Janet's pale figure cut across the dark.

5

The morning mist rose from the earth like smoke as Steven drove along the Acle Straight. The landscape stretched out, endlessly flat to his left and his right, tapering off to blue in the distance. It was impossible to see for sure where the marshes met the horizon. Ahead, their outlines sketched on the sky in dark blue ink, were the industrial shapes of Great Yarmouth. Steven drove at a steady speed on the single carriageway towards the seaside town. Old towers that looked like windmills, but were in fact ancient water pumps for draining the marsh, littered the ground on either side of him. Passing centuries had made little impact on this neglected corner of Norfolk. Dotted among the pumps and the grazing sheep, medieval church spires kept their vigil from an earlier age of faith.

Before getting into Yarmouth, Steven turned right, following an old sign to RAF Breydon and taking the narrow road across the marshland. He headed over the bridge a touch too fast, his stomach lurching as the car jumped on the descent. He hit the brakes. The road was barely more than a track, framed by twisted willow stumps and waterlogged ditches. The vast openness of the landscape ahead made him feel as if he was driving straight into the sky. It didn't make you feel free, this closeness of the clouds. Steven thought of the medieval Fathers, with their love of comparing men to worms, tiny and exposed on the earth's surface, under the watchful eye of God. He wondered if any of them had experienced the loneliness of East Anglia.

After passing through the villages of Halvergate and Halverton, the road descended into lower ground, scrubby bushes hiding the view. The old airfield lay behind the trees. At least here the sign had been updated, with the board to the left announcing that he'd arrived at HMP Halvergate. The prison was named after the nearby marshes, not for the Air Force. Steven passed through the outer gates, exchanging hellos with David the security guard. Crossing the airfield, his car bumped over the poor surface, one wheel dipping off the track into the mud and scraping the undercarriage against the tarmac. He winced, thinking of his battered old car's suspension. When he pulled into the staff car park, he noticed that Janet's silver Mini was already there.

Steven thought about their encounter in the church. The intensity of pain – or was it anger? – in Janet's face had startled him when he first approached her. He'd rarely met anyone who radiated emotion like that, but it didn't invite intimacy. Instead it had surrounded her like a wall of glass.

He smiled to himself. On the other hand, she had laughed at his jokes, which made her the most promising of his colleagues so far. Halvergate wasn't somewhere you could be too choosy. His friendly overtures to everyone else had fallen comically flat. Terry had taken fright after reading his suggestion of going for a drink as a romantic proposition, while Keith, the Band 4 officer on A wing ... Well, he was just a bastard. Steven reminded himself, piously, that Keith was probably a very effective prison officer, who had had a tough life. But he was still a bastard.

'The Polack was asking for you,' said Keith.

Steven's least favourite person in Halvergate was squinting down at him. Built like a nightclub bouncer, with multi-layered scowls wrinkling his bulldog face, Keith Lawson would be more terrifying to meet in a dark alley than most of the inmates. Steven put down his cup. He had hoped to enjoy a brew in the staff canteen and prepare himself with some quiet reflection before his shift started, but Mr Lawson clearly had other ideas.

'Sorry, you'll have to remind me who that is.' There were a number of eastern European inmates at Halvergate, all of whom were 'Polack' to Keith.

'You know, Arnie Whatsit, the blond bugger. A wing. In for ABH. He's a regular of yours, always asking to go to church.' Keith spat the last words. He made no secret of the fact he thought all churchgoing prisoners were employing it as a ruse to get recommended for parole. Doubtless many were.

From the description, Steven guessed Keith meant Arnas Kazlauskas, who was Lithuanian, not Polish. Technically he was one of Father Dunstan's charges, but like several of the Catholic prisoners from eastern Europe, Arnas seemed unconcerned about which denomination the chaplain belonged to.

'Did he say what it was about?'

Keith shrugged unhelpfully and walked off. Steven downed his tea, burning his tongue, and followed him.

Arnas looked agitated when Steven walked into his cell. The smell of stale air and tobacco added to his sense of claustrophobia. Arnas darted forward. 'Father, thank goodness you come!'

'Good to see you too. How's it going?'

'Is very bad place here, Father, you must help make clean.' Arnas loomed into Steven's personal space, towering over him. He took a step back.

'Mind if I sit down?' he asked, settling onto a plastic stool. Arnas didn't take the hint and continued pacing about in the tiny room.

'What's not clean about the place?' Steven asked, sensing his companion probably wasn't going to have a whinge about the cracked lino or the smelly loo parked in the corner.

'There is bad here, I feel it. Not for me, for others it already come. But you must say prayers make the velnius go away.' Arnas leaned over him, sweat beading over his bare shoulders and pooling at the centre of his vest. 'Make sure it not come here. It not come for me.'

Steven looked at Arnas a little uneasily. He'd had to look up 'velnius' after a past visit. It was the Lithuanian for devil. This wasn't the first time he had been asked to keep evil spirits away and it always left him feeling uncomfortable. Steven believed in evil, not as a vague descriptor but as a potent reality. For him it was a force as real as gravity, one that tormented the human heart and might well be felt more profoundly in the cells and corridors of a prison, even if, as a Liberal Christian, he baulked at the idea of actual devils capering about with horns. But he was also aware that a preoccupation with demons could be a sign of mental illness. Arnas stared at him.

'Of course we can say some prayers together,' said Steven.

Arnas sat heavily on the edge of his bed. 'You will say prayer of protection?'

'Yes, we can say them together. Not so much about keeping the velnius out of the cell, but we could pray to keep him out of our hearts?'

'Out of hearts yes, but also out of cell so can't get into heart,' Arnas said, frowning. 'Already in other cells.'

'OK. Let's ask God to bless this place and to be always in our hearts and watch over us.'

Arnas murmured devoutly in his own language as Steven prayed. The chaplain left a period of silence at the end, and the pair of them sat with their heads bowed.

Eventually Arnas looked up. 'Will you bless me also, Father?'

'Of course.' Steven stood over him, placing his left hand on Arnas's shaved head, bristling with stubble, and made the sign of the cross. 'May the blessing of Almighty God, the Father, the Son and the Holy Spirit, be with you now and remain with you and with those you love, this day and always. Amen.'

As he moved to go he saw that Arnas had stuck a postcard of the RAF chapel's Virgin Mary on the wall above his bed. The picture couldn't do justice to the beautiful white statue, but Steven smiled to see it.

'I see you've got Our Lady looking over you.'

'Yes.' Arnas laid his hand on the picture, his face fierce. 'She keep the other one away.'

Michael Donovan sat in Janet's office like an old friend. He had leaned back in the soft chair, expanding into all the available space, one leg balanced across the other, a hand draped over his ankle.

'I like what you've done with the place,' he said, looking up at the cheap Holbein print she had hung opposite her desk. 'Since Helkin was here, I mean. And that's a nice touch.' He pointed to the good-luck card. 'From family?'

'From former colleagues,' Janet said, pleased there was nothing more personal in the room for him to pore over. 'Look, Michael, I'm going to be straight with you. The reason you're here is because I wasn't sure from our last meeting whether you're entirely committed to the aims of the treatment programme.'

'Oh? Thinking of replacing me with choirboy Fendley?' Michael said. 'No need to look surprised. Amazingly enough we do all talk to each other. Ian's been positively *gushing* about you.'

'There's no question of a replacement,' Janet said. 'Ian is joining the group regardless.'

'But I'm not? Well, that's a bit hurtful.' He leaned forward, blue eyes twinkling. 'What do I need to do to convince you?'

'The programme is for people who accept their guilt and genuinely want to change their behaviour,' she told him, folding her arms. 'You seem like a man who's quite pleased with himself just the way he is.'

'Are you calling me smug?' Michael laughed. 'Of that I probably am guilty. But really, who are you to judge the state of my soul on such a short acquaintance? I don't deny I raped Karina. Simply because I'm not wailing about it doesn't mean I feel no remorse.'

'Last time we met, you said all men want to rape women.'

'Did I? How very dramatic of me.' He bit his bottom lip. 'I was obviously trying to impress you.'

Janet felt anger pressing at the edge of her professional calm. Her nails dug into the palm of her hand. She knew Michael was studying her. 'Perhaps you can tell me why you want to join the group. Other than the increased chance it offers for parole.'

'Well, as you've probably gathered, I exhibit psychopathic tendencies,' he said, his tone non-committal, as if they were discussing the weather. 'And you're right, I am pleased with who I am. But I'm well aware, Janey, that society is not. If I'm to have any hope of getting out of here I need to change. And who knows? Perhaps the sessions will help me feel the remorse you so cunningly deduced is currently lacking.'

Janet turned the pen round and round in her fingers. If Michael had continued to insist he felt sorry she would have had no difficulty in spotting the lie, but there was just enough of a whiff of the truth about this speech to make her waver. He sensed her indecision and pressed his case.

'And everyone deserves a second chance, don't they? Isn't that what the Good Book says?' He looked at the hollow between her collarbones, where they both knew the forbidden cross lay hidden under her jumper.

Janet laughed. 'Forgiveness not seven but seventy times? It may say that in the Bible, but I'm afraid the Ministry of Justice didn't get that memo. And neither did I.' She met his eyes and felt a flicker of understanding pass between them. 'I'll discuss this with Terry and let you know our decision later today.'

She knew, even though his face gave no sign, that Michael was angry. He leaned forward, just touching on the edge of her personal space. 'I'm sure if anyone can fix me, you can. Though of course, you're not the only woman to exercise her charms at Halvergate.' He took in her puzzled expression. 'But I wouldn't worry. I'm sure she's no match for you.'

Terry was sitting with his own pre-packed sandwiches when she found him in the staff canteen. Janet wondered if he had made them himself. The bread was cut into meticulous squares with no crusts, and a red apple sat beside the neat little pile in his Tupperware box. Three o'clock was an unsociable time to have picked for lunch. In a sea of plastic white tables, he made a solitary dark shape. She pulled up a seat opposite. He didn't look especially pleased to have company.

'So I saw Michael again.'

Terry glanced up from his sandwich. 'Oh?'

'I can't decide whether he would be a liability in the group or not.'

'Your call.' Terry took a swig of tea.

'It's a big deal to kick somebody off the programme. I don't think he'd be the easiest man to work with, but that doesn't mean he should be denied the chance to take part.'

'Keep him in then,' said Terry, still not looking up from his food. Janet felt like snatching the sandwich off him to grab his attention.

'What I'm trying to say, Terry, is I need your advice. You know him better than me. I took Ian Fendley on because you recommended him. I value your judgement. I'd appreciate your help here.'

Ian's name seemed to rouse Terry from his bad temper. He finally looked her in the eye. 'If you really want my advice ...' He was cut off by another figure joining them.

'Well, this is nice. Having a *cosy* chat?'

It was Richard Smith, Janet's line manager and the prison's deputy governor. In the dingy canteen, whose windows were half covered by scaffolding, his bulk looming over the table blocked out even more of the light.

'We were just discussing the sex offender treatment programme,' she said.

Richard sat down next to Terry, shaking his head slightly, rippling his mane of chestnut hair. Long and flowing, it curled at the edge of his shoulders in a majestic wave. It was an attractive man's hair, but it framed an ugly face. Folds of flesh encased his tiny brown eyes, and underneath them squatted a small snub nose, like a snout. 'Oh yes? Not planning on *missing* the performance target, I hope.'

Janet supposed he was attempting a bit of banter rather than being rude. Or at least she hoped so. She glanced at Terry. Although he was the taller man, he seemed to have shrunk in the presence of their line manager, as if in a bid to escape his attention.

'We were just discussing one of the men, Michael Donovan, and whether he should continue on the programme.'

'That sounds a bit *drastic*.' Richard had a habit of stressing individual words, as if his sentences were weighed down by their own importance. 'A lot of paperwork involved, if he's to be denied treatment. Not sure how *good* it would look in reports.'

'That's why we were discussing it. I was just asking Terry what he was like in Helkin's sessions.' At the mention of her predecessor's name, Richard stiffened. He turned to the man beside him.

'And what does *Terry* say?'

Janet had an unpleasant feeling that she had somehow put her colleague on the spot, though she couldn't understand why. Terry's face was tilted away from her, making his expression impossible to read.

'Nothing untoward happened in Dr Helkin's sessions,' he said. 'Not with Michael or anyone else.'

'There you are, Dr Palmer, nothing to *worry* about. This Michael chap can have a reprieve.' Richard's smile was not reflected in his hard piggy eyes.

A loud scraping noise made her jump. It was Terry pushing back his chair. 'If you'll excuse me?'

He left so abruptly Janet had no time to join in with her own excuses and escape. Instead she was left stranded with Richard, the pair of them facing each other over the crumbs from Terry's sandwich. Without saying anything, Richard fished around in the bag by his feet and brought out a newspaper, spreading it across the table.

'I'm sure you have *plenty* to be getting on with. The first week in the job can't *all* be fun and socialising.'

Richard bent his head to read. She got up, disorientated by his rudeness. 'Yes, of course. See you later.'

As she made her way out of the canteen, a group of prison officers barrelled through the swing doors, one of the men thumping his elbow into her chest. He scowled. 'Mind where you're going, love.'

The doors closed behind her. Janet was left standing in the empty grey corridor, with only the deep pulsing hum of the prison's ventilation system for company.

6

Behind rolls of barbed wire, the sky shone pink. The yard was empty as Janet walked to the VP wing, followed by numerous CCTV cameras perched on top of high poles. She had skipped breakfast in her eagerness to get out of the house, but arriving at the prison didn't make her feel any better. HMP Halvergate sat watchful in the yard's open space, its silence at odds with the hundreds of men locked inside. Even on the outside, she could sense the claustrophobia.

'Dr Palmer!'

She stopped, startled by the shout. A prison officer came jogging towards her along the path.

'It *is* Dr Palmer isn't it? The new psych?' The man was enormous. Despite the winter chill, he wore a short-sleeved white shirt, showing off forearms like pistons.

'Yes, and you are . . . ?'

'Keith Lawson, senior officer on A wing.' He looked down at her. 'Made you jump, did I?' He didn't look very apologetic if he had.

'No, it's fine.'

'You got a sec to come over and see one of the guys?' Keith walked as he talked, leaving little alternative but to follow. 'We've got one of the cons moaning about needing meds. For anxiety or some such crap. The nurse from the in-reach team is off sick, so you'll have to talk to him.'

'I can do an assessment if you need one, but it's not really—'

'No call for all that.' He pulled the keys out of his back trouser pocket. 'We know he's a troublemaker. All I need is for you to tell him he doesn't need any pills. Then we can say he was seen.'

'I'm not sure—'

Keith ushered her into A wing, slamming the door behind them with a clang. 'It won't take a moment.'

Janet followed him along the corridor of the unfamiliar wing, his silver key chain jangling in time to his swaggering walk. The rumbling from the ventilation system sounded louder in this part of Halvergate. She looked up at the pipes on the ceiling, wondering which was the gas. They turned a corner, reaching the cage-like gate that led to the ground floor of the landings. Beyond the bars, she could see that the association area was deserted, the football tables and foam chairs unused, all the cell doors shut.

'I thought it was already past the time for full unlock?'

'Not the staff for it today.' Keith shut the gate. 'They'll just have to stew in there a bit longer with their PlayStations. Shame.'

Janet's feeling of misgiving grew. 'What's he called, the guy I'm seeing?'

'Baz Gridley. Former dealer, in for GBH.' He set off along the left-hand set of doors, shadowed by the landings above. Posters on the wall warned about the dangers of legal highs.

'You say he's difficult?'

'Why? You worried?' He snorted. 'I'll leave the door open. Me or one of the other lads will be just a call away.'

Janet had had enough. She stopped. After carrying on for a few paces, he walked back to her with a sigh. 'I don't know what you expect from me,' she said. 'But I'm not happy about this.' He looked surprised. 'Since you're short-staffed I'll do an assessment, but it will be a genuine examination of this man's needs. Which I intend to log.' She put her hands on her hips. 'And I used to work in maximum security, so I don't appreciate having my concerns about personal safety scoffed at.'

Keith shrugged. 'Log what you like. Nobody's stopping you.' He walked further down the corridor and banged on a cell grate. 'Baz! Psych's here to see you.' He unlocked the door, holding it open for her with a flourish. For a moment she considered refusing to go in. Then she thought of the man inside. Keith was hardly the most sympathetic of officers. Perhaps the prisoner was gripped by a genuine mental health crisis, in desperate need, with nobody but her to help. She walked into the cell.

Clothes lay strewn across the floor and there was a strong smell of feet. In the window plastic cartons of milk and Ribena sat crammed on to the sill, almost blocking out what little daylight made it through the bars. Baz Gridley sat in the foetal position, crouched by the sink. Janet remained standing near the door.

'Baz? My name's Dr Janet Palmer. I understand you've been having some trouble with anxiety.'

There was no sign of acknowledgement. She took a small step forward. 'Are you OK? Can you get up please?' No answer. Raising her voice, she tried again. 'Mr Gridley?'

Without any sound or warning, the man sprang at her. If she had been any closer, he would have had her on the floor. As it was, she staggered back, barely making it to the other side of the door. She tried to slam it shut, but Baz already had one shoulder through and was trying to shove his way out. Up close she saw his pupils were wide and black. The man was high.

'Keith!' she screamed.

Baz gave another shove and the door slammed into her chest. She jumped back, running towards the empty association area. There was no sign of any prison officers. 'Keith!' she yelled again. Baz circled her round a football table, his arms stretched out as if it were a game of tag. She darted to the side, picking up one of the foam chairs and thrusting all four legs towards him.

'I'm warning you,' she shouted. 'Stand back! Don't get any closer.'

From the walkway above, Janet heard a prison officer's whistle, followed by the clatter of heavy shoes on the stairs. Baz lunged towards her, then crashed to the ground, tackled from behind by Keith. The prison officer raised his baton in the air, bringing it down hard as Baz tried to rise. Blood splashed at Janet's feet.

Elodie Harper

'Thought you'd have a go at a girl, did you?' Up went the baton again. 'Fucking scumbag!' Keith was battering the screaming man on the floor, who now had his hands over his head. 'I'll go medieval on your sorry fucking arse!'

'That's enough!' Janet raised her hands in a futile gesture. 'Enough!'

Two more prison officers arrived, bundling on top of Baz and dragging him to his feet. Between them, the three men put him in restraints. He lolled unsteadily. There was blood on his chin and it looked as if he had lost a tooth. All the noise had alerted other prisoners to the fight going on and the landings reverberated to the sound of yelling and hammering from inside the cells, leaving the air thick with agitation. Keith, sweating heavily, wiped a hand over his face. 'You pair all right to take him to segregation?'

'Doesn't he need to see the nurse first?' Janet was shaking.

'Nah. He'll live,' said one of the officers holding him, a young blond man with a crew cut.

'He's high as a kite.'

'Yeah? Funny that. I reckon we just brought him back down to earth.' Keith stowed his baton back in his belt. The other men laughed.

Janet stepped forward. 'Mr Gridley? Can you hear me?'

Baz raised his head, swaying slightly, trying to focus his gaze. His eyes found hers and he stiffened. 'Fuck you! Fucking bitch. I'll fucking kill you . . .'

'You see, love,' said the older officer, wrestling him away. 'He's not such a nice chap. Come on mate, you've had your fun for the day.'

'She's not going to fucking get away with it! Not like the last one. She'll have to watch out . . .' Baz continued protesting as they dragged him off. Janet and Keith were left alone.

'Where *were* you?'

'Sorry. Just stepped out for a piss. No harm done.' Keith stared at her, unrepentant. Janet had a sick feeling the man had left her

48

alone on purpose, as revenge for the lecture she'd given him. She brushed it aside. Surely that wasn't possible.

'He nearly had me.'

'He never touched you though, did he?'

'I could still report it to the police.'

Keith leaned on the side of the football table. 'I wouldn't do that. It didn't do Dr Helkin any good.'

'What do you mean?'

'He wasn't too popular with the inmates either. Made a bit of a fuss. Still . . .' Keith sauntered off towards the gate, forcing her to follow. 'He won't be reporting anything from where he is now.'

In her office Janet paced up and down, jittery and upset. She had had several close shaves at work before, but never anything like that. The horror did not lie in the attempted assault but the feeling of abandonment. When she yelled for Keith the second time, part of her had been afraid that nobody would ever come.

Her gut instinct had been to go ahead and call the police, but without the support of a key witness and only a few days into the job, she didn't feel the stress would be worth it. Instead she had put a call through to Lee requesting a meeting. His secretary told her the governor was out, but Richard would head over instead. Her heart sank at the thought.

Before he arrived she read again the troubling email that had been waiting for her when she logged in. She was in the process of printing it out when Richard opened the door. He didn't bother to knock.

'Sounds like you've had an *eventful* morning.' Hands in his pockets, he sat down with a groan. From the peevish expression on his face, she could see he wasn't going to be offering her tea and sympathy.

She sat opposite him with the printout in her hand. 'You could put it that way.'

'It's lucky you were with somebody as *experienced* as Keith. I understand he saved the day in his usual *style*.' Janet was about to make an indignant reply when she realised Keith must have got to the deputy governor first. He regarded her with narrowed eyes. It was clear where his loyalties lay.

'A shame he was in the toilet at the crucial moment,' she said. 'But he was certainly enthusiastic in his use of restraint. When he finally did arrive.'

Richard smiled his unfriendly smile, lips pursed together. 'I think we should be *grateful* no assault took place, rather than looking for problems. Don't you?'

'I'm surprised nobody realised Baz Gridley was stoned,' she said, ignoring his provocation. 'The man was completely off his face. You only had to take one look at him to see it.'

'Well, maybe *you* only needed one look. But then you're the psychologist. One would hope you'd have an eye for such things. If, indeed, he *was* high.' Richard folded his fat fingers together into a steeple. 'We'll have to wait for the urine test to confirm that.'

'I was interested to hear that Dr Helkin had also been assaulted,' she said. 'What happened to him?'

Richard looked surprised. 'Who told you that?'

'Keith hinted as much.'

'*Hinted?* I think you must be mistaken.'

'So Dr Helkin wasn't assaulted?'

'There's no record of it as far as I'm aware,' he said, tossing his hair. 'And since Helkin is no longer with us, I don't see what *relevance* this has to you *now*.'

'No longer with us?' It was Janet's turn to be surprised.

'No longer at *Halvergate*.' Richard tutted. 'Really, you do *quibble* over words. It's hard to say anything without you leaping to extraordinary conclusions.' He stood up. 'Was that all?'

'No.' She handed Richard the printout, which he took without looking at. 'This email came from the Courts Service this morning,' she said. 'It seems Helkin had already requested and received exactly the same documents on Michael Donovan, Duncan Fletcher and several other prisoners as I have. Six months ago.'

Richard leaned over and placed the paper on the edge of the table, still without looking at it. 'So it would *appear*.'

'Yet none of these records are at Halvergate now.'

Richard rolled his eyes. 'I imagine the good doctor took the papers home with him for some *instructive* reading. Perhaps we should issue him with a late library fine.'

Janet picked the paper up from where he had discarded it. 'These are confidential documents. I can't believe that Helkin wouldn't have kept them here.' Richard said nothing. Feeling increasingly hopeless, she ploughed on. 'Is there anywhere else they might have been stored or anyone else who had access to them?'

'Isn't this a question for Terry?'

'Terry's off today. He's been doing some overtime. And besides, he's already told me that he's not aware of any other files.'

'There's your answer then. Dr Helkin *must* have taken them home.' He paused, his piggy eyes narrowing, shadowed by folds of flesh. 'Unless you think somebody here . . . *got rid* of them?'

Janet felt her face flush red, and cursed her pale skin for betraying her thoughts. It was exactly what she had been wondering, but she didn't trust Richard enough to admit it. She looked down at the papers. 'Why would they do that?'

'Why indeed.' Richard smirked. 'Well then.' He patted his pockets, heading to the door. 'Anything else?'

'Nothing major,' said Janet. She sat back in her chair, scanning Richard with a cold middle-distance stare. 'I've also requested the results of the mandatory drugs testing over the past year. Just to keep on top of things. With Baz so obviously high on *something*, I thought it was worth a look.'

Her words sent a ripple across Richard's face, like a rock thrown into a stagnant pond. Anger perhaps. Or was it fear? 'You are a *busy bee*,' he said. 'Don't work *too* hard, will you? I've heard it's not good for your health.'

7

Friday night, and she had a date. Well, if you counted dinner with a chaplain who was almost certainly gay as a date. Janet smiled to herself. After such a stressful day, she felt even more grateful for Steven Finch's invitation. The thought of an evening with somebody friendly, somebody who laughed, had buoyed her through the long hours of the afternoon.

Now on the way from Halverton to Norwich, she was surrounded by darkness. Used to London's orange skies, Norfolk's heavy black was a novelty to her, the way it rolled out and spread across the marshes. It was only when she turned to look back that she could see a brown tinge discolouring the skies above Great Yarmouth. A few long-necked cranes with winking red eyes hovered above the town. She knew a vast forest of wind turbines were turning out at sea, invisible in the darkness. The wine bottle rolled against her feet in the footwell of the taxi as she settled back in her seat. She had decided not to drive to Steven's flat.

'Where was it you said now?' asked the driver.

His accent was so broad it took her a few moments to understand him. She squinted at Steven's scrawl. 'St Giles Street, above the gallery.'

'I know the one. Exhibition on, is there?' His eyes, reflected in the rear-view mirror, looked inquiringly at her.

'No, I'm visiting a friend.'

'Having a few beers?'

Janet was perplexed. 'I'm sorry?'

'A. Few. Beers.' The driver spoke slowly but kindly, as if she were deaf or stupid. 'A few drinks.'

'A few drinks, and some dinner.'

'Where you from then? Not local, are you.'

Janet wished the driver's eyes were focused on the road, not peering back at her.

'London.'

'Ah, London!' the driver chuckled, as if that explained it all.

Driving into Norwich, the city seemed almost deserted. The streets were poorly lit, casting a sickly yellow haze over the medieval buildings. Janet felt a touch of surprise when they passed a Tesco. It looked like a visitor that had sidled in from another age, or bad continuity on a film set. The cab pulled up on St Giles Street.

'There you go.' The driver handed her his card with the change. 'Enjoy your evening,' he said cheerfully as Janet scrambled out.

'Found it all right then?' Steven asked when he came to the door. She skirted a huddle of bikes dumped in the hallway and followed him up a scruffy, poorly lit communal staircase with an overpowering stink of rubber. ''Scuse the smell, it won't follow us into the flat.' He reached the top of the stairs, where a low door sat propped open by a trainer. 'There we are.'

Janet walked into a warm studio apartment. Cheap bookcases clambered up every possible space, except where they parted to make room for a couple of impressively large paintings.

'This is great,' she said as Steven took the bottle off her. 'I was going to ask you to mine at some point, but Cherry Tree Drive will be a bit of a let-down after this.'

'Ha! I'm sure it's not that bad.' He handed her a glass. 'Mind this while I get the bottle opener.'

Steven headed to the galley kitchen. He was wearing a sleeveless white T-shirt, a tight and revealing choice. Every scrap of his skin seemed to be covered in ink. She could make out the corners of a giant tattoo spreading over each shoulder, a dagger drawn up the back of his neck, and Latin script curving from his wrists to his biceps. Janet had a moment's misgiving that the bulging muscles might be on display for her benefit, but no, she didn't really think so. She wandered over to one of the paintings. It was of St Sebastian, on black card in different shades of blue oil pastel. Painted at an unusual angle, from below, the light caught Sebastian's ribs and cheekbones as he waited for the barrage of arrows. Janet turned to the painting opposite.

'Wow,' she said. 'I love this.'

The same model stood astride a demon, his sword at the monster's throat in a recreation of St Michael's defeat of the devil. The archangel's wings spread right across the canvas in a dazzling array of red and gold, and above the saint, writhing to the top of the painting and curving off beyond the frame, was the demon's silver-green tail. The whole picture was made up as a mosaic, made from tiny squares of coloured paper.

'Is it the same artist?' Janet turned to Steven, who'd arrived with the bottle.

He poured red wine into her glass. 'Yes,' he said, looking pleased.

She recognised his delight. 'Did you paint them?'

Steven nodded. 'The only downside is looking at my ex every evening.' He gestured at the model.

'They're amazing.'

'That one,' he said, pointing at St Michael, 'I had copied as a tattoo on my back.'

'Can I see?'

Steven turned round and she realised that the shadows poking out from the T-shirt were the angel's wings, and what she had taken to be a dagger on his neck was in fact the demon's tail.

'Can't I see all of it?'

'Only here five minutes and you're already trying to get my kit off.' Steven grinned, and pulled up his shirt.

Janet pursed her lips. 'I promise not to drool over you too much.'

The tattoo was in blue ink, and without the bright colours the design looked more sinister than the painting. The demon's scales and the angel's feathers moved over Steven's ribs when he breathed, as if alive.

'Very impressive.' Janet helped him pull his T-shirt down. 'And the tattoo's not bad either.'

Steven made a face. 'Right, dinner. It's only pasta I'm afraid, but at least I made the sauce myself.'

Janet sat at the rickety IKEA table. It looked as if it had shuffled off into the corner out of shame and was trying to hide in the bookshelves. The slanting floor meant one leg was propped up by a dog-eared paperback. It was a treatise on Foxe's Book of Martyrs. Steven spooned out the food and topped up her wine.

'Red suits you,' he said with a smile. It was the colour of Janet's jumper, but also of the cross resting between her collarbones. She felt deceitful, knowing he must be drawing the wrong conclusions.

'Thanks. Nice-looking guy.' She pointed at St Sebastian. 'How long has he been your ex?'

'Don't hang about, do you!' Steven laughed. 'I split from Paulo about nine months ago. No hard feelings, really. Not easy going out with a dog collar.' His smile turned a little bitter. 'And the good old C of E might be liberal, but not so much that you can just rock up anywhere with a boyfriend – Ooh, hello, Father, and who's your charming companion? It's a lot to ask of someone, that sort of life.' He paused. 'How about you?'

'Oh, don't ask.' Janet grimaced. 'I've managed to leave my boyfriend in London. He's not very happy about it.'

'He didn't fancy moving to Norfolk?' Steven spooned in a huge amount of pasta, his cheeks expanding like a chipmunk.

'No. But it's not just that. He's put up with a lot over the years.' She took a mouthful of arrabbiata sauce, suddenly overwhelmed by the thought of all Arun had been through. All she had put him through. 'He wants us to start a family. We've just hit our thirties and all that. But me moving to Norfolk stuffed up that plan, at least for the time being. We've been together for ever and always talked about it. But I'm not sure I'm ready yet. I'm just not sure.'

'Well, who'd fancy building a future with the love of your life when you can hang out at Halvergate with me and Terry, eh?'

Janet laughed. 'When you put it like that.' She drank her wine, savouring its warmth. 'But my work's important to me. I've put a lot into the job over the years, too much just to chuck it all in after getting a promotion.' She sighed. 'Though after days like today, I can't help wondering if it's worth it.' She saw his enquiring look and ran a hand over her face, suddenly tired. She hadn't particularly wanted to darken the dinner by talking about what had happened that morning, but Steven was so friendly it was hard to keep it to herself. 'Bad day on the landings,' she said. 'One of the guys on A wing went for me.'

'Shit.' Steven momentarily paused his demolition of the plate of pasta. 'Are you OK?'

'I'm fine, he never touched me. It was more the prison officer, Keith Lawson.' She realised she had started shredding part of the label off the wine and pushed the bottle away. 'This is going to sound crazy, but I felt like he left me alone on purpose and held back from helping until the very last moment. Just to give me a scare.'

'Keith's a bastard, I mean a real bastard,' Steven said. 'But that sounds messed up even for him.'

'It's probably my imagination,' she conceded. 'It's the stuff of nightmares, calling for help on the landings and nobody coming.'

Steven wound up a forkful of spaghetti. 'The worst. Sorry you went through that. Bloody hell, what a first week.'

'That wasn't even the half of it,' said Janet. 'The guy who attacked me, Baz Gridley, do you know him?' Steven shook his head. 'He was high on something. Which I find hard to believe nobody spotted.'

He snorted. 'I don't. Keith hates the prisoners so much, sometimes I think he barely sees them. Like they're another species.'

'If only. They're all too human unfortunately.'

Steven looked at the cross round Janet's neck. 'Is that your professional judgement talking, or vocation?'

Janet put her glass down with a thump. 'Why does everyone assume if you work in the prison service you must have a *vocation*?'

Steven raised his eyebrows. 'That's me told. But you've got to admit, it's rarely for the princely pay.'

Janet forced a smile to cover her rudeness. 'Fair enough.' She fingered the necklace round her neck, not for the first time wishing she could yank it free and throw it away. 'Look, this is misleading,' she said, putting her thumb over the cross. 'I don't believe in God. I wear it because it belonged to somebody who was special to me.' She ran the small beads through her fingers. 'If I have a vocation,' she added, her expression hardening, 'it's to make the men I treat understand just a fraction of the harm they've caused.' She paused, thinking of Baz Gridley lunging at her when she asked him how he was feeling. 'My job isn't to spend all my time sympathising,' she said. 'I know some of the prisoners have had unimaginably traumatic lives, but you can't let that distract you. It would drive you crazy. I'm there to protect other people from them, and the best way, the safest way, of doing that is to get them to recognise what they've done and feel remorse for it. Redemption doesn't come into it, not for me.'

'Well,' said Steven, unruffled by her irritation. 'That makes a change from the usual speech. I normally get psychologists telling me that the prisoners are unwell, that they need helping, that the stuff they've done is the symptom of an illness, or addiction, or their difficult past. All of which is true, but it's not everything.' He tipped some more cheese over his pasta, stirring it vigorously. 'To be honest, we're probably closer than you think. I don't buy all that illness stuff. Pathologising evil just makes light of it, which isn't helpful. And getting people to feel remorse, well, we're in the same business there.'

'Is that why you do it? Saving souls?' There was more of an edge to her voice than she'd intended.

'Not primarily.' He poured her some more wine. 'My dad was in prison when I was growing up. The chaplain made a lot of difference to me and Mum. The work's not just about the prisoners. When somebody's locked up it's a family affair.'

'Oh.' Janet felt her skin prickle with embarrassment. 'That must have been difficult.'

'I wasn't the only kid at school with a dad in jail.' Steven shrugged. 'Part of town I'm from, it's not that unusual. My uncle's a bobby though, so that did make it all a bit awkward for poor old Mum, husband and brother looking daggers at each other over Christmas dinner, epic sulking over the sprouts.' He took another bite of spaghetti, chewing as he spoke. 'Dad was always a tough bastard, we never got on. I probably had a better time as a kid when he was banged up.' He saw Janet's face. 'Not violent or anything, he was in for burglary. I just meant ... I just mean I was never ashamed of him. Funny, really, he was more ashamed of me. Manchester might be pink now, but it's fair to say gay pride hadn't spread to Runcorn in the 1990s.'

'Are you still in touch with him?'

Steven took a swig of wine, and Janet saw that the blue Latin script running round his arms went all the way to his knuckles. She wondered what it meant. He put down the glass. 'He died a couple of years ago.'

Janet felt her face go red again. 'Sorry.'

Steven started laughing. 'No, I'm sorry. What a cheery tea this is turning into. You might as well have hung out with Terry and Richard. And I'm a pretty rubbish chaplain, aren't I? Rabbiting on about my childhood. It ought to be you fessing up, not me.'

'Well, psychologists are in the business of extracting confessions too, so there's still time for me to lay you out on the couch.' She caught Steven staring at her deadpan face, trying to work out if she'd intended the double entendre or not. Janet kept her expression demure and glanced over at the books crowding against her elbow. Poking out at her, the frayed spine of Dante's *Purgatorio* nudged shoulders with Amistead Maupin's *Tales of the City*. 'Sorry for my rant earlier. I'm interested in what you said about pathologising evil. Do you think some people can't be saved then?'

Steven propped both elbows on the table, tilting it. 'Not that they can't be helped, or "saved" even, if you prefer. Just that they're not ill. It's a mistake, this idea that the church thinks good always wins and everything in the world turns out for the best. Evil is a powerful force – pretending otherwise can be dangerous. Take a prisoner I spoke to today, Arnas. Now he might be one of yours, a mentalist or something—'

Janet couldn't help laughing. 'A mentalist?'

'OK, not very PC, but you know what I mean. He thinks the devil is loose in Halvergate, that it's hanging out in other prisoners' cells. Now that might be a delusion, or he might have picked up on the real presence of evil and given it a name he understands.'

Janet's brow creased with anxiety. 'Did he strike you as delusional? He ought to be getting support if that's the case.'

'No, not at all, don't fret. I would have called you or the in-reach team if I thought he was unwell. And I'll be popping back to see him in a few days.' Steven reached for the bottle again and topped up their wine. 'To be honest, it might be an indicator of madness where you're from, but prisoners fearing the devil is pretty standard in my line of work. Occupational hazard of the God-bothering business.'

'Sounds a bit unorthodox for a priest. You don't believe in real demons, then?'

Janet asked the question lightly, but Steven didn't take it that way. The candlelight played over his face as he sat thinking. He shrugged. 'I don't know. Not a good answer for a chaplain, is it? Especially one with the devil printed on his back. But I just don't know.' He leaned over and took her empty plate, piling it on top of his own. 'If there are demons, I can't help thinking they'd be right at home in Halvergate. It isn't a happy place.'

If Steven hadn't worked in the prison service himself, Janet would have been inclined to laugh. But she knew exactly what he meant. 'No. The staff particularly. And I don't just mean Keith.' The image of Richard smirking over the table in the canteen came into her mind, and for a moment she felt the cold of the empty corridor, the greyness of Halvergate, the sense of something inexplicably *wrong*. 'I wish you'd known the psychologist there before me,' she said. 'It bothers me knowing so little about him. Keith dropped some dark hints about him getting attacked.'

'Dr Helkin? What did he say happened?'

'That's just it. He didn't say. In fact, *nobody* says anything about him. It's like he just disappeared.' She made a face. 'And his notes along with him, which makes life interesting. It wouldn't be so bad, but I don't feel I can talk to anyone.'

Steven raised his glass to her. 'You can always talk to me.' He downed his wine. 'Enough of all that. Work can wait till Monday. How about some ice cream?'

8

To wake up alone in Cherry Tree Drive on a Saturday morning was a far from pleasant feeling. Not only was there
Arun's absence to contend with, but also the strange sensation
of lying in a bed she had never shared with him. It occurred to
Janet that the last man to sleep on Mrs Slaney's hard mattress
in the pale blue room had been John Helkin, a thought that made
her even less inclined to linger between the sheets.

Sitting in the kitchen eating toast, watching thin lines of water run
down the condensation on the windowpane, Janet thought of Steven's
homely flat. She liked him enormously. At some point past midnight,
a couple of bottles of wine down, he had produced a gramophone
out of an improbably small cupboard and the pair of them had sung
along to his records. There couldn't be many people who owned Take
That on vinyl. She looked at the pile of novels sitting beside her.
Steven appeared to be one of those people who feel a friendship can
only be solidified by an exchange of favourite books.

At the bottom of the pile was a guide to Norfolk that he had
lent her to get her bearings. She picked it up and leafed through
the section on walks. Arun loved the countryside and she had
decided to spend the day casing places he might enjoy. Though
she wasn't sure whether the county's flatness was going to appeal
to such a devoted fan of the Lake District. The first holiday they
ever spent together had been a long weekend in Grasmere.

*'You don't notice the cold after a bit, I promise.' Arun stood on the
muddy bank, wrestling off his jumper. The rest of his clothes were
already kicked into an untidy pile.*

Janet looked doubtfully at the water lapping against the shore. It was clear at the edge but seemed to deepen into blackness after only a few feet. On the other side of the lake the green banks and tree-lined fells rose steeply. 'Are you sure it's OK to swim in?' She was already shivering in her costume.

'Of course it is,' Arun said, splashing in. He crouched down up to his neck, blowing out sharply. 'The trick is to get in quickly and then wait a moment while your body gets used to it.'

Janet stepped into the water. It felt like she had plunged her bare foot into a snowdrift. The things I do for love, she thought. Gritting her teeth, she sloshed onwards, her feet registering the stones and twigs in the mud, then she crouched down as Arun had done. The cold hit her in the chest like a physical blow, leaving her gasping for breath.

'Jesus, Arun!'

He laughed and put his still-warm arms round her. 'Honestly, just wait a minute. When we start swimming you'll see.'

Still freezing, but less shocked, she swam with him from the bank. Almost instantly she became aware that the floor of the lake had dropped well out of touching distance. Izzy would never believe she had done something like this. The pair of them were such townies. Beside her Arun had a huge grin on his face, and looked even younger than his nineteen years. And suddenly she understood why. With the movement, she no longer felt frozen. As the blood rushed to her skin, it brought a huge burst of endorphins. She was high on the cold.

'It's amazing!'

Arun laughed. 'I knew you'd love it. We can't swim to the other side at this time of year, but just a little further, wait till you see the view.' They carried on swimming and then he caught hold of her arm. 'Just here.'

She looked down, treading water, and was almost overwhelmed by a feeling of vertigo. She could see nothing beyond the pale pink of her feet. Beneath was endless darkness, plunging hundreds of feet below. If she sank, nobody would ever find her.

'Don't look down, Janey, look across, look there.'

She followed the line of his sight and Helm Crag reared up above them, golden in the evening light. And below it was its double, reflected perfectly in the vast glass surface of the lake.

'Helm Crag and its twin. I thought you'd like that.'

Janet smiled at him. 'It's beautiful.'

Underneath the water he took hold of her hand. 'I love you,' he said.

How different three words can sound, thought Janet, even though the same person says them. She stuffed the book in her coat pocket as she grabbed her bag and headed for the door.

Janet drove out of Halverton and joined the Acle Straight, travelling towards Great Yarmouth. Making her way past its industrial outskirts, she crossed the River Yare. Over the bridge, a seamless expanse of sky and water filled her whole vision with grey. Glancing towards the town, she thought about Ian Fendley and Alyssa Petrovic, the assault on the seafront. Her job had changed the way she saw places. She could map an area by the crimes committed there, though she knew that landscapes, unlike people, didn't retain the emotional aftermath of violence.

The roads became more residential, then fields began to take up as much space as houses. Every time she turned a corner she expected to climb a hill, or even a gentle incline, to give her a better sense of the place, but instead she was constantly surprised by the flatness. She passed a holiday park, its rows of empty caravans exposed by the leafless winter trees, before her satnav guided her to the place she had chosen from Steven's book. Burgh Castle.

Parking up, she ignored the medieval church and cut straight across the fields to the Roman fort. It was a trudge across uneven grassland, fighting against the wind. When she arrived, the ruins were little more than a perimeter wall, battered down to a few feet in height. Janet had the peculiar feeling she always got from the remains of ancient buildings, a sense of double vision, that the dead who'd lived in them were both impossibly distant and yet also close by, no further away than people who had died yesterday.

Tramping through the ruins she thought not of Arun but her childhood, all the educational trips to historical sites she and Izzy had been on with their parents. She was tempted to phone their mum and dad, but as always the idea of the inevitable barrage of anxious questions put her off. She could imagine their appalled reaction if she told them what had happened with Baz Gridley. They had been dismayed enough by her solo move to Halverton. Her chosen career had always been a source of family tension and the thought of her leaving Arun in London to take charge of a wing of sex offenders in the middle of nowhere had met with a predictable response.

'I don't know what you're expecting, that you're somehow going to "find yourself" wandering about the Norfolk moors,' her father had said. 'It's just too selfish. We'll all be worried sick.'

'It's broads, Dad, there aren't any moors in Norfolk.'

'Whatever they are, you know what I'm saying, don't change the subject . . .'

And on and on it had gone, Janet thought, leaving her annoyed and her parents upset. Though she had to admit, alone in the deserted fort, that the arguments she had given her father about career progression and unique opportunities seemed less clear now than they had from the warmth of her London flat.

At the far side of the ruins she took a path that led to the marshes. Crossing the narrow footbridge, she had difficulty distinguishing land from water: both seemed covered in corn-coloured reeds. They spread out in a swaying horizon, with only the river cutting across them in a fat brown line. Even here the water was not contained, but ran thin fingers into the sandy stems. A row of black teeth sticking out from the mud showed an earlier ill-fated attempt to stake out the river's edge with wooden posts. The only building Janet could see was a windmill, so far off that its white top looked no bigger than the pale heads of the reeds beside her.

She knew somewhere out in that vast sea was the pub the guidebook recommended as the end point for a long walk, but without Arun she couldn't face it. Without him, she might really sink to the bottom, as she had feared in the lake all those years ago, and never be found. She stood for a while, watching the wind roll across the reed heads in waves, before turning and taking the road that led back to HMP Halvergate.

9

Siobhan Trant stood in the prison fish tank, waiting to be buzzed in. Even several feet away and through the thick glass, Janet could sense her fear. It was in the young woman's pinched expression, the way she clutched her bag as if she might have to use it as a weapon. She didn't look like an ideal candidate to facilitate a sex offender treatment programme, but she would have to do.

The glass slid to the side and Janet stepped forward to greet her. 'Siobhan, hi. I'm Janet, we spoke earlier on the phone.'

Siobhan shook her hand. She had the large protuberant eyes of a frightened hare. 'Thank you so much for giving me this opportunity. I'm really excited to be here.' She looked anything but excited.

'It's OK.' Janet smiled. 'Everyone's nervous on their first placement.'

Siobhan seemed put out rather than reassured. 'I really am pleased to be here.'

'Of course. And it's great to have you.' Janet guided her out through the sterile area into the yard. The brightness of the enormous sky, even though it was veiled by cloud, made her companion squint. 'Today we'll go over a few things in my office,' she said. 'Just so you have a chance to see how everything works before we start the sessions.' They walked across to the VP wing. Janet had spent Sunday afternoon noting down topics she might discuss with Siobhan, but casting a sidelong glance at the girl she wondered if one pep talk was going to be enough. Siobhan jumped as she secured the door behind them. 'What made you want to work in the prison service?' Janet asked.

'I think everyone deserves second chances,' Siobhan said earnestly, trotting alongside her as they walked down the corridor. 'Prisoners are just the same as everyone else. I like the idea of being able to help people be better versions of themselves.'

Janet hoped her mentee had made the speech to impress her, rather than believing it all. 'You're right, rehabilitation is a very important part of the job,' she said. 'But above all, this particular programme is about risk assessment and management. About ensuring the men aren't going to go out into the community and cause more harm.' She held open the door to her office. 'After all, you don't want to recommend a man for parole only to hear later that he's attacked someone.'

Janet headed over to the sink to get out the digestives and make them both tea. When she turned round with the mugs, Siobhan was still standing in the doorway, looking more like a nervous rabbit than ever. She felt a mixture of sympathy and annoyance.

'Do take a seat, get comfortable. There's milk and sugar on the table. And help yourself to a biscuit.' Janet handed her a mug. 'I thought it might be a good idea to talk about boundaries today. Is that something you discussed as part of your degree?'

Siobhan nodded, looking relieved to be on familiar territory. 'Yes, we talked about not being too friendly, not giving loads away. That sort of thing.'

'That's right. You're building a therapeutic relationship, and that means talking a bit about yourself.' Janet sipped her tea, glad to see the other woman starting to look more relaxed. 'But you mustn't make yourself vulnerable. You have to think carefully about what you wouldn't share. Where you live, for instance. What else might you avoid?'

'Boyfriends? Where you like hanging out maybe?'

'Definitely boyfriends, or whether you have a partner. That can be an obvious minefield. Also information about your children if you have any. But the main thing is to understand that what's safe to disclose is different for everyone. You have to be aware of your own vulnerabilities. For one person it might be siblings, for another hobbies.'

'Why would talking about my brother make me vulnerable?' Siobhan asked with a frown.

'It might not. I was just using siblings as an example. On the whole, for new staff, it's best to give away as little information as possible.'

Siobhan pulled a face that might have been agreement, or might not. Janet tried not to feel irritated and carried on. 'With sex offenders, you have to be particularly vigilant. They tend to have a higher IQ than the average prisoner and be more adept at manipulation. So look out for grooming behaviour, like paying you compliments, or going out of their way to be nice—'

'But what if they are just being nice?'

'They might be. That's not the point. You're not adding years to anyone's sentence by being aware of these things, are you? Just protecting yourself.'

Siobhan took a swig of tea, half of her face screened from view by the mug. 'I guess.'

'And then there's conditioning behaviour. That's even more serious. It could be a prisoner threatening you, or trying to isolate you, claiming your colleagues don't like you. If anything like that happens, tell me straight away.'

'You seem very down on the prisoners,' Siobhan said, shuffling her Converse under the chair. Janet felt as if she were talking to a vaguely mutinous teenager.

'It's not a question of being down on them,' she said gently. 'It's just remembering some men want to reform and need support, but others are extremely dangerous and would like nothing more than the opportunity to mess with your head.' Siobhan stared at her, wide-eyed, as she nibbled on a digestive. 'You said they're people just like everyone else, and that's absolutely true. But not everybody has committed violent sexual crimes, and it doesn't do to forget that.'

Siobhan looked crushed. 'It's just some of the men I've met here seemed quite nice.'

'You've been to Halvergate before?' Janet was surprised. Here was another piece of information to add to the ever-growing list of things her colleagues had failed to tell her.

'Only as a volunteer, when I was a student. The prison put out an advert for people to visit the sex offenders, because some didn't get any family coming to see them.' Siobhan shuffled her feet again, looking embarrassed. 'I thought it might give me some experience, you know, help me apply for jobs.'

'You didn't strike up any long-term correspondence with any of the men, did you?' Janet had a sudden unpleasant memory of Michael Donovan's mischievous smile as he warned her about a female rival at Halvergate.

Siobhan looked terrified by the idea. 'Of course not!'

'That's good. It would be unfortunate if anything you said in those visits came back to haunt you—' Janet was cut off by a knock. 'Come in.'

It was Terry. For once he didn't hover on the threshold but barged in, looking out of breath and flustered. 'It's Ian. He's not well, you need to see him.' He stopped, noticing Siobhan. 'Sorry,' he said, his eyes darting between them. 'Didn't mean to interrupt.'

'That's OK. What's wrong?'

'Hard to say, exactly. He's disturbed, not himself at all. I don't like it.' He ran a hand over his short hair. Janet thought he might be shaking. 'I think you need to see for yourself. Now.'

'OK.' They both turned and looked at Siobhan, who blushed, aware that she had just achieved the status of unwanted nuisance.

'I can come back another day.'

'No, don't worry. Terry, could you take Siobhan to the canteen and have a chat with her? We've just been over boundaries – perhaps you can outline anything else she needs to think about before the sessions.'

He nodded. 'I'll get Ian sent straight up to see you.'

★ ★ ★

Nothing about the young man who walked into Janet's office recalled the Ian Fendley from last week. Dark circles pulled down the skin under his eyes and he shuffled with a walk that was not just diffident but dazed. No wonder Terry was worried, she thought, guiding Ian to the soft chair recently vacated by Siobhan. He hunched himself into the corner of the seat, thin arms cradling his head. He rocked back and forth, his breathing heavy. Janet sat down opposite him.

'It's OK, Ian. Just take a moment. It's OK. Terry tells me you've been having a bad time. Is there something you'd like to talk about?'

He started, looking around as if somebody else might be listening.

'It's just us two, I promise. Nobody else can hear. You can talk to me about whatever you like.'

Ian's skin was an unhealthy grey colour, shining with sweat. She'd seen patients in secure hospitals look better. He continued to stare, his gaze unfocused. Janet was about to speak again when he leaned forward. 'She's back.'

Janet's heartbeat was loud in her ears in the silence that followed. 'Who's back?'

'The white visitor.'

'White visitor?' she repeated, puzzled. Ian said nothing, only gaped at her. The flat light from the window drained even more colour from his face, and his hair lay lank against his temples. 'Do you mean someone you knew outside, who's visiting? I can speak to Terry if you don't want them coming to see you.'

'Terry can't stop her.' Ian began jigging his knees up and down with agitation.

'Ian, who are you talking about?'

'She's so angry. All night she wouldn't let me alone.' He gripped the outsides of his legs, clamping himself down to the chair, but his feet still drummed on the carpet. 'I close my eyes and I open them, and there she is, leaning over the bed. Standing over me.' He blinked slowly, repeatedly, as if trying to erase an image from his mind's eye.

Janet felt a jolt, like hitting a pothole at speed. It looked like

Ian was suffering from a psychotic episode. She gave a small smile, hoping to encourage him, and took up her notepad. 'Can you describe her to me?'

'It's her eyes. They're black, completely black.' Ian screwed up his face and started to cry. 'But I know she's looking at me. She fucking knows what I done, I'm telling you, she fucking *knows*. She's so angry, she won't let me alone, it'll be like before.' His thin shoulders rose and shook as he wept.

Janet pushed a box of tissues towards him. 'It's OK, it's OK, just take your time,' she said, unsure whether she was soothing the prisoner or herself. 'Ian, could you look at me?' Gulping, he turned his face to hers and she studied his pupils. They weren't dilated. 'Have you taken anything, any skunk or spice maybe, that might have brought this on?'

He shook his head.

'You're sure about that? It's really important you tell me.'

Ian hunched forward, balling his fists between his knees, his legs rigid. He shut his eyes and shook his head again.

Janet nodded, not sure she believed him. 'You say this woman's angry. What do you feel she's angry about?'

He looked over to her without lifting his head. Hair hung over his face and the whites of his eyes shone in its shadow. 'It's Alyssa,' he whispered.

'The girl you assaulted?'

'I'm sorry, you know I'm sorry.' His voice rose to a whine. 'I offered to write, but they said she didn't want to hear nothing from me, she wanted to forget it. I'm sorry,' he said, looking down again. 'But it's not enough, is it?'

'You feel this woman is here to punish you?'

'I don't *feel* it, I know it.' Ian slammed his fist down on the arm of the chair. 'For fuck's sake, you've got to help me!' He was sweating so much his T-shirt was sticking to his skin as if he had been out in the rain.

'I will help you. It's just important you try not to get too upset. I understand that you're frightened by what you've seen—'

'Understand? *Understand*?' His voice went up several pitches. 'It's all right for you, what do you have to be frightened about? She's not here for *you*, is she?'

'I know she seems very real, but do you think the fact you're the only person who's seen this woman might also be a comforting thought?' He'd hunched forward and covered his face with his hands. She continued even more gently. 'It could mean that she doesn't exist, couldn't it?'

Far from providing comfort, the question caused her patient to slump over like a rag doll and start crying again, great gulping sobs that left strings of drool hanging from his mouth. She waited until he was a little calmer, then tried again. 'Sometimes when we see something that frightens us, but which seems very unusual or unlikely, it can help knowing nobody else has seen it. Then we know it's not real, it's just in our minds, perhaps because guilt or another strong feeling is bothering us.'

'But it's not just me, is it?' Ian sat upright, sniffing hard, staring at the ceiling. 'What about the others?'

'What others?'

'You know who.' He looked at her, his eyes welling with hate. 'They're all dead, *you know* they're all dead.' He punched the arm of the chair again. 'She made them do it. That's why, that's why they're dead.' His voice quivered and he began wailing, an unbearable sound, his mouth opening wider and wider, collapsing his face inwards like rotten fruit.

Janet sat, transfixed, his cry piercing her through.

Ian covered his mouth with balled fists, trying to choke off the sobs. 'Dr Helkin couldn't stop her and nor can you. And now it's me she's come for. It's me, it's my life, it's *me*.'

10

The strange light of the cloud-filled day made everything in Janet's office look washed out, like an overexposed photograph. Terry held a hand up to shield his face, while Richard lost even more of his tiny eyes squinting in the glare. His face had a waxy look surrounded by his carefully groomed hair, like an effigy on a medieval tomb that had been intended as a cherub but ended up as a gargoyle. As she spoke, he nodded along, but she had already learned that with Richard this did not always signal agreement.

'If Ian Fendley's urine tests come back clean,' she said, 'I think we may need to consider a referral to a secure hospital.'

Richard interrupted. 'Like Ryan Spalding?' His tone was pleasant, but Janet sensed the sting curved into his question, like a scorpion's tail.

'Like Ryan in that Ian's referred to hospital, but obviously not like him in escaping. I'm sure we could make the necessary precautions clear to the medical staff.'

'I don't think *Lee* would like it.' Richard pursed his lips into a wet little pout.

'If Ian is suffering from psychosis, we'll need to consider whether Halvergate is the most suitable setting.'

'The crucial word there, I think you'll find, is *if*,' Richard said.

'I don't see what alternative there is. He's in severe distress.'

'Don't see an alternative?' Richard clasped his hands in mock concern. 'Let me spell one out for you. Ian Fendley is *pretending*. Perhaps, at an *august* institution like *HMP Leyland*, you never encountered such things, but here at Halvergate I think you'll

73

find it's quite common.' Richard darted his piggy eyes towards Terry, as if sharing a private joke. It wasn't the first time he had sneered at Leyland; he was clearly annoyed Janet had worked somewhere prestigious and determined to take her down a peg or two.

'From what I've seen, it's highly unlikely he's pretending.'

'I think it's best we wait for the test results, before *leaping* to that conclusion.' Richard shook his beautiful hair, seemingly unaware that she had suggested the same thing only a few seconds before.

Janet didn't trust herself to carry on speaking to him. She turned towards Terry, who was sitting blank-faced, his chair pulled a little away so that he seemed to be hovering at the edge of the conversation rather than sharing it.

'One thing you might be able to help with,' she said. 'Ian believed other prisoners had seen this white visitor. He said they later committed suicide. I'm sure it's just another delusion, but I have to ask. Did John Helkin ever mention anything like this?'

Terry opened his mouth, then froze as Richard caught his eye, leaving his jaw hanging like a beached guppy.

'*Really,* Janet, I hardly think you can take the ramblings of some half-baked prisoner *seriously.*'

'I'm not taking the contents of the delusions seriously,' Janet said, stung. 'Obviously. But if there's been a cluster of acute mental health problems here, shouldn't we consider the possibility there are legal highs washing around? It does seem the most obvious culprit. Spice has been behind enough deaths in the prison service, and it's not going to show up in any urine tests. I'm sure Baz Gridley was on something.'

Richard folded his arms. 'There's no evidence whatsoever that Halvergate has a problem with legal highs.'

'What *was* behind the suicides last year, then?' she asked. 'It seems odd to have had a cluster like that, all on one wing.' Richard shrugged and Terry stayed silent. Janet took a deep breath and made an effort not to lose her temper. 'In the absence of any other explanations and until we have evidence that it *wasn't* connected to legal highs, perhaps we could at least increase the number of cell searches? And I don't know if there's a drugs dog present during visits, but it might be advisable.' She saw Richard's furious expression and added quickly, 'If you say there's not a problem, I'm sure that's correct, but no harm in taking extra precautions.'

Richard's snout quivered, his lips puckering in a sneer. 'No *harm*? With budget cuts of five per cent a year, taking *extra precautions* without any obvious need is hardly a *harmless* policy.'

Janet flushed. Richard had just rocketed to the top of her list for least favourite colleague. A position that faced increasingly stiff competition. 'Of course, you know best.' She forced a smile. 'Legal highs aside, we need to put a care plan in place for Ian immediately. The fact suicide is preying so much on his mind is alarming.'

'Of course, *of course*, we can't have you and Terry here feeling *alarmed*.' Richard shot a filthy look at Terry, who went red.

She ignored his tone and drew out her notes. 'I put together a provisional plan after my assessment earlier.' She looked down the list. 'Regular therapy, I'll try CBT first. Checks every hour—' Richard cut her off with a snort.

'Every *hour*?' He shook his head in disbelief. 'Where are the staff to carry out all these checks? Can we please be *mindful* of finances? I would question *anything* more than checks four times a day. As for the rest of it, I leave that in your *capable* hands.' He stood up. 'If that's all?' He treated them to an oily smile.

They sat in silence for a moment after Richard had shut the door, both savouring his absence. But with her adversary gone, Janet felt her shoulders sag a little. Everything in this place made her feel tired.

Terry coughed. 'Will you be wanting me to get my notes now, so we can plan the life story sessions?'

She roused herself. 'Yes, great. Thanks.'

Terry moved to get up, then stopped. For once, he looked her straight in the eye. 'He'll be watched, Dr Palmer. I'll make sure he's watched. Ian Fendley's not going to hurt himself.'

The threat of violence on A wing was as palpable as the pulsing drone of the ventilation system. Even before Janet had been attacked, Steven had always felt uncomfortable here. He climbed the stairs to the landings, a network of metal spiders' webs spreading out above him. On the ground floor, the battered football tables and foam chairs still sat unused and empty. He knew staff shortages meant prisoners' association time was severely restricted. There weren't enough officers to supervise the men safely, so they spent up to twenty hours a day locked in the cells. It had a predictable effect on everyone's mood.

As he made his way along the corridor to visit Arnas, Keith in front of him, Steven could hear angry yells and thumps of frustration from inside the cells. Staring straight ahead as he sauntered past, Keith kicked a door, provoking a frenzy of swearing and hammering in response.

'That one's a fucker. Always moaning,' he said.

'Yeah, well, nobody likes being locked up all day.'

'Shouldn't do the crime if you can't stick the time. Though I'm forgetting, your old man was a con, wasn't he?'

Steven ignored him, though he could feel tension coil round his arms like the ink of his tattoos. No wonder the men were violent. Keith was almost enough to tip a chaplain over the edge. He was relieved to reach Arnas's door.

'Ta,' he said as Keith let him in. The prison officer only grunted in response.

'Good to see you, Father.' Arnas leapt to his feet as Steven walked in. He had been doing press-ups on the floor. The cell stank of sweat. So did Arnas.

'Hey,' said Steven, pulling up his usual stool. 'Thought I'd drop by after our chat last week. I wanted to check how you're doing.'

'Good. Much better.' The prisoner flopped down on the bed. He looked like he hadn't changed the grey vest he had been wearing last time Steven visited.

'No more trouble with the velnius?'

'Ah, Father, it not come for me.' Arnas smiled broadly, stretching out. He reached over to the shreds of tobacco and paper laid on the bed beside him, rolling them into a cigarette. 'No, she prefer the nonces. I hear already she found one.'

'She?'

'Not all velnius take male form.' Arnas lit up. In the dim light of the cell, the top half of his face was in shadow.

'How do you know "she" is on the VP wing?'

'News get around. He not last long.' Arnas placed his hand over the grubby postcard of the Virgin Mary on the wall. 'Maybe your prayers help me or maybe velnius only take nonces.'

Steven began to feel nervous. Arnas's belief in the physical form of the devil seemed very literal, even for a devout Catholic. Perhaps he was mentally unstable, as Janet had feared. 'What do you mean the velnius takes nonces?'

'You know. The dead ones.'

'You mean the suicides?' Steven leaned forward, rocking the stool. 'I really don't think that was the devil. People get sick and depressed and they find it hard to imagine reasons to live. It's very sad, but it happens everywhere.'

'You talk to anybody.' Arnas sounded annoyed. 'Everybody at Halvergate know it's the velnius. Even when the man run, she come after him. No escaping. She take what she want.'

Steven knew how hated sex offenders were in prison. It was why they got a wing to themselves. But for a rumour to be going round that the devil was seizing them one by one was extreme. He looked up to see Arnas staring at him from the pool of darkness in the corner of the cell, his roll-up glowing red.

'You should be careful, Father.' Arnas took a deep drag, blowing out smoke. 'Velnius hate the church. Nobody safe.'

II

The LinkedIn page on Janet's computer gave little away. Alone in her office, she stared at it. Dr John Helkin had never uploaded a photograph to his profile, remaining a generic grey silhouette. He hadn't updated the page recently either, since according to the website he was still the forensic psychologist at HMP Halvergate. Before that he had worked for over a decade in a Scottish prison with a reputation for more experimental forms of therapy. Janet didn't have any contacts there, so no chance of asking a few discreet questions.

During Helkin's time at the prison, five men on one wing had died violently. She glanced over her notes. Kyle Reeder and Ahmed Ali had both hanged themselves, but the others had chosen more unusual methods. Ryan Spalding escaped to Thetford Forest only to puncture his carotid artery, Liam Smith managed to get hold of bleach, and most horrific of all, Mark Conybeer stabbed himself through the eye with a pencil. The last three deaths suggested the balance of the men's minds was seriously disturbed. She thought of Ian Fendley, the way he had blinked to blot out the terrifying visions only he could see.

The men's crimes suggested no particular pattern. Besides Ryan the serial rapist, Ahmed had been convicted of statutory rape, Mark and Kyle were guilty of sexually motivated murders, while Liam was a paedophile who had worked as a teacher. It was possible that none of their suicides were linked, though so many deaths in such a short timeframe did raise the odds of psychoactive substances being involved, whatever Richard said. But without any notes from Helkin or a steer from Terry, who had certainly not been in a mood to talk about it all yesterday, this was just a guess.

After they had drawn up Ian's care plan in the late afternoon, she had returned to Cherry Tree Drive and ransacked the house for traces of her predecessor. Her lack of information about him was making her increasingly worried. She felt certain he must have played a role in whatever had happened, and she wanted to know how he had treated the men. Her search had thrown up two more things to set beside the shirts and the head – a pair of engraved silver cufflinks and the paper half of his driving license. Both gave her an uneasy feeling. They seemed unusually valuable objects to have left behind.

She stood up and wandered over to the sink to make a cup of tea. It was another foggy day and the bright sunshine behind the mist created a glare that made her eyes water. As she stared out of the window, lost in her own thoughts, the phone on her desk rang.

'Yes?'

'Toxicology from the lab here. I understand you wanted the results for Barry Gridley?'

'That's right.' She fished out a pen, ready to write them down.

'They came back clean.'

'Really? You're sure?'

'Quite sure.'

She thanked the lab and put the phone down. That was another complication she didn't need. Janet drummed her fingers on the desk. She had no doubt that Baz Gridley had been off his face, but with clean results, he must have been taking some sort of legal high that the tests couldn't detect. At Leyland her professional judgement would have been respected, but Richard had made it more than obvious yesterday that he would not be so accommodating. She checked her watch. It was almost time for the first group therapy session.

The nine inmates sat huddled in a circle. Looking round, Janet was reminded of the drama club she and Izzy had attended briefly in their early teens. It had been held in a damp church hall, and provided a similar combination of scuffed furniture and awkward emoting.

'Today is really a getting to know you session,' she said. 'We're going to go through everyone's life stories individually, but this afternoon we thought it would be good to chat about the whole programme and what we all hope to get out of it.'

Her speech met with a predictably unenthusiastic response. The room they had been crammed into was masquerading as a friendly space, pretending it wasn't really a prison. Someone had painted the walls a lurid shade of apricot in a mistaken attempt at cheer, and a poorly drawn picture of a bowl of fruit hung behind Terry's head. But there were no windows or carpet and a pungent smell of BO and disinfectant lingered in the soft furnishings. Siobhan was sitting as far away from the men as possible.

'It's fortunate you're here to join us, Dr Palmer,' said Michael. 'I heard you had a spot of bother on A wing.' His tone sounded sympathetic, but his eyes were full of mischief. Michael was sitting next to Terry, yet managed to look more like the facilitator. Unlike his fellow inmates, who often failed to shower and shave, he was, as always, exceptionally well groomed. His pressed white shirt and smart jeans stood out like a beacon amidst the others, all dressed in the unofficial prisoners' uniform of drab jogging bottoms and colourful trainers.

Janet didn't smile back at him. 'I'm fine, thank you.'

'Sounds like he was a scumbag, Miss,' said Majid.

'I'm sure Dr Palmer appreciates your concern,' Terry said. 'But we'll just leave it there, shall we? As you can see, she's perfectly all right.'

'Shame the same can't be said for poor Ian. We were all expecting him to be here,' said Michael. 'Why isn't he? He was so *keen*.'

'Ian's not well,' Terry replied. 'He might be able to join us later in the programme.'

'Gone quite mad. That's what I heard,' Michael said. 'Hope

he's being well looked after. You seem to have a talent for losing prisoners at Halvergate.'

'Is Ian going to be OK?' asked Jamie, a young man about the same age as Fendley, with spiky gelled hair. Janet noticed the other men turn anxiously to Terry for an answer. Ian must be especially popular, she thought.

'I'm sure he's going to be fine,' she said.

'But is he mad, though?'

'He's not well, like Terry said. I understand you're concerned, but we can't discuss other people's health. It's private.'

'Yeah, right. Sure you *understand our concerns*,' said Kamal, a heavily built man slouched on Michael's other side. 'Like he says, you got a talent for losing people.'

Two minutes in and already Michael was disrupting the group. Janet could sense him watching her, malice crackling from him like electric static. 'All right, point taken,' she said. 'If we can move on, what do people think the main aims of this programme are?'

'Risk assessment and rehabilitation,' said Siobhan in a shrill voice.

The group exchanged smirks. Siobhan reddened, realising too late the question was meant for them, not her.

'Thanks, Siobhan,' said Terry. 'What does everyone else think?'

'Is it a box-ticking exercise by the government so they can claim they're making society safer?' Michael gave his most charming smile. This time there were a few laughs.

'Of course,' said Janet. 'It's true. Some people do treat it as a box-ticking exercise. But that doesn't do their chances of parole any good.'

'Touché, Dr Palmer.'

'Anyone else?' said Terry.

'It's helping you turn your life around, like, learning how to do things differently,' said Majid.

'Controlling your moods,' said Greg, one leg bouncing

furiously up and down. 'And seeing stuff from someone else's point of view.'

'Yes, all of that,' said Janet. 'Especially Greg's suggestion. In particular, we'll be looking at things from the victim's perspective.'

'We did some of that with the other bloke,' said Majid. 'Role play stuff.' He gestured at a middle-aged man in a beige cardigan. 'I was about to be Duncan's daughter and then that Helkin guy just went and left. Nothing from anyone about why.'

'That was *strange*, wasn't it, the way he just disappeared?' Michael said. 'Don't suppose you could tell us what happened, could you, Janet? Nobody here seems to think mere prisoners are important enough to be informed.'

There was an expectant pause, which she had no means of filling. Michael stared at her, head cocked on one side in a parody of a man waiting for a reply. In that moment, Janet realised he was fully aware of her ignorance.

'We're not here to talk about Dr Helkin,' said Terry. 'Let's stick to the topic, shall we? What do you think are the benefits of role play, of looking at sexual offences from the victim's point of view?'

'That's obvious. Learning what women really want,' said Michael, smiling at Siobhan. She turned scarlet.

'I think the way we'd put it,' said Terry, 'is learning to treat women as human beings with feelings, not objects to be manipulated.' Janet saw that his knuckles were pale from clenching his notepad.

'I think that's a little unfair,' said Michael. 'If we're talking about manipulation, perhaps we should take a look at who is running a course to reprogramme people?' He stared at Janet. 'I don't think you'll find it's me.'

The return to Cherry Tree Drive was almost a relief. Janet headed straight to the shower, standing under the water at its hottest temperature, washing away as much of Halvergate as she could. After her scare last week, she had been feeling uncharacteristically on edge, not just around the men but also with her colleagues. She had run numerous treatment programmes at Leyland, but never with facilitators like Terry and Siobhan. Terry was clearly good, but had shared so little information with her she found it hard to trust him, and Siobhan was hopeless. She did little more than blush, giving Janet a queasy feeling she might have been foolish enough to lie about whether she had met some of the men before.

Flinging on a fluffy dressing gown, a present from Arun that reminded her of home, Janet wrapped her hair in a towel and padded down the stairs in her slippers. Once in the kitchen, any feeling of comfort began to fade. She had forgotten yet again to buy fresh food for dinner.

'Beans on toast it is, then,' she said, reaching for the tin. She couldn't remember how long it had been since she had only herself to cook for. She and Arun had been together over a decade, and before that there had always been Izzy.

'You can't even read Italian, how are you going to make a cake from a packet?' Janet had come down to the family kitchen in her pyjamas to find Izzy covering the big wooden table in eggs, sugar and flour. She was trying to put together a cake mix the pair of them had brought back from Florence.

'Auto translate on the internet,' said Izzy, waving a sticky printout at her.

'Oh, nice one,' said Janet, pulling up a stool and watching her sister beat eggs.

'Aren't you going to help?'

'I'll help you eat it. What's with the baking mania anyway?'

Their holiday together had been the first time she'd realised Izzy was keeping things from her. To begin with it had just been new interests she hadn't told her about, like the baking or photography, but then she had noticed her sister texting somebody at night when she thought Janet was asleep. It was an odd feeling, Izzy having secrets.

'It's just something nice to do at uni.'

'Well, that must be a first, students cooking.' Janet yawned, thinking of the kitchen at her own halls of residence, where nobody had tried anything more complicated than pasta. 'Your kitchen didn't look much nicer than ours. Hasn't it only got a microwave?'

'I don't cook in halls.'

'Where, then?' Janet looked at her sister bent over the bowl of eggs, beating away, and felt a pang of annoyance. It was meant to be her cutting ties, with her new life and Arun, but somehow Izzy had already drifted away without her noticing. 'I can tell you're dying to tell me something. It's this mystery bloke you keep hinting at, isn't it?' Izzy didn't say anything. 'I've told you everything about Arun. Why won't you talk to me? I don't understand.' Janet could see her sister wavering and took her hand, stopping her as she reached for the flour. 'Izzy, please.'

They stared at each other and Isabel finally gave in. 'It's just he asked me to keep it private.'

'Is he married or something?'

'No, but he wants to keep it between the pair of us.'

'That sounds creepy,' said Janet. The realisation her sister was part of another pair, one that excluded her, hurt her more than she could have imagined. 'He must be dodgy. Why else keep it a secret?' Izzy said nothing and Janet felt suddenly furious. 'God, you're so naive. You've obviously got involved with some creepy older man with his own kitchen. Or more likely his wife's kitchen.'

Without saying anything, Izzy put down her spoon and walked out of the room. Janet was left staring at the mess on the table, realising she had just got her sister to open up to her, then closed her down again with spite.

'Aren't you going to finish the cake?' she shouted.

The only answer was the thump of Izzy's footsteps on the stairs, followed by the slam of the front door.

In Mrs Slaney's kitchen, Janet felt her sister's absence as sharply as she had all those years ago when she first pushed her away.

And now it was too late to say sorry. She looked at the pan, realising she had burned the beans while staring into space. She couldn't face opening another tin, so she scraped the best of them on to her now cold toast. Glass of wine in hand, she headed into the living room.

From the grubby sofa, she faced the vacant stare of Helkin's ceramic head. 'Not much company, are you?' she said. It continued to stare blindly at her and the joke felt lame. She looked at her phone. Arun still hadn't answered her last text, but that was often the case when he worked late. She flicked through the channels, settling for a cookery show as an ironic companion to her baked beans.

The television had switched to a makeover programme when she woke up. Her mouth was dry, her neck sore from the odd angle at which she'd fallen asleep. 'Bloody hell,' she muttered, eyeing the wine glass. She hadn't drunk that much. Her eyelids felt sticky and uncomfortable. Heaving herself up, she padded upstairs to the bathroom. The cheap striplight above the mirror flickered as she splashed water on her face.

Janet glanced up at her reflection. Then froze. Staring back at her was a stranger's face.

She stepped backwards in surprise, but the other face didn't move. A pale woman, her skin so white it seemed bloodless, looked out from the mirror. There were no whites to her eyes and no pupils, only blackness, like holes in a mask. But even though it was impossible to read any expression in those blank eyes, she could feel the heat of the woman's rage burning through the glass. Janet shrank back against the edge of the bath. The stranger's face peered forwards, searching for her. A white hand pressed against the wrong side of the mirror.

Janet's mobile rang, ripping through her dream and jolting her awake. She was still sitting on the sofa, her skin plastered with sweat. On the chipped lacquer of Mrs Slaney's coffee table, the phone buzzed and vibrated like an angry wasp.

She grabbed it, her heart hammering. 'Hello?'

'Dr Palmer, it's Terry. I'm sorry to call you so late.'

'What is it?'

'There's been an attempted suicide.'

'Ian Fendley?' she gasped.

'No, not Ian. David Sneldon. I'm really sorry to disturb you, but David's in a terrible way, very distressed. He asked for you. Can you come to the prison?'

'Of course. I'll come straight away.'

Terry hung up. Janet sat for a moment, gripped by nausea and fear. Upstairs, in the silence, she could hear the bathroom tap running.

12

'He tried to hang himself from the light fixture,' said Terry as they headed past the cells. Along the walkway, the familiar stench of tobacco and male body odour hit Janet's nostrils. The smell of the unwashed – or, as she thought of it, the unloved.

'Who discovered him?'

'His cellmate, Donovan. Sneldon kicked against the bunk bed, waking him. God knows how he managed to keep so quiet up till then.'

As they passed the cells, a few inmates thumped against their doors or called out, and somewhere down the corridor one man was wailing. It wasn't the aggressive wall of sound she'd heard when Baz Gridley attacked her, but a disturbing chorus that shifted between melancholy and menace.

'As you can tell,' said Terry, 'it's got everyone very upset. Impossible to hide something like that, everyone rushing about the corridor, Donovan shouting at the top of his lungs.'

'Where's Michael now?'

'We moved him to the prison hospital for the night. I'll take you there after you've seen Sneldon.'

Janet suspected she looked even more drawn than usual. It felt as if she had woken from one nightmare only to walk into another. The shock focused her mind, but she had a terrible headache.

'How bad is Sneldon? Physically, I mean?'

'Donovan caught him early, held him up and hollered for help, so the hanging didn't progress far. He didn't even lose consciousness.' Terry patted the fish knife hanging from his belt. 'I cut him down with this. And he was kicking out like a bastard, so we had to tranquilise him.'

'I've only spoken to David Sneldon once.' Janet stumbled slightly as she tried to keep up with Terry. 'Nothing unexpected came up when I saw him last week. I know he was disappointed not to get on to the programme this time, but you know him better – have you noticed anything?'

'Nothing. He's only been here a few months, but far as I could see he was a bit of a joker, hardly the moody type. I don't understand it at all.'

The prison nurse was bringing David a glass of water when Janet arrived. Halvergate's hospital consisted of only four beds, but even this was a luxury for such a small institution. As she approached his bed, Janet could see ugly scarlet bruises circling his neck. He lay back on the pillows, heavily sedated but awake.

'Tim Ashton,' said the nurse quietly, turning and holding out his hand to Janet. 'Earlier David was insisting he wanted to see you, but he's calmed down since then. I've just asked him if he wants to speak to you now, or if he'd rather wait. I think it's fine as long as we don't tire him out.'

'Thank you,' said Janet, as she pulled up a chair to sit by David Sneldon's bedside. He didn't look at her. 'David, can you hear me? It's Janet Palmer, we met last week. I'm very sorry to hear about what happened.'

He stared at the ceiling and said nothing. His eyes welled with tears.

'We don't have to talk about anything now. It's important you get your rest. But I'm here if you want to talk to me.'

'No choice,' David murmured.

'You felt you had no choice?' Janet repeated. Without warning, his hand shot out from under the bedcover and grabbed her by the wrist. His grasp was surprisingly fierce as he pulled her towards the bed, his eyes wide and bloodshot.

'Now then, David, let go of Dr Palmer.' Janet heard Tim's voice behind her, before she had a chance to say anything. He leaned over and gently prised David's fingers from her wrist. David watched him, his jaw working as if he wanted to say something, but no sound came out.

'Perhaps I should come back when he's had some more rest,' she said to Tim. Gently, she pushed back her chair, but as she stood up David snatched at her.

'Don't leave!' He gestured frantically at Tim. 'She's so angry, she's so angry!' His mouth crumpled into a sob of distress.

'Now then,' said Tim, 'leave off grabbing at her, the doctor's not angry with you, she's just going to come back later when you've had a rest.'

'No rest, no rest,' he wailed.

'I don't mind staying for a bit if it calms him down. I can just sit here, it's fine.' She pulled her chair out of reaching distance. 'I'm here, David, try to relax. If you need to talk I'll be just here.'

'Keep her away,' David murmured.

Tim sighed in exasperation and rolled his eyes. 'Sorry,' he mouthed. But Janet kept her eyes on David.

'Keep who away?'

He looked at her accusingly. 'You know who! You know who I mean!'

Tim moved between them. 'Dr Palmer, I really am very sorry you were called in. He was insisting he wanted to see you, but I'm afraid he's changed his mind.' He ushered her away from the bed. 'Would you mind seeing Michael Donovan though? Since you've already made the trek out here. He's in the safe cell. He was also asking for you. Seems to have taken it pretty well, but you can never tell. Particularly given it's the second time.'

'The second time?'

'One of the suicides last year was Donovan's cellmate. You must have heard how he died? It was Mark Conybeer, middle of the night, very traumatic. I'll call Terry to take you over,' he said, turning back towards David, who'd started wailing again.

Michael was sitting cross-legged on the bed reading when she went in. He looked up and smiled at her. He was even more attractive than she remembered.

'How are you?' Janet asked, taking the seat furthest from him. 'Sounds like quite an evening. I understand from Terry that you saved David's life. Everyone's very grateful.'

Michael shrugged. 'I'd do anything to get a room of my own for a bit of private reading, without some snoring suicidal cellmate.' He held the book out to her. It was a copy of John Donne's sermons. '*No man is an island,*' he quoted. 'Definitely true in prison.'

'You certainly have unusual reading tastes,' said Janet, before she could stop herself.

Michael raised his eyebrows. 'Unusual for a sex offender, you mean? Perhaps you think I should be reading *Lolita*.' He leaned forward. 'Amazing the paths an Oxford education opens up for you. Though perhaps in my case all roads would have led to Halvergate.' He sat back again, eyes narrowing. 'I can't imagine what brought you here, though.'

'What's brought me here tonight is you. Tim Ashton said you wanted to talk to me.'

'It's the cell you should be looking at, not me. Before they have a chance to clean the walls. I was too busy holding the kicking maniac off the floor to check, but I'll bet you it's there.'

'What's there?' she asked, a sick feeling in her stomach.

'What the suicides here always scrawl somewhere, usually on the wall.' He gestured her over. Janet sensed he was playing games and stayed where she was.

'Nobody's listening but me,' she said. 'You can speak normally.'

He shrugged. 'Suit yourself. I'm sure Terry will tell you. He's been keeping you helpfully informed so far, I imagine?' Janet tried to keep the annoyance from her face, but clearly didn't succeed. Michael held up his hands in a conciliatory gesture. 'OK, fine. It's gibberish anyway, no sense to it. Just the letter E. It got them all foxed last time round. And no point asking David – he'll just deny writing it.'

'Perhaps you wrote it?'

'Of course. I popped out of prison and sprayed a big E on the tree near where Ryan Spalding was found.'

Janet looked at him doubtfully. 'How do you know there was an E on the tree?'

'It's *amazing*,' he replied, in a sarcastic drawl. 'Besides reading "challenging" books, I also watch the local news.'

'Why are you telling me this?'

'Well, this is wonderful.' Michael's voice bubbled over with laughter. 'You come here to check on how traumatised I am, I help you out, and you act as if I tried to murder David rather than save him. No, don't apologise,' he said, holding up a hand to stop the apology she had no intention of making. He grinned. 'I rather like you anyway.'

'Do you want to talk about what happened? I understand that you've had a similar experience before.'

'They told you about that, did they? Terry must be soft on you. Yes, that was pretty unpleasant. This evening was just a surprise, frankly. One moment David's boring on to me about some stupid centrefold bitch, I doze off, and the next thing I know he's doing the dance of death.' He rubbed his ribs, looking down. 'Gave me quite a kicking.'

'So David didn't seem suicidal at all?'

Michael snorted. 'I doubt he could even spell the word. He'd certainly done some droning on about how he was innocent, the usual aggrieved routine, but no. Not suicidal. But then neither was Ryan. Mark, on the other hand, was less of a shock.'

'That was the cellmate you found before, when it was too late?'

He nodded. 'He was always wailing on about how remorseful he felt. More a banshee than a cellmate.'

'Did he say anything about . . .' Janet trailed off. Michael's eyes were sparkling.

'Go on. About what?'

'Did he . . . seem to suffer from delusions? See people who weren't there?'

'Perhaps you should be asking Dr Helkin that question.' Michael looked down, smoothing the bedclothes beside him, the corners of his mouth twitching in a smile. 'If you can find him, that is.'

Sweat prickled on Janet's forehead and she felt as if the walls were closing in on them, bringing them ever closer together. 'What do you know about him?'

'A lot more than you by the looks of things.' Michael laughed. 'Poor Janey. You're desperate to ask for my help, but you just can't bring yourself to do it, can you?'

'How will I know if you're telling the truth?'

'You won't. But ask yourself, how do you know if anyone at Halvergate is lying or not?'

Janet felt trapped. She'd already blown a hole in her own safe disclosure rules by allowing Michael to guess how ill-informed she was. 'OK, I'll ask again,' she said. 'What do *you* think you know about John Helkin that *I* don't?'

Michael sat back on the bed, stretching his arms behind his head. 'I'll give you one word. Hypnosis.'

'You're saying he practised hypnosis on prisoners at Halvergate?' Janet was incredulous. 'You can't expect me to believe that, surely.'

'I said I'd give you *one* word. For now. Besides –' he smiled – 'you're a clever girl. I'm sure you'll find out if it's true or not.'

Terry was forced into a jog to keep up as Janet hurried along the corridor to David and Michael's cell. His face was drawn from lack of sleep. Staff shortages meant he was working a double shift.

'I already checked it,' he said. 'Dr Palmer, there's no need for this.'

'I just want to see if there's anything in the cell that might give us a clue why David tried to kill himself. A note, maybe.'

'There's no note,' Terry said, puffing as he joined her at the cell door.

'There's no harm in checking again.'

Terry reached into his back pocket with a sigh and fished out the key. Janet pushed past him into the cell. The room smelt rank with stale sweat. She ran her eyes around the dingy walls. There were some photographs and crumpled pictures from a lads' mag on the pinboard and, pinned incongruously in the middle, a printout of Psalm 23, 'The Lord is my Shepherd'. Janet stared at it. But the psalm was the only writing on display. The board had no notes on it and no E. She stepped over to the desk, looking through the pile of magazines.

'There's nothing. I already checked.'

Janet knocked a magazine off the table and bent to pick it up, then squatted, scanning the lino beneath her feet and the walls where they met the floor. Her eyes stopped at the base of the sink. The plaster was soft where the pipe had leaked, and scratched into it, perhaps with a fingernail, was the letter E.

'There is something,' she said. She knelt down and peered closer, damp powder coming off on her fingers as she gently touched the wall. 'Look at this.' Terry hung back. Janet sat on her haunches. 'It's the letter E.' She paused. 'I understand it's not the first time it's been found on the walls here.'

'Who told you that?' said Terry, shortly. 'Donovan? He probably wrote it himself.'

'Maybe he did,' said Janet. 'But even so, it's interesting, isn't it? Given a letter E was found written near the other Halvergate suicides. Could it be drugs-related? A code for some sort of legal high doing the rounds?'

'We never found any significance,' Terry said, folding his arms. 'The only one who wouldn't stop banging on about it was Michael. At one point, Dr Helkin thought it could even have been a copycat thing.'

At the mention of her predecessor, Janet stood up. 'That was another thing Michael said. About Dr Helkin.' She faced her colleague. 'Terry, did he practise hypnosis on any inmates here?'

He frowned. 'You ought to be careful listening to Michael. You've seen yourself how manipulative he can be.'

'Is it true, though?' Terry said nothing but she read the answer in his eyes. 'Jesus, he did, didn't he? Why didn't you tell me?'

'I don't see why it's relevant. It's unorthodox, I suppose, but people do use it in therapy.'

'Not in prison they don't.' Janet walked to the door. 'Forgive me for taking the E a little more seriously in that case, even if it *was* Michael who told me about it.'

As they left the cell, she caught Terry off guard, looking at her. His expression was unmistakably hostile.

13

A small window above David Sneldon's bed showed the blue sky of a winter's morning. Dried water marks from the rain had stained the pane in lines, echoing the white bars that partly blocked out the sunshine. David was propped up on his pillow, purple rings beneath his eyes.

Steven sat near the bed, sipping the tea the nurse had brought over. He noticed that David wore the prison-issue plastic rosary that so many inmates at Halvergate requested. When he'd started working in the prison service, this popular piety had taken him by surprise. Later the chaplain at his first placement explained that prisoners wore them to inspire respect when they left. Everyone on the street would know they'd done time.

David kept running the beads and the plastic cross through his fingers. Maybe it was a nervous habit, or maybe he was one of the few men who actually wore the rosary out of devotion to God.

'Thanks for coming,' David said, looking down at the beads in his hands.

'Not at all. How are you feeling?' Steven asked, his kind eyes focused on the man lying beside him.

David shrugged. 'Been better.'

'Have you spoken to your family at all? Tim mentioned your mum was coming to visit later this week.'

David leaned his head back, closing his eyes. 'Don't know why she would. I've always dropped her in the shit.'

'Well, everyone disappoints their mum and dad,' Steven said. For a moment he was back in Runcorn, standing in the hallway of his childhood home. He could hear his own father's voice shouting that he was disgusting, yelling at him to get out of the house, as a bag of belongings crashed down the stairs. He turned his thoughts back to the present. 'I'm sure your mum loves you, all the same.' He paused before continuing, choosing his words carefully. 'Do you want to talk about last night? I'm worried about you. Nobody should feel that alone.'

'It's not being alone that bothers me!' David sat up and leaned towards Steven. 'I know you believe in God and that, don't you? But what about . . . what about the other stuff?'

'Evil, you mean? I believe in that too,' said Steven. 'But evil doesn't get the final say. I also hope and believe that God never abandons anyone who asks for His help.'

'Why would God look out for me?' David flopped back on his pillows.

'None of us deserve God's love, but it's there all the same,' Steven replied. David's preoccupation with evil drew his mind back to Arnas and the velnius he claimed was stalking the VP wing. Stalking prisoners like David. He watched the man for a moment, trying to assess his fragility. 'David, have you . . . have you seen anything or anyone that frightened you?'

'Have you seen her too?' His voice was a whisper, eyes wide with fear. Steven shifted in his chair but didn't answer. David seemed to take this as a yes. 'It's what she said, Father, that's how I know.'

Fear seeped under Steven's skin like cold water. 'What did she say?'

'Over and over, like a hiss.' David covered his ears as if still hearing it, his hands trembling. 'I kept closing my eyes, I lay in bed thinking it's a dream, she's not real, but every time, *every time* I opened my eyes her face was closer, staring at me.' He started to cry. 'I couldn't stand it. I had to make it stop.'

Steven realised his own hands were sweating. 'What did this woman say?'

'I didn't understand . . . Sounded a bit like ring yes or in yes.

But then something else too, so I knew I had to, I had to . . .' David's voice trailed off with distress.

'It's OK,' said Steven, 'it's just me.'

David held out his hand. Steven took it and felt his fingers crushed by the other man's grip. 'Vengeance is mine,' David said, looking into his eyes. 'And I will repay.'

Lunchtime, and Janet sat alone in her office, eating a sandwich. She had lost count of the number of coffees she had drunk to stay awake. They did the trick but left her feeling jumpy. It had been close to one in the morning when she finally made it back to Cherry Tree Drive, and even then sleep had eluded her. She couldn't imagine how she was going to tackle Michael's bombshell about Helkin, not with so little help from his former colleagues. And alongside stress about work, her nightmare lay like a shadow at the edge of her mind. She knew that after seeing Ian Fendley it was perfectly normal to dream about what he had told her, but it still unnerved her.

She pressed her hands to her temples, trying to force herself to concentrate. Great Yarmouth General Hospital had finally emailed over their notes on Ryan Spalding. They made for a confusing read. Terry had told her Helkin had referred Spalding for severe depression, but according to the hospital he had also been psychotic. All his drugs tests had come back clean. Most puzzling of all was one line that suggested the consultant, Dr Gupta, thought Spalding was faking his delusions. Little wonder the hospital had been reluctant to pass on the notes, she thought. If the prisoner was only pretending to be ill, it made their security failings even worse.

Janet dialled the consultant's extension. 'Hello, it's Dr Palmer from Halvergate. Can I speak to Dr Gupta? He's expecting my call.' She waited while the receptionist put her through.

'Dev Gupta speaking.'

'Dr Gupta, hi, it's Janet Palmer. Thanks for talking to me. Like I said in my email, I'm hoping you can tell me a little more about Ryan Spalding, if you remember him?'

'Hard to forget a patient who's the subject of an investigation.'

'This is all in confidence. I'm just trying to understand the high rates of self-harm at Halvergate, see if there's any pattern.'

'So you've obviously read my note about him faking the psychosis,' said the psychiatrist, drily. 'But it was actually more complicated than that.'

'In what way?'

'Ryan Spalding admitted that he had invented his delusions, but his reasons for doing so suggested he was having an acute mental health crisis nonetheless.'

'He told you he'd invented them?' Janet turned to the window, stared at the grey silhouette of the perimeter fence shimmering against the pale sky. 'I don't understand.'

'Ryan came to the hospital claiming he was being tormented by a vengeful woman who was determined to make him pay for his crimes. When I spoke to him he confessed he hadn't actually seen any of this, but he was desperate to get away from her all the same. Even though he hadn't *seen* this woman, he *believed* in her.'

Janet felt her heartbeat quicken. 'Believed in her?'

'Yes. Ryan Spalding believed Halvergate was haunted. He was convinced a ghost had driven other men to their deaths. At the time I put this down to a delusion on his part, but on reflection I think at least one other prisoner must have been suffering from a psychotic episode. That explains why Halvergate referred Ryan Spalding to us. Even though *Ryan* hadn't been hallucinating, if another man had already reported similar delusions, I'm less surprised that your last psychologist was taken in.' Dr Gupta paused, obviously finished and waiting for a reply, but Janet found herself unable to speak. 'Does that help at all?' he added.

'Yes, very much,' Janet said, her mouth dry. 'And you don't feel with hindsight that Spalding was lying about thinking Halvergate was haunted? Given you think the hallucinations were faked?'

Dr Gupta sighed. 'It's a difficult one, I know. Of course he could have been faking that too, but in my judgement he was genuinely afraid.'

'I see,' she said, though the situation felt far from clear. 'One last thing. I know his results were clean, but did Ryan strike you as someone who had been taking drugs recently, or might have been using legal highs?'

'No. Which puzzled me. As you suggest, that's what you'd look for in a patient with his symptoms. And that wasn't the only peculiarity. For me his suicide was truly surprising. Ryan Spalding seemed desperate to escape danger. He was the very last person I would have suspected would self-harm. But when people are delusional, these events are very hard to predict.'

'That's true,' said Janet. 'Thank you.'

'No problem.'

She put the phone down and sat staring at the wall in front of her, then stood up and walked to the window. In the unforgiving light of the crisp winter's day, the Portakabins looked even shabbier. A procession of men snaked their way across the yard from one of the workshops, heading back to the prison. There were surely few groups of people more vulnerable to being manipulated into believing imaginary terrors than those cooped up in a closed community. Especially one where men were confined to their cells for hours on end.

John Helkin was no longer just an outline of a man, a blank space as absent as his notes. But the more he came into focus, the more troubling he became.

14

Another Saturday morning in Cherry Tree Drive, but this one felt less bleak. Arun was coming, and Janet hoped his presence would exorcise the house of at least some of its troubling atmosphere. Not willing to leave it to chance, she decided to give him a helping hand by unpacking as many boxes as she could.

With the radio on full blast, Janet attacked Cherry Tree Drive with Dettol and polish. Her mood was bolstered by having enjoyed a relatively normal Friday at work, by Halvergate's standards at least. Richard had sent her a predictably snotty email after he'd learned that neither Baz nor Ian's tests showed any sign of drugs, but the latest group session had gone well and Terry was confident that David and Ian's moods remained relatively stable.

By the afternoon the place looked marginally more like a home. The living room was scattered with photographs of holidays she and Arun had been on together, and she had replaced one of Mrs Slaney's terrible twee prints of big-eyed Victorian children with a framed art nouveau poster she had once had on her wall at university. Perhaps it would remind Arun of happier times. And after a spot of hoovering and dusting, the house looked almost habitable.

Determined to cook a proper dinner, Janet set off in the car towards Norwich. Steven had suggested some fancy food shops for her to investigate.

Out of habit she looked left at the turning when she reached the prison. To her surprise she saw a figure filming the sign at Halvergate's entrance. Hunched over a video camera and tripod, almost drowned by a heavy mackintosh, it could have been a man or a woman. A battered Peugeot was parked badly behind the stranger, one wheel in the air and its nose poking into the hedge. Janet slowed her car and wound down the window.

'Can I help you?' she called out.

The figure lifted its head from the camera, pushing the raincoat's hood back as if only just realising it had stopped drizzling. A woman with cropped brown hair was revealed. She looked over at Janet and smiled.

'I'm OK, thanks, won't be long,' said the stranger, perhaps wilfully ignoring the intent of Janet's question.

'Sorry,' said Janet. 'Who are you? Why are you filming?'

The woman gave the tripod a precautionary shake before striding over to the car, gumboots squelching in the mud.

'Zara Hyde,' she said, sticking out her hand as Janet turned off the engine. Zara squinted into the car, 'I'm a reporter for the Eastern Film Company, the local telly news.'

Janet stared at her in dismay. Surely it was impossible for anything about David to have leaked to the press.

'I'll be out of your hair in a mo,' Zara continued blithely. 'Just getting a few shots for the inquest.' Although she could only have been a few years older than Janet, Zara had a no-nonsense manner reminiscent of a 1950s games mistress.

'Inquest?' said Janet, faintly.

'Ryan Spalding. It's his inquest coming up soon. We don't have any recent shots of the prison, so I'm being shockingly organised. They've only just put up a sign saying HMP Halvergate – it still said RAF Breydon when we were here for the escape.' Zara looked at Janet, her gaze shrewd and calculating. 'Do you work here?'

'I'm the new psychologist. Janet Palmer.'

'Gosh, I imagine that's quite a job. After all the ... well, not easy following Dr Helkin. Crikey. I interviewed him, so, um, yes. Must be difficult.'

Janet gaped. 'You interviewed John Helkin!'

'Yes, well,' said Zara, mistaking her tone and stepping back from the car defensively. 'We never broadcast it, you know, as was agreed.'

'Sorry, I just had no idea.' Janet stopped. She was desperate to find out more but couldn't think of anyone she was more reluctant to confide in than a journalist of five minutes' acquaintance. And then there was Arun's dinner to make. She hesitated. 'I'm quite new here. Well, very new. It's my first month.' She looked up at Zara Hyde, her friendly un-made-up face and sensible trousers. She decided to take a gamble. 'This probably sounds a bit crazy, but do you fancy a coffee?'

Zara looked at her watch, unperturbed, as if requests from random psychologists for coffee were nothing new. 'Why not?' She shrugged. 'I doubt the news desk will call now. I've sent everything for today, it's an early programme. Shall we head to the Woodsman at Halverton?'

Janet nodded. The Woodsman was her landlady's pub, so it wasn't an entirely welcome prospect, but at least she wouldn't have to ask for directions.

Zara started squelching her way back to the tripod. 'I'll just stow the gear in the boot,' she called back over her shoulder. 'I'll meet you there.'

Janet chose a table in the corner, as far from the bar as possible. The Woodsman was a dingy place. Tacky tables and the smell of sweat and stale beer were not offset by any quaint beams or crackling fireplaces. It was an unlovely, single-storey 1930s building, with the same 70s-style carpets as Cherry Tree Drive. She fiddled with her phone as she waited for Zara, then turned it over to dismiss the troubling feelings raised by Arun's picture. Perhaps she ought to stick to her original plan to make him a proper meal for when he arrived, rather than sit in the pub chatting to a stranger.

It was too late to back out now. Zara marched into the bar, scanning the room. As she flung her mac over a chair, Janet scrambled to her feet.

'What would you like?'

'Tea would be nice, thanks. It got a bit chilly out there. I'll get the next one.'

'Meeting a friend?' asked her landlady as Janet ordered the tea and a glass of orange juice for herself. Mrs Slaney nodded at Zara. 'Have I seen her somewhere? She looks familiar.'

Janet smiled and took the drinks without answering.

'This is pretty ghastly,' said Zara. 'Bum choice of mine, sorry. I've never been in before. It just sprung to mind as it's close.'

Janet wished Zara's voice wasn't so loud. She looked up at the Artex ceiling, familiar from her rented home. 'At least it saves a drive,' she said.

There was an awkward pause. Zara stirred her tea, waiting.

'Look,' Janet began. 'Can we talk sort of off the record. I mean totally off the record.'

'Of course!' said Zara, visibly restraining herself from seizing the notebook poking out of her bag, a hungry gleam in her eye at the thought of an imminent scoop.

Janet almost felt guilty. 'I don't actually have anything to tell you. I just wanted to ask you some questions about Dr Helkin.'

Zara sighed. 'I always get the ones *asking* questions!' she said, pulling a face.

'If there's anything I can tell you in the future, I will,' Janet lied. She thought of the attempted suicide that would have Zara and her colleagues scurrying off to Halvergate.

'It's fine,' said Zara, smiling, as if spotting her insincerity. 'I said yes to the drink because you looked a bit lost, frankly. A scoop would be nice, but I'm not a completely heartless news-hound. Fire away.'

'Well, off the record, I don't have much information about Dr Helkin. What was he like when you interviewed him?'

'Mad As,' said Zara emphatically, putting down her tea. 'Quite bonkers. And I interview some crackpots in my line of work, especially Yarmouth way, so that's really saying something.'

Janet looked at her doubtfully. 'Mad in what way?'

'You really don't know this?' she asked. Janet shook her head. 'No, obviously. I guess I'm just surprised nobody told you, especially given all the palaver over the tape.'

'Halvergate were angry you'd interviewed him?' This was less surprising. Janet could picture Richard's fury on finding out some reporter had been talking to his staff. He barely liked the staff talking to each other.

'You could say so. To be honest, the interview was unbroadcastable. Ofcom would have been all over our arses. Duty of care and all that. He was so clearly deranged.'

'What happened?' asked Janet, hoping to find out what Helkin had said. Zara mistook her meaning.

'Our editor's a really decent chap. He called the prison to say we're a bit worried about one of the employees, he seems pretty disturbed. Then the governor, Webster, isn't it?' Janet nodded. 'He went ballistic. Talked about injunctions, wanted the tape destroyed, all completely over the top. Then in the next breath insisted Helkin wasn't mad and threatened to sue for libel.'

'What did your editor do?' Janet was interested in spite of herself at the thought of anyone standing up to Halvergate. There was something infectious about Zara's gossipy tone.

'Bearing in mind there was an investigation going on into the escape at this point, Charlie mentioned that involving the police might be no bad thing. Some of the stuff Helkin said was pretty incriminating as far as the prison was concerned. You know, to have such a mad psychologist.' Zara couldn't help smirking. 'Amazing how quickly that shut him up.' She took a sip of tea. 'Next thing we know, Helkin's gone, off with stress. Allegedly.'

'What on earth did he say in the interview?' Janet said, not even bothering to keep the curiosity out of her voice.

Zara blew out a long breath. 'I can't remember it all. It was one of those interviews you want to end as soon as possible. The cameraman was making faces at me when I turned round, as if to say, who *is* this loon? Normally I'd have called it a day after the first question, but I was hoping Helkin would come up with something relevant. It's not often you get someone like that agreeing to talk on the record. And then I thought even the madness might end up being revealing.'

'But what did he actually say?' Janet asked in frustration.

'Most of it was some nonsense about demonic possession. It was really crazy stuff.'

The feeling of dread that had been lurking at the edges of Janet's mind began to close in on her, like shadows chasing the dimming of a light. She gripped her glass.

'Possession?'

'Yes, he felt he was the victim of an attempted demonic possession. Pretty hysterical about it. God knows how he was doing his job. The man was completely ... well, off his head.'

'Did he say who was trying to possess him?'

Zara looked at Janet for a moment, taking in her pale face. 'Can I ask why you're so interested?'

Janet paused, struggling to think of what to say. 'I ... I'm just surprised my colleagues never mentioned it. Any details would be helpful. I'm trying to work out what happened under his care.'

Zara nodded. 'I don't actually recall all the details. But I remember it was a woman, an angry woman. She tried to possess him in his sleep, apparently. I think he'd been watching Babestation late at night after one too many whiskies.' Zara looked at Janet more seriously. 'What I do remember is that he felt this woman was responsible for prisoners committing suicide. That's what rang real alarm bells. It was another reason we called the prison.' She fiddled with her cup on the table, then laughed. 'Well, that's it. What a rubbish hack I am, you're much better at asking questions!'

Janet gave Zara a tense smile. She was desperate to ask more but sensed she couldn't go on without offering something, however tenuous, in return. 'I really appreciate your help,' she said. 'I'm very limited in what I can tell you, but if we keep in touch. I'll try to help you with any questions you have.'

'You've not been at Halvergate long,' Zara said with a wolfish grin. 'I'm holding out for a future gratitude scoop.'

Janet finished her orange juice. 'It's just a shame you destroyed the tape.'

'Destroyed it?' asked Zara, incredulous. 'You don't think Charlie took any notice of that old goat Webster, do you?' She poured herself some more tea. 'I kept it. You never know when something like that will come in handy.' A slight smile played on her lips as she looked up from the cup to read the inevitable question in Janet's eyes.

15

Janet had intended the meeting to be brief, but ended up spending two hours at the Woodsman. A group of locals turned up while she and Zara were talking, giving the unattractive place an almost lively air. Janet found herself caught up in Zara's entertaining gossip as she drank her way through a second pot of tea, lamenting that it wasn't something stronger.

She told Janet with some relish about being first on the scene where Ryan Spalding had died – 'all covered by a white tent by the time I arrived' – which was, she claimed, the same patch of forest where a local woman had been found murdered some years before. 'I filmed that too,' she said. 'God I've been doing this job too long . . .' Janet thought Zara was going to recount every single murder she'd covered in East Anglia, but at last, after draining her cup, she reached for her mac. Before parting, they agreed to meet again at the Eastern Film Company. She had refused to give Janet a DVD copy of her interview with Helkin but agreed to let her watch it on an edit machine in the newsroom instead, 'as long as Charlie gives the idea the thumbs-up.'

As Janet headed back to her Mini, a message from Arun bleeped up on her mobile. He had sent it a few hours ago, but the phone had only just picked up enough signal.

Getting there earlier, see you soon xx

'Shit,' Janet muttered. Perhaps he was already sitting outside the house, fuming. No time to go to Norwich and pick up supplies.

She was relieved to see an empty driveway when she arrived at Cherry Tree Drive. She sat in the car for a minute. Without Arun there, she suddenly felt less eager to go in. It wasn't the dark outside that bothered her, but the thought that some remnant of Dr Helkin's presence lingered in the house, as pervasive and unwelcome as the damp. Discovering that he was not only unorthodox but also delusional had come as an unwelcome revelation; it left her even more perplexed about what might have happened at Halvergate.

'This is ridiculous,' Janet said to herself as she got out of the car. She wondered how gradually John Helkin had lost himself, and what had pushed him over the edge. That wasn't going to happen to her.

Janet almost felt she was back at the Woodsman when she turned on the hall light. Mrs Slaney had clearly had lots of the old carpet to spare. As she headed into the kitchen, Arun called her.

'I'm about twenty minutes away. I've been calling to say I finished work early, but your phone rang out.' His voice was hard to hear. 'What's for dinner?'

Janet's stomach sank. 'I thought maybe we could go out?'

'I've been driving for ages. I thought it would be nicer to crash and have an evening in.'

Janet opened the fridge, not feeling hopeful. A few sad-looking carrots and a packet of pasta parcels. Arun didn't much like pasta. 'I can rustle something up,' she said.

'Great, see you soon.'

On his arrival, Arun looked thoroughly discontented. 'Sodding A11 goes on for ever,' he said, dropping his bags in the doorway with a thump.

'I should have suggested you get the train,' Janet replied, giving him a hug. It was strange to see him here. He didn't make Cherry Tree Drive feel safer; instead its damp atmosphere seemed to shrink him.

He held her close and she breathed in the familiar aftershave, closing her eyes for a moment, imagining herself in the past. 'Never mind,' he said. 'What's for dinner?'

Janet disentangled herself and turned back towards the kitchen so she wouldn't see his frown deepen. 'Ravioli.'

The table felt dank and tacky to the touch, even though she had tried to cover most of it with some faded Monet placemats she had found in one of Mrs Slaney's cupboards. Janet realised she had never actually sat in the kitchen to eat a proper meal until now. Not that pasta parcels were fine dining. She hoped turning off the overhead lamp and adding a few tea lights might pass for making an effort.

Arun heaved himself into a chair and poured a large glass of wine as she dolloped out the cheap supermarket meal. 'Work been all right?' he asked.

'Not really,' Janet said. 'Trouble at the prison. How was it at the lab?'

He grunted. 'The usual.' He looked preoccupied, stirring the pasta without eating it. They both continued to play with their food, the reason for his visit hanging over their meal like a shadow. 'Actually, one thing has come up.' He paused and she looked at him expectantly. 'I've been offered a six-month placement in the States. At MIT.'

'America?' Janet was stunned.

'It's a big opportunity. I'd be leading a team while someone's on sabbatical.'

Janet knew she couldn't possibly complain, having just moved miles away to Norfolk for her own job, but the idea of Arun across the Atlantic was depressing. 'That's fantastic,' she said with false enthusiasm. 'And six months will go quickly enough. I can ask about taking some leave to come visit.'

'That's the thing.' Arun put his cutlery down, abandoning all pretence of eating the now congealing ravioli. 'If it goes well, there's every likelihood I might get a more permanent offer.'

'Move to America? Permanently?'

'This isn't a break-up visit.' He made a feeble attempt at a laugh. 'I'd obviously want you to come too.'

'But what about my job?'

'You could get another job, couldn't you? I'm sure the qualifications for practising psychology must be the same. It would be a perfect chance to get out of the prison service.'

'I like working in the prison service.'

'Come on, Janey,' he said impatiently. 'You look like a wreck, you're living in this dump of a place. Can't you just admit that this job was a mistake?'

Janet stood up, scraping back her chair. Unsure whether she was angry at his arrogance or because he was right, she walked out of the room. In the comfortless living room, she flung herself onto Mrs Slaney's floral sofa. Arun followed close behind.

'I don't want to watch you doing this to yourself any more,' he said, his voice rising. 'It's like picking at an open wound. You know what your doctor said about staying in the prison service. It's not good for you, it doesn't do you any good.' He tried to put an arm round her but she shook him off. 'At least at Leyland you had Stuart, some support. I don't like you being out here on your own. I don't want you making yourself ill.'

'Don't do that,' Janet said, turning her face away. 'Don't make my mental health the excuse for you pursuing your own ambitions.'

'I'm sorry, I didn't mean to upset you.' He took hold of one unresisting hand. 'But don't you want a new start together, somewhere completely new? Seriously, don't you think that would be better? This place on your own or Massachusetts with me. Is it really that hard a choice?'

Opposite them, looking down from the 1970s cabinet, was John Helkin's blank-eyed head. In her mind's eye Janet imagined the face tilting to one side, one eyebrow quizzically raised, asking the same question. *What am I doing here?* She closed her eyes. Sensing she might be weakening, Arun edged closer. 'Why don't you think about it while I'm away?'

'OK,' she muttered. Arun squeezed her shoulders in a bear hug and breathed his relief into her hair.

'That's my girl.'

Arun spent the rest of the evening talking at Janet about the post at MIT, about where they might live together, about his hopes of a permanent job. If he was harbouring any doubts over her final decision, he kept them to himself. Between her garrulous boyfriend and the heavy atmosphere of the house, Janet felt herself shrinking into invisibility.

To try to stop the flow of his chatter, she turned the television on to a film she had no interest in watching. As Arun sat, quiet now and absorbed in the action, she felt her mind drifting back to the perfect boyfriend she had never met.

'He's called Raphe,' Izzy said, her eyes shining. They were walking in Regent's Park, the rose garden in full bloom, as Isabel spilled the beans on the man she had been secretly seeing. It had taken a week of pleading to bring her round after the cake episode.

'Why doesn't he want you telling people about him?' Janet said. 'I'm sorry I was such a cow before, but really, do you think he might be married?'

'No, it's nothing like that. I've been to his place often enough. He just wants it kept special between us, no nosy friends or family. He says he wants to keep me all to himself.'

Izzy looked delighted by this romantic gesture but Janet had always had a more suspicious nature. 'Hmm,' she said.

'Honestly, you wouldn't doubt him if you met him,' Isabel said. 'He's so intelligent. I could just listen to him for hours. He seems to have read everything. And he got a first in maths.' She broke off from her hymn of praise to look at the flowers. With her head bent to smell the blooms, she looked like a Pre-Raphaelite painting. She had always been the better-looking of the two sisters, despite their similarities. Isabel's mouth was in an almost imperceptibly deeper bow, her eyes somehow wider, her gait more languid than Janet's, whose movements always seemed sharp and sudden. It had never bothered Janet before;

her love for her sister had always made it impossible to feel jealous. So she didn't recognise the unpleasant feeling now in her chest.

'And he's really that good-looking?' She tried not to think of Arun and his geeky glasses.

'Like you wouldn't believe.'

'So have you ...' She trailed off, not sure she wanted to hear the answer.

'Not yet.' Isabel seemed uncomfortable, turning from the flowers and heading back along the path.

Janet followed. Thinking of her own first sexual experience, Arun's endearing, if not very sexy, eagerness, she felt relieved. 'Why not? If he's so amazing. And if you love him and everything.'

Isabel looked away from her sister's prying gaze. 'I just think you need to be completely sure you can trust someone, that's all.'

'I thought you said you did trust him, that I'd trust him?' Janet stopped, catching Isabel's hand. In the sunshine, she felt suddenly cold with fear. 'There's something else about him isn't there? Something not nice.'

For a moment, Janet read the truth in her sister's eyes. Then it was gone, before she had a chance to understand what she'd seen. Isabel smiled at her. 'Don't be silly,' she said.

Lying next to Arun later, Janet thought back on all the years she had relied on him, trusted the stability of his love, just as she relied on the warmth of his body, now, in the cold bed. He had long been the anchor in her life. It wasn't something she could cut loose, even if she was no longer sure how deeply she loved him.

Listening to his heavy breathing as he slept, her eyes followed the dark shades of the Artex on the ceiling, grey ridges leaking into black. She tried to imagine a new path curving off to a life in America, but instead she found herself walking down the landings at Halvergate. In her mind's eye she followed Terry, his back always retreating, getting further out of reach. She thought of Michael Donovan curled up like a Buddha on his bed and felt a stab of anxiety. Her own breathing quickened. There was something about Halvergate she didn't want to leave, not for Arun, not for the East Coast, not even for her own happiness. She didn't want the place to succeed in driving her away. Whatever darkness hid at Halvergate, she would find it.

16

In the grey morning light, Janet left Arun in bed and made an early trip to Londis for bacon and eggs. Back at the house, as she cracked the eggs into a boiling pan her mobile rang. It was Steven. She perched the phone between her shoulder and ear and carried on cooking.

'Are you all right? I went to see David Sneldon on Friday. I know how hard these things hit everyone, just wanted to check you're OK.'

'I didn't see it coming at all,' she said over the sound of the sizzling bacon. 'And he still hasn't told me why.' She pressed down on the rashers to get rid of the water. Pieces of Teflon came off the battered old pan. Taking the phone in her hand, Janet turned up the gas. It shot upwards with an alarming whoosh. 'Did David tell you anything? Anything that wasn't in confidence, I mean.'

'Yes. That's also what I wanted to speak to you about.'

'Really? Sounds ominous.' Janet moved around the kitchen, clumsily putting breakfast together as she juggled the mobile.

'Whatever's up with David, I think it might be linked to that other prisoner I told you about. You know, Arnas? The one who thought an angry woman was stalking some of the guys.'

Janet stopped, leaning against the sink. 'A woman? I thought you said a demon?'

'A demon woman, then. I've no idea what it is, but I think something weird's going on and there's really nobody else at Halvergate I trust to talk to about it.' Steven waited for her reply. 'Janet, are you still there?'

'Yes,' she said. 'Sorry. It's just very worrying. I don't know what to think.' The water bubbled away, boiling the poached eggs. Janet turned off the heat. 'Hallucinations of a demon woman seem to connect Ryan Spalding, John Helkin and another prisoner I'm counselling, Ian Fendley,' she said. 'And now David too.'

'Seriously? Bloody hell.'

'I know. I was thinking of going to the spot where Ryan Spalding was found – one of the prisoners suggested something I'd like to check out. It's just off the A11 near Thetford Forest. Do you want to go together this afternoon?'

'Not much.' He laughed. 'But I'd like to get to the bottom of this. I'll be taking the morning service at Halvergate, then any visits that come up. Are you OK to pick me up at the flat around three? We could grab a bite on the way back.'

'Three should be fine. See you later.'

She put down the phone and turned to see Arun standing in the doorway in his dressing gown.

'That was someone from work.' Janet flushed, unsure how long he had been there. She wondered if she ought to have put off seeing Steven in case Arun had wanted to stay later.

'I guess that decides when I'm leaving,' he said, sitting down heavily.

'I can push it back to another day if you want to stay longer.' Janet pried the burnt bacon off the pan and on to their plates. The eggs looked sadly solid as she fished them out of the water.

'It's fine. I could do with missing the Sunday night traffic. And there's lots to sort out back home, it's only a couple of weeks before I have to head off. I was thinking of letting the flat out to Mike while I'm away. That way we can keep hold of it if the MIT job doesn't work out.'

'Good idea,' Janet said, washing down some overcooked egg with a swig of tea.

'I suppose it's worth you staying on in this job, for the next six months anyway, while you look at other options.'

She felt herself fading again, her individual outline rubbed out by his plans. 'I haven't decided whether to leave this job yet,' she said. 'Not in six months or at all.'

He made a face. 'I thought we talked about all that last night.'

'No.' She banged her fork against the plate in irritation. 'You talked about it. I said I'd *think* about it.'

'Exactly.' Arun shrugged.

Against all her good intentions, Janet felt her temper flare up as suddenly as the gas had leapt into life on Mrs Slaney's old stove. 'I'm not abandoning this job. It's taken me years to make chartered psychologist,' she said. 'And there are major problems at Halvergate. I don't want to walk away without even trying to sort things out. America will just have to wait. I'm not ready to think about it yet, there's too much going on here.'

'What about me? Am I too much to think about?' It was more an accusation than a question, but as he spoke, the words clicked into place in Janet's head.

'Yes,' she said, surprised to hear her own answer. 'Yes, maybe you are. Maybe we should just take a pause for six months.'

'You mean a break?' A lonely piece of bacon hovered forgotten on Arun's half-raised fork.

'No, that's not what I meant.' Janet put her hands to her eyes, overwhelmed by weariness. 'It's just it *is* too much to be thinking about you right now. I'm really sorry, but maybe you need to enjoy America and think about whether you want your life to be there, and I need to concentrate on my job here and see whether I should pursue it.' Her words were met with uncharacteristic silence. 'I don't mean for ever, just for the next few months, while we try to work out what we want.' She stretched out to take his hand but he pushed her away. To her distress she saw his eyes were wet.

Arun stood up from the table. 'I know what I want,' he said and left the room.

Janet was running a little late. Steven stood in the street waiting for her, stamping his feet to keep warm. The bright winter's day had brought out the Sunday shoppers, who loitered on St Giles Street looking in at the jewellery stores. A few hardy students muffled in woolly scarves waited to get into the Waffle House, its windows steamed up from the customers inside.

He looked up the hill towards the church. Eventually the silver nose of Janet's Mini turned the corner and she pulled up in the loading bay, looking flustered.

'Sorry I'm late,' she said, turning the radio off as he got in.

'No problem. So what's with the jaunt to Thetford Forest?' Steven settled himself into the car, shoving aside the Sunday papers that Janet had dumped on the seat.

Janet barely checked the road as she pulled out. 'I'll tell you on the way.'

By the time they left Norwich, Janet had filled Steven in on Zara's interview and Michael's revelations about Helkin and the letter E. He found himself distracted from the story by her terrible driving. The journey to Thetford Forest was flat and monotonous, punctuated by the occasional roundabout, but Janet approached them all with the innate aggression of a London driver, revving past tractors. She seemed in a bad mood but Steven didn't feel able to ask her why. Instead he focused on trying to ignore her disregard for the speed limit and alarming weaving between lanes.

'Ryan made it quite some way,' he remarked, staring out at the barren scrubland.

'I've been reading up on it in the local press,' said Janet, swerving in front of a honking van. 'He hitched a lift with a lorry driver. The guy pulled in for petrol after getting through the Elveden estate and when he got back to the truck, Ryan was gone.' She pushed her hair behind her ears and the car drifted to the right. Steven gripped the side of his seat. 'Zara told me the police waited twelve hours before telling the press there'd been an escape, so the driver didn't notice anything suspicious.'

'Bit lax, wasn't it?'

'She thinks they were hoping to pick him up quickly, before anyone knew he'd gone.' Sneaky bastards, Zara had added.

Janet slowed the car to seventy as the road changed to a single carriageway at the Elveden estate. The trees crowded towards the traffic, in sparse clumps at first but then more thickly, their trunks pale in the winter light. She turned the radio on, and soothing piano music competed with the rumbling of the car. After they'd made their way slowly through the village of Elveden, the woods thinned out again. The estate stretched out in desolate waves, marked only by gorse and a few pines, their bent silhouettes marching like a line of black giants across the horizon. As the car climbed a slight hill, a tall stone column, topped by an urn, rose into view on the right-hand side of the road. It looked sinister and out of place: a lone thin finger poking out from the earth and pointing at the sky.

'What's that?' Janet said, repelled by the sight.

'I think it's a war memorial for workers on the estate,' said Steven, turning to look back at it as they passed.

'Bit odd having it in the middle of nowhere.'

The trees crept up on the road again towards the end of the estate, and they were engulfed in pine woodland by the time Janet turned off on to a roundabout with a petrol station and fast food outlet. She pulled into the car park.

'I guess this must be where the trucker stopped. It's called Barton Mills, I think,' she said, reaching over for her bag and rummaging for her notes. 'It's not far from here that he was found.'

Together they set off across the field Janet had marked out as the one Ryan must have crossed to reach the woodland. The road was sheltered from view by the pine trees, but the wind was freezing and so loud they could hardly hear one another without shouting.

Concentrating on keeping her footing in the tussocks of long grass, Janet nearly missed the fissure opening in front of them. She stopped, flinging out an arm. 'Hang on, watch out!' The ditch was partially covered by reeds. 'How deep d'you reckon that is?' she asked, pointing at the muddy water lurking at its bottom.

'Deep enough, let's go round.'

It was a relief to get out from under the weight of the grey sky. They felt the wind drop as they headed into the woods. The light was fading rapidly, and Steven reached for his torch. Twigs cracked underfoot, partly muffled by the fallen pine needles, as they headed through the undergrowth. His ears were burning red from the cold.

'I read he was found on the outskirts, so it can't be far,' Janet said, steadying herself on a branch as she skirted a puddle at the roots of a tree.

'I really can't get my head round this,' Steven said as they trudged on.

'What, you think it's a bit ghoulish for a Sunday outing?'

'No, I mean, why here? I don't get it. Why come all the way out here, work so hard to escape, just to kill yourself?'

Janet said nothing. The thought had been growing in her mind too, ever since her conversation with Dr Gupta. 'It must be somewhere round here,' she muttered. 'Unless Michael was winding me up.'

Sticking to the damp path, they came to a flatter space that looked as if it might have been trampled down, perhaps when the police taped off the area. With their breath coming out in white puffs, they spent the best part of fifteen minutes scrambling through dead fern and peering at tree trunks. The wind was quieter here, but crows in the branches above kept up a steady chorus of cawing.

'This is ridiculous,' Janet said, heaving herself up at last. 'We may have had a wasted journey. This is needle in a haystack territory. And maybe Michael did scrape the E in his cell, like Terry said.'

She got no reply. Looking round, she saw Steven had wandered some distance away and was standing with his back to her. Janet hurried over. He pointed at the tree in front, its silver trunk pocked and criss-crossed with dark lines where the bark had peeled off. At first Janet didn't see it, but then she started forward with a gasp.

Steven walked closer, and ran his fingers softly over the crudely marked letter. Janet joined him. The straight painted lines of the E were as black as the bark underneath the tree's peeling silver surface.

Under the bright lights of the fast food café, Janet warmed her hands round her bitter coffee as they waited for their food. A song crackled out inanely as Steven leaned over the table. It had started to drizzle on their way back from the wood, and his dark hair was covered in fine silver droplets that were beginning to run down his forehead in the warmth.

'I think we've got several alternatives,' he said, tapping a finger on the table. 'Ryan made his way especially to a tree that was marked. It's just a coincidence, some random graffiti. Ryan made the mark himself. Or somebody else made it, either when they found him, or ... after they killed him.'

'There was no sign of any struggle, no trace of anybody else before he was found,' said Janet. 'The police ruled out a murder inquiry. He must have done it himself. Though God knows where he got an aerosol can.'

'Unless ... is it possible someone encouraged him to the spot, encouraged him to escape even, with that in mind?' Steven asked.

Janet stared out of the window. In the twilight everything looked grey. The wet tarmac, the blocks of trees, the traffic through the rain. 'I guess so,' she said. 'Hypnosis can be used to treat delusions, even though it's not cleared for use in prison. There's every chance Helkin meant well. But there's also a nastier possibility. I mean, he could have hypnotised the men who killed themselves and planted the whole idea of a white visitor himself. It might explain why Terry saw him writing notes, and why he didn't leave those notes for whoever came after him.'

'That's an interesting idea,' Steven said. 'But people aren't machines. Even with hypnosis, surely you can't just programme them to see the world the way you want.'

Janet raised an eyebrow. 'Says a man of the church.'

Steven tutted. 'Very funny,' he said, rummaging in his pocket and bringing out a crumpled envelope. 'I suppose it's not as way-out as some of the other possibilities. Have you got a pen?' Janet handed him a biro from her bag. 'So. Who has had visions of this demon?'

Janet ticked them off on her fingers. 'Helkin, obviously. Though I suppose he might have made it up. Or maybe he really was deluded and wanted others to share his delusions. I'd have to watch the interview to judge which seems more likely. Then out of the prisoners I've met, there's Ian Fendley and David Sneldon. We can't know for certain about the earlier suicides, but after my conversation with Dr Gupta it looks like at least one other man may have suffered delusions. Your guy Arnas seems to think so too.'

Steven made a list of names on the envelope. 'Is there anyone else?'

A few bars of music piped out in the pause that followed. Janet thought about her dream, but it seemed too trivial to mention. 'Not that I can think of,' she said.

'Two fish and chips?' The waitress stood at Janet's elbow, holding out plates weighed down by rubbery battered fillets and chips shining with grease.

'Thanks,' said Steven as she set them down. He started to tuck in, gesturing with a fork when she failed to join him. 'Nothing's bad enough that it can't be fixed by a good tea,' he said, crunching through the leathery skin. 'And you look like you could do with a few more dinners.'

'Not sure I'd call it a good tea,' said Janet, poking at her own sweating fish fillet. 'So if it wasn't Helkin, what are the other options?'

'Depends how open-minded you're prepared to be.'

Janet made a disgusted face. 'You're not going to suggest an actual haunting, surely.'

'It's worth considering, isn't it?' said Steven with a smile. 'Where else would an avenging spirit lurk if not a prison?'

'You've got to be joking,' Janet said.

'Only partly.' He waved his fork at her again, his mouth half full of chips. 'Just hear me out. I'm not necessarily talking about an actual ghost, more like an aftershock of a trauma, a strong sense of evil. And there's no need to sneer, you're lucky I'm from the C of E. Father Dunstan would be on the phone to an exorcist at the Vatican by now.'

Janet shook her head. 'But how would an aftershock manifest itself as a delusion?'

'I don't know,' Steven admitted. 'I've heard other ministers and priests talking about traumatic events, like murders, that leave a sense of sadness behind, a disturbing feeling others can pick up on. But I admit an actual apparition or manifestation seems a bit less likely.'

'I'm not convinced,' said Janet. 'You'll be telling me it was that murdered woman from Thetford Forest next.'

'What murdered woman?'

'Oh, Zara told me a body was dumped in the woods a few years ago. A local woman.'

'Really? That might be relevant.' He caught sight of her expression. 'Until we have anything more concrete to go on, I don't think we can rule anything out.'

When she closed herself into the dank little house again, Janet felt Arun's absence acutely. Even the scent of his aftershave had been obliterated by the all-pervading smell of damp. It was as if he had never visited, never left in anger; as if their difficult conversation had never happened.

She dumped her coat on the rack and stood, uncertain, in the hallway. Steven's talk of a haunting had unsettled her more than she cared to admit. His mention of an aftershock, a sense of horror left in a place, seemed, in Cherry Tree Drive, all too plausible. As an act of defiance she decided to take a long soak in the bath, to reclaim the space and prove that she was not afraid of the house, or its bathroom mirror.

She walked into the living room, grabbed a book and headed upstairs. In the bathroom she ran the taps, forcing herself to look in the cheap glass over the sink as she undressed.

'See, nothing there but your own stupid face,' she said, pulling off her tights and climbing into Mrs Slaney's avocado tub. She lay back in the hot water with both taps still on, staring upwards. Light from scented candles at the foot of the bath and the reflection of the water cast dancing shadows on the ceiling. It wasn't the loveliest place to relax. The mould in the grouting and constant drip of the tap undermined any sense of luxury. All the same, she spent an hour topping up the hot water as she read an old favourite, Robert Bolt's play about Thomas More, *A Man For All Seasons*. She found herself wondering if Michael Donovan had watched the film of it and if he was still reading *Utopia*, then pushed him from her mind.

Eventually she shifted herself and stood under the shower as the water drained from the bath, the small room filling with steam. Wrapping a towel round her hair and rubbing it dry, she headed to the mirror to take out her contact lenses. It was misted up from the shower, but as she got closer, she saw that there were marks in the steam.

Shock shot through her like a jolt of electricity as she read the letter J in the glass, followed by a messy squiggle that could have been a d or – more likely – an a. Janet drew in her breath and leaned forward, gripping the sink. They definitely looked like letters, not just chance condensation.

A shadow passed across the opaque surface, as if something had moved in the room behind her. Janet whipped round. There was no one there.

She turned back to the mirror. Her face was erased by the veil of steam, a grey silhouette confronting her. Hairs prickled on the back of her neck.

'Don't be ridiculous, there's nothing there,' she said, forcing herself to wipe her hand across the glass. Her own anxious eyes looked back at her. She stepped away, feeling her shoulders sag with relief.

Janet sat on the edge of the bath, her heart thumping, angry she had let herself be frightened, even as she blinked away tears from her eyes.

17

'You say I wrecked her life, but who's the one really paying for it? Whose fucking life got ripped apart, who lost their job, their home? She was back at work the next day. It can't have been that fucking terrible.' Jamie leaned forward belligerently, his short spiky fringe wet with either gel or sweat and his baby face pink with anger.

This was supposed to be Jamie's life story session, but he had chosen to launch straight into his version of the offence, leap-frogging over the usual preamble about his upbringing. Janet had decided to let him rant a while before trying to lead him back to his own life. She turned to Duncan, a quiet man in his fifties who was sitting next to her, huddled into his cardigan. He'd said very little all session.

'What would you say to Jamie?' she asked. 'Do you think that's fair?'

'Well,' Duncan began, almost inaudibly. 'I suppose he had a choice, whereas, what was her name? Amy? She didn't have a choice.'

'That's true,' said Janet. She turned to Jamie, noting again that he looked much younger than his twenty-five years. 'It's not Halvergate that took your flat or your job,' she said. 'You gave them up when you raped Amy.'

There was a pause. Jamie looked sullenly at the floor, avoiding eye contact. Terry cleared his throat. 'And do we really think you can judge how Amy was feeling because she went back to work? The doctor's report said she had a cracked rib. How did she get that?'

Jamie shifted on his seat, uncrossing his legs. 'It was an accident. I didn't mean to push her so hard.'

From the corner of her vision, Janet saw Michael Donovan lean back further in his chair. He looked utterly out of place in the group sessions, his body language that of an observer rather than a participant. All he needed to complete the impression was a notebook. She had seen prison inspectors carry themselves with less self-assurance. It was as if Donovan admitted his guilt in words, while his demeanour issued a constant denial.

'Jamie raises an interesting point there,' Janet said, turning her thoughts back to the group. 'He says he didn't mean to push Amy so hard. Is it ever acceptable to push someone?'

'Self-defence,' said Michael, looking at her as if there were only the two of them in the room.

'When they, like, really, wind you up,' said Greg, who she'd already marked down as having anger management issues.

'What sort of thing do you mean?' asked Terry. Janet had been watching her colleague with growing respect. She could already see he was good at facilitating, firm but not dominating.

'Going on at you, like, properly in your face. Or saying stuff they know just gets you, you get me?' Greg looked furious simply imagining it. Janet guided the conversation back.

'Even if somebody aims to wind you up, even if they're a bully, if they haven't physically attacked you and you're not in danger, there are better ways of dealing with the situation,' she said. 'We'll be talking more about handling anger in other sessions. But I want to think about Amy now, who we seem to have forgotten. Wasn't Amy a friend of yours, Jamie?'

Jamie shrugged. 'Guess so.'

'What sort of qualities do people expect in their friends?' Janet asked, looking round at the prisoners ranged about her. They were a motley crew, she thought, she and Terry and their various charges, sitting in the smelly apricot room. She almost did a double take when she noticed Siobhan, chewing on a pencil, sitting on the edge of the group. She had barely managed a word all session, and Janet kept forgetting she was there.

'Loyalty,' murmured Duncan.

'Watching your back and that,' said Greg, bouncing angrily in his chair.

Michael Donovan smiled slightly, a flicker of contempt in his blue eyes. Janet felt angry, annoyed by his disdain for the other men, as if he weren't himself a sex offender. She turned to him. 'What does friendship mean to you, Michael?'

He leaned his head sideways on his left hand in a theatrical gesture, as if she were asking a philosophical question at an Oxford tutorial. She found herself wondering which college he had been to. Then he sat upright and stared at her. 'When Thomas More was executed, Erasmus wrote that he felt he had died himself. He said that between them they had but one soul.' His eyes drank in her discomfort. 'I suppose a friend is a kindred spirit, somebody with whom you share your most intimate thoughts, your feelings, all the important things. Somebody who might share your taste in reading, for instance.'

Exhausted as she was by a sleepless night, Janet found herself lost for words. Noticing her hesitation, Terry stepped in. 'So we've got loyalty, looking out for each other, shared interests – care and respect, basically. Isn't that what Amy had a right to expect from you, Jamie, since you were friends?'

Janet knew without looking that Michael Donovan was still staring at her as she turned to hear Jamie's reply.

'Maybe,' said Jamie, looking unconvinced.

'Although,' Michael Donovan broke in, 'it depends on whether Amy provoked Jamie, doesn't it? Whether, as Greg put it so eloquently earlier, she wound him up. It's just a thought,' he finished with a self-deprecating shrug.

'Yeah, she did,' Jamie said, looking animated again. 'Not just what she had on and that, I mean her whole attitude, leading me on—'

Janet interrupted. 'Are we saying you can lead someone on to rape? Forcing yourself on a friend and cracking her ribs, leaving her traumatised? Is that what she was asking for, or did she cry and ask you to stop?'

'Maybe she should have thought of that when she got dressed in the morning,' Michael said, answering before Jamie had a chance. A couple of the men exchanged smirks.

'So, Michael,' Janet said. 'If you met friends dressed in shorts and an open shirt, would you be asking for it?'

He raised an eyebrow and smiled suggestively. 'I might be. Depends how attractive they were.'

The group exploded into guffaws. Terry turned to Michael. 'I think what Dr Palmer means is, would that be an excuse for somebody bigger and stronger than you, like Greg here, to knock you about and rape you?'

Tension shot through the group. Every head turned expectantly to Donovan. He paused, savouring the moment.

'Well,' he said, pursing his lips. 'I guess it's fortunate that I'm not Greg's type.'

All the prisoners, even Greg, sniggered. Michael smiled.

After the session finished, Terry, Janet and Siobhan were left alone in the stale room. Terry got up to start stacking the cups. Ever since their conversation in David and Michael's cell, his attitude seemed to have shifted. At first she had thought it was nervousness, but now she sensed an edge of resentment.

'I can see what you mean about Michael being manipulative,' she said. 'Was he like that in Helkin's sessions?'

'Helkin didn't let Donovan get to him.' Terry glanced at her and Siobhan as he loaded the last two cups onto the tray. 'He's more of a ladies' man, I think.'

Siobhan went red with embarrassment. To her annoyance Janet felt herself flushing too. 'He's a convicted rapist,' she said.

'That too.'

Janet stared up at him as he clattered spoons into a bowl, his

128

mouth set in a thin line. There was no mistaking his antagonism. She turned to Siobhan. 'Can you collect the recorder and head to my office? I'd like to go over your role in the sessions together. I'll be there in a minute.'

Sensing the tension in the air, Siobhan slunk gratefully from the room.

Janet watched Terry loading up the tray. 'Have you got a moment?' she asked. He made no move towards her and for a second she thought he might decline. 'Please.'

He thumped his tray down across two chairs, making the cups clank. He perched opposite her, barely taking up any of the seat, poised to leave. There was a short silence.

'These groups are only effective if the staff coordinating them are united,' she said. His face was blank. 'I don't know why we seem to have got off on the wrong foot, but I'd like to put it right.'

Terry shrugged. 'I don't know what you mean.'

'I know it must be trying starting the sessions from scratch, but we had no choice—'

'The tapes shouldn't have been wiped,' Terry interrupted, irritated. 'Yes, I know.'

'Wiped?' Janet blinked. 'I thought you said no recordings were made? That Helkin thought tapes were unnecessary?'

'That's what I meant,' he said, scratching his nose.

Janet felt her words were sliding off him, a glass wall of lies between them. His expression of ill-disguised dislike made her even more uneasy. 'Maybe you can help me with what the sessions involved,' she said. 'I was really thrown when Michael told me Helkin practised hypnosis.'

Terry restacked a couple of the cups, fussing with the tray rather than looking at her. 'If he was, it must have been in the one-to-one sessions. We never did any of that in the group.'

'So you don't know what he was doing? You didn't discuss it?'

'I know John saw some of the men one to one, and hypnosis

was mentioned.' Terry shifted his weight on the chair. 'It was his business what he asked them. We never spoke about it.'

'Can you at least let me know which men he saw individually so I can ask them about it?' During the long silence that followed her question, understanding dawned. 'They're all dead, aren't they? The men he saw are the ones who killed themselves.' Still Terry said nothing. Janet felt cold. 'Why did John Helkin really leave Halvergate?'

'You'd have to ask him.'

'I don't understand. You were his closest colleague.' She sat forward, forcing him to meet her eyes. 'Didn't he mean anything to you, as a friend?' She thought of her own colleagues at Leyland, hoping to appeal to Terry's loyalty, which she was sure she'd sensed before. 'You tell me he kept notes, then that he didn't. No tapes were made, then they were wiped. I know you understand the difference and what it means for Helkin's reputation. I feel he was a friend of yours, and that something happened you're not telling me about.'

From his face, Janet realised that she'd miscalculated. Terry stood up, his shoulders tensed as he gripped the tray.

'Your job is to analyse the prisoners, not your colleagues.' He looked down at her. 'If you feel I'm withholding any information, your best call is to speak to Richard or Lee.'

Watching Terry close the door behind him, she felt a wave of despair.

By late afternoon exhaustion weighed heavily. She was sitting with Ian Fendley in her office. It was raining, and the water streaming down the windowpane distorted his reflection into a shifting pale shape. In her imagination, his grey face wavered, the dark hollows under his eyes recalling the black holes from the face in her mirror. She looked away, shuffling her papers, to hide her discomfort.

The real Ian, rather than his grey double, sat silently weeping. He looked thinner and more fragile than the last time she had seen him, though his anxiety was still punctuated by outbursts of animosity.

'I want to go over the more likely explanations for what you think you've seen,' Janet said. 'If you accept, just for a moment, that this woman's not real, why do you think you might be seeing her?'

Ian said nothing, just continued to cry. So far the cognitive behavioural approach was having little impact.

'Could it be because you are feeling guilty, that your mind is finding ways to make sense of the guilt?'

He didn't raise his head. 'She knows I'm guilty, I told you. She *knows*.'

'I know you feel that, but would somebody else's anger matter if you weren't so hard on yourself?'

'You're not listening to me.' Ian's voice was muffled, his face buried in his hands. 'If it were just me it'd be different. But she got to all the others, didn't she?'

Janet watched him. Every time she tried to question the woman's existence he brought up the other men as proof. Behind her, the rain hammered, a thousand tiny hands battering against the pane, pleading to be let into the darkening room. It ought to have been a comforting sound, a reminder of the warmth within, but instead the electric light seemed to fade, disheartened by the gloom outside. She leaned towards Ian, speaking gently. 'It sounds to me like there are a lot of rumours flying around.' She paused but his face stayed hidden. 'Which people have told you they've actually seen her?'

He looked up, his gaze suddenly focused, malevolent. 'Haven't you?'

An image flashed across Janet's mind, searing in its intensity. A pale, eyeless face, twisted with fury. She stood up, making Ian jump. The vision ebbed, losing itself in her rational mind like salt dissolving in water. There was no face, no white visitor, just a lonely psychologist and her delusional patient, together in the grey room. Janet looked at him again and saw no malice in his eyes, only bewilderment.

'You haven't seen her?'

'No, and I don't think she exists.' Janet sat back down. 'Why did you think I might have done?'

Ian wiped a trembling hand across his wet face. 'She got to the other one, didn't she? The bloke before you.'

'You mean Dr Helkin. Did he tell you about the white visitor?'

'No, I never spoke to the guy. But he's gone, isn't he? She must have got to him.'

'I think he just resigned,' said Janet, aware that she had no idea if this was true. 'People leave jobs all the time.'

Ian slumped back in his chair. He looked empty, his body a deflated sack. 'It doesn't matter if you leave though. She always comes. Look at Ryan.' Janet opened her mouth to argue but Ian cut her off. 'It doesn't matter who you are. Halvergate won't ever let you go.'

Ian had left her office over an hour ago, but something of his presence lingered, infecting the air. His delusions seeped through cracks, pooling on the windowsill, mingling with the rain. She knew it was impossible, but she couldn't escape the feeling that, somehow, the white visitor had leapt from his mind to hers. She tried to brush it off, but the idea clung to her. It crusted over her thoughts like lichen, its ugly grey spread distorting their shape.

She stood up with a sigh. Since seeing Ian, an unorthodox idea had been forming in her mind. Scanning the shelves, she stopped at a text she hadn't read since university and pulled it towards her, leafing through its pages.

A black and white medieval woodcut on the title page showed a woman burning at the stake. She put the book down on the desk, smoothing the picture with her palm. Badly drawn devils danced around the pyre, grinning, while the woman cursed the pious neighbours watching her fry. '*Vade Retro Satana*,' ran the Latin inscription beneath: 'Get thee behind me, Satan.' The print was a product of seventeenth-century mass hysteria, when neighbours would infect each other with their imaginary tales of witchcraft and some poor woman paid the price. Perhaps a prison now, she thought, wasn't so different from the claustrophobic villages of the past.

Janet flipped through the notes she'd made on Ian's appearance, replaying in her mind his pauses and distracted gaze. She stared at the words on the page until their letters danced. Was it possible she had stumbled on a community of men suffering from shared psychosis?

More than ever, she longed to speak to somebody from her old team at Leyland. She glanced at the good-luck card. Her fingers hovered over the 'New' button on her email. She clicked open a message and began typing.

Dear Stuart,
　　How are you? I'm missing everybody at Leyland and hope life's treating you all well.
　　This job has turned out to be quite a challenging post and I wondered if I might run a few ideas past you?

Janet paused. Stuart would wonder why she didn't discuss this with her current team. And that word 'challenging' covered a multitude of sins. How much could she tell him? That she hated her line manager, her closest colleague was a blank wall and her predecessor mad? She sighed and carried on typing, losing confidence with every word.

From what I can tell a number of men here have been suffering from the same delusion, namely hallucinations of an angry, vengeful woman. This recurrent delusion seems linked to self-harm and suicidal ideation. It may also be linked to the suicides of several men at HMP Halvergate before I took up the job. I've been assured by senior staff that this is unlikely to be related to drug abuse.

Not that their assurance was worth much.

I'm working on the hypothesis that it may be due to shared psychosis, meaning that we could be looking at a situation of mass hysteria, or trying to find an inducer.

Stuart's eyebrows would be shooting up at this point. Shared psychosis was a rare and controversial diagnosis. Almost as rare and controversial as hypnotherapy in the prison environment.

I've been told that my predecessor here, Dr John Helkin, practised hypnosis on a number of inmates, but I don't have much information about what form these sessions took.

All the above information came courtesy of a convicted rapist who is utterly untrustworthy.

I assume Dr Helkin tried this as an unorthodox means of combatting the delusions, but I can't discount the possibility that he planted the delusions himself. If this were the case, in your opinion, is it also possible that prisoners here could now be transmitting the same delusion among each other, even among men Dr Helkin had never met?

And by the way, I'm renting the man's old house and have been dreaming of the same vengeful figure myself. Am I going mad?

Janet looked at the words on the screen, at all the gaps she had left, and realised that even by telling Stuart only half the story, it still looked far too crazy to send. The image of the white face in her dream flitted across her thoughts. She deleted the draft.

18

'*Too high, can't come down, losing my head, spinning round and round ...*' Sweat pooled between Steven's shoulder blades as he pedalled faster. He was glad he didn't have the breath to embarrass himself by humming along to the tinny recording playing in the gym. Britney Spears' 'Toxic' was always a guilty pleasure.

In front of him four different screens played Sky News on mute. He'd never understood the point of television in gyms, unless the aim was to mesmerise you into working out harder. Steven kept going, watching the reporter in the red scarf talking in tandem on multiple screens, and tried to push Halvergate and its troubled inmates from his mind.

He turned his head slightly. The guy on the left was definitely checking *him* out, rather than his tattoos. He frowned. It had been a while since that had happened. Norwich was not, he had discovered, a gay Mecca. Not that he was allowed to get up to much anyway; he'd long since decided anything outside the most committed relationship was off-limits, and even that was taboo as far as the official Church line went. Being gay was fine, allegedly, just as long as he wasn't 'practising'. An odd phrase, Steven thought, prim and obscure, as if being homosexual was like playing the trombone after hours. A loud ostentatious nuisance that might wake the neighbours.

He had a sudden memory of Paolo prancing around the bedroom, naked, striking ridiculous poses. 'Would this count as practising?' Hands on hips. 'Or this?'

Steven looked down towards the floor, watching his own

knees move rhythmically up and down. Celibacy was not much fun.

The guy on the left was getting ridiculous. He was a bit younger than Steven, perhaps in his early twenties, and kept glancing towards him. Stretching theatrically, the boy raised his arms in the air, flexing his muscles, still pedalling away furiously. Steven snorted to himself. What a show-off.

His timer bleeped. Ten miles – not too bad. Steven jumped off the exercise bike, heading towards the changing room. His shadow nearly fell off his bike in his hurry to follow, the wheels still spinning as he hopped on one leg.

Steven's heart beat a little faster. He pushed open the door, feeling hunted. He didn't want this unsettling stranger gawking at him as he took off his jogging bottoms. He stood in the changing room, uncertain of what to do. Sure enough, the show-off burst through the doors with the flustered air of a latecomer to the cinema. Steven folded his arms and looked at him.

'Fancy a drink?' he asked. The boy flushed with embarrassment. There was a pause. Steven didn't blink.

'Yeah, why not?' the stranger grinned. 'A few beers sounds good.'

Steven winced inwardly. His stranger might have the physique of a Greek god, but there was nothing sexy about the Norfolk accent.

Steven and the stranger, who'd introduced himself as Dan Avery, sat opposite each other in Frank's Bar on Bedford Street. Even though the place was packed it had a relaxed vibe, with students and regulars crowded together, books on the walls and candles dotted about in mismatched teapots. The rain outside made the air heavy and warm.

'I work just near here.' Dan looked around nervously. He had dark hair, and grey eyes set wide apart on his face. The candlelight was flattering, but Dan's high cheek bones would have been attractive however badly they were lit.

'Really?' said Steven, sitting back casually. 'Where's that?'

'East Anglian Constabulary.'

A sudden ridiculous image of Banksy's kissing coppers popped into Steven's head. Clearly one of them should have been wearing a dog collar.

'What's funny?' asked Dan, the anxious furrow deepening on his brow.

'Nothing. I was just thinking it's interesting we're both in law enforcement.'

'Really? You police?' Dan didn't look pleased at the prospect.

'No, I work at Halvergate.'

'Prison officer?'

Here we go, Steven thought. 'No,' he said. 'I'm the chaplain.'

'You're a *priest*?' Dan goggled at him.

The waitress arrived with their drinks. 'One white and one lager?' she asked. Dan claimed his beer and stared expectantly at Steven.

'Not a priest, no. I'm not a Catholic. I'm a Church of England minister.'

'Is there a difference?' Dan asked.

'Yes,' said Steven. Not everyone in the C of E hierarchy think you and I are hell-bound, he thought. And then there's the small question of celibacy. But he didn't say that. 'There are differences,' he said. 'But it's the same God, ultimately. That's what matters.'

'Not sure I believe in God,' said Dan morosely.

Steven gave him a look of mock offence. 'I'm not sure we should be having a drink then.'

'Sorry! I didn't mean to be rude.' Blundering, Dan reached out a hand to touch Steven's arm, then withdrew it.

'Mate, no worries, I was joking. It was a joke.'

'Oh,' said Dan, reddening. He pulled a face and laughed. 'It's not easy being a bobby. A few beers in the force . . . if somebody says a few beers, it doesn't mean . . .'

Steven started to laugh. 'Tell me about it!' he said. 'But it's no big deal. This really is just a drink, OK?'

Dan took a swig of his drink, his eyes fixed on Steven. 'You seem pretty normal for working at Halvergate.'

'It's got a bad name?' Dan nodded. Steven gave a lopsided smile. 'It's certainly not the friendliest place I've worked.'

'My DCS and your governor are like that.' Dan crossed his fingers.

'In what way?'

Dan lowered his voice. 'These suicides you've been having. Interesting way of gathering evidence there.'

'Really?'

Dan looked around, his eyes shifty. 'Let's just say some of it seems to have "got lost" but not been reported as lost, if you get me.'

'Like what?'

Dan leaned in even closer. 'I was sent once and there was a whole stash of spice in the dead guy's cell. I saw it all taped up in a bag. But somehow it didn't get recorded. I mentioned it at the station and got bollocked. Never been sent back.' Steven and Dan had both leaned so far over the table their noses were almost touching. Dan noticed and blushed, then downed the rest of his drink. 'Another beer then?'

It was half eleven and more than a few beers later when they left Frank's Bar. Dan had drunk considerably more than Steven, sinking his nerves a little deeper with every bottle. There was a pause while they stood in the doorway, Steven wondering how he could extricate himself and say goodbye.

'I'll walk you home,' Dan said, clapping him on the back. 'Your own police escort.'

They walked the five minutes to Steven's flat, Dan putting all his energy into keeping upright on cobbles slippery from the rain. When they reached his front door, Steven stopped and turned towards his sozzled companion. It had begun to drizzle again. 'Hey,' he began. 'It's been fun—' Dan lunged at him, ineptly, like a teenager. Steven started in surprise and a wet kiss hit him on the ear. Undeterred, Dan tried again, grappling with him like an overeager puppy. 'Hang on!' said Steven, laughing. Through his beer-filled haze, Dan began to get the message and turned pink.

'I thought . . .' he mumbled.

'It's fine,' said Steven. 'Just take it easy, that's all.' He put his hands to Dan's face and kissed him. They looked at each other, their noses close together. Steven saw that Dan's pale eyes were framed with unusually long lashes. The street was silent. He stepped backwards. 'But I am saying goodnight here,' he said quietly. 'There's no rush is there?'

'Sorry,' said Dan. 'I've not . . . I don't usually . . .' He trailed off, even more red-faced.

A late-night confession of virginity was the last thing Steven wanted to hear. 'It's been fun,' he said. 'No pressure.'

'We could meet up again, maybe? Have another drink?' Dan stared at him, his eyes wide from either beer or hope.

'Definitely,' Steven said, smiling. Then, to his infinite surprise, Dan leaned forward and enveloped him in a bear hug. They stood for a moment, Dan's grip showing no sign of loosening as he sighed into Steven's collar. Not sure what to do, Steven patted him on the back. Dan let go. 'Bye then,' he said, heading off unsteadily down St Giles. Steven watched him turn the corner with a smile, water dripping into his eyes as the rain picked up.

'Goodbye,' he said.

Janet needed to sleep, but she still wasn't in bed. She sat in the living room at Cherry Tree Drive staring periodically at her phone. She poured herself another glass of wine. The faded orange curtains closed her into the room, rather than keeping the damp out. At the bottom of their frayed edges, water collected in a brown stain on the carpet. It had seeped through the cracks in the window's rotted PVC frame and trickled down the wall.

Arun had still not replied to any of her texts. His complete silence gnawed at her. She looked at his blurred photo on the screen, then dialled, a sick feeling in her stomach. It rang for a while but just as she was about to hang up, the ringing stopped.

'Arun's phone.'

It was Jean.

In the background Janet heard Arun's voice, muffled but close by. *'Who is that? Give me the phone,'* then, as he realised who was on the other end of the line, *'For fuck's sake! What are you doing?'* and her angry reply, *'You're on a break, why should she care?'*

Janet sat, shocked, the mobile to her ear, a voyeur to her own break-up, before Arun finally spoke. 'Janey, are you there? God, I'm sorry, it's not what it sounds like, I promise it's not—'

'How long?'

'What? No, it's not like that. It's just I was angry, I thought you didn't care—'

'So you thought you'd sleep with Jean?'

'It was you who suggested a break—'

'I meant let's work out where we wanted to live, not shag someone else!' Janet shouted.

'I'm sorry, please let me—'

'I don't want to fucking hear it.' She pressed the button to end the call.

Almost immediately Arun rang back. Her hands shaking, Janet switched off the phone. She stared at the blank screen, then dropped it with a thunk on Mrs Slaney's coffee table.

Upstairs the bedroom was freezing. She turned on the death-trap blow heater and peeled off her skirt, dropping it onto the chair along with her sweater. It was too cold to take off her tights; she kept them on and eased herself under sheets so cold they felt damp. She lay there shivering, from both crying and the cold, listening to the heater's steady hum and waiting for the warmth to spread from her body to the mattress beneath.

She leaned over to turn off the spluttering heater and the light, then hesitated. It was too cold and she felt too depressed to get up again to take her make-up off and brush her teeth. Exhausted, she flicked the switches and flopped back onto the pillow.

Janet woke up, her head pounding, her eyes sore and her mouth parched. She looked blearily for her glass of water. It was empty. She checked the alarm clock. The luminous green figures told her it was 04:21. She sank back on to the pillows, weighing up her thirst against her desire to go back to sleep. She tried closing her eyes, willing herself into unconsciousness, but her tongue stuck to the roof of her dry mouth, and images of Arun and Jean ran round in her head. With a sigh she switched on the heater, which whirred itself into life before setting up its soporific hum. Steeling herself, she clambered out of bed, throwing on her fluffy dressing gown, and headed to the bathroom across the landing.

She downed a glass of water from the tap, her tired panda eyes staring back at her as she gulped. She brushed her teeth, spitting in the sink, and went to turn off the light above the mirror, only catching her reflection out of the corner of her eye. But as she reached upwards, she realised that the right arm in the mirror remained motionless by her side.

Not moving, Janet listened to the distant hum of the blow heater in the bedroom. Dread washed over her. She turned her face towards the centre of the mirror, where her own reflection should be.

The black eyes staring at her were not her own. Janet stepped back, but the figure in the mirror leaned forwards, its breath misting the glass. Its skin was unnaturally white, while the dark eyes, wide with rage, locked on to Janet's own.

The blood pounded in her ears, drowning out the heater's hum, as Janet and the stranger stared motionless at each other.

'This isn't real,' she said, her voice barely getting above a cracked whisper. 'I'm imagining things, I'm asleep, I'm—'

The figure in the mirror let out a scream of fury. Janet shrank back and covered her ears, but the shattering howl of rage cut through her. The creature's dark eyes remained fixed on hers, its high-pitched wail jarring through her bones. Unable to look away, Janet saw the black eyes were heavy with tears. Its scream ending in a shuddering cry, the creature fell forwards, white palms pressed against the glass. Tears fell from its blank eyes, marking lines of blood across the white face.

Janet screamed.

The half-strangled gasp of her own cry tore her from sleep. She struggled to breathe in the dark of her room. Her face was wet from tears, but her mouth felt furred and dry. Gasping, she turned on the light. The clock read 04:21.

For ten minutes Janet lay rigid with fear, unable to move. Then her rational mind began to assert itself. With an effort of will, she got out of bed and reached for her dressing gown. On the landing, she hesitated, looking at the closed bathroom door. Then she headed over and pushed it open.

The old-fashioned cord clicked as she yanked it, then the light flickered on. Janet couldn't tell if the buzzing in her ears was from fear or the bedroom heater. She walked to the mirror.

Her own face stared back at her.

Janet put her hand out and softly touched the glass. 'Don't leave me,' she said.

19

She stood in the doorway of Duncan Fletcher's cell. She knew that a scuffle was taking place behind her, that Keith was shouting, but all sound seemed to have receded to a great distance, drowned out by the roar in her ears. Duncan sat slumped on the floor, wearing the same cardigan he'd had on at their last group session. He had his back to her and had fallen sideways, so she couldn't see his face. The white wall in front was spattered with red, marked by the spray from his severed artery. In her agitation, Janet made out a pattern. Splashed in blood, about a foot in length, she saw the letter E.

The prison nurse pushed past her and knelt to feel Duncan's vital signs, as if checking again would change what they already knew. He shook his head.

Janet felt a blow to her ear and the present crashed back into her consciousness, carried on a wave of sound. An inmate she didn't know was shouting at her, so close she could feel the warmth of his breath on her face. Keith was grappling with him, had caught him by the arms, but just behind him other prisoners on the landing were crowding round, shouting, trying to push past to see in. In a moment there would be a stampede.

Adrenalin shot through her. Janet held up an arm to defend herself. Then the ear-splitting sound of a prison officer's whistle cut across the mayhem. 'Everybody back in their cells, now!' she heard Keith bellow. She could see other officers running up the stairs. Keith shouted down at them, 'I don't want anybody else up here, close this section off, get everyone back in their cells!'

143

Janet swayed. She felt as if she might be sick. Terry caught her arm and propelled her out of the doorway.

'There's nothing we can do for him now,' he said. 'D block will go into lockdown before the police arrive. Have you called Lee?' She shook her head.

Keith had blocked the doorway to their left, and already other prison officers were closing off the landings from the right. Janet knew one advantage of a vulnerable prisoners' block was the inmates' passivity and general disinclination to riot, but this time, she felt relieved to have Keith's brute strength at her back.

She glanced into Duncan's cell, saw again the E drawn in its monstrous ink and turned away once more as nausea rose in her stomach.

She was jostled forward as Terry caught hold of a man to her right. He was trying to persuade Duncan's neighbour back into his cell. It was Michael Donovan. He caught her eye, smiling as if they were meeting at a garden party.

'Bit of a commotion?' he said.

'Not now, Michael, we need everybody back in their cells,' she replied, as Terry bundled him out of the way.

He locked Michael's door, then leaned on it for a moment. He looked exhausted. 'We need to discuss this with Lee and contact his family,' he said.

As they headed out of D block, Janet could hear the repeated clang of doors, a metal chorus drowning out the shouting and chaos. A superficial sense of order was being restored.

Lee sat back in his chair, scrutinising them, eyes shielded by his Miss Marple glasses. Behind him clear skies spread out in a sparkling canvas. The airfield beyond the perimeter fence shone like a silver mirror from its covering of frost. Light from the window cast his face into shadow and glinted off his spectacles, making him hard to read. Janet resisted the urge to perch forward nervously on the edge of her seat, as Terry was doing beside her.

'And you saw no sign of this, either of you?'

'No, Governor, absolutely nothing,' Terry croaked.

Even to Janet, who knew he was telling the truth, it sounded unconvincing.

'Duncan Fletcher participated fully in the last group session,' she interjected. 'Nothing indicated that he was feeling suicidal. The same in the one-to-one assessment we conducted when I arrived.'

'And nothing was said to either of you privately that should have been reported?' Lee asked.

Terry shook his head, swallowing. 'Nothing,' Janet said.

'I can't say I'm pleased with this,' Lee said, looking petulant, as if they had brought the news purely to inconvenience him. 'One less nonce in the world is hardly something to cry about, but this isn't what Halvergate needs after all the fuck-ups last year. The ombudsman here yet again. Are his family likely to cause trouble?'

'Duncan's not had any visitors for several months,' said Terry. 'He abused his daughter, his wife left him, the only person with any contact is the son, and I wouldn't say they were on good terms.'

Lee sighed. 'Well, that's something.'

Janet felt increasingly angry with the direction of the conversation. 'But it's likely the ombudsman will investigate the links to the previous suicides,' she said. 'What with the E in Duncan's cell being identical to the marks left at previous incidents.'

'E? What E?' Lee said. The question was directed at Janet, but he had turned to Terry as he spoke.

'The E Duncan Fletcher wrote in his own blood,' Janet replied. 'The E I understand was found at the other suicides while Dr Helkin worked here.'

'I think you must be mistaken,' Lee said. 'What you most likely saw was blood sprayed in what looked like an E to your distressed imagination.' He turned to Terry. 'Did you see an E?'

The question sounded full of quiet menace. There was a pause as she and Lee both stared at their unfortunate companion. Terry looked at the floor. 'No,' he said.

'There you are, Dr Palmer. I doubt the police will see an E either. It's not surprising you were mistaken, a very upsetting scene, of course.'

'And the other suicides?' she asked, angrily.

'Were you there? No, you were not. Have the staff told you about these Es?' Lee waited for her answer, then, when she stayed silent, smiled to himself. 'No, I imagine it was the inmates, wasn't it? Playing a little trick on you most likely – they're like that, they like to manipulate an easy target, a nice young woman from the city with liberal sensitivities. Let's just play a little trick on her, that's what they'll have said to themselves, and then in the heat of the moment, Duncan Fletcher dead before you, you saw things that just weren't there.' Lee pushed his spectacles forward on his nose, peering over them at her, his expression avuncular and kind. 'I don't blame you for it, but I wouldn't go talking to the police about your imaginary sightings. We can't have them thinking we've employed somebody hysterical at Halvergate, can we? I've known DCS Clarke for years,' he added nostalgically, 'and I wouldn't say he's a man who takes kindly to fancies.'

'But what about—?' Janet stopped. Suddenly she didn't want to tell Lee about the E she had seen in David Sneldon's cell.

'Just think about it mathematically,' Lee snapped. 'There's only one person who's seen this E, once. Does that sound like a pattern to you?'

This time it was Janet's turn to feel two pairs of eyes fixed on her. She folded her arms. 'When you put it like that, no.'

'Good.' Lee stood up. 'I suggest the pair of you contact Duncan Fletcher's family while I get on to DCS Martin Clarke.'

As soon as they were in the corridor Janet rounded on Terry. 'What the hell were you—?'

He cut her off with an angry gesture and pulled her towards him, making her wince. 'Not here!' he hissed.

They marched down the corridor in silence, Janet seething,

her arm still sore where he'd grabbed it. As they turned the corner, he pushed open a door. Janet followed him. They stood cramped together in a store cupboard, the walls covered from floor to ceiling with shelves of towels.

'Would you like to explain what all this is about?' she said.

'No!' Terry spat with fury. 'No, I would not. Why did you have to go and bother Lee with all that prisoner nonsense about Es? I warned you to drop it, I told you it was nothing. It's just Michael trying to wind everyone up. Why can't you *listen* to me?'

'Are you seriously telling me you didn't see the E in Duncan's cell?'

'I didn't see *anything*. There was no E there.'

'You're lying,' Janet said. 'That's bullshit and you know it. What are you afraid of, for God's sake?'

'There was no E!' Terry shouted, his intensity taking her aback. 'Do you want to go the way John did? Do you? Seeing things? Stuck out on your own, nobody believing a word you say?'

Janet swayed slightly, her elbows brushing against the thin towels. The silence in the stuffy storeroom was suffocating. She wanted to push her way out of the room, out of Halvergate, out of Norfolk, but she didn't move. Instead she stared into Terry's eyes until he looked away.

'Are you threatening me?'

'No,' he said, desperation flitting across his face. 'I'm warning you, not threatening you.' He looked at her again. 'Can't you just drop it? Nobody will miss Duncan, you know we didn't ignore any signs, you know you did your job properly, just leave it.'

'Are you asking me to lie to the ombudsman about what I saw?'

'The ombudsman will just go straight to Lee or some other manager and ask them about it. You weren't here for the earlier suicides, nobody reported any Es then. What's the bloody point?'

'The point is that it's an offence to withhold evidence. And tampering with a crime scene amounts to perverting the course of justice, which is what happens if that E is destroyed. Are you

147

really happy to be a party to that? Do you feel like being on the other side of the cell door for a change?'

'It doesn't work like that in Halvergate,' Terry said, pity in his eyes. 'Don't you understand I'm trying to help you?'

The change of tone confused her. Doubt began to dampen her anger. She felt claustrophobic, not only in the narrow confines of the storeroom but in her own skin.

'I want to go back to Duncan's cell,' she said. 'I want you to look at that E and then tell me you don't see anything.'

Terry looked relieved. 'Fine,' he said. 'And when we've done that can you just drop it and we'll call Robert Fletcher about his dad?' Already he was trying to push past her, eager to get out of the store cupboard and out of the conversation.

A flash of anger returned. 'Fine,' she said. 'Apart from one thing. Don't ever grab me like that again.'

The bloodstains on the wall were already turning brown. They stood stark against the bleached white of the brickwork, a random pattern thrown up as Duncan's heart pumped his life out against the cell. Perhaps one long streak and some spatters could be mistaken for an E if you squinted. Perhaps.

Janet drew in her breath, panic rising inside her chest.

'Excuse me!' she said, pushing past the protesting forensic officer into the cell. She bent over, her fingertips lightly touching the bloodstained wall. There was no smearing to suggest it had been wiped. The splattering of drops looked untouched.

'Get away from there!' The forensic officer was shouting at her, his eyes angry, his voice muffled by the mask over his mouth. Janet stumbled, backing her way out of the cell.

Terry steadied her as she stepped out into the corridor. 'I'm sorry, officer, she's new. This whole situation has upset her.'

Janet turned desperately to the man in white. 'It's not that. It's the evidence, it's been tampered with. Duncan wrote an E on that wall. I'm sure if you examine it, you'll find traces. There was an E there.' She could hear her own voice rising.

'She's crazy, more like,' the officer said to Terry. He turned to Janet, pulling down his mask. His teeth were yellow from smoking too many cigarettes. 'You're lucky this is unlikely to be anything other than a suicide,' he told her, enunciating slowly as if she were an idiot. 'Otherwise, you'd just have contaminated a crime scene.'

20

Every light in the house on Cherry Tree Drive was on. She knew that, upstairs, the bathroom door was closed. In her mind a series of images revolved round and round, spinning faster and faster. Jean and Arun, the stranger in the mirror, the blood in Duncan's cell, the E that was there and then wasn't. And, even more horrifying than the possibility that somebody at Halvergate had destroyed it, the thought that she had hallucinated it.

Janet sat back on the sofa and ran her fingers through her hair, breathing out heavily, trying to calm herself. A man had died today, a man had died in her care and she had seen absolutely no sign that he was suicidal. She pictured Duncan slumped in his cell, still wearing the pathetic woolly cardigan, his blood sprayed across the wall. Tears sprang to her eyes. It wasn't just Halvergate that had failed him.

She tried to recall the advice Stuart had given her before she left Leyland, that she could only do her best, that ultimately there is nothing any psychologist can do to stop a patient who is truly determined to take his own life. Yet even as she tried to focus on his words it was Lee that she heard, breaking in and drowning out her friend's voice. '*One less nonce in the world is hardly something to cry about.*' Janet flushed with shame. Lee's words had upset her because in the privacy of her own heart, she was afraid some part of her thought the same.

The photos of Arun she had failed to take down only made her feel worse. He had left countless messages, apologising, shouting, begging her to call. She had ignored them all. With a pain in her chest, she picked her phone up off the coffee table. She stared at it, willing it to ring with the number she knew she would never see again. Against her will, she found herself back in the memory that tormented her above all others.

Her phone rang. Crammed into a single bed with Arun, Janet reached for it. Izzy's number was on the screen.

'Speak of the devil,' she said.

Arun leaned over to see. 'Aren't you going to take it?'

Janet had spent the entire university term trying to speak to Izzy, but apart from a few evasive text messages, her sister almost never got in touch. She was desperate to hear her voice, but hurt and anger stopped her from pressing the button. She let the phone ring out. Isabel could wait for a change.

'I'll call her later,' she said.

Alone in Cherry Tree Drive, Janet dialled a number on her mobile.

'Hey,' said Steven's voice. 'I heard about Duncan. Are you OK?'

'Not really. Are you busy?'

'What's up?'

Janet looked down at the carpet, struggling to find the words. 'Hard to say, really.' She stared over at Dr Helkin's head with its mapped-out model of the brain. 'I know this is a pain, but would you mind coming over? It's not just Duncan's death. I think I sensed something in the bathroom, something linked to that "velnius" of yours. Would you mind . . .' She trailed off, feeling foolish.

'I can come over no problem,' said Steven. 'But would I mind what?'

'Could you bring some holy water or something?' Janet asked. She cleared her throat. 'Just in case.'

She stood outside the bathroom door as Steven said prayers. He'd brought holy water as requested and sprinkled it around.

It was the first time she'd seen him in his role as a priest, and as he stood there praying so earnestly she found that his faith unnerved her. She left him to it and headed downstairs to put the kettle on.

She heard Steven come into the kitchen behind her as she poured out the boiling water. 'Thanks for that,' she said with her back to him. She handed him the tea. 'Do you fancy sitting in the other room?'

'Sure,' he said, smiling.

Janet hadn't lied about the house, Steven thought, as he followed her along the corridor and looked up at the grimy ceiling. Apart from the terrible decor, he had felt nothing sinister as he prayed in the avocado bathroom, but Janet's admission she had seen Halvergate's white visitor in the mirror, even if only in dreams, made him deeply uneasy.

He sat down beside her on the sofa, clutching his mug, and they both contemplated Mrs Slaney's 1970s cabinet in silence.

'Oh God, it's not mine!' Janet burst out.

'What?'

'That awful psychiatric head thing. You must think I've no taste at all.'

Steven laughed. 'I hadn't even noticed it.' He got up and headed to the cabinet. 'Mind if I have a nosy? You had a good old poke around mine.' He looked back at her, his expression arch. He picked up one of the photographs. It had been taken on a beach. Janet looked pale as ever in the bright sunshine. Her mouth was smiling but sunglasses hid her eyes. An Asian man was laughing beside her; he wore spectacles and had slightly receding hair. His friendly expression made him more attractive than his features, which were, in Steven's expert opinion, quite plain. His arm was tight round Janet's shoulders. 'Is this Arun?' he asked. She nodded. 'He looks nice.'

Janet didn't reply.

Steven picked up the photo at the front. It was Janet in the hills above Florence, some years ago. She was wearing the red cross and had blonde highlights that suited her much better than her current style. But most of all he was struck by the look of joy on her face. He realised he wouldn't have thought it possible for Janet to look so happy. 'That's a lovely photograph.' Janet said nothing. 'When was it taken?'

'About eleven years ago.' She got up from the sofa and stood next to him.

'You look great – the hair really suits you.' He turned to look at her. Janet took the photograph from him.

'Thanks,' she said, holding it tight in her hands.

Steven sensed he shouldn't continue, but something in her face drove him on. 'Who took it? Arun?'

There was a long pause. 'I took it,' she said.

He was momentarily puzzled. She walked to the gas fire, still holding the picture. Steven went back to the sofa and picked up his tea. Janet was twisted away from him, her face half hidden by hair. 'It's my sister, Isabel.'

From the catch in her voice Steven realised, too late, where the conversation was heading.

'She's my twin.' Janet looked at him, her face drawn. 'It's one of my last photos of her.'

Like an image clicking into focus, Steven saw her for the first time, the wall of glass gone. 'Oh God, Janet, I'm sorry,' he said.

She turned and went on as if she hadn't heard him, looking instead at her sister. 'We went to Florence for a week at Easter, in our final year at university. It was perfect.' Janet stroked the surface of the photograph. 'Then in the last term, she stopped calling. She had this new boyfriend, I think he must have been married. He was a heartless bastard at any rate, he never got in touch after she died. And that last year she was so caught up in him, I thought she was just ignoring me, having too much fun to be bothered. So when she finally phoned, I didn't take the fucking call. We'd always been so close, you see, and I just wanted to be something on my own, to prove she wasn't as important as she thought.' She caught her breath. 'Ironic really. Now I've had years to be on my own and I find I'm half a person without her.'

'I'm so sorry.'

'When I called back, she didn't pick up, just texted saying she'd like to see me. We'd just finished our exams, and I put off going to visit her for a week.' Janet stood very still, her knuckles white as she gripped the frame. 'By then she was dead.'

Steven leaned forwards. 'You don't have to talk about it.'

Janet looked at him, her face unreadable. 'They say grief gets easier, don't they? And I guess it does. I mean it gets easier to function. But the longing. Sometimes it's too much even to breathe, just the wanting, the longing.'

Steven paused, knowing anything he said would be inadequate. 'It's so much harder on those left behind—' he started.

'That's bullshit,' she said, furious. 'I'm alive, here, talking to you. And I will never feel the pain she went through, never. Do you understand me, Steven? Izzy was murdered.'

He stared, too shocked to reply.

Janet turned away. 'I'm sorry,' she said. She covered Isabel's photograph with her hand, as if she wanted to shield her sister from hearing what was going to happen to her.

'Did they catch who did it?' Steven asked.

Janet headed over to the sofa and sat down heavily beside him. 'Yes,' she said. 'Or rather, the suspect hanged himself after he was arrested. The police said at least we were spared a trial. A man called Neil Martin. He confessed.' She paused. 'I've read some of the file.'

'Oh God, that's terrible.'

'He said an angel told him to put her in the bath, that she'd wake up if he put her in the water.' Janet's eyes were heavy with tears. 'My sister did voluntary work at a day centre for people with learning disabilities and Neil was very attached to her. Izzy took him out for the day once, to the park, she was fond of him. Nobody realised he had schizophrenia.' She looked at him, her cheeks flushed. 'I have to remember that sometimes, when I'm doing this job. When I'm working with men who've killed, who've destroyed other families. I have to remember that Izzy saw some good in Neil, that she knew what a hard life he'd had.' Her voice cracked. 'And I have to remember that he felt sorry afterwards. That he didn't understand what he'd done.'

She stopped. Steven could tell she was struggling not to cry. 'You know,' he started, 'your sister sounds a wonderful person, and she died very young.' He looked at Janet's thin shoulders and put an arm round her. 'But even though she was very young,' he said softly, 'her life was still so much more than the ending of it. And her death doesn't define her, her life does.'

They sat together in silence, in Mrs Slaney's cheerless room, their tea going cold.

On St Giles Street a fight was taking place outside the YMCA. Angry voices rang out, their tone slurred by distance and drunkenness. Steven crossed over to the window and drew the curtain back slightly, letting in the moonlight. He saw a police officer get out of the car that had drawn up and walk over to the scuffling teenagers. His words were inaudible but their low note played like a deep bass against the fluctuating chorus from the group.

With a sigh he let the curtain drop and went back to the table. After his conversation with Janet, he had been unable to shake off the fear that he might be dealing with an evil more terrifying than anything he had previously allowed himself to imagine.

He read the verse from Romans again.

'*Dearly beloved, avenge not yourselves, but rather give place unto wrath: for it is written, Vengeance is mine; I will repay, saith the Lord.*'

Steven thought back to his conversation with David, the only person, unless he counted Janet's dreams, who had actually seen the velnius or white visitor. If he were hunting an actual demon, this verse from the Bible was one of his only clues. That and the mysterious vanishing E. David told him he had never been to church before his conviction, but Steven supposed it was a relatively famous phrase, littered through a number of popular films. He stared at his own painting of St Michael defeating the devil. Rage and fear flickered over the demon's face in a mosaic of green and silver.

'Vengeance is mine, I will repay,' he murmured. Said without reference to God, the words changed from a command to put aside anger into a personal vow of revenge. He glanced over at the other book on his desk: *A History and Origin of Belief in Demons*. He leafed through the index for the second time. 'Ring yes, in yes,' he said to himself, repeating the words David claimed to have heard. There was nothing listed for either.

From the street below came a woman's steady wailing. Steven crossed to the window again. Fiery shadows played over the group's movements, the orange street lights illuminating their faces. They were surrounding the officer, who had arrested a girl; she was twisting in his grip and her screams cut through the cacophony of angry shouts. Steven thought of Dan and wondered if he was on patrol that night. Then the flashing blue lights of another panda car lit up the street and the crowd scattered.

Steven remained standing at the window. 'Avenge not yourselves, but rather give place unto wrath.' Janet had told him the woman in her dream was full of fury. Ian and David were so terrified by her anger they felt driven to contemplate suicide. And now Duncan Fletcher was dead, not to mention the men who'd gone before. Could Halvergate really be possessed? He had little time for demon lore and felt unequal to dealing with this medieval vision of evil. He wasn't even sure he believed in it.

Watching the last police car pull away from his doorway, he thought of Janet alone in the house on Cherry Tree Drive, haunted by grief. The last thing she needed was a haunting of a more malignant kind. He pictured Izzy's red cross round Janet's neck and took some comfort from the image. In his mind he recited the words of Psalm 23, praying to God for Janet's protection: *'The Lord is my shepherd; I shall not want. He maketh me to lie down in green pastures: he leadeth me beside the still waters. He restoreth my soul: he leadeth me in the paths of righteousness for his name's sake. Yea, though I walk through the valley of the shadow of death, I will fear no evil: for thou art with me ..'*

21

The visitors' waiting room was painted olive green, an ugly colour Steven imagined must have been chosen for its low price. The room was as cold as every other space in Halvergate, its windows set too high to give a view, instead letting in the sickly light of a grey day.

Robert Fletcher sat beside him on the low vinyl sofa. Steven had known Duncan only slightly, but Robert had asked to see him after learning that his father had started attending church. Steven had no intention of telling him he had suspected this was down to the boredom that drove many inmates to the chapel. After all, he had no window to peer into Duncan's soul.

'Did he ever say he was sorry?' Robert asked, his head bowed. 'In private, I mean.' He tilted his face slightly to look up at Steven, his eyes puffy and red-rimmed. 'I still couldn't forgive him, but it would help to think he felt some remorse, that he understood what he'd done.'

Robert was softly spoken, as unmistakably middle-class as his father, with the same hazel eyes and sloping chin. Steven imagined the close physical resemblance gave Robert and his family yet another cause for pain.

'He had started going to chapel on Sundays,' said Steven. 'He never spoke to me about his reasons for going, mostly he just wanted to talk about the hymns and the music, but I imagine he spent some of the time there reflecting on the life he'd lived.' As always, his words sounded inadequate to his own ears, an ineffective buffer against grief and the ferocity of its storms.

'He never admitted it, not really.' Robert drew his arms around himself, hunching over as if to knot himself into a smaller, tighter space. 'He always said my sister exaggerated, that she imagined things. I'd like to hope he understood what he'd done, how he ruined her life. Lucy barely even speaks to Mum, you know. I've told her none of us knew anything but still.' Robert paused. 'This sounds awful, but on some level it's almost comforting to think he felt bad enough about it to, to . . .' He petered out, unable to finish. 'But then not to leave any note, not to apologise. That's just his old selfishness again.'

'Maybe he felt your sister wouldn't have wanted a message?'

'If that was his thinking, it's the first time he ever bothered to consider her,' Robert said bitterly. 'And what about me?' He sat upright, gripping his thighs, his eyes shining with tears. 'I really tried. I came to visit, not often, but I came. Nobody else in the family wanted anything to do with him. Mum sent all his letters back. I really tried . . .' Robert's shoulders started shaking and he sank back down again, resting his head in his hands.

'It's not your fault,' Steven said, speaking quietly and bending over so he was on the same level. 'None of it is your fault. Your father made his own choices, all his life. There was nothing you, your mum or your sister could have done.'

There was a nervous cough. 'Mr Fletcher?'

Steven turned at Terry's voice. Robert looked up blearily, wiping his face. Terry sat down in the chair opposite and held out his hand. 'Terry Saunders. I'm very sorry about your dad.'

'Really?' said Robert angrily. 'Everyone loved him here, did they? A great guy you all enjoyed spending time with?'

Terry blinked. 'He was a very quiet man, Duncan, always polite,' he said, as if Robert had asked a genuine question. 'He liked listening to music. I think he was the first opera fan we've had at Halvergate. Yes, he had friends here, who will miss him.'

Robert began crying again, sobbing this time. His grief was raw in the waiting room, adding to the weight of unhappiness that permeated Halvergate's every stone.

Terry waited until the weeping subsided. 'If you'd like to talk more about – about what happened, the governor is expecting you. Any questions you have, anything like that, we'll try and help.'

When they reached the door, Terry looked back at Steven and nodded. It was an innocent gesture, nothing more than an expression of thanks, or perhaps a sign he could leave. But he remembered Dan's remarks about the lost evidence and felt uncomfortable. It was as if he had become complicit in something larger and darker than he could understand.

Janet arrived at Lee's office just after Robert and Terry had left. She caught a glimpse of Terry supporting the young man out of the doors at the end of the corridor. After Steven had left last night she had needed a few glasses of wine to get to sleep, and now, for the first time in her professional life, she had arrived at work with a hangover. Watching the two men leave, she felt a surge of anxiety. She must have got the time of the meeting wrong.

She looked down at her watch. No, Lee had definitely said to meet at eleven in the email, and it was 10:55. Flustered, she knocked and pushed open the door before waiting for a reply. Her boss sat, unsmiling, behind his desk. The wide, white window behind him drained all light from his face, throwing him out of balance like a photographic negative. His glasses reflected the pale sky, hiding his eyes. He didn't rise to greet her.

'I'm very sorry, I seem to have missed Robert Fletcher. I'm certain you said eleven in the email,' she began.

'There's no mistake. Your presence was not required at the meeting with Mr Fletcher.' He smiled. His lips, drawn back over long, yellowing teeth, reminded Janet of a bear's snout. 'That's not why I asked to see you.' She hesitated in the doorway. Lee pushed his glasses down his nose, squinting over them so she could see his eyes. 'Please, take a seat,' he said, waving a paw.

She sat down, smoothing her trousers and brushing a clump of hair from her eyes. Lee leaned on his elbows and continued to stare at her, folding his hands before him as if in prayer. Behind him the landscape was almost washed out by white fog from the marshes. The control tower, always visible from his office, had half dissolved in the mist. Even the barbed wire of the perimeter fence was scarcely visible, creating a false image of freedom. But the fog also made Halvergate feel hidden, cut off from the rest of the world. All that remained was Lee, a dark shape against the whiteness. He dropped his chin on to his knuckles as he stared. Minutes seemed to pass before he spoke. 'How do you feel your time at Halvergate has been so far?'

Janet paused, thinking of all the strangeness of the past few days, wondering how honest she could afford to be. 'Well, I've only been here a fortnight,' she said. 'Clearly Duncan Fletcher's suicide raises some significant questions, but as for giving an assessment of the system here I think it's too early to say—'

Lee shook his head. 'No, no. I mean how has it been for you *personally*? I hope you don't mind me saying, but you seem, well, not altogether happy.' His eyes, peering at her above the lopsided glasses, were screwed up in concern.

Janet frowned, surprised by the question. 'Not at all.'

'You sure?' he pressed. 'No problems at home?' He seemed perplexingly eager for her to agree, his knuckles white as one calloused hand grasped the other. He was trying to be sympathetic, but the hunger in his eyes made her feel queasy. It looked like the concern of a wolf circling a wildebeest, watching its movements, waiting to spy an injury. Pushing a lank curl of hair behind her ears, she was aware that it needed a wash, that there were dark circles under her eyes. Self-doubt constricted her stomach like a belt pulled too tight.

'Mr Webster,' she began, her voice steady with a strength she did not feel. 'Duncan Fletcher is the first inmate to commit suicide under my care. Clearly it's a distressing situation, but I am no more perplexed by it than you or anyone else at Halvergate. My sole focus is to discover how his depression went undetected and what lessons we can learn for the future. I appreciate your concern but it's entirely misplaced.'

Lee looked down at the desk, pursing his lips. 'Of course,' he said. 'Of course. But you must see why I had to ask, eh? That little incident yesterday with the forensic officer, your, what shall we call it? Overexcitement? Hysteria?' He raised a hand to cut off the sound of protest that rose in her throat. 'If you were under stress at home, perhaps we could overlook such a lapse in professionalism . . .' He bared his teeth again. This time it made an even more unconvincing smile. 'And with the ombudsman's visit tomorrow, I thought it best we try to avoid such scenes.'

To her dismay, Janet could feel her hands shaking. She clasped them in her lap, meshing her fingers together. 'It wasn't a scene. I believed the cell was tampered with between Duncan's suicide and the arrival of the police.' Her voice wavered and she coughed, before continuing with greater firmness. 'I was looking for evidence to demonstrate this.'

There was a long silence. 'And did you find any?' Lee's voice was barely above a whisper.

A nerve jumped in Janet's cheek. She swallowed. 'No. I didn't.'

Lee inclined his head to acknowledge her discomfort. Then he sat back further in his chair, folding his hands over his stomach. The glasses whited out his eyes again. 'What do you know about your predecessor Dr Helkin?' he asked.

Janet's heart beat faster. She felt seasick at the change of tack, sensed the room dip and sway as if the ground had shifted beneath her feet. 'Very little. Nobody's been keen to talk about him.' Janet couldn't tell whether the twist to his mouth was a smile or not.

'You remind me of him,' Lee said, his voice so low she had to lean forward, anxious to hear. His gaze wandered past her shoulder, as if picturing her predecessor standing behind her. 'Yes, you do. Very trusting. Helkin was forever chasing fantasies, chasing here, chasing there. Until he grew sick on it. Poor John. It can be dangerous to get too close to the prisoners at

Halvergate. Don't let their lies take you in.' Without warning, he slammed his fist down on the desk. Janet jumped back. 'I will not have it, do you understand me?' he shouted. 'Not from Helkin, not from you. Halvergate turned into a laughing stock, busybodies from London coming up here, telling *me* how to run *my* prison.'

Lee's fury caught Janet completely off guard. Winded, she gripped the edge of her seat. She was used to psychological games from prisoners, even expected them, but the governor's rage sent her spinning, rudderless, into uncharted waters.

'I'm doing everything I can to minimise the suicide risks here—' she began, shakily.

'I'm not talking about that,' he said, cutting her off. 'We're a prison, people kill themselves in prisons. They're not holiday camps, in case you hadn't noticed, and nobody cares about a few dead sex offenders. Escapees like Ryan Spalding, yes. The fact that he topped himself, no. Suicides aren't part of our performance targets. Ryan's death was the biggest favour he could have done Halvergate. But what I will not have, Dr Palmer, is unnecessary fuss and hysteria.' Lee thumped his desk for emphasis again. 'Of course you should work on preventing suicides. It's not the sort of attention we need. But if some nonce hangs himself, you let the police do their job and you keep your nose and your crackpot theories out of it. And I *particularly* don't want you spouting any of your nonsense to the ombudsman.' His clenched fist came to rest on the desk between them.

Janet found herself unable to speak. Behind her angry boss, the blank landscape reflected nothing back at her, no clue or steer on how to proceed. Halvergate was a new world; none of her previous experience would help her navigate its hostile waters. She sat back in her chair, folding her hands in a gesture that mirrored her boss's. She stared into the white rounds of glass in his face.

'I understand you,' she said.

* * *

The living quarters at D block were bleached white like the skeleton of a long-dead animal. Janet headed up its spine, the iron stairs leading from one walkway to the next, bars stuck out alongside it, like ribs holding her in. A pale metal mesh hung between landings to prevent prisoners jumping into the hall below. Light filtered in from the glass on the ceiling, a sickly glow compared to the orange flare of the striplights.

Lee's anger, Duncan's suicide and her own vivid nightmares felt like a multiple assault on her sanity. And now doubt had gripped her, a gnawing fear that she had been infected by delusions too. She quickened her pace, her shoes ringing out on the metal as she reached the walkway. Behind her a female prison officer puffed to keep up. 'Michael's due to start work, are you sure you have to see him now?' she asked. The woman, Lisa, sounded disgruntled at the change to the prisoner's routine. She had a prison officer's natural distrust of non-uniformed staff encroaching on the world of the landings.

'Quite sure,' said Janet.

Scowling, Lisa shouldered past her, breathing heavily in annoyance. They passed Duncan's locked cell, and Janet shook off the feeling that if she opened it, his body would still be there, slumped forward, his blood on the walls.

Lisa's keys clanked and scraped against the lock. The cell was just his now, since David was still in the prison hospital. The door swung inwards and Janet saw Michael over Lisa's shoulder. He didn't turn as they walked in but sat staring at the blank wall in front of him, an open book hanging over his leg. For the first time since she'd met him, Michael looked neither assured nor calculating, but vulnerable, shrunken by sadness.

'Michael,' said Lisa. 'The doctor wants to see you.'

He started when he saw Janet, then grinned, his face lit up with pleasure. 'Now that is a shame,' he said. 'And I was so looking forward to a morning of sewing curtains.'

* * *

'I was wondering when I'd hear from you again,' he said when they got to her office. 'How did you get on with my clue?'

He plumped himself down in Janet's seat, uncomfortably close to where she was making the tea, boxing her in by the sink. It would be impossible to get past without brushing her leg against his elbow.

Janet ignored him. 'If you wouldn't mind taking the other chair,' she said.

'Oh, of course.' Jumping up, he peered at the cheap print of Thomas More by Hans Holbein that she had stuck to the wall. He smiled to himself before sitting down.

'You know my favourite of all his books,' he said, 'is *A Dialogue of Comfort against Tribulation*. He wrote it in prison. There's a particularly interesting bit about God as the jailor of the world. Meaning we're all prisoners in one way or another.' He picked up his mug. 'Have you read it?' He asked the question innocently enough, but Janet could see the malice in his blue eyes. She was struck by a sudden suspicion that someone had seen the Holbein print in her room before she met him and told him about her love of Thomas More. From his first mention of *Utopia*, it all seemed an impossible coincidence. She frowned and looked down at her tea. Who would know to tell him? It was a paranoid idea.

'Yes, I've read it,' she said. 'Though of course More was a prisoner of conscience, making him somewhat different to anybody at Halvergate.'

Michael shrugged. 'I think the experience of being locked up is universal. Whatever the reason.'

Janet sat for a moment, trying to calculate her next move. He took a sip of tea and when he lowered the mug she saw a smile hovering at the edges of his mouth. 'You win, Michael,' she said at last. 'You're right. I am going to ask for your help. It turns out you were telling the truth about Helkin practising hypnosis. I believe you may also know something about the suicides that happened during his time here, something that could have relevance to Duncan Fletcher's death.'

'Something?' Michael raised an eyebrow. 'You couldn't be more specific?' He sat leaning comfortably against the arm of the chair. His blue eyes reminded her of a cat's, watchful, reflecting nothing back.

'Do you believe in demons?' she asked.

Michael laughed. He seemed as unsurprised by her question as he was amused. 'So it's that, is it? Our lady of the black eyes?' he asked. Janet didn't reply, but he guessed the answer from her frown. 'No, Dr Palmer, I don't believe in demons.'

'But you're clearly aware that others at Halvergate do?'

He inclined his head. 'Hard to be unaware of the fact, though most of the staff are valiantly attempting it.'

'Who has seen this . . . lady, as you describe her?' Janet opened her notepad.

Michael bit his bottom lip suggestively and leaned forward. 'You know, Janey, it's not so long ago since Dr Helkin and I sat here while he asked me the exact same question. Things didn't go too well for him. Are you sure you want to do this?'

Janet stiffened at the use of her nickname. 'Are you threatening me?'

He gave her a look of mock surprise. 'Threatening?' he said. 'No, just trying to be helpful. Still, I suspect you know the answer already. As far as I'm aware, all the suicides claimed they had been persecuted by a white-faced woman with black eyes. Not that I had a chance to ask Duncan or Ryan, who seem to have jumped the gun. The others tolerated one or two sightings before . . .' He drew his finger across his throat. 'Not much of a persecution as far as I can see. I'd be delighted to have a late-night lady visitor. And if you're wondering if that's a hint,' he smirked, 'it is.'

'You believe prison staff ignored these delusions, but Helkin didn't?' Janet said. 'Is that right?'

'Yes.' Michael leaned back again.

'And he discussed all this with you?'

'He did. So you see, you're not the first psychologist to ask for my help. Though his approach was rather novel.' Michael yawned. 'He wanted my permission to hypnotise me.'

'Why did he want to do that?'

'I was, in his opinion, the sanest man on the VP wing. He thought that if he could implant a delusion into my mind, then remove it, he might be able to do the same with men who were genuinely psychotic.'

Even though she had suspected as much, confirmation of what Helkin had been doing made her afraid. She thought of his empty shirts, still swaying in the heat of her airing cupboard, and wished she lived somewhere else. Everything Helkin had touched felt tainted. 'He tried to get you to see the white visitor?'

'No, he wasn't quite that ambitious. He started on a much smaller scale. He tried to get me to see his face when I looked in the mirror.' Michael saw her expression and stopped. 'There's no need to look so appalled. Apparently that's textbook hypnotherapy when treating delusions.'

Janet gripped her notebook so Michael couldn't see her hands were shaking. 'And did he succeed?'

He smiled. 'Strangely enough, and much to his disappointment, he made no impact on me at all.'

Janet remembered the '*unaffected*' from the few remaining files. She felt conscious of Michael watching her write her own notes. 'If he tried to plant the delusions in your head,' she said, 'what's to say he didn't do that to the other men?'

'Oh, I see where you're going.' He laughed. 'Wouldn't that be neat and convenient. No. Helkin only tried hypnotherapy *after* our pale friend was on the scene. I think he was desperate to try anything by that stage. I don't know who was more frightened of her, the inmates or the psychologist.'

With each question she asked, Michael seemed to swell with the power her lack of knowledge gave him. Everything he said sounded like a lie, but then nobody else at Halvergate was telling her anything. It was hard to imagine anyone managing to influence this man. The strength of his will radiated out like a physical force.

'You and John Helkin seem to have known each other very well. How do I know you didn't help him? Reinforce ideas he had planted in other men's heads?'

'Are you suggesting I did myself up in drag? That Helkin got me to go haunting?'

'You're a very charismatic man. I imagine many of the insecure men on D wing look up to you, or would be influenced by what you say.'

He grinned at her as if she'd just paid him a compliment. 'Now who's making threats? You know, Janey, I'm flattered that you see me that way, that my charms haven't gone unnoticed. I must say, the feeling is entirely mutual. But you're barking up the wrong tree. If you want to find Helkin's little helper, I don't think you should be looking at the inmates. You'd be better off asking yourself why everyone at Halvergate is so keen to hide what's going on.'

'I take it you have some theories on that?'

He stretched himself out, raising his arms in the air, yawning again. 'It's quite something when a psychologist has to ask a prisoner about the staff. What does that say about your colleagues, I wonder? Or about you.' He rolled his shoulders and relaxed backwards. Then he caught her eye, and his expression softened. In another man she might have taken it for sympathy. He moved his head to one side in a conciliatory gesture. 'I'll keep an eye out for you.'

Silence grew between them. Janet felt wrong-footed, unsure if his sudden warmth was genuine or another trick. She brushed the feeling away. Nothing about this man was genuine. 'It's true not all my colleagues are as communicative as I might expect, but at least one of them has passed some information on about *you*,' she said. He looked at her in surprise. 'John Helkin left a note. He said the treatment wasn't having any effect on you. He didn't mention anything about hypnosis, so I guess that would be your word against his.' She paused, letting the implications of this sink in. No effective treatment meant a diminishing chance of parole. 'But don't worry,' she said. 'I'm going to suggest to Terry that we have one-to-one remedial therapy in addition to the group sessions.' She made sure to betray no emotion as she looked at him. She closed her notepad, bringing their meeting to an end. 'Thank you for your help. I think I'd better let you get back now.' She stood up. 'I'll call Lisa.'

Moving so quickly she had no chance to step out of the way, Michael pushed her back into her seat, his arms imprisoning her in the chair as he leaned over her. He was so close she could feel his breath on her face.

'And what about you, Dr Palmer? Have you seen her?'

'What?' she gasped.

'Our Lady of Halvergate.' His blue eyes, inches from hers, prevented her from looking away. He smiled as her face betrayed her answer. Then he stepped backwards, moving out of her personal space as suddenly as he'd invaded it.

'Best be careful then,' he said.

22

Steven sat alone in the near empty restaurant. He had suggested meeting in Great Yarmouth because of the town's fantastic chip shops, without considering that a seaside resort in winter is rarely at its best. The stalls on the seafront had been transformed into rows of closed eyes, the paint peeling off their shuttered lids. Some had come loose and flapped and thumped in the wind. On his walk along Marine Parade, the loud jingles and flashing lights from the slot machines in the arcades had only emphasised the lack of people inside.

The restaurant's only other customer, an elderly man who sat silently working his way through a mound of battered fish, was clearly a regular. Steven's own arrival seemed to have taken the teenaged waitress by surprise. She kept hovering back and forth between him and the counter with an awkward smile, waiting to take his order. Steven was beginning to worry that his date might not turn up when Dan came through the door, his face pink from the sea breeze.

'Glad you could make it,' Steven said as Dan plonked himself down opposite.

'These chips better be legendary,' said Dan. 'What a choice for date two.'

Steven laughed. 'I know. Sorry. It's great in the summer.'

They smiled at each other. Dan looked more confident than Steven remembered, or perhaps he was just over his first-date nerves. Skinny jeans suited him; he had an amazing body. Dan was just leaning over to say something when the waitress popped up with her pad. 'What'll you be having then?'

'Not seen the menu,' said Dan. 'But I'm guessing two fish and chips?'

'Sounds good to me,' said Steven, folding up his plastic card and handing it back to the girl. 'And a couple of beers.'

'Sorry I got a bit pissed last time,' Dan said, grimacing. 'Well, more than a bit. Hope I didn't make too much of a prat of myself.'

'Don't be daft. I'm no teetotaller myself,' said Steven. 'How's life at the station?'

'Well, your lot's been giving us grief. One of the prisoners did himself in. Though I guess you knew that.' Dan waited while the waitress poured his beer, then took a swig. 'I spoke to one of the guys who saw the cell, and there was no spice or anything, but they're all pretty jumpy. Seems somebody might have cottoned on to something. A woman came into the cell blathering on about evidence being destroyed.'

Steven realised Dan could only mean Janet. 'You reckon the suicides are related to spice?'

'Seems likely, doesn't it? That stuff seriously fucks with your head. Much stronger than weed.' Dan lowered his voice. 'And I told you a big bag went walkabout, so maybe some of the staff are dealing it, or turning a blind eye, anyway.'

Steven felt a surge of relief. Drugs would certainly be easier to deal with than a demon. But then he thought of Duncan Fletcher, with his fastidiousness and his cardigans and his love of opera, and the explanation felt less plausible. 'I hear what you're saying. But the guy who just died didn't seem like a user. I knew him a little, and he was always sober.'

'Well, I'll keep an ear out for you, if you like.' Dan took another swig of beer, his eyes not leaving Steven's. 'But we're not going to talk about work all night, are we?'

Janet leaned back on Mrs Slaney's sofa, holding Isabel's picture. Arun had left more messages on her phone, but fewer than the day before. She'd hoped he would have driven up from London, been waiting on her doorstep, desperate to fight for her. Instead his last message had told her he was flying out to the US for a series of meetings. His voice sounded weary and she was afraid he was giving up.

She looked down at the photo of her twin. In her mind's eye, the well-loved features of Izzy's face blurred and bloated into the dead body she had never seen. She blinked, staring at the picture again, willing herself to remember her twin as she had lived, to remember their walk up to San Miniato that morning. She thought of Izzy's comedic efforts to buy the enamel cross from the monks with her limited Italian, and the wild flowers they'd picked to take back to the cheap pensione where they were staying. The old man who ran it had been unable to resist the charms of the two laughing English girls, and the wild flowers had littered their room with a ragged carpet of pollen, leaves and petals.

But the memories slipped away, and instead she remembered the first time she had come across her sister's 'case history' in a psychiatric journal. Reading it, she finally understood how much detail the police had chosen to withhold to protect her family's feelings.

She had been doing research at the Bodleian Library in Oxford. It was Izzy's old university and she had spent a bitter-sweet morning wandering the city's honey-glazed streets, remembering the times she'd visited, half expecting to see her sister's face among the students passing on their bicycles. She was leafing through the latest volumes on sex offender profiling when she came across the case of 'P', a young woman strangled by a man with schizophrenia and learning difficulties. Sitting in the beautiful library, light flooding through its high windows, Renaissance frescoes gazing down at her, Janet learned that her sister had been raped.

The post-mortem revealed 'P' had been a virgin at the time of the attack. Bruises and cuts on the victim's hands, arms and torso suggest she put up a violent struggle. There was no semen recovered from inside the body but the coroner ruled that any DNA from the attacker was likely to have been lost due to the length of time the body had been left in the water.

'*Traces of latex inside the victim's vagina were deemed to be too small, and the decomposition of the body too advanced, to determine whether the attacker had used the barrier method of protection. Given the offender's level of mental competence, such a degree of foresight and calculation is considered unlikely.*'

At the time, Janet had been so overwhelmed at reading the details of her sister's assault that the last line had been lost on her. But in the years that followed, as she worked more closely with sex offenders and tried to understand them and to make them safe, it was this line, as much as the horror of Izzy's suffering, that haunted her. In it she sensed the possibility that Neil Martin was more cunning than his mad tale of an angel's instructions had suggested. She grasped the possibility that despite his learning difficulties he had planned to dispose of evidence, that if the police hadn't caught him, he might never have confessed. That his schizophrenia, which nobody, not even her sister, had previously detected, might have been faked. And she knew in her heart that such a man, while living, could never be made safe, however many treatments he received.

'But he's dead,' she murmured, closing her eyes as tears pricked at their edges. It was always this way. Grief rose and fell like a dangerous tide at the margins of her life, constantly threatening to burst its banks and overwhelm her, marooning her in the dark place she had inhabited when she first learned of Isabel's murder.

She was barely conscious of the two years after her sister's death. Looking back, they shifted in and out of focus, a kaleidoscope of fragments with sharp edges. Each morning had brought a heartbeat of blankness before memory crashed over her, submerging her. She knew Isabel was dead, yet her heart refused to accept it. Underwater, she looked up through the dark at her past life, yet she knew, even as she struggled, that there were no means to reach it. Instead grief pushed her back beneath its surface, a weight impossible to shift.

Although the passing years brought greater calm, Janet found that her grief was bottomless. Ten years on and she was still falling. She passed from not caring whether she lived, to believing she would die, to the dull realisation that her life was moving relentlessly onwards, away from the day of Isabel's death towards that inevitable moment when she would have lived more of her life without her sister than they had lived together.

Time washed over her memories of Isabel, blurring their precision, making it harder to see her. She searched for Izzy's features in her own mirror, tracing the lines in her face, wondering if they would have drawn themselves on her sister in the same pattern. Yet as time passed, her reflection also took her further away from the person she had been. She realised she was losing herself, even as she had lost her sister. She felt sometimes that a stranger was living her life.

She sat for a moment in Mrs Slaney's living room, overwhelmed and longing for the past. The thought of Duncan Fletcher's death and the ombudsman's visit on Friday made the present even more oppressive. All of it had to be faced alone. She stood up and replaced Izzy's photograph, touching it gently, before she turned to leave.

Closing the living room door, Janet crossed the hall and stood at the foot of the stairs. At their top, the bathroom door was ajar, a faint glow seeping out from the strip light above the mirror.

A dark sea of rage rose in her heart. She ran up the stairs and pushed open the door, heading straight to the mirror. Gripping the sink, she stared into the glass, willing the white woman to appear. But it was her own eyes, wide with fury, that stared back at her.

'Do you think I'm afraid of you?' she whispered. She pressed her palm to the glass, mimicking the gesture of the creature in her dreams. 'Whatever you are, whether you're in my head or out of it, I've seen worse than you. Do you understand?'

She stood there, puffs of breath misting the outline of her second self. For a moment it seemed to Janet as if her reflection wavered, the shadow of another face dark beneath it. She leaned forward, staring, but there was nothing unusual, except perhaps the wild expression in her own eyes. She thought of John Helkin and wondered if he'd spent time talking to himself in the same house, staring in the same mirror.

'Crackpot,' she murmured. At the door, she looked back before turning off the light. As she plunged the room into darkness, the mark from her palm gleamed on the surface of the mirror.

23

Janet watched the tall figure cross the yard, accompanied by one of the prison officers. All she could see was the top of the woman's head; her office window was too high up to afford a view of her face. After her meeting with Lee on Wednesday, she found it hard to believe it was only coincidence that she was the first person to be interviewed that morning. That way Terry or Lee would know from their own interviews if she had said anything to provoke difficult questions.

Yesterday had been a quiet shift at the prison, giving her some space to reflect on Duncan's death before the interview. She had spent time agonising over what to say and what to leave out. She no longer felt confident that she had seen that letter E on the wall in his cell, but neither was she entirely sure she had imagined it.

The phone rang on her desk, vibrating in its receiver. Her stomach clenched with anxiety as she answered. 'Janet Palmer.'

'Dr Palmer, can you go to Room 21A please? Ms Gardner from the ombudsman's team is waiting for you.'

Room 21A was the freezing shoebox where Janet had held her first assessments. Ms Gardner looked uncomfortable in the small plastic chair, a shiny magenta suit buttoned high up to her neck to keep out the chill. She clutched a cup of coffee, no doubt trying to warm her fingers. As Janet walked in she put it down and reached out her hand with a pleasant smile.

'Dr Palmer, good to meet you. Please take a seat.'

Janet sat at the wrong side of the desk, feeling like a sixth-former in front of the headmistress. She had never been involved in anything to warrant an interview with the ombudsman before. Her nerves increased at the sound of a loud click as the other woman started the recording. Ms Gardner looked off to the side rather than at Janet as she spoke, in the strange, universal habit of people delivering a recorded message.

'Present at this meeting are Eleanor Gardner from the ombudsman's team, interviewing Dr Janet Palmer, registered psychologist at HMP Halvergate, regarding the death of Duncan Fletcher.' She turned back to Janet. 'I'm sorry for everybody here about Mr Fletcher's tragic death. I know these events are difficult for a community to deal with. I understand you've not been here long?'

'Two weeks.'

Ms Gardner nodded. 'And in that time, what was your contact with Duncan Fletcher?'

'I conducted a one-to-one assessment with him in my first week, since he was expected to be on the sex offender treatment programme. And then we had a number of group sessions. He had already been through part of the course with my predecessor John Helkin, but we decided to restart the programme, in a shortened version, to try to ensure the treatment's integrity.'

'And how did Mr Fletcher appear to you, when you spoke to him?'

'Nothing alarmed me.' Janet tried to keep her eyes on Ms Gardner's face as she spoke, rather than glancing at the recorder with its unwinking red light. 'He didn't seem depressed, he told me he was involved in the musical life of the prison chapel and enjoyed that. Overall, he seemed to be well adjusted to the routine in Halvergate.'

'And do you know if he had been through the victim empathy section of the treatment programme with Dr Helkin? I understand Mr Fletcher was convicted of raping his daughter over a period of several years in her childhood. Could anything have disturbed him after delving into those offences in the group role play?'

'Mr Fletcher told me he had not yet completed that part of the programme—' Janet stopped, overwhelmed by the urge to add that there were no tapes or notes on the sessions, no means of checking whether this were true. But she thought of Lee's fist on his desk, the rage behind the whited-out spectacles, and said nothing. The moment passed and Ms Gardner moved on.

'And how did Mr Fletcher appear to you in the group sessions?'

'We've not held that many so far, and none centred on Duncan, on Mr Fletcher, I mean. In both he seemed reasonably engaged, if not the most vocal member of the group. Certainly he didn't appear either indifferent or distressed,' Janet said, her voice quavering. 'I'm so sorry, I've been over and over every exchange I had with him, and I really can't think of anything that would have been a warning sign.'

Ms Gardner nodded again. 'And do you have any theories about what might have caused a sudden, undetected deterioration in mood?'

'I hope that we'll be looking at the possibility of drugs or legal highs. That's the only obvious cause that I can think of without further evidence.' Janet felt her breath quickening, waited for the question on whether she had any ideas about less obvious causes. But it never came.

'Thank you, Dr Palmer, I think that will be all for the moment. I will be in contact should we require any further information.' Eleanor Gardner reached out one magenta-encased arm and ended the recording with a click.

Janet had no chance to ask Terry privately how his interview with Ms Gardner had gone, and nothing in his manner indicated a man eager for an exchange of confidences. Due to the relentless pressure to complete the programme by the end of the year, they had been obliged to go into the next group session as soon as Eleanor Gardner had finished her interviews. With ill-fated timing, it was Michael Donovan's turn to be the centre of the life story session. Janet couldn't have felt less like confronting her most difficult prisoner. At least it was Friday and the hideous week was nearly at an end.

Janet tried not to think about her last meeting with Michael, his breath on her face, his arms pinning her into her chair, while she, Terry and Siobhan sat in the apricot room before the inmates arrived. She had been forced to have a pep talk with Siobhan after the last session, as the young woman had remained entirely mouse-like, contributing almost nothing. Now she sat biting dry lips, eyes darting nervously between Terry and Janet as they discussed the strategy for that day's session. Janet knew she should make more effort to bring her out.

'So today, Siobhan,' she said, in what she hoped was an encouraging tone of voice, 'I'll take the lead with Michael, but that doesn't mean you shouldn't get involved. I know he's not the easiest member of the group, but I want you to try and contribute a little more to the session, even if it's just to ask some of the other men for their input, OK?'

There was a knock at the door, and Siobhan darted up to open it. The inmates began to file in. Michael took a seat directly opposite her, next to Terry. He didn't look up or smile, which was unusual, but instead sat with his head bowed as if waiting to be led in prayer. Seeing them side by side felt disorientating to Janet, as if they might be in league, even though she knew that was a ridiculous thought.

When everyone had settled, she started talking. 'I know it's a difficult time, our first meeting without Duncan. Terry and I are always here if anyone wants to speak about what happened, or about how you are feeling.' The men exchanged glances.

'Never would have thought it,' Majid muttered. 'Such a quiet bloke. Apart from all his bloody opera.' A couple of people laughed.

'Not so surprising though,' said Greg, screwing up his face in disgust. 'Fiddled his own daughter, didn't he? Fucking out of order.' His leg began to jig up and down with nervous energy. In the hierarchy of sex offenders, paedophiles were several thousand leagues below the rest. Particularly those that preyed on their own children.

'Yeah, well,' Jamie started up. 'He was all right, I thought. Always had a fag to spare, if you asked, and all for nothing.'

'Top bloke, then.' Greg snorted.

Michael lifted his head and stared straight at Janet. 'I heard he had a visitor.'

She felt the ripple of unease pass through the room. She thought about their last meeting, his taunts over the dark lady of Halvergate, and regretted giving him a window on to her fears. Now he had a perfect opportunity to wind everyone up. Terry opened his mouth to speak, but she cut across him. 'What do you mean, Michael?'

'I heard a woman had been to see him.' He paused, looking round and savouring the fear. 'Perhaps his angry daughter. I imagine that must have been who it was. Must have driven him over the edge.'

'We all know Duncan abused his daughter,' Terry broke in. 'There are many sides to a person. Duncan didn't hide what he'd done, there's no need to act like he did. You know we've talked about that before. Everyone has a good side, their best side.' Janet watched him as he spoke, wondering if he could possibly believe what he was saying after years of working at Halvergate. 'And the key to getting to your best side is understanding the whole of yourself better.'

'And it's my turn for "show and tell" today, isn't it?' A couple of sniggers rewarded Michael's facetiousness, though the atmosphere still felt tense and clammy after his mention of Duncan's visitor.

'It's so we can all get to know each other better,' said Janet. 'Everybody's had a go. Nobody here will give you a hard time.' Sensing the contempt Michael had for the rest of the men, she was aware that this was the least of his concerns.

'Yes, there's nothing to be worried about,' blurted out Siobhan in a shrill voice. Everybody turned and stared at her, surprised by her sudden interjection. She blushed.

'Well, that's *very* reassuring, Siobhan, thank you,' Michael said, making her turn even redder. 'But I'm afraid there's nothing exciting to tell you. A comfortable childhood in Sussex with doting parents. No woman-hating issues from my dear mother, whose only fault was to bore me senseless.'

'Were you an only child?' Janet asked.

'No, I have a younger brother, who I'm sorry to say is an absolute cunt.'

'Why's that?'

'Self-satisfied and thick as a plank. He's a fighter pilot in the RAF, so at least my parents have one darling son they can brag about to the neighbours.'

Janet wasn't sure that the RAF let too many idiots fly their million-pound machinery, but let Michael's judgement on his brother go. Part of her felt angry, as she always did when people hated their siblings, a hatred that only the ungrateful can afford towards the living. 'Did you fight much as children?'

'I made his life as miserable as I possibly could. Destroyed his homework, stole his girlfriends, which was never difficult, even planted cigarettes on him once in primary school – which was a huge joke, he'd never have had the balls to smoke one. He nearly got expelled for that.' Michael made no effort to hide the pleasure he felt in recollecting his brother's pain.

'And what did your mum and dad say to all this?'

'He never snitched. If he had, I might have stopped. Our darling parents feared he might be a delinquent after the ciga-rettes, but he never said anything. I'm pretty sure he knew it was me. He just ploughed silently through it all, like a little martyr. No surprise when *he* went into the military, duty above all else, and all that crap. Or maybe he's taken out all his impotent rage by bombing the fuck out of wedding parties in Afghanistan.' Michael smiled to himself. 'That's a more pleasing thought.'

'Yeah, well maybe the Taliban will shoot him down, mate,' said Majid, shaking his head in disgust.

Michael shrugged. 'Here's hoping.'

'What do we all think about the way Michael treated his brother?' Terry interrupted. 'In fact, why don't we give him his own name. What's he called?'

Michael looked reluctant to reply, as if begrudging his brother any humanity. 'Peter,' he said at last.

'What do we think about how Michael treated Peter?' Terry repeated.

'Well, it's shit,' said Greg, his face flushed red. 'What'd he done to piss you off so much?'

'Breathe,' said Michael.

'Why d'you reckon he didn't tell anyone?' asked Jamie. 'Did you smack him up or something?'

'I never *hit* him, that would have been far too obvious.' Michael looked at Jamie pityingly, as an amateur in the arts of sadism.

'Do you think he didn't tell your parents because he loved you?' Janet asked. 'Because he was protecting you, making sure nobody knew what you were doing?'

'I never bothered to think about it. But that's just the sort of pathetic motive he might have had. Certainly whatever I did never stopped him following after me like some pathetic puppy, craving affection.'

Janet felt the longing for her own sister as a dull ache in her chest. 'Is that what you feel for all the people who love you, contempt?'

'That's a bit deep for me, Dr Palmer.' Michael smiled at her. 'Certainly I don't have much respect for people who don't stand up for themselves. They're just encouraging you to hurt them.'

This was the time to bring it back to the group, ask what they thought, but she found herself unable to stop questioning the man in front of her. 'And how did Peter react when you were sentenced for rape?'

For the first time since she had met him, Janet saw a flicker of anger pass over Michael's beautiful face. 'That's not something I want to discuss.'

'Why?' asked Janet. 'Was it unexpectedly painful when he

finally did reject you?' She was almost certain this was not the answer but hoped to goad Michael into a reply. For once, she had played him right.

'Rejection?' His tone was cool, but she saw the anger in his eyes. 'That I might have respected, if the patronising little shit had finally showed some backbone. No, he wrote and told me he *forgave* me, that he hoped I found peace in prison and learned to be a better person. That he'd visit whenever I wanted. As if he were Jesus fucking Christ.'

Many of the men in the group were still suffering from the rejection of their friends and family. Others had endured childhoods of abuse. Michael's remark did not go down well. Kamal, who almost never spoke, shook his head, his dark eyes unfriendly. 'You should be thankful. That's your brother.'

Far from riling him, the other prisoners' hostility seemed to snuff out Michael's anger. He gave one of his infuriating smiles. 'Please, any of you, feel free to adopt him.'

'Going back to something you said earlier.' Janet glanced down at her notes. 'You mentioned that you stole Peter's girlfriends. I'm wondering what you thought of the girls involved?'

'Can't say I remember them.'

'So they were just a means to an end? You didn't like any of them or want a relationship with any of them?'

'No, I just fucked them. That was generally enough to spoil things for him. There was one he really liked, I forget her name, when he was about fifteen. I went out with her for a while, just to wind him up. Nothing like knowing your brother's shagging the love of your life in the spare room.'

'And what did you think of these girls?' Janet persisted. 'They must have been quite a bit younger than you.'

'Not so much. Two years, maybe. I told you, I didn't think of them. They were sluts. In fact you could say I was doing Peter a favour, selflessly weeding out the chaff from the wheat.'

'And what about your relationships with women when you

went to university, when you were working? Did you have many girlfriends or female friends?'

'Women can't even be friends with each other, let alone men,' Michael said. 'And no, strangely enough, I never had any problem attracting women.'

'What about keeping them?' asked Terry. Janet glanced at him, conscious of how little she knew about his family life. She wondered whether he ever told his wife about the men he worked with.

'Can't say I ever felt the need.' Michael stared at the wedding ring on Terry's finger as if it were a badge of shame.

'So Karina was your first serious girlfriend?' Janet said. 'That's quite a jump. No long-term relationships, then you move in with a woman at the age of thirty-two?'

'We worked together. I thought Karina was different.'

'How, different?'

'We worked in the games industry. We were both coders on the same programme.'

'You work in computer games?' said Jamie, impressed. 'Cool. Which one, like *Call of Duty*?'

'Afraid not, no. I worked at a Cambridge-based company, Minotaur. Their main programme is huge in the States. *Mythos and Logos*. It's based on characters from classical Greek myth.' Michael's tone was casual, but Janet caught the hint of pride in his voice.

'How did working in the games industry make Karina different?'

'Do you know what it takes to programme a top-quality game?' Michael asked her. 'You have to foresee all possibilities, your maths has to be outstanding, your invention razor-sharp.' Now he wasn't bothering to conceal his pride, his sense of superiority. 'I thought Karina was different because I thought she would be immune from all the cloying sentimentality that makes women so unpleasant to be around. Present company excepted, I'm sure.'

'Was raping her your revenge for finding out she loved you?'

Michael laughed. 'How naive and predictable you are, Dr Palmer.'

Terry coughed. Janet looked round and saw the other men were looking bored and restless. She needed to bring them in rather than treat the session as if Michael were the only other person in the room. 'Well, you'll have more of a chance to give your side of the offence later in the programme. For now I think we should start some role play, looking at some of the things you've said about your brother and his girlfriends.' She looked over to her colleague. 'Terry, do you want to take the lead on this?'

Unwilling, as always, to relinquish control, Michael turned too. 'What a good idea. Perhaps you could be me, Terry? I can't *wait* for you to find my better self.'

24

Snow had transformed the village of Halverton; its plain houses stood frosted and glittering in the Saturday morning light. The tracks on the tarmac had been erased, and the road painted white with possibility. Ice hung from the plastic guttering on Cherry Tree Drive like coloured glass, refracting all the shades of the rainbow as Janet stared out of her bedroom window, the rattling blow heater gently lifting the bottom of her nightdress. She drew her dressing gown tighter around her shoulders. The day was beautiful but bitterly cold.

Looking down, she saw that the scrubby little hedge, normally nothing more than an obstacle to parking the Mini, was creeping into colour. Clusters of red berries were starting to form in its branches, as if somebody had tipped pots of paint over it. Janet thought of how she and Izzy would have loved to pick the dripping twigs as children, stuffing the branches into jam jars on the kitchen windowsill of their Pimlico home. She had an image of the pair of them standing impatiently in the hallway, trussed up in their bright red coats, hardly able to move for the layers of leggings, socks and 1980s legwarmers, begging their mother to let them play out in the snow. She could see Izzy make a face as a woolly hat was crammed over her head, half covering one eye, before she grabbed her by the hand and raced out into the garden. As they grew older, the girls would realise how small the space was, barely big enough for the obligatory annual barbecue, but aged five the backyard was a magical landscape, an endless white powdery playground to explore. Their first snow.

The old house had long since been sold. Her parents couldn't bear to live there, haunted by all the memories of their daughters' happy childhoods. That was before they learned that memories are not tethered to the spot where they were born, but pursue you from place to place. Even to Halverton.

Janet sat frozen with grief. Beside her Arun clutched her hand, his head bowed. Across the kitchen table where they had shared so many family meals sat her father, his face seeming to have aged ten years since the news of his daughter's death. Upstairs her mother lay on the bed, prostrated by despair and a high dosage of diazepam.

'I want to see her,' Janet said.

'Janey, it's not possible.' Her father's eyes were rimmed red from weeping. 'She doesn't look how she should. She had, she—' He broke off, trying not to cry in front of his only remaining child. He managed to collect himself. 'She had been in the water a long time.'

Appalling images flooded Janet's mind, her beautiful sister's face bloated and destroyed. 'No, she can't, she can't be ...' She started crying again, not a quiet grief, but a loud agony that tore her heart. Her father got up and stood behind the chair, holding her shoulders to stop the shaking.

'There, sweetheart, there. She was still our Izzy. She still had her faith. I told you she was holding that prayer she always kept in her wallet. She was still holding on. He didn't break her.'

The hum of the heater rose and fell as it breathed hot air across her ankles, rotating in a noisy tide. The snow's redemptive powers were only temporary, a brief reinvention of the landscape into something more palatable. Janet wished she could redraw her mind permanently in its reassuring blankness.

With an effort, she pushed away the past. Across the fields, she knew, Halvergate was being transformed, the lies ingrained in its fabric whited over. Those lies were slowly drawing her in. Although there was nothing technically dishonest about her interview with the ombudsman, Janet still wondered whether she should have brought up the missing notes. Not only that, but she hadn't reported Michael Donovan's threatening behaviour in their private meeting to anyone, either officially or in confidence. It was an act that would have been unthinkable at Leyland, but at Halvergate there was nobody in management she trusted with the information. If she reported Michael, Richard or Lee might prevent her from carrying out one-to-one sessions with him, and she was convinced that he knew more about the prisoners' troubles.

This omission was the first time Janet had deliberately broken her professional code and it made her feel oddly weightless, like the pilot of a hot air balloon cutting one of the ropes that kept her tethered in place. Just a single rope for now, but she wondered where she might drift off to if she cut them all.

Sitting back heavily on the bed, Janet reached for her phone, scrolling through to the journalist Zara Hyde's number. Perhaps it was time to sever another rope.

The Eastern Film Company stood in the centre of Norwich like a giant from the past, withstanding the flow of cars that swept round its stone island in a dirty, encroaching sea. It was an imposing red brick building, the same style as Halvergate, and every detail spoke of decayed grandeur, from the faded lettering proclaiming its name to the dusty windows of its now empty offices.

It took Janet some time to navigate her way across the lines of traffic to reach the enormous building. At first there seemed no obvious way in. She walked round several times in confusion.

'You all right, love?'

Janet turned. A tall security guard was looking down at her.

'I'm trying to find the newsroom.'

'Thought so. This way.'

The guard headed off under a brick archway. Janet saw she had missed a set of glass sliding doors, hidden in the shadow beneath. She walked into a modern reception area, all glass and chrome, at odds with the building's crumbling facade.

The guard picked up the phone behind his desk, leaving Janet standing uncertainly in the doorway. 'Who are you seeing?'

'Zara Hyde.'

'Just a minute.' He rang through to the newsroom and spoke briefly before hanging up. 'She's on her way.'

Janet contemplated a large plastic tree stationed at the entrance, looking at the dust on its leaves. She was just wondering if her visit were really such a good idea when Zara appeared.

'Hello!' The journalist stood by the reception desk, backlit by the room behind. She shook Janet's hand vigorously. 'Come on in.'

The newsroom was long and narrow, stretching the length of the building. Its emptiness made it seem even larger. Row after row of unmanned desks stood between her and the opposite wall, while a mess of newspapers, tapes, teacups, wires and computers lay strewn across every conceivable surface like the detritus left in the wake of a natural disaster.

'Is it always this empty?' Janet asked, aghast. 'Are they all out on stories?'

'As if. It's the weekend, skeleton staff, just me and that pair.' Zara waved amiably over in the direction of two people slumped over their screens in a far corner of the room, who Janet hadn't noticed before. 'Anyway, better that way, we can watch the tape without a crowd.'

Zara sauntered over to her desk. Her camera was parked next to a wheezing computer, sitting lopsided in an old-fashioned metal mail in-tray, a Post-it note stuck on the viewfinder. The word 'BATTERY?!' was written across it. She bent down and began rummaging through a box of tapes on the floor. 'The tape's here somewhere. I saw it earlier.'

Leaning against the table, Janet accidentally nudged the mouse, and glanced at the screen as it flickered from darkness into life. She froze. Isabel's face smiled at her from Zara's browser. It was the photograph her family had released to the police. Alongside it ran a familiar, hated newspaper headline: AGONY OF IZZY TWIN.

The story published the day after her sister's funeral.

The picture hit her like a punch to the stomach. She straightened abruptly, knocking against the chair. Zara looked up in surprise, then caught sight of the screen. She scrambled to minimise the window.

'Shit, I'm sorry. I wasn't snooping . . . Well, I mean, I was snooping but not for any sinister reason.' She ran her hands through her cropped hair. 'I was going to ask you about it, tactfully, some other time. I thought I recognised you from the coverage of the murder, you see, when we were talking before. It was such a terrible case.'

Janet's lifelong distrust of journalists rose in her throat like bile. Zara's bluff, hearty manner, which had so disarmed her, now seemed disingenuous. She didn't trust herself to speak but clicked on the screen to bring the headline back up. 'The wonders of the internet,' she said. She stared at the hated page until it began to blur before her eyes. She heard Zara shift uncomfortably behind her.

'We're not all like that heartless headline.' Zara reached over to the mouse and closed the viewfinder. 'Sorry to spring that on you. I really didn't mean to.'

In the far corner of the room, Janet saw that the two other journalists had stopped their work and were looking over. She sighed. Her anger at Zara began to evaporate. The woman wasn't her friend, and her nosiness wasn't a crime.

'You're not the first,' she said. 'Every now and then people recognise the face, the name, whatever it is. I just wasn't expecting to see her.' She slumped down in an empty chair, exhausted. Zara perched nervously on the desk alongside her.

'It must be difficult,' she started, not quite keeping the hint of curiosity out of her voice. 'Doing your job, surrounded by—'

Janet cut her off. 'I don't want to talk about it.'

'Of course. Sorry.' There was an awkward pause. Zara forced a return to her usual brightness. 'I think I've found that tape of Helkin, if you still want to watch it?'

* * *

The room must have been one of the Company's many spare offices. The lighting had been set up blue and moody, the background plain. Then the shot moved from wide to close, blurring the backdrop and focusing all attention on the man who had haunted Janet since she first came to Halvergate.

The lighting isolated and exaggerated the details of his face, revealing him in fragments. A short, greying beard. Neat and close-cropped. The hair on his head was much darker, showing up his sallow skin. A sheen of sweat on his face. And the nervous gestures. Glasses taken off and rubbed, replaced, taken off, rubbed, replaced. Blue eyes, darting to the camera, flitting back to the unseen interviewer, roving the room, distracted.

He had an unremarkable face, but the cameraman's stagecraft made his nose larger, his short brow squarer and cut the sagging line of his cheeks deeper around his mouth.

Janet leaned forward, headphones on. John Helkin. At last, John Helkin.

She heard Zara, out of sight, behind the camera. 'Just your name and title for the tape please.'

No answer. Helkin stared straight down the barrel of the lens as if he were searching for her, for Janet. Instinctively she sat back.

'Your name, if you wouldn't mind. For the tape.'

He turned back to the unseen journalist, swallowing. He seemed to have difficulty focusing his attention. Then he spoke with the deep, rasping voice of a heavy smoker. 'John Helkin, forensic psychologist at HMP Halvergate.'

Janet felt a sense of dislocation at hearing her job claimed by someone else. And yet, as she heard him speak, she realised on some level she had always thought of the job as belonging to him, not her.

'As we discussed, I'd like to ask you about the circumstances of Ryan Spalding's escape—' Zara didn't get to finish her question.

'I know who.' Helkin leaned forward, gripping his knees, his knuckles white. The intensity of his stare, the tension of his posture, reminded Janet of Ian Fendley.

'Sorry?'

'It's not just Ryan, she wants them all. All the ones she calls for.' The contrived blue lighting caught the whites of his eyes, making his urgency even more disconcerting. 'There's no escape. That's it for them and they know it.'

'Who wants who? Did somebody help Spalding escape?'

'She's everywhere, don't you understand? She's invaded every space, every moment of my life.'

'I, um, really don't—'

'At first I thought it was the house. That's where I saw her. But I resisted and she punished me. She punished me for not believing her, for not doing what she wanted . . .'

Helkin's gaze shifted away from Zara as he spoke. He began to stare into the lens again, his blue eyes looking straight at Janet, even though she knew he couldn't see her. Janet felt as if she was facing a mirror, Helkin's madness infecting her soul.

'. . . That first night she came to me in the bedroom, in the dark, while I lay there, unable to move. I saw her white face in the darkness, her eyes like bullet holes in her head. She leaned over, so low, so close to my face. I saw nothing, do you understand? No light in her eyes. I was paralysed, then she took my—'

The tape jumped.

The shot was even tighter on Helkin now. He sat looking off at the invisible Zara. The tape restarted in the middle of a question, as if they were already mid conversation. '. . . and is that when you realised this . . . demon wanted them dead?'

Janet took her headphones off. 'What happened? Why did the tape jump?' Sweat prickled against the back of her shirt. Her hands felt slippery.

Zara pressed pause. They were sitting together in a stuffy, dimly lit room. The journalist had called it an edit suite. Helkin's face was frozen across the two screens of a massive computer.

'The cameraman switched it off record for a bit. We thought

he was a loon, or about to launch into a porno or something. We got the important stuff, don't worry.' Zara put her own head-phones back on. 'Shall I restart it?'

Inwardly cursing Zara's sensible cameraman, Janet nodded. Helkin began speaking again, but she felt so disorientated, she missed the first part of what he was saying. She forced herself to concentrate.

'. . . it's her, she kills them, she drives them mad, she drives them to kill themselves, her rage, her demands for vengeance, they can't stand it . . .' Helkin took his glasses off, rubbed them, replaced them. His hands were shaking. 'I can't stand it.'

'So the demon wants the prisoners to kill themselves, but what does she want from you?'

Helkin's eyes darted across the room, as if he were searching for another listener. Shifting in his seat, he looked into the lens, then back at Zara. 'My body,' he whispered.

'OK, thanks for your time, Dr Helkin . . .' Zara sounded annoyed.

'No, you don't understand. I mean she wants my help. She needs my body to kill him.'

Janet heard a sharp intake of breath, perhaps from the camer-aman. There was a pause. The light reflected off Helkin's face, glistening with sweat.

'The demon wants you to kill prisoners?' Zara asked slowly.

'No.' Helkin sat very still, as if, even in his unbalanced state, he grasped the seriousness of what he'd just said.

Zara's deep voice went up by several octaves. 'Who does the demon want you to kill?'

'Nobody.' Helkin paused and for the first time in the interview shifted his gaze to the floor, obscuring his expression. 'Myself.'

'Right, OK . . . Well, I think we might have to leave it here. Don't take this the wrong way, Dr Helkin, but I really think you need to talk to somebody senior at Halvergate about this. It sounds . . . well, like something you need help with . . .'

'You think I haven't tried?'

'You've told people at Halvergate what you've just told me?' Zara sounded doubtful.

'They don't believe me.' Helkin covered his face with his hands, his shoulders collapsing inwards with despair.

'OK, Ray. I think Dr Helkin's had enough.'

Rainbow bars filled the screen, and a loud tone sounded in Janet's ears.

Janet hurried to her car, sliding on the slush in her haste to get away from Zara and the Eastern Film Company, as if putting distance between them would get her away from what she'd seen. She struggled with the Mini's door, her hands sticking to the freezing handle. Her coat caught on the runner as she scrambled in and shut out the street.

She gripped the wheel, staring out at the busy road, but John Helkin's face came back to her. She saw his sweat in the drops of condensation on the windscreen, his grey skin in the snow on the road. Nausea gripped her and she pushed the car door open, bending over the kerb, retching. She hung low over the gutter, too ashamed to look up, aware of shoppers' legs hurrying away from her.

Her cheeks flushed with embarrassment, she closed the car door and started up the engine, pulling into the road as quickly as possible. She headed out of Norwich with the taste of bile in her mouth.

The fields passed flat and white either side of her, the snow reflecting back more light than the sky, giving off an unearthly glow, making the familiar drive to Halverton feel alien. At the roundabout that would take her down the Acle Straight, Janet found herself passing the turning. She couldn't face going back to Cherry Tree Drive, back to the house John Helkin had rented, the house where he lost his reputation and his sanity. The house where he had, perhaps, plotted the deaths of several prisoners. She took the turning to Winterton-on-Sea, a coastal town she'd never been to.

Unlike the Acle Straight, the ancient road was narrow and lurching, and her tyres spun as she took the Mini too fast round an icy bend. Sweat sprang up on her forehead as she struggled to regain control of the car, aware of the marshes, sunken but lethal under their sugary dusting of snow.

The path wound round to the left and began to climb a slight hill. The luminous white, flashing past, was mesmeric. It amplified distance, pushing the horizon outwards. Under a sky heavy with sleet, the car felt like a tiny silver beetle, exposed and easily squashed. At the brow of the hill, Janet became aware of giant white shapes against the sky. Six wind turbines stood, silent yet turning, like sentries watching her approach. She passed between them, their wings dipping towards her then rising. Then she headed into the village of Winterton-on-Sea.

The road drifted between the stone cottages until it petered out at a high ridge of dunes. Beneath them, across a stretch of beach, was the sea.

Janet slammed the door, her parked car rocking gently behind her. It was bitingly cold and the wind cut at her ears like a razor. The beach didn't look inviting. There was an ugliness about the freezing grey water, the way it churned a path up the snowy shore and left behind a dark slop of sand and stones. A few hardy souls were out walking, but even from the relative shelter of the dunes, she was finding the wind unbearable. She had pictured herself walking beside the sea to clear her head, calmed by its vast expanse, but the bleak Norfolk coast defeated her. Instead she headed to a weather-beaten cafe perched on the edge of the ridge, trussed up with plastic windbreakers.

It was surprisingly warm inside. She ordered a coffee and sat at a plastic table, her hands soon starting to sweat in her gloves. She was the only customer. From her corner, she watched the waitress fire up the coffee machine, her mind playing over the tape. There seemed no question now that John Helkin had been mentally ill by the end of his employment at Halvergate, and it was not the type of illness that could have gone unnoticed. Janet no longer felt surprised that the prison had tried to destroy all trace of him. The only question was why they'd let him work there so long.

She toyed with the yellow sugar bowl in front of her. The bars on her telephone flickered between one and zero. Not really enough signal to make a call. She started to text Steven. As she typed, another customer came in. She heard a woman's laugh. 'Stamp your feet, boy, don't bring all the snow in!'

Janet looked up. A plump woman with dyed red hair nodded at her and smiled. She was wrapped in layers of padded clothing, her round face as pink as her scarf. A small child with curly dark hair swung from her gloved hand, pulling her back towards the door. It opened again and a tall man stamped his way in, shaking off the snow. With a mock growl he swung towards the child and scooped him up in the air to delighted shrieking. Janet smiled in spite of herself.

'Your coffee?' the waitress called, raising the mug above the counter as if making a toast. Janet stood up, scraping her chair, and the man turned round. It was Terry.

They stared at each other. He looked completely different out of uniform; his cheeks flushed from the cold, his son squirming in his arms, the embers of his smile snuffed out by the sight of her.

'Terry?' the redhead asked, looking from one to the other. Her eyes were circled with electric blue eyeliner, giving her the quizzical expression of an owl.

'It's Dr Palmer, she's just started at Halvergate. The new psychologist,' Terry said, finally.

'Hi, I'm Janet.' She stepped forward, feeling awkward. He couldn't have looked less pleased to see her.

'Nikki,' she said, holding out her hand with a friendly smile entirely at odds with her husband's frozen expression. 'He's making you welcome, I hope?'

'Daddeeeeeee! I want a chocolate!' The boy began kicking his little legs, struggling to be put down.

'Not now, Jo, you've had two already, what about one of those buns?' Terry turned away from them to point at the counter, talking to his son.

'Why don't you join us?' Nikki ploughed on. 'Unless you're with someone?'

'I wouldn't want to—' Janet started.

'Of course you should, shouldn't she, Terry? Tel? Shouldn't she?'

'Mmph? Yes, of course.' Terry turned his back completely and busied himself putting an order in for tea and buns.

Nikki made a face, shaking her head. 'I don't know how you get on with all those men up there. Not the liveliest lot, are they?'

In twenty minutes with Nikki, Janet and Terry learned more about each other than either had managed to cough up over the previous weeks. Terry had met Nikki at school, he hadn't much wanted to go into the prison service, but it was a steady job and there wasn't anything else around. His wife wanted to go back to work as a teaching assistant, but it was hard finding the right post. In turn Janet found herself fielding questions about Arun and why she'd left Leyland. Terry looked like he wanted to stop Nikki's flow of questions, but any attempts he made to distract her were scuppered by Jo, who insisted on sitting on his father's knee and monopolising his attention.

'So you're all on your own here? All the way from London? That's no good. You should come round some time, shouldn't she, Tel, we're only up the coast at Scratby. You can tell me what goes on up there, what he gets up to. He never tells me anything.'

Terry opened his mouth to reply and Jo stuck a piece of soggy bun in it, giggling.

'Don't do that,' Nikki scolded, grabbing his small sugary hands and wiping them vigorously. Terry picked the piece of bun out of his mouth and surreptitiously put it under a napkin on the plate.

'So what does your boyfriend do again?'

'Medical research. At Imperial in London.' Janet had decided not to mention Arun's trip to America. Or their break-up.

'And he didn't mind you coming up here?'

'London's not so far away . . .' She trailed off. Even Terry was looking curiously at her now.

'Well, I hope Tel looks out for you.' Nikki turned towards her husband. 'You do, don't you?'

'Terry's been the most welcoming to me out of everyone at Halvergate,' Janet said. It wasn't technically a lie, but Terry had enough grace to look embarrassed. Nikki seemed pleased.

'That's good. I know they're not the friendliest. It was so hard for him after what happened to John. What a shame that was.' She sat back and sighed, shaking her head at Janet as if John Helkin was an old friend of hers too.

'Not now, Nikki,' Terry said.

'Well, it was a shame. Lovely man. He had such a high opinion of Terry. Gave him some extra training. He said he could have done what you're doing, psychology, I mean. Well, he did, Tel, there's no need to be shy about it. You're always putting yourself down.'

Janet smiled, trying to look at ease, as if she and Terry were in the habit of gossiping about her predecessor. 'So you knew John too?'

'He came round a few times. Lovely man. I can't bear to think of him out Peterborough way on his own. It's a shame.'

'Peterborough?' Janet said in surprise.

'You know what I mean, whatsit, that place outside, where the mental hospital is.'

'We have to go, he's getting really restless.' Terry pushed his chair back abruptly, swinging Jo up in the air so that he started wailing.

'Oh for goodness sake! Let me take him then. Sorry,' she said to Janet, and bundled Jo to the door to get his coat. Terry and Janet were left at the table.

'Psychiatric hospital?'

Terry just stared at her. She remembered Helkin captured and humiliated on Zara's tape and felt a sudden rush of rage. 'It's your fault,' she whispered with a viciousness that made him step back. 'You saw what he was like, you could have stepped in. Instead you let him get sicker and sicker and spread his delusions to all those men in his care. You're a coward.' Her voice broke slightly and she realised her hands were shaking. She headed to the door, shrugging on her coat as she walked.

'It was lovely to meet you,' she called to Nikki.

Before Terry's wife had time to answer, she shot rudely out into the snow, the door swinging backwards on the other woman's friendly goodbye.

25

In Steven's warm flat, steam collected on the edges of the window frames like indoor snow. The smell of fresh coffee rose from a metal pot balanced precariously on a coaster by his elbow. He poured himself a cup, spooning in extra sugar for comfort. In front of him sat a pile of books, fresh from the internet. They had been recommended to him by his tutor from theological college during a particularly embarrassing email exchange. He felt ridiculous even looking at their titles. *Demonology; a precise compendium*, *A history of Demons* and, most mortifying of all, *What's YOUR demon?*, a yellow, garish-looking volume from America. Since his second date with Dan, Steven had felt a little less fearful that Halvergate was haunted, but now he had the books, he might as well do the research.

He picked up the first volume, a 1920s encyclopaedia, in which demons were helpfully indexed under their associated sins. 'Self-murder' seemed a reasonable place to start. Steven sipped his coffee and began reading. He learned about the demons Acedia and Tristitia, most commonly associated with melancholy and suicide, but their medieval depiction, taking the form of sleeping men, didn't seem to fit with anything.

Self-murder was a bust, then. Next stop, rage. Interested in spite of himself, Steven looked up 'Wrath'. Here he met the familiar names of Satan and Moloch and then the unfamiliar Alecto.

ALECTO, Ancient Greek: Ἀληκτώ. One of the three ERINYES.

Steven paused. He heard David's voice. 'It sounded like ring yes, in yes . . .' With a sense of growing disbelief, he read on.

> *In Greek mythology this is the name given to the deities of vengeance; probably personified curses visited upon a guilty criminal, but possibly in their origin ghosts of the murdered; in Roman literature they are called Furies. The name Erinyes derives from the Greek erinô or ereunaô, I hunt or persecute, or from the Arcadian word erinuô, I am angry. Sometimes one Erinyes is mentioned, sometimes several. Euripides was the first to speak of them as three in number. Later Alexandrian writers gave them names; the first, Alecto, translates as unceasing in anger; of her two sisters, Tisiphone is vengeance, Megeara, grudge.*

Then Steven came across a line that made his heart stop.

> *In myth, the wrath of Alecto manifested itself in diverse ways, but the most severe was a tormenting madness, visited upon the accursed, which drove the remorseful to their deaths.*

'Shit,' Steven said, sitting back in his chair. He read the passage again to make sure he had understood. With a growing sense of disbelief, he scanned through the rest of the entry. He skipped over the details on how the Erinyes had crossed from classical mythology to the Christian tradition via Dante, and a brief description of Alecto's depiction in art, sometimes with black snakes for hair, dripping blood. Another passage caught his attention.

> *Though mostly silent figures, we can hear the voices of the Erinyes as imagined by Aeschylus in* The Oresteia *where, in a scene of great menace, the three sing* 'The Binding Song', *designed to drive the guilty protagonist to madness:*

> *Over our victims*
> *We sing this song, maddening the brain,*
> *Carrying away the sense, destroying the mind,*
> *A hymn that comes from the Erinyes,*
> *Fettering the mind, sung*
> *Without the lyre, withering to mortals.*

Steven put the book down. Whatever he had expected to find, it was not a near match for the hallucinations at Halvergate. He wanted to pray, but for the first time in years found he lacked the words. Instead he picked up his mobile and walked over to the window, scrolling down for his former tutor's number.

To his relief he heard her familiar clipped tones after a couple of rings.

'Yes?'

'Sarah, it's Steve.'

'Hey, how are you? Enjoying your demons?'

Steven wiped his sleeve against the condensation on the glass, back and forth, creating a space to see out. 'That's the thing. I'm not. Enjoying them, I mean. I'm crapping myself to be honest.'

'Why, what's happened?'

'It's those hallucinations I told you about. The angry woman some of the inmates and my psychologist friend have been seeing.' Steven leaned against the window, looking down at shoppers slipping and sliding along the snowy street. He ran a sweaty palm through his hair. 'I just found her in one of those books.'

There was a pause on the other end of the phone. 'Are you there?' 'Yes, I'm here.' Steven could hear her shuffling. 'Which demon is it?'

'Not something I'd ever heard of before. Alecto, from ancient Greek mythology. One of the three Furies.'

'Really?' Sarah sounded surprised. 'They're not strictly speaking even demons, not in the Christian tradition anyway, just stories from the classical age.'

Steven laughed. 'A few weeks ago, I'd have said all demons were "just stories". I *still* think that, but then why are all these people seeing the same thing?' He wandered back to the table, where the book lay open on the troubling page. 'I don't know what to do. I feel completely out of my depth. How can I be the right person to take on a demon if I'm not even sure I believe in it?'

'Disbelief's not a bad place to start. It may not be a demon. How similar are the descriptions in the book?'

'Not exactly the same, but similar enough. And their Greek name matches the Es found in various places where men have died. But it's not just that. There's something really wrong at Halvergate, the whole place feels wrong.' There was silence on the other end of the phone and Steven knew Sarah expected him to fill it. He looked at the photo of a Greek vase on the page. It showed a stylised woman with wings and snakes for hair. 'Maybe it's not a demon,' he said. 'I've heard the place has a drugs problem. But I don't think this is only about some stoned inmates. It feels like everyone at Halvergate is frightened. The staff are creepy, the inmates all seem scared, nobody ever cracks a smile. It's an awful place.'

'There's another minister, isn't there? Have you tried talking to him?'

'Father Dunstan? Yeah, but he's a really old guy, retired. He only comes in once a fortnight or so. He looks like he might have a heart attack any minute. I wouldn't want to worry him with all this.'

'And the psychologist?'

'Janet.' Steven thought about her laughter as they got drunk together in his flat, singing along to his records. She had felt like an old friend that night. But he also remembered her face, full of grief, when he first saw her in the chapel. 'She's more of a friend,' he began, hesitantly. 'But not the ideal person to talk to about this. She's got a lot to deal with, personal stuff. And she seems a bit conflicted about what she believes. About the Church, I mean.'

Sarah snorted. 'Aren't we all? The point is, you do need to discuss this with somebody sensible, and she sounds like your best bet. I think the thing is not to be so hung up on the idea of demons, and whether they exist or not. We *know* evil exists, we know it's powerful and we know it mustn't be underestimated. You don't have to understand everything about this. It's not up to you, it's up to God. The only thing you can do is to pray for guidance, pray for God's grace, and pray for His protection for Janet, and all the others who are being troubled by whatever this is.'

Steven swallowed. 'Thanks. I appreciate that. Could we pray together now? I've been struggling with what to say.'

'Of course we can. And Steven? I'm always here. Always.'

Janet stood in John Helkin's old house. The air felt heavy with his absence; all that was left of him were meaningless fragments, like the ugly ceramic head. She walked to the cabinet and cupped its face with her hands before tracing the line of the frontal cortex with her finger. There was something pathetic about it now she knew its owner was in a psychiatric hospital.

She stared into the blank porcelain irises, badly drawn in blue paint. 'What put you there?' she asked.

The head gazed back at her, pop-eyed and vacant. Suddenly she didn't want it up on the mantelpiece like some sort of shrine to Cherry Tree Drive's last tenant. It could go in the airing cupboard and keep company with Helkin's shirts.

She scooped it up, leaving a clear circle in the dust where it had sat. Turning it over to examine the grime, she saw it had an air hole on the base. At the same time, she heard a gentle thunk, as if something had dropped against the inside of the skull. Surprised, Janet shook it. The blank face gave off a gentle rattling, as if something small and hard was bouncing off the china inside. The noise continued in her ears even after she stopped shaking the figurine and it was motionless in her hands. It was probably nothing, she told herself; perhaps a piece of china broken off and trapped inside the cheap cast. She lifted the head, sliding it back and forth above her, and saw a glint of red plastic as it dropped from side to side. It looked like a USB stick.

Janet felt unsteady. She walked to the sofa, gripping the head to her stomach as she sat down, her knees wobbling. Lifting it again, she scrabbled her finger round and round the hole in the base. The edges of the ceramic were rough and it was impossible to get a grip on the solid sliver of plastic rattling about inside.

She put the bust down on the floor and walked to the kitchen. In a dusty cupboard under the sink she found a small saucepan, the Teflon burnt from its base. Janet took it into the living room and knelt by the head. Guilt made her pause with the saucepan raised mid-air above the ceramic cranium. Memories of Helkin's haunted expression on Zara's tape caught at her arm, reducing the force of her blow. A clang, and the head cracked over the medulla. Janet screwed up her face and brought the saucepan down again, hard. The skull crumpled inwards, fragments breaking off like the shards of a novelty Easter egg. She shook the head gently upside down and pieces of porcelain and white powder scattered everywhere. In among the broken pottery sat the memory stick. Janet picked it up and blew the dust off. Gingerly, as if it might burn whatever it touched, she placed it on the coffee table.

Without bothering to clear up the mess, Janet sat on the sofa and powered up her laptop. It cranked into life, limping online with the aid of her super-slow broadband. She looked at the wavering bars of her connection. Helkin's paranoia must be infectious, she thought, as she disconnected her computer from the internet. When the screen had finished blinking at her, she inserted the flash drive.

Two folders came up. One blank, the other titled 'Confidential'. Janet clicked on the second. Up came row after row of files, named after the prisoners in her care, along with a few other names she didn't recognise. Scrolling down, Janet clicked at random on a prisoner's file. Inside, she saw, Helkin had scanned in all his handwritten notes. They appeared to make up a body of information on almost every inmate in his care, which would take her hours to work through. Overwhelmed, Janet leaned back. Considering the possibility that Helkin's notes had been destroyed was one thing, but having the proof was another matter.

For a moment she felt too afraid to read on, as if she might hear a knock at the door and see Richard waiting outside. She put the computer down, crossed to the window and pulled the curtains, shutting out the possibility of prying eyes. Sitting back down, she saw that her hands were trembling with adrenalin. She breathed out, fastening her hair back into a tighter ponytail, trying to calm herself.

Before ploughing through the notes, she decided, she would check out the blank folder. Inside sat a single untitled Word document. Janet opened it. It was a copy of an email sent to Lee Webster, dated six months previously.

Dear Lee,

I must request an urgent meeting with you regarding my concerns about the mandatory drugs testing procedure (MDT) at HMP Halvergate.

I have received allegations from one of the prisoners that, on several occasions, the randomly generated list of men required for testing was not followed. Instead 'safe' urine samples were supplied by prisoners who were known to be drug-free.

Mark Conybeer, an inmate on the VP wing, has complained to me that he became suspicious after being asked to give a sample almost every month, but was promised access to a smartphone in return for keeping quiet about it. The prison officer in question, Keith Lawson, apparently never gave him the promised phone, which is why Mark reported the situation to me.

Mark claims another inmate, Ahmed Ali, has also been
supplying urine samples with suspicious frequency, though
Mr Ali denies this.

I can only conclude, therefore, that there is a high risk that
the MDT data has been doctored.

I'm aware Halvergate has a low positive rate in its MDT,
and has been doing well in this particular key performance
target, which will make the discovery all the more
disappointing to you. But as I have suggested before, the
positive rate in the prison does not seem to match the
number of inmates I have come across who appear to be
symptomatic for substance abuse.

I know you will want to start a formal investigation into
this matter, and would welcome your instructions on how you
wish me to proceed.

John

Janet read the letter again. The written voice rang out in her
head, clear, hard, dispassionate. Nothing in it seemed to fit with
the deranged figure from Zara's interview. There was no absolute
proof that the email was genuine. Yet somehow she knew he had
sent it – and that Lee had read it. She thought about Keith
Lawson, the man who had left her alone with Baz Gridley. If
Mark had been telling Helkin the truth, it wasn't surprising that
Baz's tests had come back clean. Keith was clearly adept at
swapping urine samples.

She clicked back on the prisoners' files, scrolling down to the
names that might hold some answers. She typed Mark Conybeer's
surname into the search bar. References to him came up in a
couple of other men's files, but nothing for Mark himself. She
searched again. Nothing. With a sinking feeling she typed in
Ahmed Ali. No files were present.

Next she entered the names of Ryan Spalding and the other
men who had committed suicide. Only one appeared, Liam
Smith, who had died a few days before Helkin left. The notes

extended to just a couple of pages, with no observations to suggest Liam was at risk of self-harm.

In frustration, Janet typed in the name of another man who might hold some answers. Michael Donovan. This time, to her relief, the computer revealed a sizeable file. She started with Helkin's executive summary of his patient, dated four months before the interview with Zara Hyde.

Serious questions remain as to whether Halvergate is a suitable environment for Michael, though Richard argues, with some merit, that a secure hospital might diminish any chance of rehabilitation still further.

The man is highly manipulative and not only shows no remorse for his offending behaviour, but appears to have little ability, or willingness, to empathise. This is all the more troubling given his formidable intelligence. It remains uncertain as to whether group therapy is doing more harm than good, since MD exercises an unwholesome influence during sessions. No history or evidence of substance abuse.

Janet skimmed through the notes, which started a short time before the date of the first recorded suicide. They were all scanned copies of Helkin's handwritten papers, written in the same uneven hand as the scrawled '*unaffected*' she had found in the official prison files. The first notes were dry and unexceptional, telling her nothing surprising, but then one entry caught her eye.

June 18th. MD has agreed to help me work on treating his fellow inmates' delusions. Proceeding with caution. Tried hypnotherapy but MD appeared entirely resistant to its effects. Prisoner asked me to teach him how to perform self-hypnosis. Interesting discussion on the real versus the imagined.
June 25th. MD seems amused by hypnotherapy. As yet no impact.

July 5th. Further sessions of hypnotherapy. Prisoner's attitude bordering on antagonistic.

July 19th. MD reported to me that he is suffering from the same hallucinations of the woman that have been troubling other men on his landing. Unlike others, he exhibits no distress over the delusions. Have ceased hypnotherapy sessions.

July 28th. MD speaks constantly of the woman, who he now calls the white visitor. Keeps asking if I have seen her. Seems unmoved by Kyle Reeder's death, despite Kyle being one of his closest associates.

August 15th. MD delights in tormenting me. Not a session passes without mention of the white visitor. At the last group meeting, MD claimed I am responsible for summoning her. Mark Conybeer became so incensed Terry had to restrain him from attacking me.

August 20th. Advised MD be placed in isolation. Overruled.

August 27th. MD admitted his own delusions were faked. He mocked the power of the white visitor, mocked my attempts at hypnosis. He is afraid of nothing.

August 31st. Confronted MD with his lack of remorse. Warned him neither of us could let it pass. She will repay.

September 8th. Are you reading this, Michael? I put nothing past you. How long do you think you can remain unaffected by her rage?

The handwriting became increasingly erratic as time passed. The last note was written a month before Zara captured Helkin's madness on camera. Janet scrolled through the rest of Donovan's file, trying to find anything from Helkin's last weeks at the prison, but there was nothing. The remainder looked like it was made up of official documents, some of which she had already received from the Courts Service, though Helkin had also managed to get hold of the pre-sentencing psychiatric report and a victim impact statement from Donovan's girlfriend, Karina Okafor.

Putting the laptop down carefully, Janet brought her feet up on to the sofa and curled them under her, hugging her knees. On the floor lay the shattered remnants of Helkin's head. She would have to be careful not to cut herself.

The garbled notes were hard to decipher, but it seemed Michael had been telling the truth about the hypnotherapy sessions. But where she had suspected the prisoner of being in league with the psychologist, it appeared the opposite was true. If anything, Michael seemed to have gloated over the psychologist's breakdown, tormenting Helkin with his inability to implant delusions in him via hypnosis.

Then there was the drugs email to Lee, which must have occurred before the psychologist suffered a full-blown mental health crisis, and opened the possibility of serious corruption at the prison. There was no way she could ask Mark or Ahmed about the allegations since they were both dead. Janet felt cold as the implications sank in.

The deletion of Helkin's notes was a disciplinary offence, and whoever was responsible would surely only have risked their career in order to hide something even more serious. Her gut told her that it hadn't been John Helkin. Although they were deeply incriminating, to have made the notes at all he must have lacked insight into his own illness. And everything about them, their unlikely hiding place, the time it must have taken to scan so many pages, even while his own sanity unravelled, all suggested that he was trying to preserve his records, not erase them. And that meant he knew somebody else wanted to make sure they disappeared.

Janet ejected the USB stick. It looked so small, like a red pebble in the palm of her hand. She knew that she was not going to report her discovery. Not until she had spoken to Helkin himself.

26

Terry was sitting alone in the staff canteen, his tall frame hunched over. Janet watched him as she waited for the coffee machine to kick in. The stooped figure was unrecognisable as the man who had burst into the cafe at Winterton, swinging his son in the air. She couldn't remember the last time she had seen Terry with anyone else at work, and thought again about his friendship with Helkin, all the time they must have spent together.

She had found it difficult to get through that morning's group session. While Majid told his story she had kept getting distracted, wondering what part Terry might have played in the cover-up. She had spent her Sunday reading through more of Helkin's notes, and his regard for Terry had become obvious. Several entries recorded Terry's observations with approval. Michael's comment about Helkin's 'little helper' played over and over in her mind.

Janet jabbed at the coffee machine, the hot milk and steam gurgling into her cup. Anger congealed in her stomach, cold and unsavoury like fat left overnight in a roasting pan. She fixed a smile on her face and walked to Terry's table, banging the chair as she sat down.

'Lovely to meet Nikki the other day.' Terry looked up, startled. She continued to stare at him, the fake smile still in place, and was pleased to see him glance away, unsettled. 'Don't worry. I'm not going to ask anything else about John. Not today anyway.' Terry looked down at his milky tea. 'I wanted to talk to you about Michael. I think we need to be particularly careful. I had a look through Helkin's notes and it seems he felt Michael was something of a troublemaker.'

Terry's mouth hung slightly ajar as she spoke. 'But I thought you said John hadn't left any notes.'

'He didn't leave many, it's true, but a few here and there.' She took a sip from her latte, leaving a frothy moustache on her upper lip. 'More on Michael than anyone else. I'm sure I mentioned that.' She frowned, wiping her mouth. 'I'd like to start one-to-one sessions with him. We'd need to go through all the usual procedures so I can set aside a time every couple of weeks. Could you set that up for this afternoon?'

Terry seemed to turn paler beneath his freckles.

'Anyway, enough about work. How was the rest of your weekend with Nikki and Jo?' Janet sat back in her chair, watching him. But Terry didn't look thrown; instead he started to laugh.

'What is it?'

'All this talk of Michael Donovan.' He shook his head. 'I think you should be careful how much time you spend together. You're even starting to sit like him.'

Janet walked down the corridor, her shoes squeaking on the linoleum, shadow wavering before her, the waxy blue floor shining in the overhead lights. On the way back to her office, she passed a couple of prison officers who neither looked nor smiled at her. For the first time since arriving at Halvergate, she didn't try to make eye contact, didn't mumble a greeting, just shouldered past them, her face as stony as theirs. In her mind she severed another rope that tied her to her old professional self, drifted a little further. She pictured John Helkin walking behind her, following, his tread silent on the shiny floor.

Janet buzzed herself through from D to A block, heading in the direction of the mandatory testing coordinator's office. She had tried going past earlier this morning, but the room had been occupied. At lunchtime there was a chance she might find it empty.

This time the door was closed. She knocked gently. No answer. Turning the handle, she slipped inside, pulling the latch shut with a click.

She stood for a moment, half-expecting the door to swing open. Then, with a long intake of breath, like a swimmer before a dive, she headed over to the desk. On it sat a printout of the month's randomly generated list of men to be tested. Janet began opening drawers and rifling through papers.

A filing cabinet sat in the corner. Her hands sweating, she pulled out the first drawer, leafing through the folders. The spot between her shoulder blades began to burn at the point where she imagined the officer would see her when he walked back through the door. She didn't stop, making her way steadily down the cabinet, kneeling on the floor to get to the bottom drawer. Here, at last, her gamble was rewarded.

The drawer held printouts of randomly generated lists going back several years. She flicked back through the pages, back to the months when Mark Conybeer and Ahmed Ali were still alive. Without pausing to think, Janet grabbed several of the sheets, folding them and stuffing them in the back pocket of her trousers.

She stood up, crossing the room as quickly as possible, then hesitated. There was no point sneaking out, or trying to check if the coast was clear. That would look too obvious. Grasping the handle, she opened the door, stepping out purposefully into the corridor. She walked straight ahead, using all her willpower not to look behind and check if anyone had seen her.

Back in her own office, she didn't dare take the papers out again. Their bulk pressed against her as she sat down. Pushing the hair behind her ears, she logged back on to her computer and saw she had an email from Steven.

Free tonight? Can do mine or yours? Sx.

Janet hesitated. Sitting there with stolen documents in her trousers, she wasn't sure she wanted to see him. Part of her longed to tell him everything; but at the same time she didn't know whether she could trust him to keep it quiet, or whether his moral compass would insist on her reporting her discovery immediately, which she had no intention of doing. That had hardly gone well for John Helkin. But there was no rule that said she had to tell Steven everything, and she couldn't avoid her only friend in Norfolk indefinitely. Janet typed back.

> Let's do mine. There's a chippie in Halverton, we can get a
> takeaway and you don't even have to risk my cooking. Janet x

His response came back immediately, making her smile.

> Only if they do gravy S x

She checked her watch. Still some time before the lunch break ended. Janet took out a piece of paper with a number on it. An internet search last night had led her to the only psychiatric hospital within a twenty-mile radius of Peterborough. She picked up the phone, tapping through the automated options until she got through to reception.

'Orton Hospital, how can I help you?'

'Hi there, this is Nikki Saunders. My husband Terry sometimes visits John Helkin, who's staying with you at the minute.' The lie sweated through her palms, making the receiver slippery. Please God let it pay off, let him have visited. Janet cleared her throat. 'The thing is, he's asked me just to check when his next visit is. We think it might clash with a school event for our son.'

'Just a moment please.' The receptionist put her on hold and a recording of the 'Ode to Joy' looped round and round in her ear.

'Mrs Saunders? There's no visit scheduled from your husband.'

'Right, thanks,' said Janet, her heart sinking.

'I can see from the visitors' log that he last visited over a month ago, but you can tell him he just needs to call the day before, next time he wants to come. I'm sure John would love to see him any time.'

'Thanks,' said Janet. 'I'll tell him. Thanks very much.'

As she put down the receiver, she had the feeling somebody was watching her. She turned, and there in the window, just a faint outline, was a white face with dark eyes, its expression blurred but unmistakably malevolent. Janet let out a cry and stood up, scraping back her chair. The figure moved with her, and she was about to flee when she realised it was only her own reflection, made indistinct by the grey light of the afternoon. 'Jesus Christ,' she breathed, sitting back down again. Halvergate was destroying her nerves.

When Michael came for his first remedial session late that afternoon, Janet made sure she had drawn the blinds, so that the window was screened from view as she poured them both coffee.

'So you made good on your offer,' Michael said. 'Or was it a threat?' He had flopped back in his chair, one foot resting on the small plastic table near the sugar bowl.

'You don't look like a man who's under threat,' said Janet, putting down his mug.

'Perhaps I'm just better than most at hiding my fear.'

'Of course, I was forgetting your brother. You don't like people showing any weakness.' Janet could still feel the printouts in her pocket as she leaned back in her chair. 'How did you manage all those sessions with Dr Helkin? Last time we met you told me he was even more frightened than the prisoners.'

Michael studied her face. 'Terror is never attractive,' he said at last. 'And that's what he became.' He raised the mug to his lips. 'Afraid of his own shadow.'

'And yet you continued with the hypnotherapy?'

'It passed the time.'

Janet looked at him, sensing the animosity beneath his relaxed pose. 'You must have known what Helkin was up to, the delusions he was planting. Why didn't you report him?' Michael said nothing, only smiled. 'Or did you enjoy what he was doing? Watching all those men die?'

Michael shrugged. 'Perhaps I didn't report him because I thought he had a point.'

'A point?' Janet frowned. 'I thought you said you didn't believe in demons?'

'Not in demons,' said Michael, his blue eyes fixed on hers. 'In evil.' He stretched his arms above his head, looking up at the print of Thomas More above them. 'Ever heard of the noonday devil, Janey? You should, as a good little fan of More.'

Janet lifted the mug, hiding part of her face from view. 'Perhaps you can remind me.'

'Thomas More described the noonday devil as the one who attacks in plain sight. The most dangerous threat of all. So I'll repeat myself. I don't believe in demons, but I do believe in evil.' He lowered his voice. 'It's everywhere in Halvergate. Haven't you felt it? Helkin did.'

Janet said nothing, and Michael smiled.

Steven stood outside the chip shop, illuminated by a pool of light from the window, clutching his greasy parcel. He had a multicoloured pom-pom hat on, pulled down low, almost covering his eyes. He knew it made him look like a teenager, but was too cold to care.

'I thought you said there was gravy?'

'I can make you some Bisto at home,' Janet offered.

'Bisto on chips?' He looked at her as if she'd just offered to piss on his dinner instead.

'Come on.' Janet gave him her arm, and they walked slowly along the slippery pavement back to Cherry Tree Drive. They passed the pub and the Londis, the only other shops in the village besides the chippie. The snow had started to thaw, losing its glistening whiteness, leaving behind a trail of sludge. In the gloom, a single orange street light only served to highlight the darkness outside its feeble reach. Steven and Janet trudged past a row of semis until they came to a stop outside Number 14's unlovely front.

Steven squinted up as Janet let them into the damp hallway. He stomped the slush off his boots. 'I hate this place. Why don't I try and scare away one of the tenants above the gallery, make unwanted advances or something, so you can move in there?'

'Thanks, nice plan.' Janet kicked off her own boots and headed down the hallway in search of plates and cutlery. She called back, 'Shall we just eat off our knees in the main room? The kitchen's so depressing.'

Installed on the sofa and stuffing themselves with chips, they sat for a while in companionable silence. Deprived of gravy, Steven instead covered everything with ketchup.

'I needed that,' he said with a sigh when he'd finished. He looked at Janet, still eating her cod, and wondered whether it was the right moment to bring up the topic he'd been avoiding. 'I've been having a think about our old friend the velnius.'

'Oh?' Janet's head was bent over the bundle of chips, making it hard to see what she was thinking.

'I've been chatting to somebody in the police about it—'

'You've gone to the police?' Now he had her full attention.

'Not in an official capacity, no. I'm kind of seeing somebody. Who happens to be a policeman.'

'Oh right,' she said. Janet looked a bit downcast by the news. He supposed she must be missing Arun. 'Is he nice?'

'Yes, I think so. It's early days,' he replied. 'But anyway Dan told me that drugs might have been involved in the suicides. Apparently a bag of spice was found in a cell, but then it went walkabout. He thinks the police are covering for Halvergate and didn't want to embarrass Lee.'

'There might be something in that,' Janet said. 'Not as a cause of the suicides, but it could explain why everyone at the place is so cagey.' She hesitated, looking uncertain about whether to go on.

'What is it?' he said.

'Can this stay between us? I don't want to go to the authorities until I've got more information.'

'Of course,' he said, hoping he wasn't agreeing to anything he'd regret.

'I found some of Helkin's stuff, including a letter about his suspicions that mandatory drugs tests were being falsified. One of the men on the VP wing claimed he and another guy had been giving clean urine samples.'

Steven raised his eyebrows. 'That's serious,' he said. 'But somehow less surprising than it should be. Have you had a chance to talk to them about it?'

'Bit difficult,' said Janet. 'They're both dead.'

'Bloody hell.' Steven put his greasy plate on the chipped lacquer table. 'You don't think . . .' He couldn't bring himself to finish the sentence. He could believe staff at Halvergate were bent – expected it even – but murder was another matter.

'No,' said Janet. 'It did cross my mind, but really, it wouldn't be worth the risk. And it was only one guy making the allegations. The other denied it. Much easier to bribe one into silence than murder two.'

'Who were they?'

'Mark Conybeer and Ahmed Ali. And this is the thing, I think we've got proof. I had a chance to go through C-NOMIS on the computer system this afternoon. It logs exactly what every inmate in the prison was doing on any given day and it looks like Mark, the one who made the allegations, really was telling the truth.' Janet spoke so fast, Steven had difficulty following her. She had sat forward and was perched right on the edge of the sofa in her eagerness to explain.

'I don't understand. How can you tell?'

Janet gestured impatiently. 'I told you, C-NOMIS tracks everyone's movements. A couple of the guys on the randomly generated list for March and April last year couldn't possibly have given urine samples when they were supposed to – one was in court on that day and another was attending a family funeral. That means somebody else provided their samples instead. And there's something else,' she said, thumping the sofa cushion for emphasis. 'If Mark and Ahmed were both clean, drugs can't have been behind their suicides.'

Steven shrugged. 'Though legal highs don't show up in urine tests.'

'True. But if you're going to falsify a load of drugs tests, I don't think you'd want to take the gamble that your clean guys had dabbled in something else. You'd go for men who didn't touch the stuff. At all.' Janet pushed her own half-eaten meal aside, flopping back on the grubby sofa. 'But then I don't understand why Helkin would pick Mark and Ahmed to hypnotise. They were his witnesses, after all. Although I guess if he knew somebody else was already manipulating them, he might think they were suggestible, easy targets,' she said. 'Also Helkin's notes suggest Mark tried to attack him, so maybe he just didn't like the guy.'

'So you still think Helkin's behind the delusions?'

'Why, you're not still thinking it's something supernatural, are you?'

Steven looked at her. There were dark circles under her eyes, and her hair looked like it needed a wash. Every time he saw her, she seemed less like the woman who had sung along to his 90s records and more like the distracted figure he had first met in the chapel. 'Sort of. Not exactly. Don't laugh, but I've done a bit of research on demons.' He stole a glance at her and noticed she didn't look as dismissive as she had the last time he raised the subject. Steven wasn't sure if this was a good sign. 'It looks like our white visitor has some similarities to the Erinyes, also known as the Furies. In ancient myth they hounded the guilty to suicide, driving them mad with remorse.'

'Demons of vengeance?' said Janet. 'Well, I guess it would explain the E.'

'You're taking the idea seriously?' Steven was not at all comforted by the thought of such a sceptical person embracing the idea of a haunting so easily.

'Of demons? No, I don't think so,' said Janet. 'Though this place does make you start to wonder.' Her gaze travelled to the window behind him. He turned and looked at the black glass, but there was nothing there. She shook her head and started speaking again. 'What I meant was Helkin might have known about the Furies and drawn on that knowledge when he hypnotised the men.'

'And you really think a belief in this Fury could be spread by hypnosis?' Steven cracked open the beer he had bought at the chippie, sipping it cold from the can.

'I've never heard of shared psychosis being spread that way,' Janet admitted. 'But it has to be induced by somebody very charismatic or authoritative within a group dynamic, and as the inmates' psychologist, Helkin would fit that bill. Also he didn't manage it with all his patients.'

'How do you know?'

'One of the guys, Michael Donovan, told me Helkin tried hypnosis on him but it didn't work. And in the notes I found, he's raving about the fact he made no impact on him. Seems Michael enjoyed tormenting Helkin with his failure.'

'That's the same guy who told you about the E, isn't it?'

'Yes.' Janet grimaced. 'I'm not surprised hypnosis didn't work on him. I've never met anyone who so clearly bears all the traits of a psychopath.' She stopped and for a moment Steven thought she was going to say something else.

'What?' he asked.

'Oh, it's nothing,' she said. 'He's just a nasty piece of work, that's all. Nothing I can't handle.'

Steven sat back, propping his feet on the coffee table and taking another swig of beer. 'Shame we're never going to be able to ask Helkin about all this,' he said.

Janet smiled. 'That's something else I've been meaning to tell you. I've found him.'

'Found who?'

'John Helkin. He's in Peterborough, at a psychiatric hospital. I've got an appointment to see him tomorrow.'

* * *

In bed that night, John Helkin refused to leave Janet's mind. In the darkness every shadow on the wall recalled the grey pallor of his face, the black silhouette he cast in Zara's interview. She heard his voice, the rasping smoker's tones, reciting his deranged note to Michael. *'How long do you think you can remain unaffected by her rage?'*

Janet tossed on the uncomfortable mattress, wondering if Helkin had lain in the same lumpy indentations, wishing there was somewhere else to sleep. She closed her eyes, trying to blot him out, but when she did a deeper dread overshadowed her. She remembered his words to Zara, his description of the white visitor leaning over him as he slept. Behind her closed lids she had the sense of being watched. In her mind she saw the pale face from the mirror leaning above her. She did not open her eyes.

27

In the distance Janet could see a squat row of buildings resting at the side of the road. It was hard to tell how close they were; the fens stretched out impossibly far and flat on all sides, making space hard to judge. As she drew nearer, she saw that one was a dilapidated service station and slowed down. This was not a road where she wanted to run out of fuel.

As she pulled in, she passed a large, barn-style building, covered in corrugated iron. Painted across the side ran the message, 'Adult Lingerie Store'. It was the third sex shop she'd seen on the Norwich to Peterborough route. She stared at it as she filled up the Mini. The place was falling apart, its windows so covered in grime it was hard to see inside. An old purple bra, which looked like it was made of plastic, hung on display, motionless. Janet was reminded of the dead chickens and pheasants she used to see as a child, hanging by their necks at the butchers.

'Somethin catch yer eye?'

A man at the pump opposite leered at her. Janet sliced through his head with her middle-distance stare, focusing on the meter ticking upwards behind him. She stood there, unmoving, unblinking, until he looked away.

Back on the road she gripped the wheel. Sinkholes at the edge of the tarmac steered her closer to the centre, tipping her wing mirrors within striking distance of the cars flashing past. She pressed down on the accelerator, the car lurching from side to side as she hurtled over the uneven surface. An oncoming truck honked and swerved to avoid her.

She hadn't always been a dangerous driver. When she was

seventeen, it would have been difficult to find anyone more meticulous on the road. It had been one of the first points of difference between her and Izzy, her desperation to get behind the wheel. Izzy hadn't seen the point when the tube could take them everywhere and they couldn't afford their own car anyway. She would sit cross-legged on the bed, watching Janet with a puzzled frown as she crossed off the days on the calendar to their seventeenth birthday. Janet had passed her test first time, then spent most weekends pleading with their parents to let her borrow the car. The speed, the control, the effortless grace of driving, so unlike the jagged clumsiness she felt in her own body, all mirrored the pride she felt in her rational mind. She'd change gear with the precision with which she marshalled her thoughts for an essay, putting her foot down, moving into fifth.

To show off, in the summer before their A-levels she would drive them both out to Kent, just so they could sit with their books in a field and revise in the open air. In Janet's memory those afternoons were all filled with sunshine, grasses waving overhead as they spread out their files and wasted time dozing and gossiping rather than revising. Still, it hadn't ignited any yearning to drive in Izzy. She would yawn and stretch on the journey home, and promise that she'd learn after university, when the pair of them could club together for a car. She died without having taken a single driving lesson.

Years later, when Janet finally heard the thump of her first car's door close behind her and the tick-tock of the indicator as she pulled out, everything felt different. She was no longer the person whose mind could casually change gear, or overtake at speed. Instead she felt herself hurtling on without knowing if the brakes would hold. Her driving took on an obsessive quality. At night, when she couldn't sleep, she would get in the car. Her speeding wasn't conscious, but with each journey it seemed she travelled faster, until on one journey at three in the morning, on a deserted Kent road, she'd realised she was travelling at 110 miles an hour and the car could go no faster.

The scream of the engine, protesting against the accelerator, had filled her ears. She recognised it as the sound of her heart. She turned off the lights, took her foot off the pedal and let go of the wheel. For a few moments she felt nothing, a pause as the car continued to plunge onwards like a blinded horse. Then the road shifted to the left and she charged off the tarmac, smashing through a fence. The car lurched through the grassy field, tipping her violently from side to side before finally coming to a stop.

The fence saved her life. Its obliteration on impact decelerated the car and prevented it from rolling. Everyone said it was a miracle that she'd survived, a broken arm her only serious injury. Nobody said the words 'attempted suicide'. Instead she read it as an accusation in her parents' eyes and felt it in the pressure of Arun's grip as he held her hand in the hospital. He never asked her to explain herself, never reproached her, but the car crash sat between them, another yawning crater opening up to lengthen the widening chasm left by Izzy's death.

Janet had no idea if she had meant to die or not. She decided after the crash that she would never kill herself, not because life held any great appeal, but because even in those brief few seconds when she let go and closed her eyes she had felt no closer to her sister. Even in death, she would not get Izzy back.

That loneliness surrounded her like armour now, on the journey to Peterborough. The satnav directed her off the main road and she slowed down as the side road sank slightly to the level of the fields. The earth of the fens was a startling shade of black, as if all the normal accessories of a landscape – hills, houses, woods – had been incinerated, leaving nothing but the scorched soil behind. The road grew steadier and a few dotted farmhouses came into view. She saw the red arrow of the satnav come to rest forty metres ahead, near a straggling row of trees.

You have reached your destination.

Janet slowed to a stop. A modern block, like a university halls of residence, was just visible at the end of a driveway beyond the branches. She edged closer and saw that fencing and an automated barrier prevented her from driving straight in. She leaned out of the window and pressed the button.

'Hello?'

'It's Nikki Saunders. I have an appointment to visit John Helkin.'

The barrier rose.

Janet was the only person sitting on the row of immaculate white chairs in the pale yellow waiting room. Every surface shone as if still wet with disinfectant. A receptionist, screened behind plate glass, looked discreetly at her computer rather than stare at the solitary visitor. Janet felt tense. She had never called in sick to steal a day off work before, and she kept expecting to see somebody from Halvergate. Though truancy was the least of the deceptions she was practising today.

A swish and the secure doors to her left opened.

'Mrs Saunders?'

She started at the name, then jumped to her feet and shook hands with the nurse. Pretty dark curls framed her round face, which dimpled as she smiled.

'I'm Laura. It's so nice you've come. John doesn't get many visitors.'

Janet gave a tense grimace that could almost pass for a smile.

They stepped into the lift. It clunked shut, leaving them to stand together with the awkwardness of strangers trapped in a confined space, unsure whether to talk or not. Nerves wiped Janet's mind blank of any possible conversation anyway. As the lift passed each floor, her heartbeat quickened. She had no plan of action if Helkin reacted badly when he saw an unfamiliar figure, rather than Terry's wife, walk through the door.

Laura guided her out on to the third floor. 'He's in the day room.'

They walked in. Light streamed into the beige, modern room, whose sofas and chairs couldn't quite shake off the careful arrangement of a clinical setting. Boredom hung in the air. A woman of indeterminate age sat mumbling softly to herself in an armchair by the window, while two young men watched sport at a low volume on the TV. Janet hesitated, unsure what to do. Then she saw him, hunched away in a corner, reading a newspaper. He looked much smaller than he had on Zara's tape.

'There you go, John, your visitor's here.'

He turned to look at her, blinked with surprise. Then an expression Janet had never expected to see flickered across his eyes. Recognition.

'It's you,' he whispered, wonder on his face.

The nurse beamed, giving Janet's arm a squeeze. 'I'll leave you to it.'

Her footsteps faded, and still Janet stood rooted to the spot. Halvergate's two psychologists stared at each other.

'I knew you'd come,' he said.

She crossed over and sat in a chair opposite him. He continued to gaze at her, tears welling at the corners of his eyes. She noticed his hands had the distinctive tremor of the heavily medicated, and his skin was so dry it looked thin, as if his defences against the outside world had been eroded. His vulnerability pained her. She forced herself to remember that he was most likely responsible for the suicides of several men, not to mention her own nightmares, and that deceiving him was necessary.

'How do you know me?' she said.

Fear and confusion clouded his face. 'No. I don't know you. Who are you?'

'I'm doing your job, John,' she said, taking hold of one trembling hand. 'I'm the new psychologist at Halvergate.'

He drew back, his fingers limp in hers. 'Did Halvergate send you?'

'No. They don't know I'm here.'

'Where's Nikki?'

'She's not here. I had to use her name. I'm sorry. I didn't think they'd let me see you otherwise.'

'You can't trust them,' he said. 'You can't be too careful.'

He gripped her hand. She didn't know if he was referring to staff at Halvergate or Orton Hospital. To her discomfort, she realised they were now whispering, leaning close, heads together like two crazy conspirators. John Helkin shuffled even further forward in his chair. 'I was starting to think I'd imagined the place; that maybe Halvergate was all in my mind.'

The grim building loomed up in Janet's own imagination. 'It's there. It exists.'

'Does it? You can't imagine what it's like in here.' He tapped his head. 'I feel sorrier for my more disturbed prisoners now I understand them a little better.' He turned his face from hers. 'Not that it matters. I'll never practise psychology again.'

As he spoke, fear and lucidity flickered across his face, like the light and shadow thrown by a candle. She steeled herself for another lie.

'I found your notes,' she said. 'They're a credit to your dedication. I see no reason why you shouldn't practise again, once you're well, once you help me expose whatever the management were doing.'

Helkin stared at her. 'How did you find them?' She saw hope in his eyes. 'Was it Terry? I thought he might have kept copies.'

Janet felt sorry to disappoint him. 'It was thanks to Halvergate's HR department recommending your old place to me when I got the job. I came across them by chance. I'm afraid I had to destroy that figurine you hid them in. I hope you don't mind.'

His sallow face was transformed by delight. 'My God, I thought Slaney would have thrown that stuff away! She certainly never replied to any of my requests to send me my shirts. I thought it had all ended up in a car boot sale.' He let out a harsh bark of laughter. 'There wasn't much time for me to collect everything when I left. Being sectioned doesn't exactly give you a great deal of space to plan.'

'What happened to the originals?'

'What do you think?' He sat back in his chair, and for the first time since she had arrived, she saw a trace of the professional assurance he must once have possessed.

'I suspect somebody, perhaps Richard, destroyed them?'

Helkin nodded. 'I must admit I had started to become . . .' He hesitated, looking sidelong at her, trying to choose the right word. 'Disturbed,' he said at last. 'So it took me longer than it should have to realise that the notes were disappearing. They got rid of the ones about Mark making accusations about the urine tests first. Then the suicides. As soon as I understood what was happening, I made copies of everything, backing it up, in case they destroyed the lot.' He smiled sadly at her. 'Just because you're paranoid doesn't mean they're not out to get you.'

'I'm so glad you did,' she said. 'When I arrived everything had gone; there were just a few pages here and there. And all the tapes wiped.'

'I expected as much. Such fools. As if the white visitor could possibly be explained by hallucinations from some petty drugs, or corrupt tests.' He turned to her, his voice rising with indignation. 'That's what they thought, you know, that the suicides were caused by the drugs Richard had turned a blind eye to. Lining his own pockets, no doubt. Such a loathsome man.'

At his mention of the white visitor, the tremor in Helkin's hands had become more pronounced. Janet shifted nervously in her seat. It felt too soon to press him on the hypnosis. 'I can't argue there,' she said, picturing her line manager's piggy eyes. 'But do you think Richard's actually profiting from the drugs? Surely it's not lucrative enough to take that kind of risk. I thought it was down to Lee wanting to protect his precious performance targets.'

Helkin shrugged. 'Possibly not for money, then. Though corruption is often more banal than we might imagine.' He started to pick at the seams of his cuffs, his fingers twitching with nervous energy. 'At that stage I believed the E might be linked to legal highs. That's what I said in the notes. They were the first of my papers to go missing, so somebody obviously didn't want them on record.'

'Did you mention any of this to the ombudsman?' asked Janet, thinking of Ms Gardner and her magenta suit.

'Not my findings on the drugs tests. I trusted Lee then. He told me there was an investigation and he had raised the issue himself. And I was never interviewed over the last suicide. Halvergate ensured I had been sectioned before that.'

He seemed to be getting more agitated, winding a loose thread from his shirt round and round one finger. She couldn't keep skirting the main issue. Janet dug her nails into her palms, trying to keep her voice calm. 'Is it true that you tried hypnosis on some of the prisoners?'

Helkin didn't look at her. 'Not by the book, I know. But I wanted to see if the delusions had been *planted* by somebody else.' He had wound the thread so tightly that it dug into his flesh, turning his fingertip white. 'I couldn't reach any of them. Hypnosis was completely ineffective at finding the source of the disturbance.'

Janet watched him. He looked like a man telling the truth, even though she knew that must be impossible. But then, a man capable of spreading delusions would have to be persuasive. 'I see,' she said. 'And what do you think caused the hallucinations now?'

'You know the answer to that. Isn't she why you're here?' He leaned forward, so their faces were almost touching again. A crazy thought that his madness might be physically contagious made her want to flinch away. She could see grey flecks in his blue eyes, and smell the cigarette smoke on his breath. Janet knew the hideous features of the white visitor were as familiar to this man as they were to her.

'Yes,' she said. 'It is.' He sagged into his chair, blinking away tears. 'You believe she gave you a message about Michael Donovan, don't you?'

'I didn't understand her at first.' He took his glasses off with a trembling hand, wiped them and replaced them, a gesture Janet remembered from Zara's tape. 'But every night she came to me, demanding, tormenting. I couldn't tell where I ended and she began. Her rage was relentless. And then finally I understood.'

'What did you understand?'

'She could manage the others herself, she drove them mad with remorse. But with Michael she couldn't do it alone. He doesn't feel it, you see. He isn't sorry.' Helkin's voice cracked. 'So she needed me to kill him for her.'

At the word remorse, Janet felt a chill of recognition, remembering Steven's Furies. For a moment she felt she was standing on the precipice of Helkin's madness, her own mind within a few steps of the edge. Inside the abyss lurked the deluded belief in a real demon hell-bent on revenge.

With the acute perception that can sometimes accompany psychosis, or perhaps with the remnants of his professional judgement, Helkin sensed her hesitation. 'This isn't news to you, is it? When you're lying in bed at night, when you see her, doesn't it ever occur to you that it might not be madness, it might not be a dream? That the reason she looks so real is because she is?'

Janet stepped back from the edge. She looked at the broken man in front of her so desperate for her to share his delusions, and felt a mixture of pity and anger. 'Sometimes,' she said. 'But it doesn't mean they are. And deep down you must know that.'

'*Must I?* Well, you go on thinking that. After all, it's what keeps you in the visitor's chair and me over here.' A tic started in his cheek and he clamped his hands to his sides, his tone unfriendly.

The television screen behind her distracted Janet's attention. Somebody had scored a goal and the commentator's voice went up several notches as the crowd cheered. She glanced over at the two young men watching the game. Both looked dopey and uninterested. 'All right.' She spoke slowly, trying to get him back on side. 'Say she's real. Why Michael, why the other men?'

He waved his hand dismissively. 'The others were just collateral damage. Michael was always the target, but anybody in his radius who felt remorse for their crimes couldn't resist her. He was the only one unaffected, the only one who felt no guilt, don't you see? That's why she needs me to kill him. She needs me, she's always asking, threatening. She can't rest until he's dead.'

Helkin's anxiety had wound him up so tightly Janet feared he was perhaps moments away from breaking down – or becoming furious. He was drumming his left leg up and down and his eyes had dropped away from her face to the floor, his breathing quickening. The professional in her told her to drop the subject, that she had pressed him far enough. But, driven by her need to understand how and why he had targeted the men, she continued to push him. 'Why Michael? Why him above the others?'

'Am I the keeper of his crimes?' he snapped. 'How should I know who he's wronged. Ask the woman he raped, maybe she can tell you.' He shuddered, as if trying to shake off the contamination of memory. 'If you've met him, you must know. The man is cursed, marked by evil. Don't you feel it?'

Janet pictured Michael, the energy he generated, the sense of unease, the fear. She sat back in her chair, angry at finding herself agreeing with Helkin yet again. 'No, I don't feel it,' she said, speaking more harshly than she'd intended. 'He's just a prisoner, like the others.' Helkin shook his head impatiently and she felt her own frustration boil over. 'Did you *want* the men to die?' The words were out before she had a chance to stop them. He stared at her, incredulous. 'They've committed appalling crimes,' she said, softening her tone. 'I suppose some people would think they deserved it.'

'Good God, you think it was *me*, don't you?' he said. '*Deserved to die?*' His voice rose. 'Nobody deserves to die, not like that, so terrified they stick a pencil through their own eye. Can you imagine the fear it takes to kill yourself like that? What poor Mark had seen? What she'd done to him?'

They sat looking at each other, both too surprised to speak. Then a shadow passed over Helkin's face, and Janet saw him turn white with fear. 'Who are you really? Why are you asking me all this?'

'I told you, I'm the new psychologist at Halvergate. I'm trying to understand what's happening there.'

He shook his head. 'You're not a psychologist. Asking if they deserved it. I know who you are. You want revenge. *She* sent you, didn't she? *Didn't she?*'

Confused, she stretched out a hand to reassure him, but he leapt upright, pushing her off. 'Get away, get away from me.' His voice rose to a shout. 'Get away!'

Janet stood up, afraid. He was backing away, making the sign of the cross, his mouth moving as he gabbled a phrase over and over. It took her a moment to understand the words, but when she did they hit her like a physical blow.

'Dead face in the water, dead face in the water, dead face in the water—'

Janet stepped forward and grabbed his arm. 'Stop it!' she said. 'Stop it! Why are you saying that?'

Helkin screamed and shook her off. She heard Laura's voice behind her. 'It's all right, it's all right, John, it's just your friend. It's just your friend Nikki come to visit you.'

'She's not my friend. She's not Nikki. It's her, I know her, she's here to test me, to see if I'm doing what she asked.' He turned to Janet, his face crumpled and pitiful. 'Leave me alone, leave me alone, why do you always come? Every night. What more can you take from me? Please, please, just leave me alone. I can't help you. I can't do it.'

Another nurse arrived, taking him by the shoulders and blocking Janet from his view. He collapsed, weeping.

Laura took Janet's elbow and steered her out of the day room, back the way they had come.

'I'm so sorry. That happens sometimes. But it's been so long – I thought he was over it.'

Janet felt her stomach drop as the lift descended. 'What do you mean?'

'John hallucinates. He sees this woman, this angry woman. Sometimes he mistakes some of the nurses for her. I'm so sorry you had to see that, Nikki, I really am. I do hope it won't put you off visiting in the future.'

28

'So then the other bobby pointed under the car. I bent down to have a look, and there he was, the lad we'd been trying to find all night, hiding under our own bloody police car. He'd been with us the whole time.' Dan laughed and Steven joined him. 'Useless dog that handler had, it never barked at all.'

Dan sat back on Steven's sofa, telling tales of his exploits in the East Anglian Constabulary. Dinner at his place on a Tuesday had felt like an unthreatening way to move their relationship on without rushing things, but if Steven had wanted to make sure their meeting wasn't romantic, he had failed. Dan was impossibly attractive and sitting far too close. Every sinew in Steven's body felt taut with longing. He didn't make a move, instead reaching over to top up Dan's glass.

'I hope they're sending a different dog round your place,' Dan went on.

'Eh? What dog?'

'At Halvergate. They've put a request in for a drugs dog to be present at prison visits. To sniff out any legal highs. They must be getting jumpy. The handler wasn't impressed by the boss ranting on at him to get the dog there next visit, like he wanted it done yesterday.'

'I didn't know they were doing that,' Steven said. 'My colleague will be pleased.'

'Who's that then?'

'Janet, the psychologist at Halvergate. She's a friend of mine.' Steven took a sip of wine. 'Though she's got her own theories about what might be behind the suicides, and it's not drugs. To be honest, I'm a bit worried about her.'

'What does she think it is?'

Steven looked at the gorgeous man next to him. He really didn't want to be talking about Halvergate. He didn't much want to be talking at all, but it was far too early to think about anything else. He sighed. 'It's all a bit complicated. You'll probably think the pair of us are bonkers.'

'I already think you're a bit bonkers, with all the God-bothering.' Dan gave him a cheeky smile. 'Not put me off so far.'

Steven pursed his lips. 'Very reassuring, thanks. Well, it looks like all the guys who died had hallucinations about some sort of demon woman. That's what tipped them over the edge. Janet thinks the last psychologist at the prison hypnotised them, planted the delusions in their heads.'

'But you're not convinced.' Dan's forehead creased with worry. 'Steve, please don't tell me you think it's a real demon.'

'I'm not going to lie, I have thought about it, but on balance that's not the sense I have.' He saw Dan's expression and shrugged. 'It's part of my job to consider it.'

'So what're you thinking?'

'I'm really not sure. But I'm not comfortable that Janet seems to have got so much of her information from one of the prisoners. I had a bit of a snoop, asked what he's in for. It was a particularly violent rape. One of the guards told me he was up for attempted murder, but got off.'

'Doesn't sound like he'd win reliable witness of the year. Can you visit him, try and suss the guy out?'

'I was thinking about that.'

Dan nodded. 'Let me know how it goes.' He put his glass down and looked sidelong at Steven's arm. With just a moment's hesitation, enough to build the tension, Dan ran a finger along the length of the blue Latin script tattooed on his skin. Steven felt his touch more deeply than he had the needle that had administered the ink.

'So you believe in demons.' Dan's finger had traced its way up Steven's arm and now rested on his collarbone. 'What's this then? A prayer?'

He hardly dared to move. 'No. It's a poem.'

'A poem? About what?'

Steven coughed, embarrassed. 'It's about love.'

Dan laughed. 'You soppy git.'

Steven smiled back at him, his lips parted to make a joke in reply. But before he could answer, Dan leaned forward and kissed him.

Back at Cherry Tree Drive, Janet paced up and down the living room, exhausted yet unable to keep still. Meeting John Helkin had disturbed her. He remained her prime suspect, but speaking to him had sent doubts scattering through her thoughts. He felt more like a victim than a victimiser. Of course, she reminded herself, his mental illness meant he *was* a victim. If he'd been unable to face his own responsibility for the men's deaths, it was possible guilt had convinced him the white visitor was real. But his strange incantation and his seeming recognition of her face set suspicion stirring in the darkest part of her imagination.

Janet sat down and read through a printout of his email to Lee again. That and her annotated photocopies of the test lists were the most incriminating documents that had ever come into her possession. All of them should already be on the desk of the area manager, along with Helkin's missing notes and her own observations. Instead she sat pondering an explosive idea. It risked severing all the professional ropes that still tethered her to Her Majesty's Prison Service, leaving her to drift off into an unknown future.

Setting aside the printouts, Janet picked up her computer and scrolled through Helkin's notes on Michael Donovan, searching for Karina Okafor's victim impact statement. His obsession with Michael seemed to be at the heart of his delusions. Michael was a master of manipulation, adept at hiding himself. One of the only people who had seen him unmasked was his former girl-friend. The question now was how to find her. There were two groups of people who were good at such things: the police – and journalists. She picked up her mobile and dialled.

'Zara? It's Janet Palmer, from Halvergate. Good, thank you. Listen, do you know somewhere private we could discuss that gratitude scoop?'

Zara's small terraced house on the Wellington Road in Norwich was dominated by an enormous black Labrador. The moment Janet set foot inside, it started charging around brainlessly, bark-ing and drooling. Never a fan of dogs, she stood tight-lipped against the wall while Zara hustled the yapping monster into the porch and shut him in among a heap of gumboots. His woofs continued to boom through the door.

'Sorry about that,' Zara said. 'The dear old thing loves a good slobber over visitors.' She waved Janet into a tiny kitchen, painted duck egg blue and bright with hanging pans. A 1930s-style radio sat on the counter. 'Tea?'

'Thanks. White, no sugar.'

They leaned against the countertop while the kettle boiled. Zara ran a hand through her tomboy haircut, an unconscious gesture, leaving a clump of hair over one eye. Janet was reminded of the scruffy dog, whose barks had finally subsided. 'So what's this favour in return for the juicy stuff?'

'I need to find somebody.'

Zara poured the tea. 'Can I ask why?'

'No. But I promise you it's not a hit or anything.'

Zara snorted. 'It shouldn't be too much trouble, as long as it's not a Jane Smith. I'm not a miracle worker. The more unusual the name, the shorter the list I can give you.' She gestured with one of the mugs, spilling hot liquid on the floor, and led Janet back into the front room. The barking started up again, and a furry black head made itself visible at intervals through the frosted glass.

'You say the documents are from our old friend John Helkin?'

Janet nodded. 'I tracked him down to Orton Hospital.'

'The loony bin out Peterborough way?' Zara raised her eyebrows. 'Well, there's a surprise.'

Janet stiffened at the description. 'I don't want this information traced either to Helkin or me – can you guarantee that?'

'You have my word, which,' she grinned, 'isn't worth so much. But I promise you the Eastern Film Company has never, ever ratted on a source. It's completely against company ethics.'

Janet put down her mug, reaching into her bag for the documents. 'These show Helkin was concerned about false drugs testing in the prison.' She handed Zara the email. 'And these are records I've found that bear out his fears. What you can see are printouts of the randomly generated lists for mandatory drugs tests over several months.' She ran her finger down the first page, pointing out a few names. 'What I've done is gone through the prison computer system C-NOMIS and noted down when and why men couldn't have given the urine tests they were supposed to.'

She handed the papers over and Zara scanned through them, trying not to appear too excited. 'And you say that another prisoner gave urine tests instead of the men marked here? Can you corroborate that?'

'It's just an allegation at this stage.' Janet picked up her mug and leaned back onto the dog-hair-covered sofa. 'But I do know that no investigation was carried out into the allegations, even though there were a number of suicides that may or may not have been linked to drug abuse. Mark Conybeer, the man making the claims, ended up suffering from hallucinations about the same woman Helkin mentions in your interview.'

'This is pretty decent stuff if we can stand it up,' Zara said. 'Ideally it'd be great to have a second source.'

'You've got Helkin's email, he's one source. Then there's me for another. Other than that I can't help. It's not like I can ask around. I've no idea who might be implicated. One of the reasons

I've passed this on to you is because there's a culture of silence at Halvergate.' She reached over and took hold of the papers again so they hovered between them. 'Speaking of which, you do realise I could be fired for this?'

'I promise it won't be traced back to you. We'll have to get our lawyers on it, make sure we can run the story. And as you're a whistleblower we have to guarantee your anonymity. That's all part of the deal.' Zara took a noisy slurp of tea. 'So what's this name you're after?'

On the journey back to Halverton, Janet felt light-headed. She had just handed over her reputation into the hands of a journalist she hardly knew, allowing her obsessions to jeopardise her career.

She rattled along the road out of Norwich in the heavy dark of the evening, undertaking and weaving past tractors, before heading onto the Acle Straight. Her mind was still running over the meeting with Helkin as she made the right turn to cross the marshes, glancing out of habit in the rear-view mirror. Two black eyes shone back, wide and angry, in the glass. They grew larger as the figure behind her leaned forwards from the shadow of the back seat.

Janet gasped and hit the brakes. Her car skidded, nearly smacking into the side of the narrow bridge. Shaking, she raised her eyes to the mirror, only to see her own frightened face reflected back. She turned round. There was nobody but her sitting in the car.

For a few moments she felt unable to move; then the headlights of a large van illuminated the Mini from behind and honked her into action. She started up the engine and slowly manoeuvred into a straight line before heading towards Halverton.

As she pulled to a stop in front of Cherry Tree Drive, her mobile rang. Everything got in the way of her nervous fingers as she rooted through her bag to find it.

'Yes?'

'Dr Palmer, it's Terry. I don't know how to tell you this. I'm really sorry. It's Ian Fendley.'

'He's not . . .' She trailed off, already knowing the answer from his tone.

'I'm afraid so. He hanged himself in his cell this afternoon.'

Janet felt suffocated. She reached for the car door, desperate to stand outside in the cool air. 'But I thought he was being watched?'

'He was being watched. This happened in one of the breaks. He must have been so quick.' Terry sounded distressed. 'It was one of the only times he was without his cellmate, too.'

'Oh, God.' Janet leaned against the car, feeling tears come to her eyes.

'I've got to go. I'm sorry. Richard wants to see you in the morning. Are you well enough to come in?'

'Yes, I'll be there.' She dropped the phone in her bag and trudged over the slushy pathway, shivering as she struggled to let herself into the house. The Yale lock was almost too much for her shaking fingers.

She stood in the freezing hallway. The open door behind was letting in the cold air. She closed it. Keeping her coat on, she went into the kitchen to make a cup of tea. She flicked the kettle on. The Monet placemats were still scattered all over the table from Arun's visit. In the sink were several days' worth of dirty dishes.

Janet put her hand to her mouth, bunching her shoulders together, forcing herself not to cry. She rocked silently for a moment, breathing deeply, the sound of the water bubbling beside her. When she had recovered, she poured boiling water into a cup, adding sugar for the shock. The clinking of the spoon was the only sound she could hear as she stood with her back to the window. A cold draught blew through the kitchen, and the nape of her neck prickled. She stopped stirring a moment, listening. Silence. Yet she was unable to shake off the feeling that she was not alone. Somebody was watching her from the garden.

Turning slowly, she faced the window. The pane was black, the light from the kitchen making it easy for anyone to see in, but hard for her to see out. She squinted. Towards the back of the small garden, a few feet away, Janet could see the grey shape of a human figure. She walked closer to the window, clasping the handle of her mug so hard her fingers hurt. The figure mirrored her movement, until it was directly outside, illuminated by the electric light.

Janet and the eyeless woman stood face to face, separated only by a thin sheet of glass and Mrs Slaney's kitchen sink.

'What do you want?' she whispered.

The stranger said nothing, but Janet could feel her rage.

'Who are you? *What do you want?*'

In a movement so swift Janet had no time to step back, the figure smashed its fist against the pane. She heard the crash of breaking glass and screamed. In her attempt to get away, she slipped and fell.

She slammed hard onto the cold linoleum, jolting her back. The pain shocked her out of her terror, and she looked up at the windowpane. There was nobody there. She sat for a moment, trembling, then heaved herself to her feet, her legs wobbly. The windowpane was intact. The crash had been from the mug she dropped, which now lay splintered on the floor beneath her. A trickle of blood ran down her shin.

Janet stood in the empty house, alone with her reflection, knowing she was awake, knowing John Helkin had stood there before her.

29

Richard had his back to her as Janet entered the room, a slight flick of his chestnut locks the only sign that he was aware of her presence. She stood in the doorway, waiting. After last night, she felt as if she were in a trance. Richard had intended to insult her by making her wait, but the gesture was wasted on her.

He turned round at last, gesturing silently for her to take a seat. His mouth was pursed into a pout, his lips wet slugs. There was silence between them until Janet's stare prodded him into speech.

'Ian Fendley.' He threw the name down like a stone at her feet. Janet refused to pick it up. Richard's mouth compressed into a hard line. 'What's your *explanation*?'

She spoke so quietly that he had to lean forward. 'I understand from Terry that during one of the breaks when his cellmate was out Ian took the opportunity to rip up his shirt and hang himself from the light fixture. It's extremely sad.'

'*Sad*,' sneered Richard, the skin puckering around his eyes. 'Is that all you have to say about it? And why was he only being checked four times a day?'

Even in her shocked state, the mendacity took her aback. 'But that was your decision. You said we couldn't afford more checks than that.'

'*Me?* Why would I decide how many times the man was checked? I think you'll find, Janet, that as Halvergate's psychologist, Ian Fendley was *your* responsibility.'

His features seemed to swim before her eyes, blurred by

loathing. She felt weightless, with none of the usual professional caution tethering her in place. 'Don't you think it's crass to use a man's death to cover your own arse?' The sheen on his pink cheeks grew brighter, but she carried on. 'Ian Fendley's death is a tragedy for his family, and a source of sadness for everyone who cared for him here. But I don't believe it's on my conscience. I asked you whether we could consider sending him to a secure hospital and you declined. You rubbished my idea of extra checks for legal highs. In the absence of those safeguards, Terry and I put in place the maximum number of checks we were told staffing levels would allow. We did everything we could.'

Richard seemed to swell with venom while she spoke. 'Is *that* what you call an explanation? And you *dare* to preach about legal highs after you went whining to the ombudsman about our procedures? Thankfully Lee was able to scupper your little *game* and tell her we already had a drugs dog, so your *lie* did not pay off.'

Janet shook her head. 'I'm not the liar here.'

Richard sat back in his chair, as if to restrain himself from slapping her. 'May I remind you that your probationary period is not yet up?' He paused to allow his words to sink in. 'If you wish to remain at Halvergate, you will need to up your game. *Two* suicides *already*? At this rate you will be outdoing Helkin's *extraordinary* record in half the time.'

'Is that a threat to my position?' she asked.

'The only threat to your position is *you*.' A fleck of spit landed on Janet's cheek. Richard waved a hand. 'That is all. I would like a detailed written analysis of all the fuck-ups leading to Duncan and Ian's deaths by tomorrow, before the ombudsman's visit next week.' Janet remained seated. 'You may go,' he snapped.

She stood and moved to the door. 'I did also put my request to move Ian Fendley to you in writing.' She spoke evenly, as if none of the previous conversation had occurred. 'You didn't reply to my email, but I will, of course, include it in my report.'

* * *

The jangling of Keith's keys and the tramp of their footsteps echoed in the cold atrium as Steven followed him along the landings to Michael Donovan's cell.

'I don't know why you want to visit this one,' Keith said. 'You'll never get *his* arse on a pew.'

'Got to offer pastoral care to everyone. Part of the job.'

Keith grunted. He stopped in front of a heavy metal door and slid the latch across with a bang. 'Donovan,' he bellowed. 'Priest's here.'

Steven stepped inside the cell, the same space where David Sneldon had recently tried to end his own life.

'Reverend Finch, what a pleasure.' Michael stepped out of the shadow into the harsh glow of the strip light. He was an unusually beautiful man, his face angelic, his body lithe, even better-looking than Dan; and yet as he shook his hand, Steven felt a wave of revulsion hit him like an electric shock. He stepped back, confused, and saw amusement in Michael's blue eyes. 'Do take a seat. How fortuitous you decided to visit. As it happens there's a rather thorny ethical problem that's been troubling me. Perhaps you can offer some spiritual guidance?'

He felt wrong-footed by the appeal. 'I'd be happy to help,' he said, stumbling slightly in his haste to draw up a stool. 'Fire away.'

Michael sat at the desk by the wall, turned towards him. Steven couldn't help picturing a spider, perched at the centre of its threads, waiting to spool him in. Sweat gathered under his hairline.

'This is rather difficult,' Michael said at last.

'Please, take your time. No rush,' said Steven. He was already desperate to leave. Get a grip, he told himself. The unpleasant premonition he felt was probably nothing more sinister than nerves, brought on by all the reading about demons he had been doing lately.

'My problem is the new psychologist,' Michael said. Steven stared at him, dumbstruck. 'You must have seen her? Attractive redhead? Very distinctive. Although perhaps . . .' Michael looked him up and down with a contemptuous smile '. . . she's not your *type*.'

'I know Janet Palmer. What seems to be the problem?' Steven tried but failed to keep the surly tone from his voice.

'I've been having *impure thoughts*.' Michael whispered the phrase with mock seriousness.

'Well, it's not the sixteenth century,' Steven said. 'If you fancy Janet Palmer, that's no business of mine and I don't need to hear about it.'

'I'm not going to subject you to any sordid little fantasies,' Michael said. 'I'm talking about dreams, or nightmares, rather.'

A bead of sweat made its way down Steven's forehead and soaked into an eyebrow. He sensed the other man was playing with him, but was too curious to cut him off. 'Dreams?'

'Janet visits me most nights in my dreams. Some of them are quite delicious, though you've told me I don't need to trouble my conscience about that. Which is a great *relief*, obviously. The troubling dreams are the violent ones.'

'What troubles you about them? You aren't responsible for them.'

'In the nightmares, Dr Palmer and I are locked in a life or death struggle. It's never clear whether I'm trying to kill her, or she me. It's always very arousing. A shame to wake up.'

Steven felt his stomach churn, but tried to treat the man as he would any other. 'Like I said, we're not responsible for our dreams. The only problem would be if you're tempted to try any of this in reality. Is that the case?'

'Opportunity would be a fine thing. Not very likely given where we are.' Michael glanced over his shoulder at the barred window.

'That's not what I asked. Do you want to hurt Janet?'

'I want to hurt lots of people.' Michael's cheek dimpled into a lopsided smile.

'OK, let me phrase it this way. Have you made any actual plans to hurt her? Is that why you wanted to speak to me?'

'So interesting that you assume it must be *me* planning to harm *her*. I told you the dreams are ambiguous.'

Steven stood up abruptly, making the stool snag against the lino floor. Michael remained seated, looking up at him in mild surprise. 'I don't appreciate being dicked about,' he said. 'I don't believe you've brought this up because your *conscience* troubles you. I think you're trying to wind me up. And just because I'm wearing this – ' he pinched the dog collar between thumb and forefinger – 'doesn't give you a license to waste my time.'

'I can see Janet's charms *have* had an effect on you. How touching.'

'Are you threatening her?' Steven's voice came out loud and belligerent.

'I'm not threatening anybody. Though *you* make for rather a menacing figure looming over *me*.' Michael peered at him. 'Are those tattoos on your knuckles?' He laughed. 'How extraordinary.'

Steven flushed and looked down at his clenched fists. He turned and banged on the cell door.

'I should make it plain,' Michael said smoothly to his back, 'that I'm not threatening anyone. I just wonder how wise it is for Janet and me to be having these cosy one-to-one sessions. I wanted some friendly advice about it, from a man of integrity, that's all.'

The cell door opened and slammed shut again, leaving Michael sitting alone.

'Sweet Jesus, what a creep,' muttered Steven, safely on the other side of the door. He had never responded to anyone with such physical revulsion.

'More than the others?' Steven realised it was Terry, not Keith, who had let him out.

'Sorry, scrap that from the record. Very unprofessional.'

'He seems to make a big impression on most people,' said Terry. 'I warned Ian not to get too close to him.' His eyes were red-rimmed and bloodshot.

'Ian Fendley was one of yours, wasn't he?' Steven asked. Terry nodded, his mouth set in a tight line, and Steven sensed he was close to tears. He put a hand on his arm. 'Do you want a brew in the chaplaincy? We could chat about it.'

'Not sure they can spare me. We're a bit short-staffed.'

'You look like you need a break. They can bollock me for it. Come on.'

The chaplaincy was little more than a broom cupboard, dominated by an enormous grotesque carving of Jesus on the cross. It was Father Dunstan's and Steve hadn't had the heart to say he hated it. As a compromise he had moved it to the other wall, so that it stared him in the eye, rather than looming, green-faced, over visitors.

'It's complicated with Ian,' Terry said, clutching an extra-strong cup of tea. 'You see, I sort of knew him. On the outside.'

'And you didn't disclose this?'

'Not entirely.' Terry looked at the floor. 'I told Dr Palmer he was from my neighbourhood but that I didn't know him personally. Which is true.' He wrinkled his nose. 'My wife knows him. Knew him, rather.'

'But you didn't tell Janet?'

Terry shook his head. 'I promised Nikki I'd look after him. She knows Ian's mum, you see, his little brother was at the school where she used to be a TA. I thought I'd done him a favour getting him on the programme, but now . . .' He rested his head in one hand, to hide the tears.

'What happened isn't your fault, you do know that?'

'But it is, that's the thing.' Terry wiped his eyes. 'I'd seen his symptoms before. When John was here. But I was too worried about my own bloody job to tell Dr Palmer about it.'

The tortured wooden face leered over Terry's shoulder. Steven felt cold. 'What do you mean?'

'Richard read me the riot act when she was hired. I wasn't to talk to her about all the crap from before, and he'd know about it if I did.' Terry ran a hand over his close-cropped hair. 'He got ill, you see. John got really sick. All that stuff Ian was saying about some angry woman hunting him down, that's what the other guys said. And in the end John believed it too.'

'If that's the case why didn't they just fire him? Why let him carry on?' Terry closed his eyes, his expression anguished. Steven began to understand. 'It was the drugs, wasn't it?' he said. 'They wanted Helkin to discredit himself, so nobody would believe him about the dodgy tests.'

'How do you know about the drugs?'

'I can't tell you that. I'm sorry.'

His shoulders sagged. 'I suppose it's best out,' he sighed. 'They wouldn't intervene when I told them John was ill, and then some journalist got a sniff of how unbalanced he was and they couldn't get rid of him fast enough. And when Dr Palmer told me his notes were missing, I realised Richard must have destroyed all trace of him.'

'It is a shame that you didn't tell Janet any of this.' Steven chose his words carefully. He felt furious with Terry but didn't want to make the other man's burden of guilt unbearable. 'But it doesn't make you responsible for Ian's death. Even if you had told her, it doesn't mean things would have been different. You still did your best to look after him.'

Terry sat back in his chair, letting out a long breath. 'I guess so.'

They sat for a moment in silence. The wooden carving stared at Steven, its mouth a twisted hollow, the eyes overshadowed by heavy lids. He thought of the dark cell he had just left, and of the man locked inside it. 'What did you mean earlier when you said you had warned Ian about Michael?'

'Oh,' Terry said. 'I don't think he has a good influence on people. He wound everybody up after Ryan escaped, claiming there was a curse that made a letter E appear in cells where the other guys had died. I think he saw some graffiti on the news and went from there.' Terry shrugged. 'If something's difficult you can always rely on Michael to make it worse.'

30

Parked outside Halvergate's main gates, Janet listened again to Zara's voicemail.

'You're lucky, we've only got two Karina Okafors. One is fifty-four and lives in south London. I can get you the address and phone number, but I think you said she was mid-thirties? The other one, who's the right age, is over Easton Bavents way. Funny little place, don't know if you've been. Near Southwold, it's slowly falling into the sea. This Karina's ex-directory, so no number, but this is the address . . .'

As Zara spoke, Janet typed the street name into her satnav. It was just over an hour away. She had expected Cambridge, but supposed Karina might not want to carry on working at the place where everyone had known, and possibly liked, her rapist.

Janet looked up at the sky from her dashboard. The evening was crisp and clear, the stars bright overhead. If she set off now, she would reach Karina's before half past seven. Not an ideal time to surprise a stranger, but at least there was a good chance she would be home.

In the dark, Janet missed much of the scenic coastal drive. Instead she could only see the dull orange glow of Great Yarmouth and Lowestoft, interspersed with the blackout of the country roads. Twisted shapes of trees and hedgerows flashed past, picked out by the headlights, and she thought of Michael Donovan with an increasing sense of dread. She remembered Helkin's claim that Michael was cursed, that the demon wanted him dead. She gripped the wheel, blinking, determined not to relive the hallucination from last night.

John Helkin had become obsessed with Michael, had wanted to kill him, but before that he had trusted the man to help him, just as she had. Yet the more she thought about Michael, the more she suspected he was the last person anyone should ever trust.

Eventually the road started winding down through Southwold to the sea. The satnav directed her round the back of the row of colourful beach huts that grace a thousand postcards and up a steep track. Even in the dark, Janet could see the path was precariously close to the cliffs. She drove more slowly, the road getting ever bumpier, the darkness ahead almost total, each house illuminated by the headlights seemingly uninhabited.

The satnav took her down Easton Lane, but then she was forced to come to a sudden stop; ahead of her, a red warning sign strung up on rickety fencing and wire blocked the path. Janet got out of the car, leaving the lights on, and walked on to the end of the road. The tarmac broke off just beyond the sign, crumbling straight down into the sea. She could hear the crash of waves in the dark. The house to her left was just feet from the edge; another few storms would likely tear it down into the water.

She returned to the car and locked it. Karina lived in one of the small red brick cottages a little further back from the edge. Light through the blinds at the window guided Janet up the front path. Her heart quickened. At least somebody was in. She knocked on the door, anxious about the reception she would receive. Over the faint murmur of the television, she could hear somebody walking across the room, and then the door opened.

'Yes?' A slim dark figure stood in the doorway, her expression partly blanked out by the light behind.

'I'm sorry to disturb you. My name's Janet. I'm hoping you can help me.' She started gabbling, afraid she wouldn't have long. 'I work at Halvergate, where Michael Donovan is being held—'

'If this is about him wanting forgiveness, I'm not interested.' The woman made a move to close the door.

'It's nothing like that.' She stepped forward. 'I think he's extremely dangerous. I think he really did try to kill you. I'm trying to make sure he doesn't automatically get parole.'

The door had almost closed. The other woman's hand wavered in the sliver of light left between them; then the light expanded.

'You'd better come in.'

The door opened straight into the living room. Janet followed her inside. Karina Okafor had a perfect hourglass figure; cornrow braids fell down the back of her bright floral pyjamas. Janet felt a pang for disturbing her when she had so obviously turned in for the evening. She picked up the remote, switching off the TV and sat on a white sofa, curling her slippered feet beneath her like a cat. Janet took the seat opposite.

Karina was beautiful in the same eye-catching way as Michael Donovan, the planes of her face matching his for symmetry, her dark lips full and curved. But while he exuded arrogance, she seemed to tuck herself into the smallest possible space.

'I'm really sorry to disturb you—' Janet started again.

'What is it you want from me?' Karina's tone was neither friendly nor unfriendly, her eyes guarded. Janet understood that it took courage to open her door and let a stranger into this, the most painful part of her life. She decided to be completely honest.

'I'm afraid of Michael Donovan,' she said. 'I don't understand him. I'm frightened that he might be exerting a dangerous influence. I believe that he tried to kill you, and I think because you saw him when he no longer had anything to hide, you might be able to help me.'

Karina looked down at her ankle, clasped in one hand as she held herself tucked into place. 'Does the prison know you're here?'

'No. This is completely unauthorised.'

'You must be worried.'

'I am. Michael frightens me more than anyone I've ever met.'

Karina shook her head. 'It's still strange for me to hear that name. When I knew him, when we were at Minotaur, he called himself Gabriel.'

Janet felt a strange sense of recognition, but it eluded her like a shadow flitting past too quick to see. 'How strange. I never knew that.'

'It was one of the things that went against him, the use of aliases.' Karina shifted position slightly, leaning against the arm of the sofa. 'I don't know how much I can help you. I still can't understand what happened. Even now I struggle to accept that the man who attacked me is the same man I lived with. I didn't see it coming at all.'

'What was he like before?'

'He wasn't perfect. I always knew he was arrogant. Sometimes he could say things that seemed callous, but then he'd smile as if it was a joke. He was always very witty, very charming, but more than that, we seemed to share so much. The same love of maths, the same taste in music . . .' She trailed off and sat for a moment. 'I loved him. Completely. And he was never anything but loving back. I don't remember him even raising his voice to me.'

The man Janet knew from Halvergate, with his humour and charm, took shape before her eyes. 'So there was nothing, even retrospectively, that warned you?'

'Nothing. And I've been over our life together a thousand times, trying to find a clue. The first I knew about another side to him was when I woke up one morning to find him tying one of my wrists to the bedhead. I wasn't scared, just surprised. I asked him what he was doing. He punched me in the face.'

Karina's words brought the shadow of violence between them. 'I'm sorry,' said Janet. 'Please don't feel you have to relive or describe what happened. Only things you feel comfortable telling me.'

'It wasn't about sex, I can tell you that. He raped me, but he could have had sex with me any time without forcing me. It was about pain and fear. He assaulted me with objects from our own bedroom, with a souvenir vase I really loved from our holiday together in Greece. At the time I was too terrified to think, I just kept crying. But since then, I've thought it was his way of showing me that the relationship meant nothing to him. It was all a lie, it was never love.'

'Did he say anything to you?'

'I kept asking him why and all he said was because he felt like it.'

Janet paused. A clock made of driftwood stood on a small chest beside her, and its ticking was loud in the silence. Karina remained curled into the corner of the sofa, watching her. She looked calm, but still, Janet hesitated before asking her next question. 'It said in the victim impact statement that you had a miscarriage afterwards. Did he know you were pregnant?'

Karina looked at the carpet, away from Janet's gaze. 'No. I hadn't got round to telling him. I'd only known a week. I wasn't sure how I felt about it yet. It wasn't planned.'

'Were you worried about how he'd react?'

'A little. Not that I thought he'd turn into a murderous psychopath, or anything like that,' she said. 'I can't describe why, but I just struggled to see Gabriel as a father.'

'Did you tell him when he attacked you?'

'Of course. It was the first time he stopped and looked at me as if he'd heard what I was saying. Then he laughed. I couldn't believe it, he actually *laughed*. And he said it was another reason it would look like a stranger attack, that after he had killed me he could play the grieving expectant father. That's when it sank in that he was wearing latex gloves. I'd been too shocked to realise the significance of that before.'

'Jesus,' said Janet.

'He smashed the vase and told me he was going to cut my throat. I kept crying and asking him why.' For the first time since she had started speaking, Karina's eyes filled with tears. She wiped her face with her sleeve. 'I don't know why but his answer has stayed with me more than anything else. He leaned over and whispered to me, like it was something tender. He said, "I've been dreaming of watching you die."'

Janet felt her skin go cold, thinking of how close that face had been to her own, remembering the feel of his hands as he pinned her to the chair. Her voice was hoarse as she asked the next question. 'That's when he was interrupted by your neighbour?'

'I'd given Marek a key to the back door. He was fixing some stuff in the spare room. I'd forgotten to tell Gabriel I'd arranged for him to drop by that Saturday. I heard him calling up the stairs and started screaming for help. Gabriel never said anything. He just left.'

'I don't understand how he wasn't convicted of attempted murder.'

Karina's mouth twisted into a bitter line. 'Do you know what his defence said? That I was into kinky sex, that it was some kind of tribal thing to be tied up like that. And you can guess how many black people there were besides me in Cambridge Crown Court, let alone on the jury. The prosecutor told me if Gabriel hadn't cut himself on that vase and if Marek hadn't given such a strong testimony about the state I was in, he might have got away with it. That and the miscarriage. The jury would have hated that, she said. The irony being that that was the least traumatic thing. As if I would *ever* have wanted his child.'

They sat quietly for a moment, the seconds ticking past. 'Did Michael – or Gabriel – ever tell you anything else about his dreams?' Janet said at last.

'His dreams?' Karina shook her head. 'No. Why do you ask?'

Janet stopped, unsure how much to say. Her fear that Michael might be cursed by a vengeful spirit was not one she wanted to voice aloud. It sounded crazy enough in her own head. 'I'm worried that something from his past might be causing a disturbance at the prison, that it's harming other people who get too close to him.'

'I imagine he'd take great pleasure in other people's pain, that he'd do anything to hurt someone again, even better to kill. But I never got the feeling he was psychic or anything.'

'He wouldn't have to be psychic as such,' said Janet. 'Just very disturbed. And everything you've told me makes me feel he's even more disturbed than I'd imagined.' She shook her head. 'I hear about crimes all the time, but what he did to you is terrible. I'm so sorry.'

'Nothing to do but survive it. In spite of him. I find living here helps.'

'You don't ever get nervous being so isolated, or so near the cliffs?' Ever since learning Karina's address, Janet had been curious about her choice to live there.

'One thing I learned from Gabriel is that strangers aren't the first people you should fear. And the erosion doesn't worry me. Mortality is around us all the time. Besides, where else would I get a place by the sea so cheaply? I work from home now, since leaving Minotaur. I like the quiet. It's the same for my partner. He's in the Royal Engineers. The peace is good for him.'

The more Janet spoke to Karina, the more she liked her. But she felt that she had already trespassed enough on her time. 'I can't tell you how much I appreciate you speaking to me.' She reached into her bag, searching for a pen and scrap of paper. 'If it's OK, I'll leave you my number, in case anything else occurs to you.'

'There was one other thing that might be interesting. About his past,' Karina said. 'When I went through the house to throw all his things away, I came across some love letters from another woman. I've no idea if they were old, or if he'd been seeing somebody else.'

'That's interesting,' said Janet. 'He denied having any serious relationships before you.'

'The letters sounded pretty serious. But that wasn't the main thing. They were all addressed to "Raphe" and "Raphael". It struck me as odd, that he had two aliases, both the names of archangels. Like some sort of sick joke.'

The bottom fell out of Janet's stomach. For a moment she sat, unable to move, unable to speak. She realised Karina was watching her, her face growing anxious.

'Do you think it's important? Do you think he's done this before?'

'I don't know.' Janet's tongue felt like lead. 'Do you remember the woman's name?'

Karina sat back, her brow screwed up in thought. 'Isabella, or Isobel, or something like that. Does that help?'

31

The Mini's engine protested as Janet drove back to Halverton in the dark, her foot pressing the accelerator to the floor. She could hardly breathe, the pressure in her chest was so intense. Fragments of her conversations with Michael came back to her, playing like flashcards in her mind. His reaction when he first saw her, the constant remarks about Thomas More, his use of her nickname, and above all, the mockery in his blue eyes. No wonder he seemed to know so much about her. He was Izzy's Raphe.

A lone car in front pulled over, honking, as Janet swerved and speeded past. She ignored the flashing lights in her rear-view mirror and continued to hurtle along the coastal road. She thought of Neil Martin's story that an 'angel' had told him to put Izzy in the bath, that the water would wake her up. It had sounded crazy, yet poor Neil had been telling the truth. All those years she had tried to forgive him, had even counselled prisoners with Neil in mind, imagining how she might prevent another attack, and all along he had been another victim. How Michael must have laughed, the innocent young man's death yet another sign of his power, the means of his escape from justice. Raphael, Gabriel, Michael. And now this dark angel was faced with another seeking revenge. Her sister.

Helkin's voice sounded in her mind, repeating his horrible incantation. The dead face in the water, the image she had spent over a decade trying to erase, had been Izzy. Her sister was trying to make Helkin understand what Michael had done.

Janet's own power over Michael was waning just when she

needed it most. If Richard fired her, as she feared he would, then she had no control over his parole. Without her, her sister's killer would be processed in time to an open prison, and after that to the outside world. And then there was no reason why, with a new name and plausible backstory, Michael might not find another Karina or Isabel to manipulate and abuse. Or even kill.

Janet took the bend too fast and briefly lost control, nearly colliding with a tree. She slammed on the brakes. The car came to a sudden stop, jolting the air from her lungs. She rested her head on the wheel, and sat for a moment in the dark, reliving the crash that had nearly killed her ten years before. She took a deep breath to calm herself, then drove slowly onwards to Halverton.

Back at Cherry Tree Drive, she ran straight to the bathroom. In the mirror, her own face was barely recognisable, her eyelids red and swollen, while the hair she usually scraped back so painstakingly had come loose, making it look as if she had been out in a storm.

She placed a palm to the glass. 'Izzy,' she said, her voice low. 'Is that you?' She searched her own features, desperate for her sister or even the white visitor to appear, but her reflection remained steady and unchanging. 'Whatever you want, you know you only have to ask me. Was it him, was it Michael? Please tell me. *Please.*'

Nobody answered.

Janet remained staring at herself, in silence. Then she switched off the light.

In the living room, she poured herself a glass of wine. She had six missed calls from Steven and a text from Arun telling her he had arrived in America and was missing her. Janet switched the phone off. She didn't want or need anybody else now, not if Izzy was going to come back to her. She closed her eyes, gripped with the longing to share her anxiety, her guilt, her fear, the way they had shared everything together, whispering at night when their parents thought they were asleep. She looked at Isabel's photograph and drank her glass down to the bottom.

Unable to summon the energy to go to bed, she lay on the sofa, the curtains still open, her coat pulled up over her for warmth, watching one television show merge into the next until sleep began to interrupt, shifting her in and out of the present. Then, at last, she was dreaming.

In the hills above Florence, she was walking to San Miniato al Monte in the baking sun. Her step felt weightless on the country path, the fields painted in the saturated technicolour of her unconscious, the red poppies and yellow grasses unnaturally bright.

She breathed more deeply, savouring the calm. She turned off the path into a field, the wild flowers touching her fingertips like the surface of the sea as she passed. In front of her was a river. A woman stood beside it, dressed in white. In her dream Janet knew it was her sister. Her chest constricted.

She pressed through the field, desperate to reach her, but now her steps were heavy and the flowers and high grasses pulled at her legs, slowing her down. Out of breath, she pushed on until she heard the familiar murmur of her sister's voice. Isabel was facing the sun, her face shining white in its blaze, her eyes closed.

'Izzy,' she called. Her sister didn't move, didn't even seem to hear her, but she raised her voice so that Janet could distinguish the words.

'He makes me lie down in green pastures, he leads me by the still waters . . .'

The bright colours of Janet's dream began to fade to grey and the flowers withered beneath her feet. Dread crept over her, buffeting her like the wind that now blew across the barren landscape.

'Izzy,' she called out, her voice choking with tears. Isabel ignored her, raising her voice still higher, relentlessly carrying out her recital.

'Though I walk through the valley of the shadow of death, I will fear no evil—'

Janet reached out and shook her sister. 'Izzy, don't you hear me?'

Isabel's eyes opened, the beloved face distorted by rage. She turned on Janet, her eyes black and empty. Janet tried to pull her sister towards her. 'Izzy, it's me, it's me!'

In fury, Isabel shook her off, her mouth open in a scream. Its pitch rose higher and louder until it was unbearable, and as she screamed, Janet fell backwards, plunging beneath the dark surface of the river. Still the sound pursued her, ripping through her heart, shattering the world of her nightmare. She opened her eyes, jolting back into Mrs Slaney's living room, but the awful sound didn't stop. Terrified, she swung her legs from the sofa, and then, as she caught her breath in a shuddering gasp, the screaming stopped. It had been her own voice that had woken her.

Janet stood drenched in sweat, staring at her pale reflection in the living room window. She had dreamed so many times of her sister, but never anything like this.

Her hands shaking, she crossed the room to draw the curtains. Before she pulled them together, she clutched the fabric in her fingers for a moment, her breath misting the glass, her own unhappiness reflected back at her. She breathed again, this time deliberately steaming up the window. A single word was just visible on the glass.

Repay.

32

'He should have been checked every half-hour.' Terry held the logbook so tightly the knuckles showed pale through his dark skin. 'Four checks a day weren't enough. And he should never have been left alone without a cellmate. I had insisted on that.'

Janet could see how much Ian Fendley's death had upset Terry. Heavy bags sat under his eyes and he had obviously been crying. They were perched close together, squashed into the two chairs by her office sink, the logbook between them. Steven's voice message, saying that Terry had some explaining to do, now made sense. He had finally opened up to her, just when she no longer cared. She was even finding it difficult to concentrate on what he had to say. On the surface she projected her usual calm, while inside anxiety clawed like rats at her ribcage. Her mind kept returning to images of Michael Donovan and her sister.

'It wasn't your fault. I know you did everything.'

'More than everything. We don't have the staff even for this kind of watch. You've no idea the grief I got for insisting. And still it wasn't enough.'

'I know.'

'He was a nice lad, Dr Palmer. I know he made some big mistakes, but at heart he wasn't bad. You met him, you know what I mean. He might actually have made something of himself after. How often do you see that?'

Janet looked at Terry's drawn face. His guilt needed to find an appropriate object. 'It wasn't up to you,' she said. 'Ian should have been in a secure hospital.' She left the accusation against

Richard unspoken. 'Once those drugs tests came back negative, that was the safest place for him. You know that.'

She thought of Richard's dismissal of Ian Fendley's psychosis as play-acting, the refusal to take his distress seriously. Terry closed the logbook. He looked at her. 'I know it's too late to say sorry. There's so much I should have told you and I can't change that,' he said. 'But I'm telling you now, you need to be careful. Richard told me to keep an eye out, to watch what you get up to. Lee thinks you're unstable.'

Janet tilted her head to one side as if pondering an abstract question. 'And what do you think?'

'I thought John was unstable. I kept telling Richard he needed time off, he needed help. Nobody listened.' Terry stopped, his jaw tightening with emotion. He got himself back under control. 'And then a few weeks ago, I thought Ian was unstable. Oddly enough nobody was interested in my opinion then either. Except you.' Terry sucked his teeth. 'So I reckon they can live without my opinions about you.'

Janet nodded. 'Thank you,' she said. 'That's good to know.'

Alone again, sitting at her desk, Janet stared at the blank computer screen. Under normal circumstances a direct threat to a job she had done so much to secure would have made her desperate. But now she simply felt detached. Lee's hostility, Richard's warning, Terry's confession – all suggested that the management had no intention of extending her contract. Yet her main emotion was not anxiety for her future, but a terrible fear that she would never understand the true meaning of the white visitor. Or what had happened to her sister. And that was all that mattered now.

She looked at her watch. There were still thirty minutes before her meeting with Michael. Terry had insisted on bringing him in after she suggested he might be able to shed light on Ian Fendley's death. She closed her eyes. If she were ever to find out the truth about Izzy and act on it, being discredited was not going to help. Any influence she might have on Michael's parole would evaporate the minute she was disgraced. Halvergate might intend to get rid of her, but there was no need to make it easy for them.

In her bag sat photocopies of the printouts she had given Zara, along with a copy of Helkin's USB stick. Picturing Richard's face as she typed, she began to compose a letter to the Chief Inspector of Prisons.

Dear Sir,

My name is Dr Janet Palmer and I recently took up the post of chartered psychologist at HMP Halvergate in Norfolk, having worked the previous five years as assistant psychologist at HMP Leyland.

When I started my position here I was informed by the deputy governor Richard Smith that my predecessor Dr John Helkin had neglected to file any notes on the inmates in his care for the last six months of his employment. However, senior officer Terry Saunders, John Helkin's closest associate, appeared confused by this claim, which alerted me to the possibility that Dr Helkin's files had been wrongfully destroyed.

I have since been able to obtain the enclosed USB stick, which contains both Dr Helkin's notes and evidence for his suspicions that data from the mandatory drugs tests was being doctored. No investigation appears to have been carried out into his claims. Also enclosed are printouts of the MDT during his time at the prison, which show evidence that certain inmates on the randomly generated list could not have given urine samples as they were supposed to.

Dr Helkin is currently being treated as an inpatient at the psychiatric facility at Orton, near Peterborough. Whether he did in fact delete his own notes, or whether, as he says, the notes were destroyed by his line manager Richard Smith, is impossible for me to determine.

I thought the matter sufficiently serious that it should be passed to your office, it being impossible for me to raise the issue

> *here at Halvergate, since the allegations involve my direct*
> *superiors.*
>
> *Yours sincerely,*
> *Janet Palmer*

The letter was a gamble, since the management might claim that she had deleted John Helkin's notes herself, but she hoped the MDT data was sufficiently damning to discredit them. She rifled through her desk for an envelope. She enjoyed the irony of sending it through the prison's own internal post system. Whether this cleared her name or not, if Halvergate intended to fire her anyway, she had nothing to lose from a pre-emptive strike.

A loud knock caused her to stuff the papers in her bag. Rather than call the visitor in, she went and answered the door.

'What an unexpected pleasure,' Michael said, pushing his way past. 'Though I must warn you that besides the odd hello on the landings, I don't think Ian and I ever enjoyed much stimulating conversation.'

Terry closed the door, leaving her and Michael alone. Janet's skin flamed hot from nerves and adrenalin. She had employed a trick of Lee's by moving her chair further away than normal, putting her back to the window. The bright winter light now shone in Michael's face, a hostile tactic she would never normally use. He blinked, moving slightly in his chair to avoid squinting. Looking at him, imagining him with Isabel, Janet felt her breath become shallower.

She set her notebook aside. 'How much do you know about my past?' she asked.

'This session's about you, is it? A piquant reversal of the norm.'

'Just answer the question.'

They stared at each other, a vast chessboard of lies between them. Michael leaned back, but the casualness of his favourite gesture was undermined by his enforced squint. 'Have you ever Googled yourself, Janet Palmer?'

'You don't have internet access.'

He laughed. 'Do you know how easy it is to get drugs in here? Imagine how much of a trial it could be accessing a smartphone.'

'You know about her, don't you?' Janet couldn't stop her voice from shaking.

'Poor little Janey and the tragic loss of her twin. Yes, I know.' He dismissed the idea with a shrug. 'The whole prison might know about it, if any of them had the wit to do some research.'

'You have an interesting past yourself. A man with many identities. Michael, Gabriel, Raphael. Perhaps you've named yourself after the entire angelic host in your previous lives.'

Michael sat very still, watching her, eyes narrowed against the sun. He said nothing. Janet could feel the blood beat in her ears.

'I never used the name Raphael,' he said at last.

'When we first met, you seemed struck by something.' She fished the cross from under her jumper, holding it out. 'I thought it was because I was wearing this, against the guidelines, but now I wonder if you'd seen Izzy's necklace and my face before.'

'Maybe I was just struck dumb by your dazzling appearance.'

'When my sister was found, she had been put in a bath. She was wearing this cross, nothing else. And the only part of her outside the water was her right hand.' Janet looked down at her own hand, turning it over as she spoke. 'She was holding a plastic card, a copy of her favourite psalm, from her wallet.' She looked up at him. 'You know which psalm that was, don't you? It's the one I saw pinned up in your cell. Psalm 23.'

'It also happens to be the most famous psalm in the Bible.' Michael crossed his arms. 'What are you driving at, Janey?'

'And there's that name. Only my sister called me that. But I think you knew that already.'

'This place is truly remarkable. It seems to be unique in the prison service for sending its psychologists mad. First John Helkin and now you.'

'You know who the white visitor is and what she wants, don't you?'

He stared at her, perplexed, before realisation dawned on his beautiful face and he started to laugh, the tension relaxing as he gave way to genuine amusement. 'Oh, that's priceless. You really think it's your murdered sister? You poor girl. She hasn't got very good eyesight, if I'm her killer. Why go for all those other poor bastards? Why am I still here?'

Janet stood up, her face rigid with fury. '*I know you killed her.*'

Michael crossed the room, taking hold of arms clamped stiff by her sides. 'You miss her so much,' he said, his voice low, almost tender. 'Poor Janey. I know you must long to join her. Why don't you let me help you?'

Janet closed her eyes. She could feel the warmth of his body. He was standing so close, their lips were almost touching.

'I've been dreaming of you, Michael.'

His breath was hot on her face, his hands moving softly up her arms, 'And what have you been dreaming?'

She opened her eyes. He met her gaze, his own eyes cold blue, sharp with desire. Desire for what? she asked herself, thinking of Karina Okafor and the broken vase. She leaned towards him, her cheek resting against his, remembering the other woman's words. '*I've been dreaming of watching you die.*'

Michael let go and stepped backwards. For the first time, he looked unnerved. He wiped his hands on his trousers as if tainted by her touch. 'You're one crazy bitch.'

'Like John Helkin?' Janet said. 'I spoke to him recently. Do you know what he thought? He thought he'd have to kill you himself, because the white visitor wasn't getting through to you. Imagine that.'

'You should be careful who you threaten in here.' Michael moved towards her swiftly, just stopping short of taking hold of her again. There was no desire in his face now. His eyes shone with malevolence. 'All this talk of *imaginary* murderers. You never know when you might meet a real killer. Because you know what they say about killers. One death is never enough to satisfy. And then, Dr Palmer, where would you hide?'

33

It was the first time Steven had been to Dan's place, a small flat on the Earlham Road. He felt a pang as he walked in. Dan had festooned the narrow hallway with candles and reeked of aftershave. He had obviously been hoping that Steven's last-minute request to pop round had an ulterior, romantic motive. And instead they were sitting perched on Dan's quilt-covered sofa talking about Halvergate.

'I'm sorry to do this to you. I just didn't know who to ask for advice,' Steven said. 'I can't think of anyone else to talk to who actually knows something about the prison.' He didn't mention all the unanswered calls to Janet's mobile. Bad enough your sort-of boyfriend calling on you for work rather than sex, without being second choice as well.

Dan put an arm round him. 'Of course. I'm glad you feel you can talk to me.'

'Thanks.' Steven looked at him, then glanced away, not wanting to get lost in his eyes. 'You know I said before that inmates had been having hallucinations about the same woman, some sort of demon figure?' He felt awkward, remembering Dan's reaction. 'Well, she appears to be a revenge demon from ancient Greek myth, one summoned by the curses of the bereaved.' He felt Dan's arm almost imperceptibly move further away.

'Right, but you were just doing research. You don't actually believe all this, do you, Steve?'

'No, but the similarity between the men's description and her description in the books had me worried. Until I started looking into one of the prisoners.'

266

Dan's arm was barely resting on his shoulder now. 'You think a prisoner summoned a demon?'

'In a manner of speaking.' He caught sight of Dan's horrified expression. 'Not literally! I think he's conjured up the idea of one. The psychologist at Halvergate, my friend Janet, mentioned a condition called shared psychosis, where one person plants delusions into other people's minds. I think that's what he's been doing.'

'Why would he do that, though?' Dan asked, scooping up his cat, a fat cream Persian with a spectacularly ugly face, on to the sofa. It purred and rubbed itself on Steven's leg, leaving fluff on his black trousers.

'He's a charismatic guy, a troublemaker, and by all accounts a sadistic bastard. I suspect tormenting people to death would be right up his street.' Steven didn't mention the physical repulsion he had felt for Michael. He wasn't sure Dan would be too impressed by unsubstantiated hunches. 'And then there's the dead men themselves. I spoke to the senior officer on his wing, and all of them seem to have had some link to this same prisoner – he either befriended them, shared a cell or was in an adjacent cell.'

'That last bit sounds interesting, although it doesn't prove anything,' said Dan. 'Being an arsehole who'd like to cause harm could be a description of any number of cons. Anything more specific?' He looked interested now, and reached for his laptop, which sat on the coffee table. 'Budge over, Princess,' he said to the cat, whose flat face crinkled in annoyance as he settled the computer on his knee.

'Not much. In for rape. Acquitted of attempted murder. The only other things I thought might be significant are that he's Oxford educated, so obviously smart, and a computer programmer. He designed games for a company called Minotaur.'

Dan typed into the search bar. 'Based in Cambridge?'

'I guess so. I'd not heard of it.'

'Well, they do a number of games. *Quest*, *Excalibur* and one called *Mythos and Logos*.'

'Really? As in Ancient Greek?' asked Steven. Dan looked blank. He felt embarrassed. 'Here, let me have a look at that last one.' He leaned over the purring Princess to see the screen. The game's home page flickered and glinted with an abundance of animations. A man in a lion-skin, his shining torso bulging with muscles, wrestled with a many-headed monster, while a red-haired woman with a tiny waist and giant breasts waved a hand and turned a foolish-looking man into a pig. Music that sounded suspiciously like pan pipes warbled out from Dan's poor-quality speakers. 'Looks crap,' he said. He'd never understood the appeal of gaming.

'Let's see.' Dan scrolled down the menu bar. 'Characters.' He clicked and a long list of dramatis personae came up. 'Does your demon have a name?'

'Alecto.'

Dan made a face and handed the laptop over. 'You look.'

Steven scanned the As. 'Nothing,' he said. 'No Erinyes either. Hang on, there we are. Furies.' He clicked on a link. A trio of hags burst on to the screen with a loud wail. Underneath a fizzing nest of snakes, three brown wrinkled faces with bulging eyes gurned and snarled their way around the screen. 'That doesn't look very familiar,' he said. 'All the men described a white-faced woman with black eyes.'

Dan read the blurb next to the animation:

Ware, Oh pilgrim, ware the three, lest you suffer agony!
Murder Friend and not your Foe, We will hunt where e'er you go.
Show remorse to break the charm, and risk your life to right the harm.

'I hope your con didn't write the lyrics,' he said. 'Not very menacing is it?'

'That bit about showing remorse though,' Steven said. 'That fits in with what I've read and with what some of the inmates at

Halvergate told me. Men are being driven to suicide by remorse. Literally driven mad by guilt.'

'Sounds like one for your psychologist if that's the case. Not sure the police could do much.' He patted the now drooling Princess on the head. 'One inmate allegedly sending other prisoners mad. Not really an arrestable offence.'

'I know, it's just this man might be having an effect on the staff too,' Steven said. He thought of Janet the last time he had seen her, hair unwashed and hollow-eyed. She had been ignoring his calls and emails ever since going to Peterborough to see Helkin. The last contact had been a cryptic text message, thanking him for speaking to Terry but adding that she no longer thought Helkin was responsible. Once he had got over feeling hurt at her coldness, he had started to worry. Her message could mean she was on to Michael too – or something infinitely more disturbing.

'You think he's making the staff ill?'

'I'm pretty sure he convinced the last psychologist there was a demon unleashed at Halvergate, and I think he's working on Janet.'

'What does she say about it?'

'I haven't been able to speak to her recently.' Steven paused and the Furies on the screen fell silent for a moment too, before continuing their wailing, clearly on a loop. He wondered how much it would be ethical to disclose. 'Janet's seen this demon too. Only in dreams,' he added quickly, catching sight of Dan's horrified expression.

'Your psychologist is delusional?' Dan sat up straight, shoving the cat aside. Even the candlelight could not stop the last threads of a romantic atmosphere from unravelling. 'If that's the case, you've got to report her.'

'But I don't know that she is. And anyway, I can't, not without speaking to her again.' Steven ran a hand over his eyes. 'I feel a bit responsible too. It was me who brought up the idea of demons in the first place.' He didn't dare mention Janet's murdered sister, the reason she might be particularly vulnerable to delusions about vengeful ghosts.

'It's too late to feel bad about that now,' said Dan. 'You've got to get a grip on this, Steve. Real people are at risk here. Get Janet away from this creep. And if that doesn't work, you'll have to report her.'

The day of the funeral was bright sunshine. Looking up, Janet saw splashes of green and white against the blue sky. Trees waving in the breeze. During the drive, she had kept her eyes down to avoid seeing the hearse in front. But all journeys come to an end. The walk from the car to the churchyard was one more impossible task on a day filled with impossibilities.

At the gate she was dimly aware of flashes. A snapshot of grief. Her face would be in the papers the next day. An extra frisson for readers, knowing her face was identical to that of the murdered girl in the coffin.

A stumble as she made her way up the path. Arun held her steady. And then they reached the hole in the ground. Unable to breathe, she heard almost nothing of the priest's final prayers and blessing. She kept her eyes shut to avoid seeing the coffin lowered into the ground. Then came the murmured condolences as people filed past her, dropping flowers into the grave.

She was aware of birdsong. She let go of the last remnants of her faith, like ash left to the wind. Then she was kneeling on the grass. Below her the smooth grey of the wood, the silver handles, the mound of dying flowers.

She had no words for her sister, no prayer to God. From the shattered remains of her heart she cursed the man who had killed Isabel, a curse strong enough to summon the devil himself, bringing down all the rage and pain in her soul.

A thousand images of her sister filled Janet's mind as she drove. Izzy running full pelt to catch the bus to school, laughing rather than swearing when it pulled off just as she arrived. Izzy rolling her eyes in a dusty classroom, a shared moment of boredom during double physics, a stifled giggle under the teacher's drone. Izzy's rapture at her acceptance letter from Oxford, the dance of glee on the doormat. Izzy's wave the last time she saw her, the swing of her shoulders as she turned and walked off down the street, blending into a crowd of students. Nothing about her bore any resemblance to the white woman in the mirror.

She pulled up and got out of the car. The squat bulk of Cherry Tree Drive loomed above her. A mean house filled with sadness. She made her way inside, breathed in the familiar scent of damp, saw the single bulb hanging from the ceiling.

She dropped her bag on the floor and walked upstairs. In the bathroom mirror she searched her features for signs of Izzy. But the face in the glass bore almost no trace of her sister's character now. Anger and pain had drawn lines in the pale skin and the dark eyes were hard. In her mind's eye the pupils bled outwards, until the whites turned black.

She and her double stared at each other in silence. From behind the glass, the familiar stranger looked out and Janet knew the face for her own. Rage burned out, and Janet recognised that that too was hers. Hatred spilled from the stranger's black eyes, and Janet felt the tears on her own face.

She placed her hand to the glass and the other woman followed her movement, so they stood palm to palm.

'All that time I thought John Helkin was the inducer,' she said. 'And all the time it was you.'

Steven knelt in prayer before going to bed. He felt like a child leaning against the edge of the mattress, it was so many years since he had prayed in this posture. He thought of Michael Donovan's malevolent presence, and the evil his imagination had let loose, and felt afraid. It was a madness that seemed to be taking on a life of its own, beyond even Michael's control, creating a hysteria that had destroyed John Helkin and was driving vulnerable men to their deaths. Worst of all was the thought of Janet, already disturbed by grief, being exposed to his toxic influence. Any relief that he might be spared from meeting a real demon was dimming with the light.

He found sleep hard to reach; his mind kept replaying the hundreds of traditional tales where a devil impersonated the beloved dead. He thought of Helkin, driven to the edge of his reason by the fear of demonic possession. Steven stifled a rising sense of panic. He looked at the clock, which read 1:20 a.m. Heaving himself up, he padded to the kitchen, ran himself a glass of water, splashed some on his face. Back in bed, he turned his fears over and over, despairing of ever getting to sleep. Yet for all his anxiety, at some point his mind slipped from the rat run of consciousness.

He found himself sitting again in the chapel at Halvergate, the evening he'd first met Janet. She walked past him, standing just as he remembered, before the beautiful Maria Dolorosa. Again he saw her shoulders shake with tears. This time, instead of calling out, he walked down the aisle towards her. She did not hear him. He called her name, but still she remained with her gaze fixed on the statue.

In his sleep Steven shuddered, a frown deepening between his closed eyes. In the dream he reached out to her shoulder, his movement slow, as if he dreaded contact. He felt the weight of her, like one dead, as he turned her bodily towards him. The tears on her cheeks were not silver this time, but red, and there was no friendship in her face. The black eyes fixed on him were full of fury. Steven tried to step backwards, away from her, but she seized his hand like a drowning woman. As he felt her cold fingers he knew she would pull him down with her, into the deep.

Steven's sleeping body lurched away from the image in his mind, waking him. He sat up, palpitations of fright and exhaustion hammering against his ribs. It was just before half past seven in the morning. He grabbed his mobile and dialled Janet's number. There was no answer. He called again and still she didn't pick up. He left a voicemail, conscious that he sounded out of breath as he tried to gather his scattered clothes and speak at the same time.

'It's Steve here. Listen, please don't go anywhere near Michael Donovan. I don't think it's safe for you to be near him. I can't tell you why, but it feels really important that you stay out of his way. Please call me when you get this.'

34

Steven's was not the only call Janet missed that morning; the shower drowned out the sound of her phone, and she was far too preoccupied when she got out to check for messages. Her mobile lay forgotten on the floor by her bed as she locked the front door behind her and set off for work.

Her hatred for Michael Donovan had expanded, leaving no space for any other thought. But rage, even the rage of the white visitor in her heart, was not enough to stop him. He would only serve time for murder if he killed again. And yesterday he had showed how much he longed to take another life. Hers.

She pictured him as she drove up to Halvergate's main entrance; his image was still before her as she crossed the sterile area, his voice and his laugh filling her mind. Everything stood out sharp and bright in the early morning sunshine, the outline of the prison clear against the blue sky, like a cardboard cut-out. In the exercise yard to the left, a huddle of prison officers were looking at the scaffolding that clambered up the building on to the roof. She slowed down as she neared the group.

'Dr Palmer!'

Janet turned at the sound of Terry's voice. He jogged towards her, his face drawn with anxiety. 'I've been trying to call you. Why haven't you picked up?'

'I didn't check my phone this morning. What is it?'

'It's Donovan. He made a run for it during the exercise circuit this morning. The bastard managed to get up the scaffolding. He was so quick, it was unbelievable, like a rat up a drainpipe. He's been on the roof the last twenty minutes.'

'He's up there now?' Janet looked, but Michael must have moved out of sight. She remembered her arrival at Halvergate, the way the unattended scaffolding had filled her with foreboding from the first, a security breach waiting to happen. 'What's he asking for?'

Terry looked uncomfortable. 'He's demanding a hostage negotiator. Been very specific about it. He's threatening to jump if he doesn't get who he wants. He's asking for you. Nobody else.'

'Me?' She heard Michael's voice. *I know sometimes you must long to join her.* In her imagination she felt the touch of his hands on her skin, remembered Karina's warning that he would do anything to kill again. And now, perhaps, she could make sure he paid for Izzy's murder, if not with the death of one twin, then with the death of the other. 'Oh God,' she said, unsteady on her feet. Terry put a hand out to support her. Behind him, Janet could see Richard walking towards her.

'I see Terry has been updating you on our *situation*.' His carefully manicured locks shone copper in the sunlight. His face was puckered with hostility. Janet could feel the pulse jumping in her neck.

'Are we sure it's wise to give him the hostage negotiator he demands?' she asked.

'Why? You don't feel up to the task?' His eyes glittered like flints. 'The cherry picker is going to take as much as two hours to get here. By that time, I imagine *somebody* will have blabbed, and we'll have the local press *scurrying* around, making a meal of it. I'm sure you'll agree there's no point drawing things out even further once the cherry picker *does* arrive by sending up a negotiator the prisoner won't *negotiate* with.'

'You don't have to do this, Dr Palmer.' Janet and Richard looked at Terry in surprise. He reddened under his manager's vicious stare, but carried on. 'It's asking too much, Mr Smith. Michael has a problem with women. I don't think we should trust his motives. He's bound to be getting some sick kick out of the whole thing.'

'Whatever *kick* he's getting out of it, Dr Palmer will be perfectly *safe* talking to him from the cherry picker,' Richard snapped. He turned to Janet. 'Won't you?'

Janet looked at Terry, whose brow was wrinkled in concern. A few weeks earlier, his support would have meant a lot to her, but now even her personal safety felt trivial. 'It's OK, I'll do it.' She turned to Richard. 'If that's what the management want.'

Janet excused herself from the conversation about the best location for the cherry picker and headed to the bathroom alongside the staff canteen. It reminded her of school: the chill, the chipped blue paint and rows of sinks facing cheap ceramic loos. No mirrors. Closing herself into a cubicle, she pulled down the plastic seat and sat on it, drawing up her feet so nobody would know she was there.

She felt certain Michael's escape on to the roof was linked to their conversation about her sister yesterday. He would be expecting the cherry picker, and all the witnesses it would bring. Might he accuse her of visiting Karina, try to discredit her before she could link him to Izzy's death? Or did he have more murderous intentions? Either way, he must have planned to manipulate both the situation and her. The key was to surprise him. The cherry picker would not arrive for two hours, which gave her an opportunity to confront Michael alone, if she were brave enough to take it.

She sat for a moment in the cold cubicle. She pictured her own face merge into that of the stranger in the mirror. There was no reason to be afraid. She was doing this for Izzy.

She walked to the window, pushing the heavy sash upwards. A cold breeze blew in. It was a long way to fall. The scaffolding's platform ran underneath, easy enough to swing herself on to. She sat down on the sill.

Without stopping to think, barely stopping to breathe, she jumped down on to the platform. It felt sturdy enough, but the drop made her stomach lurch. The roof was just out of reach; even by jumping up she couldn't quite get a grip on the ledge.

The guttering was little use; it was so old it had buckled from the wall. To her right, there was a spare spike of pole sticking up about a foot over the top of the platform. Balancing on that was going to be the best way to give herself enough height.

If she hesitated, fear would overwhelm her. Without looking down she pushed herself up from the pole and made a grab for the ledge. Something metal, perhaps a vent, caught at her hand and she clung on. She hoped it was solidly attached. For one moment she stood balanced, one foot on the pole, both hands grasping the roof. Then she pushed upwards again, her spare foot scrabbling against the brick. For a hideous moment she was suspended, both legs kicking the empty air; then she pressed against the guttering with her knee and managed to haul herself on to the roof.

For a moment she lay still, feeling the concrete against her cheek. It was noisier than she'd expected. The wind flapped against her clothes and she could hear the loud hum of several ventilators. She stood, swaying slightly as she regained her balance. Her hands shook, but not from fear – she felt high on hatred.

She raised a hand to shield her eyes from the sun and scanned the roof. Michael was watching her, the light behind him, a slender silhouette. She picked her way towards him, stepping over shattered glass where a skylight had been smashed. The dark figure waited. As she drew closer she saw he was holding a long shard of glass with a jagged edge.

'So you came.' Michael laughed. 'I can't believe you actually came. I must be irresistible, after all.'

'What do you want to say to me?'

'I wasn't planning on talking much. That's not why I asked for you.' He spoke lightly, as if discussing a date at the cinema. 'Once a killer always a killer, isn't that what you lot believe, despite your pious little programmes of re-education? Don't pretend you don't know why I wanted you. I was hoping you might have the guts to confront me, and here we are.'

Michael stepped closer, but she circled around him to avoid facing the sun. Her heart beat faster. 'Tell me about my sister.'

'I never met your sister.'

'We both know that's a lie.' Then she smiled, understanding his silence. 'You think I'm wearing a wire, don't you?' The wind froze her skin as she lifted her top, exposing her stomach. She turned slightly so he could see her back, her eyes never leaving his face. 'Satisfied?'

Michael gestured with the sliver of glass. 'Let's entertain your deluded fantasy for a moment. Say I did kill her. What can you possibly do about it now? Another man was convicted. The police aren't going to reopen the investigation, not without DNA, which you obviously don't have.'

'Izzy told me about you. The wonderful new man in her life, the older maths graduate, the extraordinary Raphael. So intelligent, so attractive, so kind.'

'We don't even have the same name and you recognise me from such a glowing description? I'm flattered.'

'I went to see Karina. She found Izzy's letters to you. Why did you keep them, some sort of trophy?'

The hum from a nearby generator filled the silence. Then Michael shrugged, as if finally letting go of the pretence. 'Charmingly old-fashioned, dear little Izzy.' Janet flinched at her sister's name. 'Did *you* ever reply to her letters, or were you as lax about that as answering her phone calls?' He paused, waiting for her to reply, but she stayed silent. 'Why do you want to know?' Cruelty twisted his face and she wondered how she could ever have thought him beautiful. 'Are you jealous, Janey? Do you want to hear how I fucked her, do you wish it had been you?'

'You left her holding the copy of Psalm 23. Why?'

'Can't you guess? Dear faithful Izzy. It was her last request when I said I was going to kill her, when it finally sank in to her trusting little skull that I meant it. *Please could she read one last prayer.*'

Janet felt tears sting her eyes. 'But it wasn't just a prayer, you do realise that, don't you, Michael? It was her way of saying you didn't frighten her. "Though I walk through the valley of the shadow of death I will fear no evil." Who else was that evil but you? And she wasn't afraid of you.'

'It had occurred to me. But she never got that far. I killed her at "lie".' He laughed. 'Don't look so shocked. If you think I raped and murdered her, what difference does it make whether I let her finish a silly prayer? "He makes me down to lie in green pastures . . ." Well, she got her wish, didn't she? Where else is she now but rotting away, the grass growing over her head?'

Janet felt unsteady, unbalanced by the rising tide of hatred inside. She tried to speak evenly, but her voice wavered. 'You think you won, but all it tells me is that even though you killed her, you didn't destroy her faith. You didn't destroy her hope.'

'No, but I destroyed yours.'

She stared at him.

'Surely it must have occurred to you how similar we are. All that rage, all that hate? I gave you that. Now you feel what I feel. Looking at you is like looking in a mirror.' He stretched out his arms. 'I took away one twin and gave you another.'

She was aware of him watching her face, reading the anxiety that flickered in her eyes. Then her anger surged, drowning the fear before it could catch fire. She remembered the woman in the mirror: her true double, her true reflection, not Michael Donovan. She felt her eyes turning black, her face whitening into a mask. She circled him again, to force him back to the edge of the roof. He blocked her and they stood side by side. 'What is it you want, Janet Palmer? Are you looking to go the same way as your sister? Join her and make sure I go down for murder?' Michael ran his finger slowly over the flat side of the glass. 'It has a certain symmetry, you must admit. You get justice, and I get . . . you.'

The wind blew Janet's hair against her neck, the curls like fingers against her skin. He was standing so close to her, as close

Elodie Harper

as he had once been to Izzy. 'I'm not here to die, Michael,' she said. 'I'm here to kill you.'

'Don't you think that's a little unlikely?' He held out the glass. 'Given I'm the one who's armed, who's killed before. You may find you don't have the stomach for it.'

'But I have killed before.' He didn't manage to hide his surprise. 'All those men who died at Halvergate. Ryan Spalding, Duncan Fletcher, Ian Fendley, all of them died because of me. All that rage I meant for you, that's what killed them, what drove them mad. Don't you recognise me? I'm the white visitor.'

'You're insane,' he said, stepping back. 'The white visitor is *mine*, a little something to entertain me at Halvergate. She's nothing to do with *you*.'

For a moment she felt afraid. She saw Michael clench the glass tighter in his fingers. Then she thought again of the face in the mirror and knew it didn't matter where the white visitor came from. She still belonged to Janet, as did her revenge. In one swift movement, she tugged downwards on the chain of her sister's cross, snapping it. She held it clenched in her fist. 'Who will you pray to, Michael? What does evil pray for in the valley of death?'

He came towards her in a single movement, slashing downwards, aiming for her neck. She blocked him with her free hand, slicing her palm open on the glass, before catching his wrist. His strength was far superior and the struggle should only have lasted seconds, but as he moved to wrest himself from her grasp, he found she had gripped him like iron. They stood body to body, in a deadlock. The veins stood out white in her neck as she put all her strength into holding him.

Slowly, she turned his wrist, trying to force him to drop the blade. He shifted his full weight against her, and her arms began to shake from the effort. Beads of sweat ran down her face. As she started to crumple he pressed harder. Rather than continue to resist him, she gave way in a feint and he fell forwards.

Glass protruded from his body, her hand still gripping his

wrist. Janet had twisted the blade towards him before letting him fall. They stood close together for a moment, like lovers. Blood from her wounded palm had splashed across her face like tears, and her eyes were black.

Janet screamed.

The sound spewed from her in a dark tide. All the pain and rage, locked inside her heart since the day of her sister's death, filled her voice. It rose above the wind, above the hum and noise, in a scream that might shatter every window in Halvergate.

Michael pulled away from her, appalled. She reached out her bleeding hand towards him, but he recoiled. He lost his footing and fell backwards off the roof.

For a moment, Janet stood alone, swaying slightly in the wind, with nothing but an endless expanse of sky before her. Then she dropped to her knees, looking over the edge. Michael's body lay on the earth below. Her hand was still clenched around Isabel's cross. She held it out, opening her fingers. The chain slipped through them, and as the enamel caught the light, she saw a flash of red.

Then it was gone.

35

'Just a few more questions, Dr Palmer.'

She lay in the hospital bed, her right hand heavily bandaged. The glass had severed a nerve and it was uncertain how much feeling she would regain. Arun sat on the opposite side of the bed to two policemen, leaning protectively over her, holding her good hand. Steven had remembered her saying Arun worked at Imperial and, unaware of their break-up, had got the university to track him down. He had flown over from the East Coast as soon as he'd heard.

For the past two days she had been in hospital with severe shock and post-traumatic stress.

'Of course,' she said. 'Whatever you need to ask.'

'Why did you go up on to the roof, against prison protocol?'

'I was concerned Michael might jump before the cherry picker arrived. I hoped to talk him down before that.' She paused. 'Obviously with hindsight that was a terrible mistake.'

Detective Inspector Tom Osmond nodded, making notes. A heavyset man in his fifties, he gave every impression of going through the motions, rather than being a keen inquisitor. The same could not be said for the younger officer, PC Dan Avery, standing beside him. Suspicion was written on his sharp elfin face.

'And how did Mr Donovan react when you tried to calm him down?'

'He told me he had no intention of jumping. He wanted to kill someone and . . .' She trailed off, looking at Arun, who squeezed her hand in encouragement. 'And he said I might as well do.'

'Grudge against the prison service, was it?'

'Something like that.'

PC Avery cut in. 'The CCTV shows you moving round him, as if you were trying to get his back to the edge. That's quite aggressive, isn't it?'

'It was the sun,' Janet said. 'It got in my eyes. And to be honest I preferred not to be the one with my back to the edge, given Michael was armed. There was nothing aggressive about it.'

Dan Avery looked unconvinced but his superior jumped back in. 'Quite. And what did you say to try and calm him down?'

'I told him that he had been making good progress, that the group therapy was going well. Killing somebody would only add years to his sentence, and there was no point. He's a relatively young man and could still make something of his life.'

'And what did he say to that?'

'He told me he had been cheated of killing before, that he had meant to kill his girlfriend Karina, and that he had no intention of being cheated again.'

'That the lady he raped?'

'Yes.' One of them, anyway, she thought.

'And then what happened?'

'He told me to take my necklace off. I don't know why, maybe to distract me, then he, well, he . . .'

'It's OK, Janey,' Arun said. 'It's OK.'

'Take your time, Dr Palmer.'

'He dived at me with the glass. I don't know how I stopped it. I don't really know what happened next, it's all very confused. We struggled, he was leaning on me, I buckled, and he fell on the knife.'

'And you never managed to take the knife off him? He was still holding it?'

'No, I never managed to disarm him. That's what I was trying to do, by twisting his wrist. But I never got hold of the glass.' She looked over at PC Avery. 'I'm sure any surviving prints will confirm that.' DI Osmond nodded curtly. 'And then we both looked down. I was so shocked, I couldn't believe it, I never wanted that to happen. I just didn't want him to kill me.' Her voice started to break. 'And then he stepped backwards and he fell.'

'But before that you screamed,' said the unsmiling Dan Avery. 'You screamed, Dr Palmer, before he moved away from you.' It wasn't a question, more an accusation.

'I'm sorry, what do you mean by that?' Arun asked. 'She was very upset, why shouldn't she scream?'

The young policeman looked at him. 'Some of the prison officers said it sounded more threatening than frightened.'

'Are you saying she screamed him off the roof?'

'No, of course not.' The detective inspector shot an irritated look at his junior. 'Thank you, Dan,' he said, his tone not matching his words. He turned back to Janet. 'There's just one more thing you might be able to help us with. Did Mr Donovan ever mention a young woman called Siobhan Trant to you?'

'*Siobhan?*' said Janet. 'No, why?'

'We found letters from her in his cell. Seems they were planning on getting together once he was out. She told us he might have mentioned it to you up there, that perhaps him being love-lorn was a reason he'd made a run for the roof.'

Janet shook her head. 'Silly girl,' she said, thinking of Siobhan's huge guileless eyes, the way she blushed. Someone like that must have been easy game for Michael. She wondered if Siobhan would ever realise what a lucky escape she'd had. 'No he never mentioned her.'

'Didn't think so,' said DI Osmond. 'But we have to ask.' He closed his notebook and stood up. 'That's all for now, Dr Palmer. Obviously we will be in touch as the investigation progresses.'

Janet and Arun watched the policemen leave. After they'd shut the door, she sighed and leaned back on the pillows.

'Jesus, as if you haven't been through enough. Complaining about you screaming.' Arun was in protective boyfriend mode. Janet decided not to contradict him.

'It was good of you to fly over,' she said. 'It means a lot, having you here.'

'I'm just sorry I didn't know how bad things were at Halvergate. I should have listened to you when you were trying to tell me, rather than making ultimatums—'

Janet interrupted him. 'If anyone should be sorry it's me.' She closed her eyes. 'You were right. This isn't the best career for me.'

'I can't believe you'd apologise to me, after . . . after what I did. I'm so sorry, Janey, I'm just so sorry.' He didn't mention Jean by name. His eyes were welling with tears. He certainly looked sorry. It still hurt, the thought of him cheating on her. She was surprised by how much it hurt. Then she thought of all the secrets she would never share, all the lies she would tell about Michael. There are, she thought, worse betrayals than infidelity. She squeezed his hand. 'It doesn't matter. We're still OK. If that's what you want.'

'Seriously?'

'One mistake. It doesn't wipe out all the years we've had together.'

'So you forgive me?'

'You forgive me, don't you, for everything in the past?'

'Of course, but you've never cheated, have you?' He looked at her a little anxiously. 'I mean, unless, while we were on this break . . .' He trailed off.

Janet saw Michael Donovan, felt again the weight of him as they fought, as he fell on the knife. 'No,' she said. 'There's never been anyone else. Not like that.'

After Arun left for the comforts of Cherry Tree Drive, Janet lay in bed alone, watching the television. He had insisted on leaving it on, to distract her from more troubling thoughts. She gazed at it listlessly for a while, half of her still on the roof with Michael, in their ungainly, fatal embrace. She closed her eyes, had almost drifted off, when a familiar voice pierced the fog in her head.

'These documents, which I can reveal are in the exclusive possession of the Eastern Film Company, show that the prison may have been aware of a widespread drug problem at the time of the suicides, but they took no action to investigate . . .'

Janet opened her eyes to see Zara Hyde, in an uncharacteristically smart outfit, perched on a pink sofa, clutching a sheaf of papers. A male anchor with silver hair and a shiny suit nodded along sagely as she spoke.

'And I understand that's not all you've learned, Zara?'

'No, the Eastern Film Company has also spoken to HMP Halvergate about the recent death of an inmate who apparently tried to kill a member of staff. The prison has neither confirmed nor denied whether this inmate, a convicted rapist named Michael Donovan, was under the influence of narcotics at the time, but we understand that will form part of the investigation. All of which I put to the prison in this exclusive report.'

At that she turned to camera with a solemn look as the screen went to pictures of the prison, shot through a red-filtered lens.

'Halvergate,' intoned Zara's voiceover. 'A prison of secrets and lies . . .'

Janet watched as the story she had given Zara unravelled in a sensationalist version. The infamous interview with John Helkin even made a brief appearance, Zara's editor obviously having overcome his scruples in the interests of the wider story. The 'EXCLUSIVE INTERVIEW' banner across her predecessor's forehead somehow lessened the shock of seeing his waxy features dominate her screen. She realised that despite Zara's promise to protect her as the source, her own email outlining all the same allegations would make it very clear who was behind the leak. That was unlikely to go down well with the Ministry of Justice.

At the end of Zara's report, Janet turned off the TV. She found it impossible to feel anything but indifference about the professional fallout. It hardly mattered now. Instinctively she put her hand to her throat to feel Izzy's cross, before remembering how she'd lost it. The flash of red as it fell, joining Michael's shattered body below. Her eyes filled with tears. On the roof she had really believed that she had the right and the power to take her revenge, but now she felt less certain. Perhaps Michael had been manipulating her to the very end, his only mistake a miscalculation of the impact of the delusions on her. Unlike his fellow inmates, it seemed her deepest instinct was not for self-destruction. It was to kill.

Janet shut her eyes, trying to blot out the memory of Michael's face as he stepped backwards. She could not be sorry he was gone, but his death brought Isabel no closer. Revenge had left its own sense of emptiness, the hole in her heart still unfilled.

Steven turned over Isabel's cross in the palm of his hand. Half the red enamel was missing, smashed in the fall, leaving just the cheap metal at the back. The shine of it, in the dirt near where Michael Donovan died, had caught his eye. He ran the broken chain through his fingers.

Steven could still hear Janet's scream.

He had arrived at the prison, desperate to find her, but by the time he got there she was already on the roof. He had asked the crowd of prison officers what was happening, but nobody was interested in talking to him. They'd jostled him aside, trying to get a better view of the struggle above their heads. He was dimly aware of Terry trying to get up on the roof from the canteen window, the guttering coming away in his hands, leaving him stranded on the scaffolding. Janet and Michael were close enough to the edge for some of their fight to be visible, but not all. When Michael fell against her, Steven had thought it was Janet who was wounded. Then she'd screamed.

It was not the cry of an injured woman; there was no fear in it, only rage, like a curse. He'd felt it was him who had been stabbed, run through the heart by the sound. He didn't see Michael step back and stumble. To him it looked as though the fury carried in her voice had impelled him off the roof. The fall was swift, so swift that he barely had time to register what was happening before the impact. The wet thud of Michael's landing.

A month had passed since then and he had seen Janet just once at the hospital. Arun had also been there, and he had no chance to speak to her properly. She had barely looked him in the eye, and never answered his message offering to chat. And now, waiting in his flat, Steven had no idea what he would say to her. She had told him she was back for one last weekend, come to collect the rest of her things, and promised to drop in on him. He was no longer sure he wanted to see her.

He knew she had been suspended from Halvergate after Michael's death and had pre-empted a disciplinary hearing by resigning and returning to London. Dan had told him the police were not pressing criminal charges against her, as it was impossible to argue from the CCTV that Janet had acted in anything other than self-defence. Michael's downward strike with the knife was unambiguously aggressive and appeared to have been unprovoked.

Janet's disgrace was not the only fall at Halvergate. The Eastern Film Company's exposure of endemic corruption brought outsiders to the prison, and like a vampire exposed to daylight, the terrifying edifice had started to crumble. Lee and Richard's resignations were surely only a matter of time. He wondered whether the institution itself would survive; with the government determined to make cuts, it seemed an obvious target for closure. He had already started applying for work elsewhere.

The buzzer rang and he walked to the door to let Janet in, waited as he heard the light tread of her footsteps on the stairs. They embraced awkwardly in the hall.

'Coffee's on the hob, if you'd like some?'

'Great, thanks.'

He turned away from her as he poured. 'Glad to see you're looking better. Is the hand all mended?'

She came and stood next to him, leaning against the countertop. 'I've not got all the feeling back, but I can still use it, which is the main thing.' She took a sip of coffee, holding the cup in her wrong hand, the left. 'How's life treating you? Are you still seeing that guy, the policeman?'

Steven looked at her. She was paler and thinner than he remembered. He thought of Dan, how their bright new relationship had withered in the frost brought by Michael's death, how they had fallen out over Janet's role in it. Dan had wanted Steven to make a statement saying that he suspected Janet was delusional. Steven had refused. 'It didn't work out in the end.' He shrugged. 'I didn't like his cat.'

'Sorry to hear that.' She tried to smile at his joke, but it didn't spread to her eyes. She took another sip of coffee. 'There's something I've been wanting to ask you.' She paused, as if gathering herself to speak. 'You left a message on my phone that morning. About Michael. What was it you wanted to say?'

He felt a chill at the dead man's name. Looking at Janet's face, he half expected to see her transform into the Fury from his nightmare, but instead in front of him was the woman he had grown to care about, his almost-friend, the one he had got drunk with, who sang along to his records. Her eyes were not black, but creased round by lines of sadness and anxiety.

'It was about dreams,' he said. 'Michael Donovan had told me that he dreamed you were trying to kill him.' Janet put her mug down on the counter but said nothing. 'And then the night before he died, I had a dream about you.'

'About me? What was I doing?'

'You were the white visitor.'

They stared at each other. Steven sensed that Janet was about to speak, but then she frowned and looked away. 'Dreams don't mean anything.'

'I don't think that's what Michael believed.'

'What are you saying, that I was possessed?'

'No, I think Michael messed with your head, like he did with John Helkin, like he did with all the men who died, like he tried to do with me.' Steven thought of the man as he had seen him in his cell, sitting in the shadows, spinning his web of delusions. 'I think he was the inducer of the shared psychosis you were looking for. But perhaps you knew that already.'

Janet half turned away from him. 'Funny, that,' she said. 'You thinking Michael was behind it all. I remember one time you told me the demon of Halvergate was a Fury, summoned by the curses of the bereaved. I didn't believe you. But maybe you were right.'

'What do you mean?' Impulsively Steven took hold of her arm, pulled her to face him. 'Janet, I'm worried about you.'

'Don't be. I wouldn't want to work in the prison service again anyway, not after that. And the police aren't charging me.'

'That's not what I'm worried about.' Steven didn't let go of her arm. 'What happened on the roof?'

She looked at him. He had never seen sadness like that in her eyes. Janet Palmer's grief was bottomless. 'He tried to kill me,' she whispered. 'That's all you need to know.'

'Of course, I'm sorry.' He let go of her arm. 'Forgive me, it must have been terrible.' He reached into his pocket, bringing out Isabel's cross. 'I found this on the ground. I thought you might like it back.' She made no move to take it. 'It's yours, Janet.'

'It was Izzy's. I don't deserve it.'

Steven took hold of her right hand and opened it. The red scar from Michael's glass knife ran across the palm. Gently, he closed her fingers around the cross. 'None of us deserve God's grace, yet it's always there, whenever we want to take it.'

Janet didn't answer him, but nor did she return the cross.

Steven poured another coffee for himself and Janet held her mug out for a refill. 'What are your plans now?'

'I'm going to America with Arun.'

'Really? That's great.'

'I guess.'

'You do love him, don't you?'

'Of course,' she said a little too quickly. 'And in any case, there's nothing for me here.' She ran her injured hand gently along the countertop. 'She's never coming back.'

Steven, who had just started to relax, felt his stomach drop again. 'Who's not coming back?'

'Izzy.' Janet looked into his face, which was creased with a puzzled frown. 'I thought once that dying would bring me closer to her, and then I found out I was wrong. And now I know that nothing will bring her closer. She's really gone.'

She was staring at him intently, and he had the feeling there was something more behind her words, something that she wanted him to understand. 'Do you remember I told you once that Izzy had a boyfriend named Raphael, who I never met?' she said, her gaze still holding his. 'It turns out Michael had a fond-ness for angelic aliases.'

He gasped. 'Janet, you don't mean that Michael . . .' He trailed off, but read the answer in her eyes. 'But that can't be right. I thought they found her killer?'

'He said he killed her at "lie". You know the line in the psalm, number 23?' He nodded and saw Janet's face harden. 'My sister was found holding a plastic card, the sort some people carry in their wallets. It was a printout of 'The Lord is my Shepherd'. Michael told me he killed Izzy when she was praying, when she reached the word lie.' Janet took hold of his hand. 'It was him or me, Steven. That was the only way to get justice. I knew he wanted to kill me, and in the end, I just couldn't let him do that. Not again.'

Steven thought of David Sneldon, of the words Michael had planted in his head. *Vengeance is mine, and I will repay.* It seemed Halvergate's most dangerous prisoner had sown a delusion darker even than he could have imagined, one whose words had returned to claim his own life. 'I understand,' he said.

'Thank you.' Janet let go of his hand. 'I think I'd better go now. Arun will be waiting.'

Steven walked her to the door. Neither of them offered to stay in touch. He stood for a moment listening to her footsteps on the stairs, then crossed to the window and watched her step out from the doorway and stand uncertain at the edge of St Giles Street. She looked so vulnerable, a slim figure in the bright light. He felt a pang, and pushed up the window.

'Hey,' he shouted. 'Enjoy life on the outside.'

She turned, laughing, the sun blindingly bright on her face. 'Who knows?' she called up to him. 'Plenty of jails in America.'

She raised her injured hand to shield her gaze, and her eyes fell into shadow. For a moment Steven's heart stopped. Janet stood before him, her eyes completely blacked out in the hard white face. Then she smiled, raising her hand to wave, and he saw it was just a trick of the light.

Acknowledgements

HMP Halvergate is a gothic nightmare of a prison, not based on any real institution, but I'm indebted to numerous people for giving me the tools to build it. Firstly, thanks to residents and staff at HMP Grendon for hosting me for a day on F Wing. The horrors of Halvergate are a world away from the hard work, humanity and dedication I witnessed there. Thanks to Andrew Barclay, former governor of HMP Norwich and HMP Whitemoor, for the wealth of stories and for the run of your bookcase. Thanks too to Revd Emma Smith, for sharing memories of prison ministry. Among those I cannot name, particular thanks to K and A. Above all thanks to R, for your time, encouragement and generosity. Not forgetting Tony Aldous who got the ball rolling.

The book's transformation into print is down to Juliet Mushens, a whirlwind of enthusiasm and support, and to Ruth Tross, whose guidance and insight made the final drafts a joy to work on. Thanks also to Nathalie Hallam at Caskie Mushens and the whole team at Hodder for their support, including Cicely Aspinall, Naomi Berwin and Rosie Stephen. Thank you to everyone who read the MS at its earlier stages, in particular Alexander Harper, Suzy Kendall, Jason Farrington, Joyce Eliason, Reg Gadney, Eugenie Walker, Tom Harper, Rena Fruchter, Linda Agran, Geoffrey Case and most of all, Ruth Grey Harper. Thanks also to everyone at ITV News Anglia, particularly Simon Wright and Terry Brennan, who literally gave me the time to write.

This book was written across two years of extremes, one of grief and the other of joy. Thank you Rosie Andrious, Peter Ryan,

Andrea Binfor, Melanie Marks and Peter Mason for helping me through.

The biggest thanks go to those closest to home. My mother Suzy for never giving up, even when I came close. My husband Jason for supporting me at every step. And my son Jonathon, for spending the first weeks of his life snoozing on my chest, listening to me type.